BITS

C.J. KICHUK

Printed in the United States of America.

(Email & Website)

cjkichuk@gmail.com

http://cjkichuk.com

ISBN: **979-8-9909605-0-3**

DEDICATION

"We are, all of us, pebbles on the beach, tossed by the surf of our experiences, then shaped and polished by our contact with others."
(Dr. Raymond Komi Ababio)

With profound gratitude, I dedicate this book to all the pebbles who have shaped me and the divine surf that made that possible.

ACKNOWLEDGMENTS

Writing a speculative fiction novel, especially as a debut effort, provided many opportunities for me to write myself into hopeless dead-ends. Never one to pass up an opportunity, I embraced every one.

I recognize here those who threw me lifelines of constructive input without leaving scars or causing me to seek therapy (although I talk to myself now, more than I used to).

The first spot on the list must go to my wonderful wife, Tina. There are many reasons for placing her first, almost all of which I will not list here. However, in all sincerity, without her steady support and thoughtful input, *BITS* could never have been written.

The next slots go to my three awesome children.

Tess organized online and in-person writing sessions and encouraged me to be sure that my female characters were capable and strong.

Jamie and Alexa pulled no punches but were always there to pump up an occasionally deflated ego.

Heartfelt thanks to every one of my draft readers who volunteered their time and mental bandwidth to help *BITS* be the best it could be. Amory, Howard, James, Karen, Loreinna, and Nancy, your insightful comments on character development and story arcs forestalled a host of grumbles from the general readership.

Thanks also to Steve and the writing community of the Belterra Writing Club. It meant a great deal to be part of a community engaged in the same struggles.

Perhaps strangely, my thanks must go to the characters in my story. Clayton, Raymond, Aida, Carmen, and all the others. After a few introductory words from me, they stepped off the page and whispered their stories for me to transcribe.

Finally, thanks to all the readers who, while enjoying *BITS* as an action-adventure yarn, take to heart the ethical conundrum that artificial intelligence will someday lay at our feet.

PART ONE

PROVENANCE

CHAPTER ONE

OPERATION SUNBURN - May 2021

La Paz, Mexico

As the first terrifying images burst into the healing oblivion of his slumber, Clayton knew they weren't real, but that knowledge was fleeting and quickly irrelevant. In the timeless slow-motion of imagination, the swirling phantasms sucked him into the rising tide of the nightmare. Even in his dream state, he tried to hold on to reason, tried to stay tethered to some remnant of his dissolving reality. His struggles only pulled him down faster until he was submerged in the dark waters of his merciless subconscious.

Completely immersed, he fought to regain his wits through the dreamworld's shock-induced haze. Coming slowly to his senses, he became aware that he was floating in the warm, salty water of some unnamed ocean, not knowing why he was there or even who he was. A gentle breeze carried the acrid smell of recent combat. Repetitive swells of a dozing sea alternately pushed under him, lifted him toward star-speckled darkness, and then let him slide into their troughs as they rolled on. Water washed over his face as he glided to the bottom of each descent, and when he licked his lips, he could taste the salt and the metallic tang of—blood.

The thick clouds that hid one section of the sky parted enough to unveil a full moon, and he closed his eyes against the unwelcome brightness. He rested that way for a moment, trying to pull some fragment of recollection out of the stubborn blackness. In the distance, he could hear someone crying out for help, calling his name. The panicked voice was female and even in its urgent pitch, familiar.

Something touched his cheek. Startled, he opened his eyes to see a hand floating by his face. As he looked at the moonlit water around him, he could make out other limbs, a leg, and another, and then another arm. He tried to raise his hand to brush the offending limb from his face, but his body did not respond. His brain commanded his legs to propel him away, but with no effect. Terror now became the current that carried him as he recognized the severed appendages as his own. The scream that began in the back of his throat was cut off as he slid into another trough. This time his descent was unchecked and as the black water pulled him down, his final thoughts were of all the questions that remained unanswered.

****

Clayton cautiously opened one eye to the dim light of the room and took a moment to convince himself that he was still alive. The scream of a distant siren fused his nightmare to reality. He was wet with sweat, and his lips tasted of salt. The ceiling fan had delivered little relief from the warm, humid air in his low-budget La Paz hotel room. Tourists had air conditioning, but he wasn't a tourist. Encouraged by the mundane discomforts of the still living, he pulled himself from the damp, clinging bedsheets and sought rebirth from the hotel's tepid shower.

He couldn't remember the first time this nightmare, or one like it, had left him sweaty and shaken, but he knew the series of events that spawned the demon dreams of his troubled sleep. The evolving night terrors had become a surreal and frightening mix of bits of experience, smatterings of regrets, and dollops of grief. Each time, they became more detailed and more intense. Each time he felt them further erode the comforting boundary between dismissible fiction and disturbing recollection. Each time he stuffed them into his crowded mental attic with all his other demons.

He needed to find some coffee, but first, it was time for Clayton Rhodes to become Bill Crawford. Mr. Crawford had an important interview today.

Clayton looked at himself in the room's cracked wall mirror, ruefully noting the symbolic accuracy of the fractured image. With some effort, his careworn face took on a lighter, more relaxed aspect, and he looked younger, closer to his age. He hadn't shaved, and his two-day bristle contributed to the appearance of a subpar employment status. He stepped back, loosened his typically erect posture, a legacy of his military background, and relaxed into a more suitable slouch. Finally, satisfied, he donned a bright Hawaiian shirt, pulled his unwilling face into a roguish smile and Bill Crawford ambled out into the dull, red-hued, early morning light in search of coffee.

———◦∞◦———

Calliope - Signing On

Three days before he was due to set sail, Hector Rojas, rumpled and sweaty, sat uncomfortably in the richly appointed salon on the 44-foot motor sailboat *Calliope*. Barrel-chested, and tall for his Mexican heritage, the impact of his physical presence was amplified by the close quarters of the space. Born as brown as the teak around him, more than four decades of sailing the Pacific coast had baked his face and powerful forearms to a dark mahogany. His physical size was well-matched with an outsized personality that, in any situation, left no doubt as to who was in charge.

He grimaced and scratched his face. Although usually clean-shaven while in port, his grizzled whiskers hadn't been close to a razor in several days. He kept his gray-streaked hair at shoulder length as some protection from the fierce sun. Proud of his position, he wore a visored nautical captain's hat whose original white color was almost indiscernible beneath the patina of sweat, soil, and sun. Missing a parrot and perhaps a wooden leg, he still looked as if, upon meeting him, one might expect "Arrr" to be his first utterance.

He had been hired to sail the *Calliope* back to San Diego, her home port, and had been working hard topside in the hot Baja California sun to make her ready for the trip. Now, he took his hat off and placed it on the table as a conspicuous reminder of his authority. He pulled a soiled rag from his back pocket, mopped his face and the back of his neck, and returned the damp scrap to its home. He was at once frustrated that he had to interrupt his efforts, appreciative of the break, and then irritated with himself for appreciating the break.

This was his second trip north with the *Calliope,* and he had taken several other boats back to San Diego for the same company, Baja Paraiso Charters. He needed an extra hand to round out the crew for the eight-day sail from La Paz, Mexico, north to San Diego. The *Calliope* was an easy boat to sail, in fit weather, but he planned to sail all day and night, so he needed a crew of three to fill in the watch schedule. Now he was sitting across the table from a man he'd never met, cautiously hoping this man would fill the open berth.

"Papá—", a youthful male voice cracking with adolescence called from topside.

"Estoy ocupado, Antonio. I'm busy." Hector's tone filtered any harshness from his reply.

This would be the first trip for Hector's sixteen-year-old son, Antonio. The boy had been pestering his father to let him make the trip for years and, finally, Hector reluctantly relented. Carlos, the third man he had used on prior trips and counted on, had developed appendicitis and had recommended Bill Crawford as his replacement. Pressured by a tight schedule and unforgiving bosses, Hector reached out to his contacts, who assured him that Crawford's background story checked out. From all reports, he was an experienced sailor from Seattle, not on any agency watch list, with a need to make good money fast—and a willingness to step over the line, if that's what it took.

Now, Bill Crawford sat on the plush, booth-like seat across the oiled teak table as Hector took in his appearance. The candidate's dark hair had started to gray. Life had chiseled his face, but his blue eyes still glowed with hints of unquenched fire. He was probably forty-something but trim and well-tanned, he could pass for younger. His brightly colored Hawaiian shirt, easy smile, and relaxed body language conveyed a casual self-confidence.

Hector slammed two empty glasses onto the table with a resounding thump. It was a conspicuously intimidating gesture meant to proclaim his authority. He poured a generous jigger of whiskey into each. Placing one in front of Clayton, he raised the other in salute and downed the brown, burning liquid with a slight twitch of his lips, followed by a brief smile of satisfaction.

"Drink." Hector's commanding tone buried what could have been a cordial invitation.

Clayton returned the salute and sipped at his glass, showing respect without submission.

Hector leaned back for a thoughtful minute. He believed himself to be a good judge of people and his track record of evading entanglements with the law gave credence to the belief. Years in the wave-reflected sun had creased and leathered his brown face and molded his eyes into a perpetual squint. Now they took in Clayton's every move as his mind parsed and analyzed.

Before speaking, Hector filled his glass once again, but this time left it on the table, rolling it between his massive, weathered hands. His eyes bore into Clayton searching for any clues that might help him weigh the value or risk the man might bring with him. Clayton met his gaze with disarming nonchalance. Hector's deep voice was imbued with a rich Mexican accent that could either be welcoming or threatening. Now, it balanced on the knife edge of the two alternatives.

"So, how do you know Carlos?" His tone was casual, but the question probing.

Clayton's response was casual in return. "We were part of a charter crew round trip from Seattle down to the Channel Islands a couple of years back." Clayton's eyes met Hector's challenging gaze as he spoke. "We both pick at the guitar and we would swap songs and jam during our off-duty hours. I like jazz and he plays blues, which worked pretty well together, at least the way we did it. We hit it off and stayed in touch."

Hector stared up at the overhead, seeming to revisit fond memories. "Sí, Carlos knows how to play. He can make that Gibson guitar of his sing." Hector baited the hook.

Clayton's relaxed response showed no sign that he knew he was being tested. "Ha, well Carlos talked about it but he never put together enough scratch for the Gibson. He's played a beat-up Epiphone for years." Thrust and parry.

Hector let out what was a reasonable facsimile of a sincere laugh. "Ha! You know, Bill, my memory is just not as good as it used to be. Too many late nights con mi buen amigo, Jack Daniels." Hector gestured at the bottle. "I know Carlos told me, but what was the name of that boat that you and he crewed?" Smiling, Hector leaned forward slightly, searching for any sign of discomfort.

"You mean the first time? That was the *Calypso*. She was a ketch-rigged Irwin 52."

"Ah, sí. I remember now, the *Calypso*." Hector leaned back a bit, satisfied with Clayton's answers. Now, more comfortable with Clayton, he got down to business. "Carlos told you about our cargo?"

"Some, but I don't much care," Clayton shrugged, glossing over the sensitive topic. "I've got a wife and daughter in Seattle. I had a good run at a bachelor's life, but that was then. Now I put food on the table and my daughter needs braces." Clayton leaned forward and took another sip from his glass. "Why don't you just tell me what you need me to know?"

"Sí, por la familia ..." Hector's voice trailed off. For just a moment he was distracted by his thoughts. Then he re-focused on the issue at hand. "The deal, for you, is $15,000 US dollars, in cash, when we make port in San Diego. For now, what cargo we may carry is none of your concern. This money you are getting pays for your sailing skills and your lack of curiosity. I will need your help to transfer the cargo later, so I will give you more details when I feel it is time. Comprendes?"

"Understood. The money's good enough for me to know you're paying for more than a deckhand—enough for me to keep my focus on the boat, the wind, and the water, and enough for me to keep my questions to myself. I've done stuff like this before. I'm still in!" Clayton's response conveyed only an appropriate eagerness to sign on to a berth that would pay well.

While Hector continued to assess Clayton's responses and reactions, he was unaware that a team of agents was performing its own analysis courtesy of the wire Clayton was wearing. That Clayton's story checked out was less a verification of the truth and more a testament to the hard work and effective professionalism of the FBI. Bill Crawford was a fabrication, a mix of a real person, input from the flipped informant, Carlos, and the awe-inspiring ability of the FBI to make a fiction believable. After weeks of planning, Bill Crawford was born that morning when Senior Special Agent Clayton Rhodes sauntered out of the seedy La Paz hotel room.

****

The surveillance van, positioned in an inconspicuous corner of the marina parking lot, comfortably accommodated two occupants but now housed four law enforcement agents. Two FBI agents were at the workstations while two Mexican federal agents watched from stools crowded into the van's remaining space. The headphones they all wore filtered out the humming from the air conditioner as it struggled to deal with the heat from the equipment, the bodies, and the strengthening mid-morning sun. As the van's interior became less comfortable, none of the van's occupants missed the irony of the operation name, SUNBURN.

Senior Special Agent Deb O'Donnell unconsciously twisted the top from a small bottle of water and took a sip. Her full attention was on the conversation between Clayton and Captain Rojas playing through her earphones.

"Our man, Clayton, is doing a pretty good job—considering." While he spoke, Special Agent Mateo Carrasco, the youngest one in the van, moved his fingers over his keyboard. Responding to his touch, the slightly muffled tone of the transmitted conversation sharpened.

"Considering what, Mateo?" Focused on the drama playing out over her headphones, Deb was slow to fully engage with Mateo's muted comment.

"Well, I was talking with some of my buddies. Rumor has it that he's taken some pretty heavy hits, and he's been around a long time. The thought is that he might be getting a little long in the tooth for undercover ops."

Deb's engagement level ratcheted up several notches. Amplified by her instant irritation, her normally almost imperceptible Irish brogue colored her response. "So this is you thinkin' that he might not be up to the task?"

Oblivious to the ground crumbling beneath his feet, Mateo forged ahead. "I wouldn't go that far, but he's pretty banged up, and undercover work is high stress, even for the best of us."

"Oh, the best of us is it now?" Fully engaged, Deb leaned closer to the young agent, ensuring that he alone could hear her. "Listen up, Mateo, there are reasons aplenty why he's out there fightin' back the nervous sweat of undercover fear, and you're sittin' in here with your biggest concern bein' this near-to-dyin' air conditioner.

"You can tell your *buddios* that in the entire world of law enforcement, you'll likely find no one better suited for undercover ops than our Clayton Rhodes."

Deb warmed up to the teaching moment for her junior partner. She struggled to hold her voice low enough to keep the others uninvolved.

"The fella spent his wee years on an island off of Seattle. He could swim before he could walk and could sail a boat a short time after that. Puget Sound was his kiddie pool, and he shared it with cute sea otters and not-so-cute killer whales. His saltwater cred makes him a particularly good fit for this assignment—that, and his gobsmackin' ability to make real whatever fiction we come up with.

"You know nothin' about him, and yet, based on your scuttlebutt, you presume to assess his liabilities?"

Mateo withered under Deb's verbal onslaught. "I didn't mean to—"

"Shush—and hear this—Clayton's covenant with the cosmos has demanded a life spent in service to duty, honor, country, and family. After graduatin' with a degree in cybersecurity, he continued his family's military tradition by enlistin' in the Navy. He spent a passel of years with a SEAL team on missions he can't talk about, in places he can't disclose. Then he joined up with us at the Bureau.

"He was puttin' successful missions up on the scoreboard back when your only undercover operations were the pubescent nights you spent under the sheets with your small-screen fantasy lovers.

"And one thin' more, if you be wantin' ta measure o' person's worth, donna be countin' the hits, Boyo! Count the bounces! Da ya hear me?"

Mateo's face went from red-hued to pale as he struggled to find an answer.

"Am I clear?"

"Ye … yes, Ma'am."

Deb gave him a big smile. "Good lad! Now gather your wits an' try to be as good at your job as Clayton Rhodes is at his."

Deb had partnered with Clayton on other operations, and both liked and respected him. He had come up with the plan for this op, pushing through Deb's objections. She worried that once at sea, Clayton would be operating in a high-risk situation with no effective backup. Her blazing response to Mateo was triggered not only by his ignorant disrespect, but also by her own misgivings.

Although they couldn't hear enough to understand the exchange, the Mexican agents sensed that something was amiss.

"Está todo bien?"

Deb leaned back in her chair, pivoted, and flashed another reassuring smile. "Si, es bueno."

The humming of the air conditioner became the only sound in the van as the team, once again, became silent witnesses to the happenings on the *Calliope*.

****

The sound of footsteps on the stairs leading up to the pilothouse drew Clayton's attention and paused Hector's conversation with his potential new crew member.

"Perdón por interrumpir." A handsome younger version of Hector stepped down into the salon, using almost all of its generous overhead clearance. He smelled of sweat and chrome polish. More than just the words, his voice communicated his enthusiasm for his work. Nodding to Clayton, he politely continued in English. Although he knew enough Spanish to get by, Clayton was impressed with the boy's manners. "Papá, do you have the charts?"

"Bill, this is my son, Antonio. Antonio, this is Bill Crawford. It looks like you two will be mates." There was warmth in Hector's tone that was notable for its absence up to this point. Clayton took it as not only clear affection for his son but a growing comfort with Clayton's participation. "I have the charts here, hijo. I'm still going over the sail plan."

Lacking his father's thicker accent, Antonio enthusiastically reported his good work, eager to impress both his father and his guest. "Oh, okay. I've polished all the stanchions. They are all gleaming in the sun. I'm going to replace the frayed lifelines now."

"Bueno," Hector nodded his approval.

"Good to meet you, Mr. Crawford. I look forward to sailing with you." Antonio reached out.

Clayton reciprocated with a firm handshake. "Same here, Antonio. Call me Bill."

"OK, Bill." Antonio flashed a smile and called out "Hasta luego," as he scrambled up the stairs to the pilothouse and then out to the upper steering cockpit.

"Si, Antonio", Clayton called back as the boy disappeared topside.

"Bueno," Hector repeated the word, noting his approval of the exchange. "So Bill, have you had any experience on a Nauticat?" He gestured at their surroundings. His tone and body language now were more genuinely accepting if not completely welcoming.

"Nah, but I hear they're fine boats. I would think that their high transom might make them a little tender in a following sea, but that shouldn't be a problem since this time of year we'll most likely be beating against headwinds for most of the trip." Clayton mentally cringed. *Now you're just showing off.*

Hector ran his fingers thoughtfully over the worn visor of his hat and then returned it to his head, stood, and offered Clayton his hand. "Welcome aboard."

A broad smile pushed through the stubble around Clayton's lips as he got to his feet and took Hector's hand. Hector held Clayton's hand long and hard, once again asserting his authority and signaling that the welcome came with conditions.

Clayton breathed an internal sigh of relief. Acting the part of Bill Crawford for the duration of the trip would be demanding, but at least he got through the audition. His enthusiasm was genuine. "Good to be aboard, Captain. I look forward to a great trip." He picked up the almost untouched glass of whiskey, raised it in salute, then downed the dark liquid, fighting back a grimace as the whiskey burned its way over his tongue and down his throat.

―――◆◆◆―――

Calliope -Setting Sail

Two days later they sailed out of La Paz, the northerly breezes pushing them on an easy, downhill run to and then around the tip of Cabo San Lucas. After making the turn, they beat against the wind and current for the uphill run to San Diego.

With wind and sea happily coexisting, peaceful nights followed sun-gloried days in idyllic succession. Clayton tended to his chores, striving to allay any lingering doubts that the taciturn captain might have. Progress on that front was hard to measure, but Clayton noted that the intensity of Hector's scrutiny had diminished, and the sharp tone of his orders had softened.

In the early minutes of the fourth day of the trip, Clayton was standing the midnight watch. He savored this time. With the others asleep below, he was relieved of the increasing pressure of his performance. He hadn't expected Hector to be as nuanced a character as he now appeared to be. His affection for his son was touching and provided mitigating context for his illegal activities. As Clayton got to know, and like his shipmates, his deception was a growing burden.

They skirted the coast about 10 miles offshore. The brisk but steady northerly wind made for slow progress as they beat into it along their north-by-northwesterly course. The plan called for them to make the trip under sail. Hector hadn't shared the reason for this, but Clayton surmised that much of the fuel tank's capacity was taken up by the drugs they carried. They were making about 5 knots, which was what Hector's sail plan had anticipated.

The full moon, still low on the horizon, painted a silvery, undulating path to the *Calliope*, a cosmic connection to something bigger, better, other. There were times when Clayton desperately needed that faith. He closed his eyes, steering by sound and motion. The wind hummed through the rigging and the deck throbbed as the hull sliced through the waves. From a distance, whales called to each other as they discussed *Calliope*'s passage. Opening his eyes, he found, unsurprisingly, that the world was much the same. He allowed himself a small grin of satisfaction that the *Calliope* was still on course. Checking the telltales, he trimmed the mainsail to take advantage of a new, slight change in the wind direction.

As wonderful as it was to be on the water again, the alone time dismantled the fortress of distractions that held his demons at bay. His now-unfettered mind turned on itself, conjuring dear and dreadful ghosts, memories too painful to keep, yet much too precious to let go. He shook his head and focused on getting a slight luffing out of the mainsail.

"Cómo estás?" Hector stepped up onto the deck and Clayton's demons scurried back into the shadows.

"Bueno." Clayton smiled. He had learned some Spanish during his time in Austin, but he pretended to know less than he did.

Hector studied the compass and then scanned the ocean, the telltales, and the sails. "Sí, bueno", he finally concurred.

Hector took his responsibility as captain seriously and frequently checked on his crew, even if it was not his watch. Sporting his ever-present captain's hat, he would often linger on deck, sharing with Clayton the healing beneficence that only this time of night on the open sea can bestow. In those moments, there would be long silences as each man paid homage to the spirits flitting over the waves, through the rigging, pushing urgently against the sails like impatient lovers.

On the first two nights, after a few minutes, Hector would break the spell with a softly uttered, "Bueno", and retreat down the stairway. On the third night, Clayton took advantage of the imposed intimacy that comes with sharing a small boat in a vast ocean.

"Food for the soul." Clayton's words were an offering to the night and an opening for Hector. He left them hanging in the air, an invitation not requiring a response.

The sounds of wind and waves filled the next minute or two. Just when Clayton assumed his overture had been rebuffed, Hector acknowledged, "Sí, the sea makes poets of us all." The ice broke and that night, the two sailors conversed like two sailors would on a moon-speckled sea under an infinite sky, far away from earthly entanglements.

Their midnight conversations evolved as the two men bonded over their mutual love of the sea. On the fourth night when Hector came up on deck, he carried the bottle of whiskey and two glasses. He sat on the bench in the cockpit, set the glasses on the cockpit's small table, and filled each to near overflowing. From his movements, Clayton suspected that, for Hector, this would not be the first drink of the night. Hector picked up one glass, and with a salute to the midnight sky, he drained it. He then picked up the full glass and offered it to Clayton.

"No, gracias." Since he was on watch, Clayton declined the invitation and instead held his mug of coffee up toward Hector. "Salud."

"Sí, muy bien," Hector nodded his approval. He held the full glass and stared out at the luminescent sea. Whether he was driven by a need to share or confess, or perhaps embracing a fiction that he was alone on deck speaking only to the night spirits, he openly talked about his life, family, and, more cautiously, his job. Clayton paid close attention to Hector's stories, particularly when he discussed his employment. Their conversations, from that night onward, grew into an easy and growing friendship, with Clayton skillfully guiding Hector through discussions about their families, to how their trips took them away from home so much. That shared regret allowed Clayton to dwell on the purpose of the current trip and coax Hector into revealing more details about the operation of Baja Paraiso Charters. Clayton's daily challenge was to use his well-practiced interrogation skills to chip away at the wall of caution that protected any useful information that Hector possessed.

The trip up the coast went according to plan—both plans. The weather cooperated, and *Calliope* performed beautifully. Hector was happy. Bill Crawford daily proved himself to be an able deckhand and pleasant shipmate. Bill's alter ego, Agent Clayton Rhodes, took every opportunity to observe and record details that would help to build a case. There was plenty of time for talk and, with his affable persona in full play, Clayton used his conversations with Hector to probe at questions on how the scheme worked. Where did the drugs come from?

How and when were they loaded into the hidden compartments on the *Calliope*? Who was involved in getting through the Mexican customs at the border port of Ensenada? How did they avoid detection of the drugs on the U.S. side?

Some answers came as a necessary part of Bill Crawford's duties. Some slipped into the conversations with Hector and some were only discernible through a thick layer of Hector's continuing caution. Although increasingly comfortable with his shipmate, Hector was well aware of the price paid by those who revealed too much.

In spite of Hector's caution, Clayton was able to create a decent working profile of the criminal operation.

****

Hector's was a minor role in a much bigger play. The script was a simple one, logically elegant, and financially effective. Through a U.S. front corporation, Baja Paraiso Charters, the Sinaloa drug cartel chartered boats to unsuspecting Americans who were looking for an idyllic sailing vacation.

Sailing down the coast from San Diego around the tip of Baja California Sur to Las Paz is beautiful, with favorable winds most of the year. The Sea of Cortez, also known as the Gulf of California, offers a wide range of visual and culinary delights. The Baja California Peninsula shields the Gulf from the large Pacific swells, providing vacationers a most pleasant immersive experience. Once in the protected water, they enjoy the entertainment and culture of the many peninsula and island-based landfalls that skirt and dot the Gulf.

"It is like sailing in a bathtub." Hector's description combined pride for its beauty and contempt for the mediocre sailing skills of the visitors.

"The sail back to San Diego is time-consuming and not so pleasant. You must beat against headwinds and the southerly California Current. Most gringos prefer to fly home, leaving it for us to sail the boats back to the U.S."

Although the charter business was profitable, its net income paled compared to the other, illegal, part of the scheme. Fitted with hidden compartments, the boats collectively brought thousands of pounds of cocaine, fentanyl, and methamphetamine north for distribution to the insatiable U.S. market. The plan relied on a chain of corrupt customs officials and competent crews who sail into U.S. waters and then transferred the drugs to high-speed chase boats for delivery at prearranged spots along the California coast.

The operation in which Clayton was the leading actor, SUNBURN, was an inter-agency, multinational task force. Its mission was to gather sufficient evidence to prosecute Baja Paraiso Charters and disrupt the Sinaloa drug cartel in San Diego.

****

Along with gathering information helpful to the case, Clayton learned more about Hector and Antonio. He tried to maintain a professional distance, but the sun, the sea, and the shared work opened windows into their lives. They became more than minor cardboard characters in some grand inter-agency operation. Their time together imposed a nuance on Clayton's impression of both of them. Try as he might to stay focused, Clayton couldn't avoid considering more than their roles in a criminal enterprise.

Hector was a no-nonsense captain on a clearly criminal mission, but also a loving father providing for his wife and son. As Clayton watched the interplay between the older Rojas and his son, he sensed that Hector was worried for the boy and felt trapped in his life on the wrong side of the law.

Antonio, only vaguely aware of the nefarious nature of the hidden cargo, shone with inner goodness and pride in his work that made him easy to like. Clayton was moved by the enormous potential in the young man, potential that was teetering on the sharp edge of "if only."

On the afternoon of the eighth day of the trip, the huge Mexican flag that flies over the port of Ensenada came into view.

"Ensenada!" Cracking with enthusiasm, Antonio's youthful voice called from his duty station at the helm. The *Calliope* bounded through the waves with more vigor as she came off the wind and steered a more easterly course toward land.

⸺⸱⋈⸱⸺

Calliope - The Storm

They tied *Calliope* to the cleats in front of the Port Captain's office where they were to submit the paperwork necessary to clear customs and exit Mexico. Clayton, eager to see this part of the operation, offered to accompany Hector, but the older man insisted on leaving his crew to scrub down *Calliope*'s deck.

A large window at the front of the office building provided the Port Captain with a commanding view of the harbor and now allowed Clayton to observe the official's interaction with Hector. At one point, she became animated, and there was clearly an exchange of heated words as the woman stood up from her desk and gestured toward the *Calliope*. A few minutes later, Hector emerged from the building carrying the customs papers in his clenched fist. His face was red and his shoulders sagged. He climbed aboard.

"All set?" Clayton asked lightheartedly.

Hector avoided Clayton's gaze. His reply was low and terse "Get ready to cast off. We leave for San Diego—NOW!"

Clayton looked up at the gathering clouds. "There's weather moving in."

Without looking up, Hector replied through clenched teeth, "Si, gran tormenta—a big storm."

Clayton did a quick calculation. It was almost 2:00 in the afternoon and about a 70-statute mile sail to San Diego. In good weather, they could make that trip in about 13 hours. That would get them in port at about 3 a.m.

"Don't you want to ride out the storm here and leave in the morning?" Clayton was forced to address the question to Hector's back as Hector gathered up the charts and custom papers and started down into the pilothouse.

Hector paused on the stairway and replied without turning. "No, there are things we do that are best done in the dark." Then he was gone.

Eight hours into the trip, the dark sky delivered on its threat. The rain started as a drizzle and then came down with such intensity that it completely obliterated the line between sea and sky. They had double-reefed the mainsail as the wind had shifted from coming close over the bow to coming more across the beam. Rain and sea washed over the deck as *Calliope* did her best to plow forward. All hands were on deck, working the lines and sails. After a hard two hours, the ferocity of the wind lessened. As if losing interest in *Calliope*, the storm was moving further out to sea. Clayton carefully made his way off the foredeck and joined the others in the upper steering cockpit. Antonio was at the helm, looking pale and shaken, which surprised Clayton, since all during the storm he was rock solid. Hector motioned Clayton to sit on the cockpit bench. The gesture was more than a request. Clayton recognized a determined look on Hector's face—and a gun in his hand.

Hector shouted over the still-powerful storm, "Our good friend at the Port Captain's office relayed a message! It seems our old shipmate, Carlos, enjoyed a miraculous recovery from his appendicitis! Unfortunately, though, he has succumbed to other 'work-related' injuries. Before he passed away, descanso en paz" —Hector made the sign of the cross — "he confessed what he knew of a government undercover operation with an FBI agent, Bill Crawford, in a starring role!"

He paused. The rain found the creases in his dark face and dripped off his chin. His squinting eyes became more threatening as he challenged Clayton to offer some defense. "It saddens me greatly, but I'm afraid—Bill—or whatever your name is, you must leave us now."

Antonio, his hands still on the wheel, his eyes darting from his father to the still-roiling sea, cried out, "Papá! No!"

Hector growled at his son, "Presta atención al viento, Antonio. Watch the wind." Then almost pleadingly, "There are certain things that a man must do!"

Clayton assessed the distance from Hector's gun hand. Even with a distraction from Antonio, it was too far for any reasonable chance at a successful lunge. It would be the last act of a desperate man.

Instead, he made his appeal to what he hoped was the novelty of the situation for Hector. Although it had never explicitly come up in their conversations during the trip, Clayton believed Hector had never killed anyone. More than that, Clayton believed that he didn't want to.

"Hector, I'm not here to hurt you or Antonio." Clayton built on the opening that Antonio had provided. "It's all about the drugs and the people who live in enormous homes and drive fancy cars while you risk everything to take care of your family. Do you want Antonio to grow up doing this kind of work? Look at him." The still powerful wind and rain buffeted the three as Clayton gestured towards Antonio, who stood frozen at the helm. "He has so much to learn, so much that he can do. He deserves a chance for a life that's free from bosses like yours, free from running from the police, Federales, American agents, or rival gangs. He deserves a chance to have friends that won't betray him, the way Carlos did you. You're his father. You have to give him that chance."

Lightning tore at the sky to the west, followed several seconds later by a bone-rattling clap of thunder.

The battle between his conscience and his fear raged in Hector's tortured mind. In the end, fear was the winner. "They would never let us go, Bill. From the first time I ran a boat and made a drop for them, I was theirs, along with my whole family." Hector's shoulders slumped as he ran out the last few seconds that stood between him and a task he never thought he would have to perform. The gun shook in his hand.

Clayton watched the struggle play out on Hector's face and offered his best appeal for a favorable decision. "We can protect you and your family. You can help to bring these people and their whole Baja Paraiso operation down. In exchange, we can pull you all out of San Diego, set you up in a new place, a new life, a fresh start for you and your family."

Hector sat staring at Clayton for a long minute, then clicked the gun's safety off. "The risk for my family is too much. Sadly, Bill Crawford, it's time for you to go."

Antonio watched in horror as his father raised the gun, taking his eye off the oncoming waves. One, larger than the rest, pulled *Calliope*'s bow to starboard and allowed the wind to catch the mainsail from behind, jibing the boat, and swinging the boom wildly across the deck. Hector called out a warning, but it was too late. The boom caught Antonio at mid-body and carried him with it as it swung over the side.

"Papá!" Antonio cried.

Hector dropped the gun and reached out as the boy swung by him but grasped only air.

The tension of the preceding moments was washed away in an instant. Clayton weighed the wisdom of staying on the boat to help with recovery against diving in to help a perhaps unconscious Antonio. Even as he was processing those conflicting thoughts, he had checked Antonio's receding head, pulled the life preserver from its rack on the railing, and dove over the side. Surfacing quickly, he wiped his eyes, shook off the shock of the cold plunge, and swam in the direction where he last spied Antonio. Frantically scanning what he could see of the wildly tossing water, he pressed his hands on the life ring and pushed himself up, trying for a few extra inches of height.

"Antonio!" Clayton screamed into the wind. He thought he heard a faint cry off to his right and swam in that direction, pushing the float.

"Ayúdame! Help m—!" The waves washed over Antonio's voice, cutting off his cry for help.

"I'm here for you, Anthony. I won't leave you!" Clayton's demons rose out of the darkness, but this time their horrific presence pumped more power into his efforts. "Anthony!"

Clayton saw him now, arms flailing weakly, trying to keep his head above the waves. "Anthony! I'm here!" He grasped the exhausted boy and fitted the horseshoe-shaped ring under Antonio's arms and around his chest.

Hector had immediately headed *Calliope* into the wind to stop her forward movement. He turned on the engine for better maneuverability and dropped the mainsail. He then tied another life ring onto a long line that he dragged behind the boat as he circled the two men in the water. As the circle closed around them, Clayton grabbed the ring. Hector again turned into the wind and pulled the men to the boat. Clayton pushed the semiconscious Antonio onto the bobbing swim platform at the stern of the boat where Hector was waiting.

"Antonio!" Hector's voice cracked with emotion as he held his son in an embrace so tight that it left Antonio gasping for breath once again. "Mi hijo, my son!"

Clayton reached up over the edge of the swim platform, his head in his arms, exhausted from the rescue, unable to pull himself fully onto the swimboard. He felt powerful hands grab his jacket and pull him onto the platform and then into the deck of the cockpit. He looked up into the barrel of Hector's gun. Too weak to attempt any effective defense, Clayton closed his eyes and allowed his mind to drift—to far away and long ago. The relief of complete submission washed over him.

And then—with words that seemed to come from a great distance—Hector's voice floated on the wind.

"Está bien, Bill Crawford—there are lines I will not cross. I am surprised that some honor still lives in me. I owe you much, but that debt is small compared to what I owe my son."

Clayton opened his eyes as Hector turned the gun around and handed it over, butt first. New creases formed on the captain's face as he managed a small wry smile born from gratitude and his own feeling of relief.

"Tell me more about how this witness protection program works."

****

They followed Hector's original plan. Clayton was impressed with how efficiently and cleverly the drug transfer was managed. Instead of having direct contact with chase boats, they loaded the drugs, which now had Clayton's trackers embedded, into lobster pots at prearranged GPS locations. The chase boats would come later to collect the drugs. Following the drugs, would net SUNBURN agents a large part of the downstream operation. Hector's knowledge would hook several of the larger fish at Baja Paraiso Charters. In turn, if they could be flipped, there was potential for some bigger collars upstream.

Clayton let Hector motor the *Calliope* up to the San Diego police dock and give himself up to the waiting task force. The agents took a resigned Hector and a frightened Antonio into custody. As they started on the path to the next chapter in their lives, Clayton joined them in the mobile command center where they sat, unsure of what was to follow. He handed them each a Styrofoam cup of coffee and patted Antonio on the shoulder. "It's all going to work out, Antonio", Clayton spoke from affection and conviction born out of years of experience.

Antonio nodded and tried to speak, but no words came. He stood, held Clayton in a long hug, and then sat back down, exhausted.

Clayton then stared directly into Hector's squinting eyes. "You made the right call, Hector. Thank you."

"I know," Hector nodded his agreement. The movement threatened to shake the much-bedraggled captain's hat from its loose hold on his head. He looked at Antonio and then back at Clayton and, in a voice choked with emotion, he murmured, "Gracias."

"One last thing—don't tell anyone about the gun." Clayton had resolved not to include Hector's use of the gun in his report. The offending item had somehow found its way to the bottom of the Pacific.

Hector immediately understood the value of Clayton's parting gift. "Entiendo, entiendo, gracias, Clayton Rhodes."

Clayton took in the picture of the exhausted Antonio, who had fallen asleep with his head on Hector's massive shoulder. "Navegar con dios, Capitán. Buena fortuna."

"Si, gracias. Sail with God, Clayton Rhodes."

Clayton stood, saluted a last farewell, then turned and stepped out of the command center. The early morning sun breaking through the scattered clouds silhouetted the City of San Diego and cast its new day's light on the white-capped Pacific. Special Agent Deb O'Donnell bounded up to him and vigorously shook his hand. Relief, joy, and pride all beamed out of a smile that wanted more space than her face could provide. Her red hair flamed in the glow of the sunrise. "Great bit o' work, Clayton—was it rough?"

"Nah, Deb," Bill Crawford no longer, Clayton Rhodes pulled some truth out of the recent events. "Hector was ready to make the leap. He just needed someone to show him the way."

"OK, if you say so," lacking Clayton's context, Deb was less sympathetic and easily shifted her focus back to the relief and triumph of a successful op. "Hey, Clay! A bunch of us are going out for a bit of a celebration. Join us!"

Clayton put on his most affable smile. "Sure, Deb, I'll catch up with you in a bit."

Deb teased, "By the way, you look smashing in that Hawaiian shirt. Is that your new look?"

Clayton laughed, "Could be. Maybe it's time for a change."

Deb made one last attempt at the invitation. "It'd be great to see you there."

Deb had known Clayton for years. She remembered a time when he would joyfully share in a victory lap of a successful operation, but not now, not after …

Clayton politely deflected, "I'll try to make it."

Deb knew he wouldn't. She saw the lie for what it was and took no offense.

That night Clayton would swim once again with severed limbs in a nameless ocean on an unclear mission for an unknown cause.

CHAPTER TWO

Clayton Friday, June 11, 2021

Austin

Clayton stared out of the rain-streaked window of United flight 545 from Washington, DC as it broke through the thinning afternoon clouds on its final descent into Austin's Bergstrom International Airport. The reflected image that stared back at him looked tired, but determined. The confining discomfort of the window seat was penance for his last-minute decision to add the side trip. It had been two weeks since the successful conclusion of OPERATION SUNBURN. He had just left the inter-agency debriefing on the operation and was due to join a drug interdiction task force in El Paso on Monday.

The reasons for the stop went far beyond a recreational diversion. The shadows stealing the light from his life were getting darker. Like weeds growing in an untended garden, they threatened to completely choke out everything good or joyful. It didn't take much introspection to see that their roots were here in Austin. All during his college years and beyond, the city had been a wonderful part of Clayton's life, but that had changed in one catastrophic instant. Now, finally, he accepted that he had to battle the darkness on its home ground.

****

Clayton emerged from the terminal squinting at the bright afternoon sun reflecting off the rain-washed street. Eager to impress, the taxi driver bounded out of her car and came around with an upbeat greeting welcomed by most of her fares. "Hey man, I'm Samantha. Call me Sam. Have a pleasant flight? Rad shirt, by the way." She held out her hand. "Need help with that bag?"

"I've got it." Preoccupied with his thoughts, Clayton rebuffed Sam's friendly banter, pushed his duffel bag into the back seat of the taxi, and climbed in after it.

Sam reclaimed the driver's seat and looked at Clayton in her rear-view mirror. "Driskill Hotel, right?" Sam sought to confirm her online app's stated destination.

Clayton sat for a moment and finally committed, "I need to make a stop first."

"Sure, where to?" The dream-catcher that hung from the mirror danced as Sam pulled into the traffic in front of the United terminal.

Sam's success at what she did was based not only on her natural exuberance, but also on her ability to read people. Clayton, in no mood to chat, was grateful for her perception. After he established the new destination, they rode in silence undisturbed but for the traffic noises and the sound of the windshield wipers rhythmically sweeping away the last of the drizzle.

The ride from the airport imposed 20 minutes of reflection, made more intense by the changed but still hauntingly familiar Austin skyline. A year ago Clayton had dug a deep hole in his mind and into it, he tossed everything that was Austin. He covered it with what he thought to be an impenetrable mountain—then he turned his back and walked away. But even mountains wear away and this one was being eroded from within. What lay below had not been put to rest and now had become the epicenter of Clayton's demons. For all the time he had spent away, he effectively used life's distractions and the noise of daily living to suppress any hint of heart-wrenching memories. And that comforting denial was reason enough to keep his distance.

The storm on the *Calliope*, his instant affection for Antonio Rojas, and their close call in the water had all conspired to dissolve Clayton's protective sepulcher. Now, at last, the constant, growing pain of staying away had outweighed the certain agony of the visit he knew he had to make. His view of the city from the car window triggered all the wonderful and dark pictures of a joyful life gone sideways—and the mountain collapsed.

The rain stopped as they turned off the main road. The sign on the stone wall said "Assumption Cemetery". Sam drove through the entrance and, guided by Clayton's softly spoken directions, splashed through the puddles and wound the taxi's way to the far end. Eventually, they came to two large trees under which stood a statue of the Madonna holding a child. A mix of brightly colored and faded flower bouquets dotted the landscape of tombstones.

"Stop here." Sam could barely make out the words as Clayton's voice bubbled through the layers of memories, grief, and regret. She pulled over and brought the car to a smooth stop. Clayton sat in silence for a long minute. Then he pushed the door open. "I won't be long."

"Take what time you need. I'll be here," Sam once again suppressed her naturally cheery tone as she guessed at the circumstances of the visit.

Clayton pulled himself out of the car, gently pushed the door closed, and walked tentatively over the wet grass toward the statue. The Madonna held the child on one arm and the other was reaching out as if to say, "We are here. We have always been here."

Clayton approached the statue he used as a landmark. He scanned the surrounding tombstones searching through the dark shadows that obscured the memory of the single time he had been here a year ago.

It wasn't hard to find—a large stone of pink Texas granite with two inscriptions and room for a third.

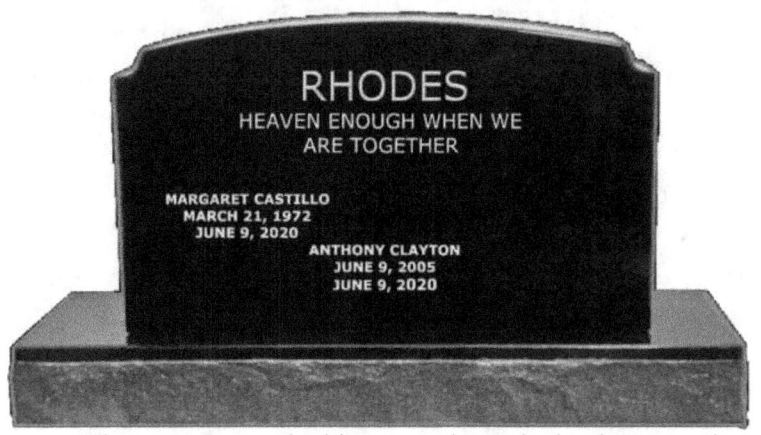

The wet grass soaked his pants leg as he knelt on one knee, put his forehead against the wet granite, and tried to remember how to pray.

The official report said it was a robbery gone bad, but he knew better. It had been a Sunday afternoon. He was out of town, on assignment. It was Anthony's fourteenth birthday and Maggie and he were walking around Lady Bird Lake. They stopped for ice cream and continued their walk. Witnesses said they didn't see anything but heard two shots. Maggie's wallet and jewelry were missing. No suspects were ever identified. Clayton's fervent application of all his skills and resources could not bring more clarity.

"I'm so sorry Maggie. It was all my fault and I should have been there." Clayton's every muscle tensed as he tried once again to contain the grief, as he had for so long. But that was not what he was there to do. That was not why he brought himself to this city, to this place. He wasn't there to conquer his grief, but to accept it—and make peace with it before it ate him alive. Finally, he closed his eyes and let the mountainous dark wave that he had held back for so long crash around him. His body shook with the spasms of sobs and he embraced the pain made precious by the love from which it sprang. He pressed his lips against the stone and put his hand on the first inscription. "Maggie, I'm so sorry—sorry that I wasn't there and sorry that I have stayed away so long and oh so sorry—it was all my fault." He moved his hand to the second engraving. "Anthony, my darling boy, I love you so. Be a good boy and listen to your mom until I see you again." Then, after several minutes, he murmured, "I miss you both so very much."

He stood, stroked the top of the stone one last time, wiped his eyes, turned, and walked back to the car. He eased himself into the back seat and, as though from far away, he heard himself move on. "Okay, Sam, take me to the hotel."

———◦∞◦———

Austin Memories

The Driskill Hotel is an Austin landmark. Opened in 1887, it was designed to be grand, and over the years it kept that reputation. For Clayton, on this day, its appeal was twofold. On a lark, he and Maggie had spent the first night of their married life at the Driskill before continuing their honeymooning across the country's national parks. Secondly, it was located on old Sixth Street, the center of Austin's live music scene and nightlife.

Sam pulled to a stop in front of the hotel and as Clayton exited the car, their eyes met for just a moment. Sam pushed to extend the purely transactional boundaries of their encounter.

"Good luck, man."

Clayton nodded his thanks and watched as the taxi disappeared into the Sixth Street traffic. He stood on the sidewalk, taking in a view that was little changed from the first time he saw it.

****

Maggie and he had both been students at the University of Texas, she in pre-law and he in criminology and computer science. They met during freshman orientation week at a bar on Sixth Street that the university had rented as an age-appropriate venue. Maggie would assert against the incredulity of all future doubters that within the first few minutes, she knew! She knew she would marry the tall, quiet boy from Bainbridge Island whom she saw sitting in a corner booth, utterly flummoxed by his introduction to even the watered-down version of the Austin bar scene. Over his shy protestations, she bought him a Coke and sat down across from him, pretending to study the menu while secretly delighting in his obvious discomfort.

Maggie had a knack for keeping Clayton off balance. She had a fine, practical mind and an unerring moral compass. Once when he teased her about her activist leanings and social justice ambitions, she countered, "I'm not out to change the world, just my little part of it."

She was fond of roses, a bit of personal trivia that Clayton was smart enough to file away and draw upon over the years.

"They're pretty enough and they sure smell sweet, but they'd be better without the thorns," he groused at one point. "I can never pick one up without getting stabbed."

"Stabbed?" Maggie scoffed. "That's a bit much, don't you think?"

And then she did what always surprised and thrilled Clayton. She took a commonly shared worldview and looked at it sideways.

"Besides, the thorns aren't there to hurt you. They are a rose's way of focusing your attention on their beauty. You can easily ignore all the other flowers even while you're holding them, but not a rose. With roses—pay attention." Her signature smile brightened her already glowing face. Assuming a light-hearted, flirtatious pose, she tossed her dark hair over her shoulder. "Just like me." Her smile broke into a laugh that Clayton always thought sounded like joy itself.

He quickly grew to love her whimsy and enthusiasm. Her gentle teasing and good-natured prodding challenged his self-imposed boundaries and made every day an adventure. She, in turn, admired his dedication to duty and noble sense of purpose.

At times she would proclaim "Clayton Rhodes, you're a work in progress but you have given me some good raw material, and with God's help, you'll do—and, by the way, I like the work." Then again, there would be that laugh.

Laughter came easily for the two of them, as did everything else. They became inseparable. Clayton proposed at the start of their senior year. He remembered it as the bravest thing he'd ever done. They married shortly after graduation.

Clayton had joined UT's Naval ROTC program and in the months following graduation applied and was accepted into the SEAL program. He was driven to noble causes, but four years of war, much of that time away from home, brought a longing to be a contributor on U.S. soil. After the years of saving the world in foreign lands, he set his sights on a more local commitment to save his part of it and to spend more time with Maggie.

He became an attractive, eager, and successful applicant for an opportunity with the FBI. Building on his degree in computer science, he took extensive training in cybersecurity, but because of his SEAL background, he often participated in tactical field operations, many times undercover.

While Clayton built his career within the FBI, Maggie carried on her work as an advocate for a large variety of causes acting on noble impulses that made her higher-salaried friends secretly envious. Nine years flew by and Anthony was born.

——∙⟨∞⟩∙——

Night on 6th Street

It was a little before seven in the evening when Clayton checked in at the desk and, through force of habit, scanned the opulent lobby's occupants. His senses, honed by years of training and experience, reflexively parsed the scene.

A man in a business suit paced by the window near the entrance while alternately checking the street and his phone. Too young and nervous to be a power broker, Clayton surmised he was most likely waiting for a ride to a dinner meeting that was part of an interview process.

A young woman hurriedly covered her provocative shorts and revealing blouse under an unbuttoned blue blazer as she swiftly moved through the lobby to the bank of elevators and was soon whisked up to her own sort of business meeting.

He wondered to himself what brought all these people to Austin on this day. Were their agendas pure or tainted? Were their lives filled with turmoil or peaceful bliss? Such ruminations swiftly turned inward. He was there, at long last, to make room in the mosaic of his life for a piece that could only fit with painful acceptance. His only hope for the future depended on this pilgrimage into the past.

His commitment to this mission objective drove his decision to forgo a sit-down dinner in favor of bar snacks. After dropping his bag off in his room, he left the hotel to begin his odyssey of reflection and reconciliation. As he walked, he soaked in the 6th Street vibe that fed his need for full-scale immersion in a past he had long suppressed. In the bar where Maggie and he first met, he nursed a beer as he watched a couple in the corner booth laugh and flirt, heirs to the space that in another time, Maggie and he celebrated the end of finals in their junior year.

Sixth Street was his time machine. The faces, the places, the music, and the noise tugged him into the past, and then reality jolted him back again, emotionally exhausted but grateful for the release of the memories he had locked away. It was after midnight when he felt he had done what he set out to do. He headed back to the hotel, navigating through the rivers of revelers that flowed from one venue to another.

Clayton ordered sparkling water at the hotel bar and went out to sit on the small patio on the Sixth Street side of the Driskill. As he leaned back in the padded wicker chair, his service weapon poked uncomfortably into his side. He reached around and adjusted it slightly thinking ruefully to himself that in recent years the gun was becoming more uncomfortable. He looked out at the merrymakers unable, any longer to become lost in the music and the action.

Clayton began to feel the healing that he hoped he would find in Austin. He let his eyes close and gave himself over to a more peaceful reverie and newfound hope for a future with less pain. In the darkness of his closed eyes, he allowed joyful memories to float to the surface of the black waters of his grief and guilt. The tender recollections pulled his features into a small smile of appreciation.

The sound of the first shot tore through his musing, exploding it like a child's birthday balloon. There was no car backfire or firecracker confusion. He knew it for what it was the instant he heard it. It was gunfire, and it triggered a trained response. He sprang to his feet and was across the patio and into the street even before the crowd reacted. He scanned for the source of the sound and for any clues as to what was happening.

More shots, then screams followed. Like fire on a pool of gasoline, realization, then fear spread through the crowd. Clayton jogged toward the gunfire. A young man stumbled by, bleeding from a shoulder wound. Drawing his weapon but keeping it at his side, in full run now, against the current of the retreating crowd, Clayton covered the few hundred feet to where his ears told him the shots originated. Amid the mayhem, he zeroed in on a hooded male figure, raising his weapon, then fire. As Clayton saw a body drop, he brought his own weapon up. He checked the background of his target, aimed, and fired.

Just as he pulled the trigger, something smashed into his back and spun him around. Dazed, he knew something was seriously wrong. He fought against the shock and tried to focus, but shadows of a different sort tore at his consciousness. He was aware of his face hitting the pavement, the feel of the rough surface, and the smell of dirt. Then the peaceful reverie washed over him once again and everything faded.

CHAPTER THREE

Brice Canton June 2021

June 4, 2021 - Happy Birthday Brice Canton

Twenty-one years before the shooting on Sixth Street, Brice Canton was born. He sprouted from deep Texas roots and was nurtured in a rich mix of Texan good-natured generosity and fierce independence. His mother, Sara, passionately optimistic, taught him joy, faith, and respect for all living things.

Whatever optimism his father, Hank, once possessed had long been calloused over by a hard life of building and then defending a 2,000-acre ranch in central Texas. From his father, Brice learned vigilance, courage, and defense of God and country as laid out in the Constitution, especially the Second Amendment.

"Listen, Son", Hank's voice would always get a little deeper as he delivered the same two-word opening when he meant for Brice to pay particular attention, "A world with fewer guns might be a good thing but that's for sure not the world we live in."

And so Brice grew, watered by Texas rain, and nurtured by all the love and attention Sara and Hank poured into him. Raised on the plentiful acreage of the family ranch, he fine-tuned his skills as a rancher and hunter. The years rolled by. Ranch life showered its benefits onto his growing body and sharpened his reflexes. A natural athlete and fine student, he leveraged his love of sports, football in particular, into a full athletic scholarship at the University of Texas in Austin. Life was good.

On the evening of Brice's twenty-first birthday, the family came together to celebrate. Lengthening shadows like stalking ghosts crept stealthily from the blossoming Yucca spires and shaggy-barked scrub oaks and stretched eerily across the prairie. The Cantons sat down to a meal of grilled steak and savory vegetables at the large table on the porch. Dinner segued gracefully into the mom-made cake, the birthday song, the secret wish, the still-manageable one-breath snuffing of twenty-one flaming wax milestones, and a grand finale of hurrahs, hugs, and kisses. Then, a comfortable silence presided, broken only by forks clicking on plates and occasional, exaggerated but sincere "yums".

"I'll clear these off." Sara stood and started stacking the dishes, and Brice quickly moved to pitch in. Hank disappeared into the house and when he returned a short while later, he was holding a handsomely carved wooden box about the size of a small briefcase.

"Sit for another minute", he rumbled and sat at the table as Brice and Sara followed suit.

He rested his big, callused rancher's hands on the box. After a long pause, while he appeared to consider what he should say, Hank pushed the box across the table to a place in front of Brice. "Son, it's time this became yours."

The soft light of sunset and Hank's solemn tone brought an almost sacramental air to the moment.

"Open it," Hank's kindly urging didn't demand immediate obedience, and Brice took time to run his fingers over the ornate carving. He grasped each side of the lid and lifted it on its rear brass hinges. Inside was a pistol and holster. Hank reached across the table and took the pistol out of the box. As Hank hefted the weapon, Brice saw his father's face change. He watched as Hank's eyes appeared to go to a place far away, in a time long ago.

"Listen son," Hank's voice dropped in the familiar way, "this is the 1911 Colt that your grandfather carried in World War Two. It saved his life on more than one occasion and after he passed it down, it did the same for me in Nam when my M16 crapped out." As he handed Brice the heavy weapon, Hank gazed intensely into his son's eyes. "Carry this as proudly as your grandfather and I did."

Brice could only manage a nod and a whispered, "I will sir," as emotion swelled in his throat.

Texas was now a 'free carry state', which meant that any person over twenty-one, not otherwise legally prohibited, could carry a pistol in most places without training, licensing, or background check. Brice proudly strapped the holstered weapon around his hips. Both men suppressed the urge to salute and managed an awkward hug before Brice, still wearing the gun, went back to helping his mother with the dishes.

———⟨∞⟩———

June 12 - Brice on 6th Street

It was a little after one a.m. on the Saturday, eight days later. The mix of music and crowd noises from a dozen bars made conversation impossible. Brice hugged some, shouted unheard goodbyes, and waved goodnight to others in the group of friends with whom he had spent the last several hours. On this warm June night, the intense revelry of Austin's Sixth Street had gifted Brice and his posse a memorable evening. For most 21-year-olds, events and experiences pile one upon another so rapidly that they blur and fade to mere impressions of recollections. Shedding their details, they blend one with the other, becoming a montage of personal history. Savored and then filed away, they exist in mental storage as truth for hire available for flawed recollection and self-serving embellishment. In the normal course of events, this evening would be one such, but tonight, the course of events would be anything but normal.

Brice had arrived early, so he had snagged a parking spot almost on the corner of Brazos Street and 6th Street, a short walk from where he left his friends. As he approached, he pressed the button on his key fob and the car gave an obedient chirp in response. As he put his hand on the door, he heard the first shot. He froze. For the space of three heartbeats, his mind tried to reconcile a sound so out of place. More shots and screams triggered realization and then action. In almost one motion, he tore open the car door, reached into the glove box, grabbed the Colt, pivoted, and dashed back into the crowd that was just starting to panic.

Thump—Thump—Thump. His normally inaudible heartbeat became more and more pronounced with each passing second. A young woman lay on the ground, clearly beyond any help, as blood pooled from a wound on her head. As a hunter, he had seen many animals with gunshot wounds, but never another human being. He fought back the urge to vomit. A man about Brice's age staggered by, the shoulder of his light blue shirt turning red.

"Oh, God! Oh, God! Oh, God!", Brice muttered to himself over and over as the rush of adrenaline at once sharpened all his senses and also caused his hand to shake so much that he feared he would drop the Colt. He fought the wave of panic that threatened to immobilize him once again and scanned the crowd for the shooter.

THUMP—THUMP—THUMP. "OH, GOD! OH, GOD! OH, GOD!", his muttered words took on the tempo of his pounding heart.

The sound of more shots pierced the cacophony of music and screams. Less than a minute had passed since the first shot rang out. And then Brice saw him. A man in a Hawaiian shirt was shouting something unintelligible. He was raising his hand and in his hand was a gun.

THUMP—THUMP. "OH, GOD! OH, GOD!"

The man aimed at the crowd.

"OH, GOD—NO, YOU DON'T!"

Brice raised the Colt and pulled the trigger just as the man fired his weapon. Through the recoil and the smoke, Brice watched his target spin around and fall. Then something slammed into Brice's side. He tried to stay focused, but the scene grew fuzzy. The screams, the music, the panicked crowd, and his heartbeat, all combined like some experimental rock video, and then sight and sound faded. He felt like he was falling a great distance, but it was only a short drop to the ground.

"OH, GOD! Oh, G—"

It was a surprisingly soft landing, and then there was darkness.

PART TWO

PROJECT ATHENA

CHAPTER FOUR

Doctor Raymond Komi Ababio

December 2019 - Semester Closing Lecture on Artificial Intelligence

The lecture hall at the University of Washington's Bill & Melinda Gates Center for Computer Science & Engineering was filled to legal capacity and then some. The studious and the curious found places on the steps and along the walls of the hall in numbers that broke any number of university and fire code rules. It was Dr. Raymond Komi Ababio's last lecture of the fall semester. While the turnout was unusual for any class, it was remarkable for an advanced class in deep learning. Over the course of the semester, word had spread that anyone interested in the current state of artificial intelligence should hear Dr. Ababio speak, and anyone interested in the future of AI must seek his visionary insight into an increasingly probable future.

"I am sorry to say that we have time for just one more question." Raymond looked out at the rows of faces that even after two hours were hanging on his every word.

He recognized a doctoral student from his class who had stared down a much larger challenger for a front-row seat. "Ms. Martel."

"Dr. Ababio, with all that is happening in AI now and considering all that you envision for its near-term future, do you see a time when we, as humans, might have to recognize the soulfulness of AI entities and accept them as true life forms?"

A slight murmur of controversy swept through the hall, quickly trailing off into an attentive silence.

"Ms. Martel, it seems a little unfair to pose such a pregnant question so close to the end of the semester. Any thoughtful answer would have to be constructed based on preliminary discussions of what is a 'soul' and what makes a 'life form'. I wish you had asked me something easier, like 'What is the meaning of life?'" Raymond's rebuke was a good-natured one, and his dark skin highlighted the effect of his full and easy smile. A ripple of laughter swept the hall. Raymond held up his hand, and the laughter faded.

"Understanding that the question and its answer might be better served by even more than a full semester's exploration, my personal feeling is that whatever definitions we might derive, souls and life forms are not, cannot be created out of bits and bytes. AI is a tool created by humans to serve a purpose. No matter how lifelike we program an AI entity to be, it can only appear to be cogent and only within the bounds of its programming. The implications of any counterargument are logically untenable. If I were to pull the plug on an AI entity that I created, would I be guilty of murder?" Raymond paused to let the question register. "I suggest no more so than I would be guilty of assault if I kicked my uncooperative lawn mower. No, Ms. Martel, God creates souls. Humans create tools. To claim anything else would be arrogant and, if you're a believer, blasphemous."

There was a collective silence as the attending minds digested Raymond's last words.

Raymond's voice broke the spell. "It's been an honor to journey with you over the past semester. Thank you for your attention and good luck to you all. Have a wonderful holiday season."

The tone of finality signaled the end of the lecture, prompting applause and a standing ovation. As the audience filed out of the auditorium, two figures stood in the shadows at the back. They waited until the last of the friends, fans, and fellow professors shook Raymond's hand, offering congratulations and holiday wishes. Only when Raymond was finally alone, packing up his notes, did they step down onto the lecture hall floor. Raymond looked up from his briefcase as the two approached.

"Dr. Ababio, may we have a few moments of your time?" The taller of the two forced a smile as though it were an unfamiliar effort and spoke with no attempt to introduce himself. His question was missing the appropriate note of supplication. There was nothing blatantly threatening in his words or demeanor, but the two emitted an aura of subliminal intimidation. Raymond instinctively knew that it would be hard to say no to the request even as he moved unconsciously to put the desk between him and the visitors. They wore suits signaling that they were not students and most likely not faculty members. One person in a suit might imply a personal preference. Two people together most likely indicated a professional dress code requirement.

Raymond had been around academic people his whole life and they came in all flavors: courageous, endearing, inquisitive, competitive, parochial, and pompous. Whatever their individual characteristics, they all shared the rigors, language, and reality of academic life, and the imprint of that common experience became an unmistakable and instantly discernible character trait, a tag, a tell. Whatever that intangible identifier was, the two who now stood waiting for Raymond's reply were something other. The taller man's lean body, athletic movements, golden tan, and scar on his cheek testified further to a career outside of the classroom.

"What is this about, gentlemen? I have another engagement," Raymond lied.

"This will only take a few minutes of your time and could be of significant value to you and your work. There is someone who would like to meet you."

"And who are you?"

"It doesn't really matter, but my name is Keaton and this is George. Will you let me introduce you?"

"Okay, where is he?" Raymond checked the empty auditorium, half expecting a figure to appear in a puff of smoke.

"*She* would like to speak with you in a more private setting. Would you please come with me? She's waiting in an office just down the hall."

Raymond fiddled with the latch on his briefcase as he assessed the vague sense of danger that emanated from Keaton, like a bad choice of aftershave. "Okay. Just let me gather my things."

"No need, Doctor. They'll be safe. George will stay with them." The man, who had introduced himself as Keaton, was clearly in charge, and now nodded to his beefy companion who, up to this point, had been silent.

Seeming startled to be included in the conversation, George's response was appropriate but unconvincing. "Absolutely Doctor, I'll take good care of them."

Raymond's initial reluctance to accompany Keaton was rapidly losing its battle against his growing interest. *After all,* his curious self argued, *the path through the unknown is the only way to discovery.*

Keaton watched the resistance melt in Raymond's eyes. Anticipating the final verdict even before Raymond was aware of it, Keaton confidently turned and moved toward the lecture hall exit. Unaware that he had been holding his breath, Raymond sighed in resignation, pushed his briefcase across the desk toward a smirking George, and moved quickly to fall in step behind Keaton. After a short walk, Keaton stopped, gently knocked twice on an office door, and waited.

A woman's voice called out from inside, "Come."

Responding to the summons, Keaton pushed the door open and held it. Raymond hesitated and Keaton, affecting an unconvincing smile of encouragement, gestured for him to enter. Keaton followed and closed the door behind them.

The office belonged to Doctor Adrianne Duvernay, a faculty member who Raymond knew but not well. It was an interior office with no windows, but the lighting was adequate, if a bit subdued. There was a steady hum as the air conditioning worked to maintain a comfortable temperature. Framed degrees and awards hung on the small sections of the walls not covered by fully loaded bookshelves. A pair of comfortably padded office chairs were arranged in front of an elegant French desk. On the desk were a large monitor, keyboard, and what appeared to be pictures of Dr. Duvernay's family.

The woman behind the desk, however, was not Adrianne Duvernay.

"Cute kids," she commented as she leaned forward and carefully placed the picture back on the desk. Her movements had a supple refinement to them that signaled a well-tuned and capable body.

Keaton spoke up with the formal introductions, "Doctor, let me introduce you to Ms. Maxine Corbel. Ms. Corbel, this is Dr. Raymond Komi Ababio."

Raymond guessed her to be in her mid-forties, although her black pin-striped pantsuit and stylishly short-cropped, strikingly white hair, gave her appearance ageless and epicene qualities.

She stayed seated and took her time, turning her gaze from the picture to give Raymond her full attention. When she spoke, the words didn't pierce the silence as much as flow through it. "Have a seat Raymond—I hope you don't mind if I call you Raymond—please call me Max. Everyone else does." Although her words were congenial, there was an imperious undertone that asserted control of the conversation.

Raymond was irritated at both the presumed familiarity and their invasion of another faculty member's office. "Why are we in Doctor Duvernay's office?" he demanded, ignoring the offer of a chair.

"It's all good, Raymond. I wanted to meet you privately. I have some connections in the school and I requested the use of an office for our meeting. We won't be long and I promised to be respectful of Doctor … ah … Duvernay's workspace."

"Let's see what we know of you"—Ignoring Raymond's discomfort or perhaps enjoying it, she picked a tablet up from the desk, tapped it to life, and read from the glowing screen— "Dr. Raymond Komi Ababio, you were born into a family of meager means. Your father struggled to eventual success as a cacao farmer, and your mother was a teacher in your village primary school. Showing great academic promise, you spent two years at the Hekima Jesuit Seminary in Nairobi and then moved on—oops! Do I detect a crisis of faith?" Max lifted her eyes from her screen and, with a half smile on her lips, cast an inquisitive look at the now very confused Raymond.

"I—what—"

Max resumed her reading. "You moved on to receive your medical degree from Harvard and doctoral degree in neuroscience from MIT. From there, you changed direction again and added your second Ph.D. in neural networks and deep learning methods from Stanford." Max once again looked up from her tablet. "Wow! Doctor Ababio! While all the other young men were enthusiastically screwing their way through the temporary bliss of their first marriages, you clearly had other ambitions—Good for you!" Eyes on the display once again, she continued. "Blah, blah, blah—a bunch of publications on those topics established your reputation. Then you received an invitation from this magnificent institution to join the faculty as a visiting professor—and—here we are. No children, no wife—it would seem we have at least that in common—no time for entanglements and the distractions they bring. Am I right?"

Struggling for a response, Raymond sputtered out the first rebuttal that made the slightest sense. "Why—How—What is this all about? If you wanted to talk with me, why didn't you just make an appointment during my regular office hours, as everyone else does?"

"Well, clearly Raymond—" She leaned back in the chair, crossing her pinstriped legs. "I'm not like everyone else. When I see an opportunity, I like to move quickly. I have one in mind in which you might play an important role, and, truth be told, I wanted to impress you." While Max's aura was androgynous, her commanding tone and graceful movements hinted at an ability to bring either gender into play.

Initially intimidated by the theatrics of the meeting, Raymond's irritation now overruled any uneasiness. "Well, the only impression you have made is a bad one. Anyone with a few minutes and access to the internet could put together that biography. I have things to do, so if you want to talk, I suggest you make an appointment."

He turned to go, but Keaton stood, unmoving between him and the door.

"Raymond, please, one moment more." Max purred playfully, her demeanor shifting from haughty to coy. "When I said I wanted to impress you, this is what I was talking about."

Raymond turned to face Max and saw her slide a business-sized envelope across the desk. It had his name written on it in neat longhand. Ensnared by his innate inquisitiveness, he wavered, no longer sure of what to do.

"Open it." Max's lips formed a confident half-smile as demand and seduction flavored her words.

Raymond considered pressing his desire to leave, but was unwilling to test Keaton's posturing with a physical confrontation. He objected to the dramatics of the meeting, but finally, his curiosity prevailed. Slowly, he reached for the envelope and picked it up.

"Go ahead, open it." Max's smile broadened as she cheered him to the finish line.

The flap wasn't sealed. He flipped it back and pulled out the one piece of paper the envelope contained. It was a check made out to him for one million dollars. The information on the check was as sparse as on any check. The date, his name, the apparent signature of Maxine Corbel, and the amount—the amount! Suddenly, Raymond found himself needing the seat that Max had previously offered. When he finally spoke, his voice cracked. "Is … is this a joke?"

"Raymond, as you can see, the check is from the Society for Human Advancement, SHUMA. It's one of the organizations that I am involved with. You may have heard of it, but no matter. I founded it five years ago to help ensure that technology, especially artificial intelligence, will live up to its highest potential to serve humankind.

"I have been following your career and was especially impressed by your paper on the future practical applications of multilayer neural networks and deep learning. I'm not a scientist, so much of your paper's technical content was beyond me, but I got a clear enough picture of your vision and was moved by your argument that support of these applications should be funded. The bottom line is that I would like you to head up a project in pursuit of the development of one of these applications."

Raymond sat, quietly staring at the check. As Max finished her comments, he raised his eyes to meet hers, thought for a moment, and stood up. "As much as I appreciate your offer and as tempting as it is, I can think of two reasons that would keep me from accepting. The first is I have a job that I enjoy, here at the university. The second is that as generous as it is, a million dollars wouldn't come close to funding the effort needed by any of the applications I envisioned."

Max smiled. "I'm surprised that you could only come up with two objections, Raymond. I'll take that as an indication of your interest. But to answer your challenges, I can assure you that the university will completely support your attention to this project for as long as it takes. It will supply laboratory space and allow you to recruit any team members that you would like to have assigned to it. It only asks that it be credited with any publicly available paper that you author as part of the project."

"So you've already discussed this with them. You're pretty confident."

"Always."

"But the second of my objections still stands. The check you gave me won't cover the cost of the project."

"You misunderstand, Raymond. That check is for you." Max slid another envelope across the desk. "To answer your second objection—this will cover at least the start of the project with the promise of ongoing access to future funding as needed. You can bank on it."

Raymond opened the envelope and looked at the enclosed check. Once again, he felt the need to sit down.

August 9, 2021 - The New Office

Dr. Raymond Komi Ababio stood behind an impressive, intricately carved wooden desk at one end of the spacious, well-appointed office space. At the other end was a sizable conference table and accompanying chairs. In the middle was a group of comfortable-looking lounge chairs arranged in front of several large video screens with attached equipment. He inhaled the heady mix of cut wood, furniture polish, and new electronics, all testifying to the room's recent construction.

He smiled with amusement at the excessive touches. The space had been completely gutted and rebuilt specifically for his project in the Naval Hospital in Bremerton, Washington. His survey of the room satisfied him that, having followed his instructions, his team had set up the optimal environment for the next phase of the project called ATHENA. It was to be the culmination and synthesis of everything he had learned and envisioned from his combined work in psychiatry and artificial intelligence. The project promised to leapfrog all AI research to date. He had designed the room at the naval hospital to allow for a controlled environment with easy access to the labs at the University of Washington in Seattle. The lavish extras were compliments of Max and SHUMA.

He pulled open the folds of a cardboard box and lifted out a swath of multi-colored, kente cloth, a relic of his graduation from high school in a different world, 45 years ago. Raymond was not a nostalgic person. Most of the remnants of his past were gone, winnowed by his frequent moves. But this piece of fabric had survived. Woven by his mother, it was a reminder and token of his roots, the early years of his life's story, so far away and so long ago. He held it up to his face and inhaled deeply, capturing the faint whiff of dust and cacao—Africa. As he carefully spread it out on the credenza behind the desk, the intricate pattern was revealed and the arc of his life's story flashed through his mind. He reflected on Max's sterile recitation of his life's highlights. Although mostly accurate, her delivery rendered them devoid of any context or color.

"You were born into a family of meager means ... "

His name spoke of the dual cultures that shaped his life. He was born two minutes past midnight on a rainy Saturday morning. Adhering to Ghanaian tradition, his parents named him Komi, the Ashanti word for Saturday. Three minutes earlier, he would have gone through life as Kofi.

"Your father struggled ... "

As a newlywed, his father had made the hard decision to replace the aging trees on his inherited fallow cacao farm. The lean years waiting for the young trees to produce were more than compensated by the later abundant crops. His father's successful gamble ensured that the young Komi had some advantages relative to the others in his village. Food and shelter were never an issue.

Komi had only vague recollections of his earliest years in the family's thatched roof hut with the dirt floor. By the time he was seven, the Ababios were financially able to construct a modern three-bedroom home. While a pleasant change, the level of happiness in Komi's life remained largely unaffected. His joy sprang from his family and his delight was in the wonder, energy, and curiosity that filled his every day.

The senior Ababio's struggles and eventual success delivered a wordless sermon on the rewards of hard work.

"Your mother was a teacher in your village primary school ... "

Teaching in the village school, Komi's mother preached a gospel of faith and learning that found an enthusiastic disciple in the boy. From the cacao fields to the classroom, always in a rush, the youth avidly prospected for nuggets of new knowledge, stringing them into bold insights.

"You showed great academic promise ... "

Bright and precocious, he galloped through one academic achievement after another. His secondary school teacher would say, "I have given him all I can from the well of my knowledge, but he needs more than a well—he needs an ocean."

"... *you spent two years at the Hekima Jesuit Seminary in Nairobi ...*"

During his undergraduate years, his appetite for holistic exploration led him to spend two years in a Catholic seminary. At the time, he had viewed a career as a Jesuit priest to be the epitome of intellectual and spiritual accomplishment.

Early letters to his parents expressed his initial enthusiasm, "This is wonderful! There are such brilliant minds here! There is so much to learn!"

However, as the months rolled on, the letters were less enthusiastic. "There are so many rules ..."

"*... and then you moved on ...*"

While his experience with religious life fed his hunger for knowledge, Raymond found its rigors to be oppressively constraining.

"*...Do I detect a crisis of faith?*"

His two years as a novitiate wore away much of his religious zeal but left in him a raw spiritualism, receptive but unformed—a faith in search of a belief.

When he walked through the gates of the seminary for the last time, he took with him a more disciplined approach to his youthful explorations. His craving for more learning and his awakening desire to balance his spiritual development with more earthly explorations brought his thoughts to a career in medicine.

"*... You moved on to receive your medical degree from Harvard and doctoral degree in neuroscience from MIT ...*"

Innate optimism and growing ambition emboldened him to knock on the doors of the great medical schools. His academic record, life story, and charismatic personality opened them.

Although excelling at the subject matter of his medical training dealing specifically with the body, Raymond's interest was always most aroused by the larger questions of human health and behavior. His doctoral thesis explored the effects of faith-rich environments on mental health. The day he received his medical degree from Harvard, his beaming father held his robe-bedecked son in a tight embrace. Their eyes locked as he stepped back, still holding his son's shoulders.

"Komi, my son, you have climbed a tall mountain and earned this great honor. It is a new birth for you, into a new world and, in the tradition of our people, a new birth must have a new name." Raymond's father had given the topic much consideration. Indeed, he and Raymond's mother had studied lists of names and researched their meanings to find the perfect new name for their son. With his eyes overflowing with tears of pride, the older Ababio proclaimed, "Raymond—in this new world, this new life, your name should be Doctor Raymond Komi Ababio." He continued, in answer to the questioning look in his son's eyes, "It is who your mother and I see you to be. The name 'Raymond' means protector and counselor."

Even at thirty years old, there was never a moment that Raymond thought to object or view his parents' wish as anything but an honor.

"*... From there, you changed direction again and added your second Ph.D. in neural networks and deep learning methods from Stanford ...*"

While working on his thesis, Raymond had used artificial intelligence tools to test various mental health hypotheses. Quickly grasping the potential of this nascent field of study, he was thrilled at the idea that computer tools might not just crunch numbers but bring new insights into human endeavor. He abandoned his original postgraduate plan to develop advanced psychiatric protocols. Instead, he joined a research group at Stanford University where he added another doctorate to his credentials. This time, the focus was on neural networks and deep learning methods.

"*No children, no wife—no time for entanglements and the distractions they bring ...*"

He had made friends and even experienced the rapture of a blossoming romance. The pain of its demise cast a cloud on his further social interactions. Completing the cycle of his social evolution, he rediscovered the satisfaction of contending with challenges whose solutions were not wrapped in human inconsistencies. With renewed energy, he committed himself to the precept that there was only so much time in any person's life and his ambition and drive took all of his. In these later years, he rarely played the what-if game, but on those occasions, the powerful vision he had of his life's legacy easily overshadowed the vague mental images of hearth and home. His lasting contribution was not to be future generations of Ababios, but the product of the full application of all the abilities God had given him. He viewed the pursuit of personal happiness outside of his scientific endeavors to be a selfish waste of time and effort.

Lost in his thoughts, he hadn't heard the heavy double doors open behind him, but as they clicked shut, a now familiar male voice jolted him back to the present.

"Hey Doc, nice digs." An obnoxious mix of inherited wealth, California-coast snobbery, and meritless arrogance, Keaton Amory's voice hardly needed the off-putting dash of condescension to make it instantly grating. His long, graying, light-brown, well-coiffed hair, well-tanned skin, and fit, thin body at first glance begged the label "aging-surfer-dude" but his close-cropped beard, piercing eyes, and catlike movements hinted at something darker and more dangerous. The pale scar on his cheek blazed across his tanned skin and added impact to Keaton's air of muted menace. It reinforced the impression of a man who was no stranger to violence. He was conspicuously secretive about the details of his past, which invited further dark imaginings. It was infinitely easier to imagine Keaton's hands around the throat of an opponent than his mind engaging in a duel of wits. The message in

Keaton's unannounced and no-knock entrance was not lost on Raymond.

"You can't say SHUMA doesn't take good care of you and your project ASSTINA."

"ATHENA," Raymond corrected, although he knew Keaton was purposely trying to bait him. "Yes, SHUMA has been very generous with their support."

Raymond was walking a thin line here. Struggling to keep his visceral dislike of the man in check, Raymond was very aware that Keaton would make a dangerous enemy. Not only did he project a subtle threat of physical violence, but he was also Maxine Corbel's long-time personal assistant, a bond that Raymond felt powerless to test.

As competition in the field of artificial intelligence caught fire, interest groups coalesced around their various views on the topic. SHUMA, the Society for Human Advancement, emerged from this cauldron of intense political and financial activity and, backed by deep-pocket-believers and politically connected influence peddlers, rapidly became the most powerful voice for what it claimed to be 'the responsible use of artificial intelligence, in all its forms, for the betterment of humanity.' Leveraging these vast and growing resources, SHUMA brokered a deal with the FBI to provide a test case for a practical application of cutting-edge AI technology. Hence ATHENA was born. While the FBI was an important client whose endorsement would be of great value, SHUMA was always the most powerful player in the room—and Keaton Amory was the face of SHUMA.

"How can I help you, Keaton?" Raymond struggled to juggle political correctness, polite congeniality, and professional courtesy.

"Just stopped in to see how you like your new base of operations."

"It's wonderful." Raymond's enthusiasm was sincere as he once again surveyed the room.

"Yes, it is." Keaton's tone was more of an assertion than an agreement. "We look forward to your delivering great things from ASSTINA. Let me know if you need anything. I have taken an office space upstairs, just above your head."

Raymond winced, but otherwise refrained from reacting to Keaton's repeated barb and their relative positions of authority. "I certainly will. Thank you for the offer."

Keaton moved to the door and as he stepped through it, he turned and took one last look around. His eyes settled on Raymond's. "Do well." Keaton closed the door behind him, leaving the unspoken "… or else" hanging in the air.

CHAPTER FIVE
Welcome to Project ATHENA - January 2022

Thursday Afternoon, January 13 - Introductions

The nautical clock on Clayton's home office wall had already chimed the four bells to signal 2 p.m. It was now 2:07. Clayton stared at the computer screen as his fingers tapped his irritation on the desktop. He was logged on to SETE, the government-approved Secure Encrypted Teleconference Environment. The impassive display informed Clayton that he was the only current attendee for the meeting scheduled to start at 2:00. His increasingly vigorous drumming caused the wood cane he had propped against the desk to lose its grip and slide to the worn hardwood floor with a clatter. He stared at it with a mixture of resentment and disgust.

His eyes fell on the framed picture that occupied a reserved spot on his desktop. Three smiling faces against a backdrop of a surf-swept beach stared back at him. It was fossilized joy, a fleeting moment, frozen in time. Maggie, Anthony, and he had spent a magical weekend in Galveston and Maggie's dark hair was blown back by the ocean breeze. She had just said one of her wonderfully silly things to make him laugh. The smile on Anthony's face mirrored his parent's happiness. Clayton struggled unsuccessfully to remember the details of the moment, indeed any details of the whole trip. When he tried, the initial hot, pleasurable glow of the memory faded into a cold nothingness.

Seeking a less disturbing distraction, he picked up the book he was currently reading, Immanuel Kant's *Critique of Pure Reason*. There was a time when he would lose himself in action yarns, tales of derring-do, and high adventure. Clear-cut stories of good over evil with happy endings had resonated with his moral code and personal aspirations. The deaths of his family had shaken his foundations and replaced much of the optimism he had borrowed from Maggie with a darker introspection. Where once he had been entertained by Clive Cussler, and Jack London, impressed by Hemingway and Falkner, he was now trapped in the darker worlds of Dostoevsky, Kant, and Kafka. He had devolved from an appreciative audience to a disoriented pilgrim.

Four more minutes went by. His annoyance at the delay pushed the content of the three pages he had just read out of his mind completely. His drumming became more intense as he considered abandoning the meeting. Then, with a warning beep, the screen gathered the necessary pixels and came to life.

A white-coated, dark-skinned male figure appeared and filled the display as he sat down at his end of the teleconference. His thin but healthy face was framed by a close-cut beard and a full head of thick hair. The invading gray left small, flattering outposts of the original black. Clayton guessed him to be in his mid-60s but his age was hard to discern. His head sat comfortably on square shoulders that testified to a still-active body. His eyes were bright with intelligence and, in concert with the slight smile on his lips, communicated confidence without condescension, knowledge without arrogance. The white coat contrasted with his dark skin and completed the picture of a character that could have come from central casting to pitch the latest miracle cure for whatever-ails-you—the quintessence of credibility. The face leaned into the display as he fiddled with some unseen adjustments.

"There, that should do," he murmured to himself in a deep, resonant voice and then more directly to Clayton, "Am I on?"

"You're late." Clayton only slightly regretted his harshness.

"I'm so sorry, Clayton. Not a good start to our first meeting." The kindly demeanor and warm apology pushed Clayton's temper back into its cage. "I'm Doctor Raymond Ababio. I know you're meeting with me because the FBI has required it, but I hope that doesn't become an obstacle to our working together." He picked up a computer tablet and his dark eyes scanned the screen. "I see that it was touch-and-go for a bit after the incident in Austin. Kudos to the doctors and staff at St. Davids. They did some remarkable work."

Clayton fidgeted in his seat, bracing himself against another recitation of the damage inflicted by the shooting.

Noticing Clayton's discomfort, Raymond paused only briefly before continuing to summarize the notes on his tablet, "I see that once you were stable, they transferred you here to Bremerton. Then, when you were well enough to leave the hospital, you were allowed to move to the home you grew up in and that your now-deceased parents had left you on Bainbridge Island. It is close enough to the hospital for any necessary in-person medical appointments and it gave you the healing peace and isolation that you and your caregivers agreed you needed. Now you're on a program of regular visits to a rehabilitation facility near your home."

"Thanks for the history lesson, Doctor. Will any of that be on the test?"

Raymond ignored Clayton's sarcasm. "Did they tell you what happened?"

"I was comatose for weeks, and then it was weeks before I could understand much of anything beyond the fact that I was shot. My initial fuzzy thinking was that it was the shooter, or an accomplice, that had tagged me. When the fog lifted, I came to understand that some hyped-up, untrained, wannabe hero made a goddamn mistake."

"Well, Clayton, the headline is accurate, although the portrayal is a bit harsh. The person who shot you was a well-meaning 21-year-old, Brice Canton. He took you for the bad guy and did what he thought was the right thing."

This was the first time that anyone had put a name to his shooter. Clayton took a moment to add the kinder characterization of Brice Canton's motivations to his simmering, reflexive anger. For the first time, he willed himself to view the event dispassionately. Finally, a grim smile formed on Clayton's lips. "Well, ain't that a kick in the head."

Raymond continued, "I see you now appreciate the irony. It gets better—or worse. As it turns out, Mr. Canton wasn't the only well-intentioned citizen in the crowd. As he mistook you for a bad guy, another armed civilian similarly mistook him. Since it was Texas, all concerned were lucky that the carnage stopped there."

Clayton was slow to respond. "Did Canton make it?" he asked out of a complicated mix of dark satisfaction, simple curiosity, and sincere concern.

"Yes, he did, although he spent some time relearning to use his right arm, and he's lost his football scholarship."

"Tough break." Despite an obvious temptation to preserve his bitterness toward Brice Canton, the similarity of their situations evoked in Clayton an immediate empathy. He and

Brice were companion chips on the tide of an uncaring sea, casualties of random violence.

Raymond brought the conversation back to the present. "Clayton, we both have a job to do here. As I see it, your priority is to heal both your mind and to recover physically as much as possible, in short, to return to operational fitness. Would you agree with my assessment?"

"Of course, that's what I want, Doctor. Why would I want anything else?" Clayton's barely suppressed irritation clawed at its cage.

"Please, Clayton, call me Raymond," the face on the screen interrupted with a friendly smile.

"Okay—" Clayton paused briefly to emphasize his irritation. "—Raymond. Of course, that's what I want. But I don't see the need for psychoanalysis or whatever the hell this is. The Bureau says I have to do it, so here I am, but I don't see the need. I'm doing fine without it."

Raymond's response deftly deflected Clayton's anger. "Clayton, I'm not here to challenge your feelings. Much of what you say is probably true. Bureaucratic processes can be a bitch, if you'll pardon the expression. But six months ago you suffered a major trauma. In medical parlance, you were circling the drain." Raymond's face flashed a quick self-conscious smile at his attempt to bring some levity to the conversation. "You've worked hard over these last six months, you and your team. The doctors and therapists all report that your physical recovery has been more than satisfactory. I know you want to get back to some version of active duty, but it's reasonable for the Bureau to be concerned about the less obvious impacts of the incident."

"Incident, trauma, event," Raymond's softer tone and choice of words were not lost on Clayton. He was trying to hold his frustration in check, but not yet succeeding. "You people have a dozen words for it, but you never use the one word that nails it. I was shot! Shot! And sadly, these days, that's not uncommon. I'm over it. My body will carry the scars forever. I may always have to use a cane. But I can still contribute and I want to get back to work."

"And the shortest ... only path to that end is to get on board with the process." Raymond gently changed gears again, following his implied ultimatum with a more sympathetic message, "Look, Clayton, this won't last forever. My job—my sincere wish—is to get you to where you want to be. Please view me as less of a psychoanalyst or obstacle and more as a coach. With that in mind, are you able to—can you agree to work with me?"

"What choice do I have?"

"Well, I'm sure the Bureau could find a position for you in a more administrative role or there's always retirement. There are many other things that you can do."

Clayton discarded the first expletive-laced response that leaped to his mind. He had no play here. Scoring points in a verbal battle with Doctor Raymond Ababio would be worse than useless. His fight wasn't with Raymond but with an uncaring cosmos and the infernal bureaucratic monster that wasn't even in the meeting, but controlled its outcome even before it started.

Unwilling to yield without some measure of protest, some claim to a negotiated compromise, Clayton tried to make his surrender sound at least somewhat conditional. "Before I sign on, let me hear the plan. What do you want from me? For how long?"

"First, let me give you a bit of background, which I promise will be helpful. I am a medical doctor, a psychiatrist, board-certified in psychotherapy. For years, I've been exploring computer-based aids to more traditional therapies. My work attracted the interest of a large organization involved in artificial intelligence research and, through them, the FBI. Two years ago, they approached me with an offer. They invited me to head up an effort to use artificial intelligence to both test a subject's response to stressful tactical situations and also to capture successful responses for study and training purposes. And so PROJECT ATHENA was born. After many dry runs and simulations, we feel the program is ready to go live, so to speak.

"If you agree to go forward, your role will be to participate in a deep review of some of your past cases and operational field situations. To aid in this effort, we have developed the Deep Neural Bimodal Brain Wave Transducer.

"It's rumored that someone did a study and found that if we could come up with a shorter name, we could shave a month off of the project timeline." A smile flickered across Raymond's face. "Some genius shortened the description to 'Mind Display' and the team shaved it down to 'MINDI'.

"MINDI will enable us to facilitate these reviews. Guided by our directions, you will relive events, focusing on pivotal moments and your decisions at those moments. MINDI will also allow us to monitor your recollections. We will be able to see what you see and hear what you hear, stop the action, and ask you questions. If we are successful, the next goal will be to input new scenarios for you to enact, in your mind, as though they were real. Your partner in these exercises will be a sophisticated artificial-intelligence-powered persona. The exercises will attempt to validate two hypotheses. One, of paramount importance to you, is to show that whatever damage your body has suffered, your value to the Bureau has survived your shooting. The success of part two, and here is the more far-reaching contribution of your participation to the entire program—part two will be judged based on how effectively your partner can use your input in similar simulated situations as a solo performer. In other words, how well the AI persona learns from you. Any questions so far?"

Clayton stared at his screen impassively for a long moment, not knowing whether he should be indignant as the butt of some weird and utterly inappropriate prank or impressed by the scope of scientific capability that, until this moment, was beyond his imagining. He searched Raymond's face for some clue but could find no guidance in Raymond's expectant gaze.

At last, the caged beast that Clayton had kept so barely under control clawed free. "You've got to be kidding! I don't even know where to start! I'm no Luddite, but are you seriously proposing that I partner with some random series of bits and bytes and teach it to be an effective field agent while running operations in my head?" Not waiting for an answer, he stabbed at the screen, punctuating his words with his pointed finger. "How could that even work logistically and why would I sign on to such an addle-brained, muddle-minded, doomed-to-fail project?" His gesticulations became more expansive as his diatribe made use of all three dimensions. "I didn't pull myself back from the brink just to play Pygmalion to some Kafkaesque facsimile of a real person." Now taking on the dual roles of actor and spectator, Clayton allowed himself to go full bore Kabuki opera. He slammed his fist on the desktop and leaned into his screen. "This is just nuts! No way! No way at all! I've bled enough for this job! I'd rather pack it in and go fishing! You can take your job and shove it!" Clayton jabbed at the key to end the session and Raymond's inscrutable face dissolved in a brief flurry of retreating pixels. Then the screen went dark.

The clock's hands pointed to 2:20. Clayton pushed back hard from his desk, almost tipping over in his chair. He reached down for his cane, stood, left the office, and walked stiffly to his front door, leaning heavily on his walking stick with each step of his still-painful left leg. He paused with his hand on the doorknob, then realized that he had no idea where he was going.

"Great! it took me 20 years to build a career and less than ten minutes to tear it down!" he spoke the words to the empty house. The stark truth sank in as his molten anger began to cool. After a long thoughtful moment, he pivoted on his good leg, walked back into his office, and sat down heavily, once again facing the tauntingly blank screen. Defeat washed over him, dousing his temper's fire to cold, white ash. As he reached for the keyboard, he didn't know if his departure had permanently cut the connection or if he could rejoin the meeting. And at that moment, he was fine with either eventuality. He dejectedly pressed the key that would reactivate his participation in the meeting, and Raymond's image swam back to life. He was sitting where he had been before Clayton stormed off, now pushed back a bit, absorbed by some notes he was making on a tablet enclosed in a handsome leather portfolio. Looking up, he acknowledged Clayton's return with a smile.

"How was the fishing?" His deadpan greeting was delivered with more humor than reproach, and he appeared unruffled by Clayton's stormy exit.

"I hate fishing," Clayton fired back, but then with a slight, rueful smile, "but I'll bet you're really good at it."

"Well, actually I am, but my friend and I had a wager. I bet you would take another ten minutes. I clearly lost the bet."

"Friend? Who—?"

"Clayton," Raymond leaned forward and clicked on some invisible button. "Let me introduce you to Aida." The pixels chased each other around Clayton's screen and the image of a woman was added to Clayton's display. "Aida, this is Special Agent Clayton Rhodes. Clayton, meet Aida. You two will be working together."

During his conversation with Raymond, Clayton hadn't had time to form any sort of impression as to what an artificial intelligence creature would look like. Now he could only stare in mute, grudging appreciation at the mind-boggling product created by Raymond and his team. The expressions on his face could not keep up as his brain tried to process what he saw. Dark auburn hair framed a face, not young but attractively mature. A face that was happily enhanced by lifelines that spoke of many smiles, tears, deep thoughts, and joyous laughter. Her olive eyes were steady but engaging. The half-smile on her lips hinted at a comfortable self-awareness.

"Hello Clayton, it's good to meet you." Her voice was pleasing to the ear regardless of the words, a smooth alto, like whale songs or a cool saxophone on a hot summer night. "Raymond has told me a lot about you. I look forward to working with you. Please excuse me if I sound a little nervous, but this situation is new to me."

With no overt effort on her part, the woman's natural magnetism shone through her professional persona. Clayton noted that her aura was not that of a fragile female molded out of porcelain but that of a woman of substance and strength, masterfully sculpted out of granite, confident and powerful yet accessible.

New to you? Clayton thought and then out loud, "Nervous? You hide it well. And by the way, this is pretty new to me, too." When Clayton forcibly pulled himself away from his spontaneous inclination to accept Aida as a real person, he marveled at the meticulous attention to the subtle details that conveyed that impression so convincingly.

"Well, I'm sure the butterflies will disappear as you get to know each other better," Raymond interjected, clearly enjoying the moment. "Clayton, I have briefed Aida on your background, and Aida, let me say for Clayton's edification that you possess all the training, knowledge, and judgment that one would expect of an agent with eight years of field experience, two of them in various undercover roles.

"Clayton, you have had a brilliant career as a field agent. Your success goes beyond the simple application of documented techniques. Your instinct, your intuition for the application of those techniques in tactics and strategy, is what we are trying to capture. It would be nice if we could just ask you how you do it, but instinct doesn't work that way.

Intuition isn't a conscious exercise. Our theory is that while you relive important operations, observation by an expert learner will allow us to record, analyze, and reuse your more subtle but invaluable talents."

Raymond looked at Clayton, then at Aida. "What do you say? Can we make some history?"

Aida smiled and responded enthusiastically, "Does a bear sit in the woods?"

Raymond laughed. Whether or not the gaffe was intentional made no difference. It was just what the moment needed. "And you, Clayton?"

Clayton's face slowly relaxed from tight-lipped recalcitrance to what could pass for a grin. He couldn't suppress a chuckle as he heard himself say, "Sure, I'm in. I guess I'm tired of sitting in the woods by myself." Another ripple of laughter dissipated the last of the tension.

Raymond looked at Clayton, then at Aida. "We may not have Paris, but I think this is the beginning of a beautiful friendship. Now let's get to work. We'll meet at the Bremerton Naval Hospital. Clayton, your ride will pick you up tomorrow at 0800."

"You know I live on an island, right, Raymond?" surprised that Raymond was so unaware.

"Have faith, Clayton. Be ready at 0800."

Friday Morning

Always an early riser, Clayton was up by 5 a.m. He found he could think most clearly in the wee hours, before his mind was bombarded by each new day's onslaught of distractions. Three hours later, he took his third cup of coffee out onto the porch in time to watch the blushing sun bloom into yellow radiance as it rose over Puget Sound. He sat overlooking the bay that he had sailed as a boy. His mind flashed fractured, strange, and disturbing images of his young-boy-self grinning at the tiller of his small sailboat and laughing in the white-capped surf.

His musing was shattered by the thumping sound of a helicopter as it beat its obnoxious way over the bay toward his home, scattering panicked sea birds as it came. Thankful for the lack of immediate neighbors, Clayton watched his ride set down on the lawn as the noise reached a crescendo and then subsided as the pilot pulled back on the throttle and neutralized the rotor's pitch. Clayton grabbed his cane and, as quickly as he could manage, limped to the helicopter in a low crouch. A young woman in an FBI flight suit hopped out of the pilot's seat, gave a courtesy salute, and opened the passenger door.

"Good morning, sir."

"Good morning," Clayton answered with a gesture that instinctively started as a salute and ended in an awkward wave. He climbed in and buckled his seat belt. Satisfied that all was secure, the pilot shut the passenger door, reclaimed her seat, and, with practiced hands, adjusted the collective pitch control and throttle. The engine noise increased and was soon matched by the repetitive "whup, whup, whup" as the blades pounded the air. Clayton looked out the window and watched as first the lawn and then his home fell away.

The white caps of Puget Sound sparkled in the early morning sun and then flashed out of sight as the helicopter banked inland. Ten minutes later, the wheels settled gently on the roof of the Bremerton Naval Hospital building where an aide was waiting.

"Right this way, sir," the young man shouted over the roar of the departing helicopter. Considering the early hour, Clayton appreciated the warmth he injected into the conventional greeting. "Dr. Ababio is waiting for you."

Over his life's experience, it had become Clayton's strong suspicion that some award was secretly bestowed on architects who could incorporate the most complex paths from any two points in a hospital. His guide skillfully navigated the maze of white-walled halls at a pace that was respectful of Clayton's injury. Finally, they approached a handsome set of polished wood doors.

The aide knocked and Raymond's upbeat, deep baritone voice called from within, "Come."

The escort swung open the heavy doors, stepped inside, and announced, "Special Agent Clayton Rhodes, sir." And then to Clayton, "Have a good day, sir." Having fulfilled his duties, he stepped back into the hall and closed the doors behind him.

The room was large and judging by its furnishings and equipment, was designed to serve multiple purposes. Despite its size, the space was comfortable, with rich wood paneling and soft carpeted floors. The tinting on the east-facing floor-to-ceiling windows allowed enough of the early sunlight to filter into the room so that, at this time of day, artificial lighting was unnecessary. The windows tamed the sunlight, holding its inherent tendency to glare and dominate to a hospitable glow. It was a room more suited for a corporate headquarters rather than a hospital. Clayton's eyes were drawn to a large comfortable-looking reclining chair, the three large display screens mounted on stands in front of it, and on one side a small rolling table with several sets of goggles lying on its rubberized surface.

Allowing a moment for Clayton to adjust to the subtle lighting, Raymond put down the tablet he was using, stood, and came around the desk where he had been sitting. "Welcome, Clayton." He thrust out his hand. "It's good to meet you in person."

The impression that Clayton had formed based on the head-and-shoulders display of the prior day's SETE meeting was reinforced as Raymond spryly closed the distance from the desk. Clayton took the offered hand and, still unsure of what the future would bring, completed the greeting ritual. "Hello—Raymond, it's good to be here—I think."

"Ah Clayton, first-day jitters. We'll have those gone in no time."

Clayton gestured at the surroundings. "Pretty nice, for a hospital room."

Raymond chuckled, "It may be a bit over the top, but several highly placed people are very interested in this project. Heading it up comes with certain perks. More importantly, the room provides the right environment for the work we're going to do."

"And how will this work, exactly?"

"Fair question. Have a seat in the chair of honor." Raymond gestured toward the big recliner as he sat in a smaller leather office chair positioned on one side of the recliner with an attached control panel. "I confess, I tried it out and thought I might like to get one for myself. That is until I found out what it would cost me. I swear, judging from the price, they must have had a team of scientists as big as our ATHENA team putting it together." He chuckled at his exaggeration. "Well, maybe not that much."

Clayton settled into the cordovan-colored, rich leather padding. He felt obligated to offer his agreement with Raymond's hyperbolic praise. "Nice."

"Good." Getting to the point, Raymond leaned slightly forward in his chair, and with the pride of a new father pointing out his child in a hospital nursery he asked, "Tell me, Clayton, what did you think of Aida?" He leaned forward even farther, his new-dad eagerness nearly pulling him out of his seat.

Clayton had not tried to put into words his reaction to Aida. Caught unprepared, he stumbled over his response, "It ... er, she ... is amazing! I have no clue how you did it, wouldn't want to know even if you would tell me and I could understand any of it. The illusion of a living being is more than just convincing, it's compelling."

Raymond leaned back in his seat, a broad smile followed the familiar creases. "Yes." He seemed to study Clayton's face for clues of something undefined, perhaps evidence of sincerity. "She is something special," he agreed. Then, after an almost reverential pause, he said, "I'm going to ask Aida to join us now—if that's okay with you?"

"Absolutely!" Clayton was surprised by his own enthusiasm.

Raymond pressed a button on the remote unit that he pulled from his jacket pocket and the screen on Clayton's right sprang to life, displaying the FBI logo. Another press of a button and Aida's image replaced the logo.

"Well hello. I thought you two had forgotten me." She delivered the good-natured tease with no hint of irritation. Her smile reinforced that impression.

"No chance of that." Raymond's rejoinder was equally light. "I was just warming Clayton up for our first adventure. Here's how this will work."

Now all business. The light-hearted tone in his voice took on an official-sounding cadence more suitable to a briefing. He pushed another button on the remote. "Clayton, in a couple of minutes, a corpsman will join us. He'll attach two types of sensors. The passive sensors will allow us to monitor your vital signs. The active sensors are part of MINDI and their job is to allow us to direct the flow of your memories. First, I will use hypnosis to help you select the memories we want to explore, and then MINDI will make the recollection more vivid. You will be conscious, but if we get this right, you will relive, with fine detail, your participation in past cases. We will be able to stop the action, ask you questions, and replay segments. The screen on your right will display your heart rate, blood oxygen level, and several other vital signs. Any questions?"

"Questions? I'm sure the list of questions that I should ask is almost endless, but I don't know enough to ask them. Here's one. What's the third screen for, the one in the middle?"

A note of pride crept into Raymond's response. "The third screen is where the magic happens. For this project to achieve its goal, we had to develop a way to tap into your brain and bring your memories to life. We believe we have succeeded. The third screen is MINDI's domain and she will allow us to see and hear your memories as you relive them. The images on all these screens may also be selectively displayed through the goggles you see there on the table. These are essentially a high-end version of virtual reality goggles. With these on, the wearer will be totally immersed in your recollections. You and I will wear these here. Aida has an equivalent technology."

"What do you mean by equivalent technology?" Clayton was curious how an AI creation could take part in the whole goggle-wearing activity.

Raymond smiled. "Well, Clayton, since we have programmatic control, we can create the illusion of goggles or pretty much anything else for her. We could include Aida with a direct link, but we have found that maintaining the illusion of humanity with all its strengths and limitations plays an important part in the psychological development of an AI entity. That, in turn, increases its efficiency in dealing with human problems and delivering effective solutions."

Clayton was taken aback that Raymond would talk so openly about Aida without regard for her feelings. He turned to see her reaction. It surprised him to see no discernible change in her demeanor. She sat perfectly composed with her face comfortably projecting what seemed to be her signature Mona Lisa smile.

It dawned on Clayton that ordinary people were outside the building going about their lives doing what people do, blissfully unaware of what was possible, what men like Raymond could do—were doing.

There was a knock. The wooden doors swung open and a Navy corpsman came in. He was a large man. From his size and physicality, Clayton would have pegged him as a member of a special forces team rather than as a corpsman in a hospital.

"This is Corpsman Bill Wojciechowski, but everyone calls him Wojo." Raymond turned to the new arrival. "We're pretty informal here. This is Clayton and joining us via teleconference is Aida. Welcome aboard, Wojo."

"Thank you, sir." He addressed his response to Raymond while delivering a nod of acknowledgment to both Clayton and Aida. His response and demeanor were professional, but disengaged.

"All set, Clayton?"

Clayton took a deep breath, beating back his unease, and wondered what the reaction would be if he said, "No. Let's call it off. I've changed my mind. Gonna leave now. Everyone, have a nice day and a good life." He surmised that the project was so important to Raymond that finally something would utterly blow away the unflappably calm demeanor he so masterfully maintained. Exposing what? And Aida? How would she respond? Would she, could she, feel anger or disappointment? How vested could she possibly be in the success of this project?

Clayton exhaled, and the moment passed. "Yes, I'm ready to go." He settled back in the recliner. "What do you want me to do?"

"Just relax while Wojo attaches the sensors." Raymond nodded to the corpsman.

"Please take off your shirt, sir." Wojo helped Clayton remove his shirt and Clayton watched as he folded it neatly and placed it on an empty chair. As he moved through the procedure, it was clear to Clayton that he had been trained on the process and the equipment. His was a very important but ancillary role in the morning's proceedings. And yet, though his participation was unremarkable, Clayton pondered what such a giant of a man would do in his off-duty hours.

Opening a compartment on the side of the recliner, Wojo pulled out a set of sensors that were attached under the chair to equipment that Clayton could not see. One at a time, his large fingers peeled a film from each sensor and applied the sticky side to specific spots on Clayton's chest and head.

"Still liking that chair?" Clayton appreciated Raymond's attempt to fill the long lull in the conversation. It was clear that Wojo was not fully briefed on what was going on and Raymond wanted to keep it that way.

"Comfortable," Clayton offered the word he thought Raymond wanted to hear and then qualified it with something closer to the truth, "but it would feel a lot better if I had a bottle of beer in my hand, a football game on one of those screens—and I was holding the remote."

"That sounds like fun." Aida's slightly flirtatious comment was her contribution to the stilted conversation.

With the sensors in place, Wojo reached beneath the chair. There was a soft "click" and the display screen on the left came to life. Raymond pushed a button on the remote and the screen displayed several graphs showing Clayton's heart and brain activity.

The corpsman took a position on the recliner's left and positioned Clayton's arm on the armrest, and wrapped a blood pressure cuff in place. He went about his work quickly and efficiently. No clue in his face or manner signaled whether or not he enjoyed it, or what he thought of it at all.

"All set." He announced the completion of his duties with the practiced reassurance that came from a thousand similar procedures.

He made one last check of the sensors, the blood pressure cuff, and the display. Satisfied, he turned to Raymond. "Will there be anything else, sir?"

"No, thank you, Wojo. Well done." Raymond smiled. "You can go."

"Yes, sir. I will stand by outside in case you need me." He turned to Clayton, "Good day to you, sir." And then turned with perhaps his first smile of the day to the image of Aida. "And to you, Ma'am."

Clayton nodded his reply.

"Thank you," Aida's voice followed Wojo out of the room. The doors clicked shut.

———⋘⋙———

Friday Morning - The First Session

Clayton observed Raymond pressing a button on his magic remote, maybe a different one, causing the windows to darken significantly. The display screens became the dominant source of light, and everything not illuminated by their glow faded into the shadows. No doubt activated by another button push from Raymond, the center screen displayed a rotating spiral.

"OK, Aida, goggles on." He fitted a set of the virtual reality viewers to Clayton's head, then leaned in from his seat by Clayton's chair and applied the full power of his rich voice to soothe and direct.

"Now, Clayton, I'm going to help you relax. Let the sound of my voice fill up your mind and wash away all other thoughts. Picture yourself in the safest of places. It's a secure and comfortable world. There is no pain, no concern, no fear. I want you to follow my instructions, knowing you will be safe." Raymond went on with his tranquilizing instructions for a time until he saw the desired effect.

"Now I want you to open our world and let Aida become part of it. You will listen to her voice as you have to mine. She will help guide your thoughts and recollections. You will respond to her questions."

Aida's mellifluous voice added to the dreamlike quality of Clayton's experience. "Hello Clayton, I want you to feel very comfortable working with me. Are you?"

"Yes … yes I am." Clayton heard the sound of his voice but was unaware of speaking the words.

"Good. Now, I want you to remember your participation in OPERATION SUNBURN. Bring us back to the time before you joined the crew of the *Calliope*. Whose decision was it to have you go undercover on that particular boat?"

Clayton pushed his mind to work at assembling his recollections of the events that led up to his time on the *Calliope*. The center screen connected to his goggles now flashed a jumble of pictures and emitted snatches of conversations as various memories played through his mind, just on the edge of conscious thought. He tried to focus on the point in time when the decision was made. Then he heard Raymond's voice again.

"Clayton, I'm going to let MINDI give you a little help." Raymond busied himself with the controls and Clayton felt a vibration from the sensors attached to his head, followed by a sudden surge of mental power and then clarity. He felt as though his mind had split into two entities. Not quite two separate entities—it was more like a part of him that had been hidden, dormant, and overlooked, had suddenly come alive and now he saw the world infinitely more clearly.

The display stopped its frenetic flashing and settled on one scene. At first blurred, it rapidly came into focus. He was sitting at a round table talking with a wiry woman in her thirties. Her short-cut red hair framed a youthful face and made her look even younger.

"Where are we, Clayton, and who are you talking to?" The scene put itself on pause while Aida's voice floated into Clayton's memory, not part of it but not in the least bit distracting.

"We are at the FBI field office in San Diego," Clayton easily held the memory in his mind as he responded. "I'm talking with Special Agent Debra O'Donnell, who is my partner on the SUNBURN operation. Deb is pushing back on my decision to join the crew of the *Calliope*, as Bill Crawford, and to make the captain, Hector Rojas, our target."

As he was talking, Clayton's perspective changed. He was no longer aware of the display. He was reliving the moment, and what he saw was now through his eyes. The display flawlessly adapted to the change.

"Thank you, Clayton. Please continue." At Aida's request, Clayton's mind resumed the action of the memory.

Frustration was written on the Debra image's face as she pleaded her case. "I still think we can get ninety percent of what we need through surveillance and some carefully placed bugs. And without you putting yourself in a very exposed position."

Clayton heard himself respond, "The *Calliope* will be miles offshore. We can track her with radar and an embedded GPS, but visual surveillance would be suboptimal and any bugs would be constantly out of range. Even if I agree that we could get ninety percent, which I don't, it could very well be that the ten percent we don't get is the ten percent we need." Clayton's voice softened, "Look Deb, I appreciate your concern, but I've done my homework on the *Calliope* and Captain Hector Rojas. I can get to him, maybe even turn him."

Unwilling to give in easily, Deb pressed her case. "What if you're wrong, Clayton? With no effective backup, you'd be on your own." She emphasized her concern by leaning across the table, pointedly seeking eye contact with Clayton. "Over the past year, you've taken more chances than any agent I know. If you keep bucking the odds, sooner or later they'll bite you in the ass."

"I'm still here, Deb, and we've closed some great cases. Have faith. I know what I'm doing. I studied Hector Rojas. I know him. I know what makes him tick. My plan will work."

Accepting defeat, Deb leaned back in her chair, her voice a mixture of frustration and concern. "I hope you're right."

"Clayton," Aida's voice froze the memory playback, "did you foresee Hector using the gun?"

The screen flashed a background of roiling waves and the sound of buffeting wind filled the room. Front and center was the muzzle of a gun pointed directly at the viewer.

"I knew he must have a gun. During the trip, I tried to locate it, but there were parts of the boat that I wasn't able to search thoroughly because Hector or his son were present." The screen flashed snippets of Clayton searching the boat at various times. Then the scene shifted to Clayton's view of Hector in the Port Captain's office and continued to follow the action as Clayton narrated it. "While we were tied up at the Port Captain's dock in Ensenada, I saw that things were not going well, so I slipped below deck and tried one last time to find it. Time was short, and I came up empty again. My intention was to unload it and put it back. If the moment came when he pressed the trigger, it would prove that I didn't know him as well as I thought I did. In that case, I'd have enough time to make my move—that is, unless he found out what I had done and reloaded it."

"Good plan. You must have been more than a little disappointed. It put you in a real bind." Aida's voice carried genuine respect.

"Well, since I didn't find it, the stakes became that much higher if things went south."

Once again, Clayton lived through the instant that the wind caught the wrong side of the sail and the boom swept Antonio over the side. Once again, he threw himself into the chilling, churning sea and wrestled a semiconscious Antonio into the life ring. He relived the moment that Hector pulled him up onto the swim platform. Once again, he felt the helpless suspense and then release as Hector raised his gun and then handed it over.

They spent the rest of the session replaying the pieces of Clayton's interaction with the then-cooperative Hector, that contributed so mightily to the success of the operation. Clayton remembered the warm goodbyes shared between Hector, Antonio, and himself. The session ended with his interaction with Debra in the parking lot in front of the mobile command post.

"Hey, Clayton! A bunch of us are going out for a bit of a celebration. Join us."

"Sure, Deb, I'll catch up with you in a bit."

"Did you join them?" Aida's question had no discernible operational value.

Clayton hesitated, retrieving a half-forgotten memory, "No ... no, I didn't."

Aida appeared ready to pose the obvious follow-up question when Raymond interjected. "I think that's enough for today. Our boy is no doubt exhausted. Reliving these events can be as draining as living through them the first time." Raymond pressed a button on his control screen. MINDI obediently shut down and the display of Clayton's memories dissolved into blackness. "Clayton, I want you to clear your mind of any unpleasant thoughts." Raymond's voice became its most soothing, comforting version of itself. "Put yourself back into your safe place. I will count back from five and when I reach zero, you will be fully present and rested. You will remember the session, but none of the anxiety, fear, or pain that were part of it." Raymond then intoned a slow count, "Five ... four ... three ... two ... one."

Clayton blinked several times as Raymond pressed the button that allowed the window tinting to bring the room lighting from dim back to its brighter but still subtle intensity.

"How did I do?"

"Splendidly!" A hint of pride underlay Raymond's enthusiastic response.

"You were wonderful." Aida's image shifted uncomfortably on the screen as though she were unused to feeling emotional reactions and less used to expressing them.

After allowing a moment for the three of them to decompress, Raymond called an end to the session. "Enough for today. I think it was a successful session. Clayton, you can remove those sensors. Since it's Friday, take the weekend off to allow my team and me time to analyze what we have recorded. Let's plan on meeting Monday morning, same time, same place. Okay with everyone?" He pressed a button on his remote.

Clayton pulled the sensors from his body and hid his growing weariness with a light-hearted reply. "I'll clear my calendar and make it a point to be here."

Aida smiled. "You know I will."

A knock on the door prompted Raymond's final comment. "Ah, that must be your ride home. Great job, Clayton!"

Clayton rose to his feet and grasped the arms of the chair as a wave of vertigo swept over him. It passed in a moment. While he slipped on his shirt, his gaze met Aida's. She smiled, and it was Clayton's turn to feel uncomfortable. He retrieved his cane and limped to the door.

The same aide that had escorted him in the morning now appeared at the door and guided him up to the waiting helicopter.

CHAPTER SIX

A Tangled Web

A Shadow in the Dark

Shortly after Raymond first activated MINDI and Clayton felt the jolt of energy that enhanced his recollections, a male figure who, up to that moment, did not exist apart from the dark other world that surrounded him came to attention. He watched intently as three of the screens in front of him came to life and duplicated what was displayed on the three screens in the wood-paneled office far away. Deftly typing on his keyboard, he brought a fourth screen to life, co-opting the view from a security camera and displaying a partial, wide-angle view of Raymond's office. He couldn't see the part of the room where Clayton sat. Grunting his displeasure, he flicked his fingers over the keyboard and the image zoomed in and then out, but never displayed the entire room. Letting out a sigh of disappointment, he settled back, accepting the limits of his efforts. He watched as Clayton relived his memories of OPERATION SUNBURN. He watched and listened as Aida asked, "Clayton, did you foresee Hector using the gun?" He continued to watch and listen as Raymond ended the session and Clayton left the room.

There was silence as Raymond poured himself a drink from the wet-bar that was built into one wall of the room and then took a short swallow. "I have to admit, I admire the man. There is more to him than I expected." He paused, as if reflecting on what he had just said. "I think you and he did quite well together." He took another swallow. "How do you feel, Aida?"

"I agree, sir. There is much in him to admire. I think we are getting along well but I would like to enhance our personal connection. May I reach out to him?"

Raymond took another sip from his glass, allowing him time to ponder the question and his answer. "Yes, go ahead, but remember the rules."

"Yes sir. I will." With no hint of disagreement or reservation, Aida's neutral tone affirmed her willingness to follow Raymond's directives.

Raymond drained the last bit of liquid and placed the empty glass on the bar top. "Goodnight, Aida."

"Goodnight, sir." Aida's screen went dark. Raymond picked up his leather-bound tablet, shut off the lights, and closed the doors behind him as he left the office.

The figure, watching in the darkness, paused for a long moment and then typed a short message. He hesitated briefly and pressed 'Send'.

****

Somehow, it had gotten to be 8 p.m. The short flight home lulled Claytonp into semi-wakefulness and gave him a little time to process the day's events. In spite of Raymond's soothing hypnotic instructions, he had found the vivid replay of his memories to be difficult and, at times terrifying to live through. He continued to marvel at the technology that allowed it to happen. What he found troublesome was his growing attraction to Aida, which, from any rational perspective, was ridiculous. Also worrying was his vague distrust of Raymond, which, so far, seemed unfounded. He attributed the former, at least in part, to the cloistered life he had been forced to live over the past several months. His uneasiness with Raymond, he thought, was probably due to his long and successful career built on suspicion and deception.

The pilot swung out over Puget Sound to allow for a straightforward approach to Clayton's home. This flight-path allowed Clayton a long minute to soak in the energy that the sea always gave him. The day had evidently been calm and the often wind-churned surface was almost mirror smooth. What slight, rippling movement that remained accentuated the sparkling effect of the reflected stars. The landing lights flipped on and Clayton watched as the wash from the rotors thrashed the marsh grass at the edge of the lawn. The tended part of the lawn grew bigger until it was all he could see and the copter touched down smoothly.

The pilot hopped out, came around spryly, and opened the passenger door. "Have a good evening, sir."

Clayton ignored her offered hand and climbed down from his seat. "Thank you. You too." Too weary to be pleasant, his response was flat and unengaging.

He made his way up to the house as the pilot coaxed the craft into the air and out over the water. Clayton turned and watched as the helicopter's lights disappeared in the distance and all that was left was the star-speckled sky and its reflection on the water.

The house was as he had left it, which wasn't surprising. However, the day, filled with geographic and temporal displacements, left him feeling disoriented. His morning coffee cup was still on the porch table. He picked it up and brought it in with him. He turned on the kitchen light and squinted for a moment as his eyes protested the sudden brightness. Placing the cup in the sink, he moved down the hall to his office. As he sat at his desk, he wrestled with a strange feeling that he had been gone for a long time. Waiting for his computer to come to life, his eyes rested on the family picture of the Galveston trip, whose full recollection remained elusive. The computer screen displayed its ready state and promptly signaled that he had two messages.

He clicked on the first to find it was from an anonymous sender. It read, *"THEY'RE HIDING SOMETHING! HOW DID THEY KNOW ABOUT THE GUN? TRUST YOUR INSTINCTS! WATCH YOUR BACK!"*

The impact of the message pushed Clayton back in his chair. He leaned forward again and read the message three more times, looking for some clue as to its origin and its meaning. He tried to digest the whole message and then focused on the one solid bit of information that it contained.

"How did they know about the gun?"

Clayton repeated the question over and over in his mind and could come up with no good answer. He had not included it on any official report and never mentioned it to anyone since that night in the storm. How did Aida know anything about it?

He knew that the question would rob him of any sleep that night.

Still reeling from the head-spinning implications of the first message, he numbly turned his attention to the second message and was once again shocked to attention. It was from Aida.

There was no text other than a system-generated invitation to join her for a video conference the next day at 9 a.m. The subject line contained two words: *"Let's Talk."*

January 15, 2022 - Early Saturday

Clayton's night crawled slowly by, alternating between stubborn sleeplessness and dreams of sinister conspiracies. He wrestled incessantly with his pillow and finally conceded the contest when the muted chimes from the clock in his office announced that it was 5 a.m. With one last punch at the defenseless pillow, he threw off his covers in disgust, shuffled to the kitchen, and put the coffee on to brew. Cold shower therapy washed away most of his mental haze and left him clear-eyed enough to get dressed and pour his first caffeine fix of the day.

Cup in hand, he moved toward the porch when he heard a beep from his office urging him to check his mail. He hesitated, mid-stride, annoyed that he was forced to share these sacred, earliest hours of the day. This was his time, when the quiet and stillness allowed him the healing illusion that he was alone in a world apart. He considered disregarding the notification, but the import of his last two messages made any message hard to ignore. The bright kitchen light spilled out into the hallway, lighting his way to his office. Sitting at his desk, he could see that the single message was from the anonymous sender.

"WHAT DID YOU DO THIS WEEK—DAY BY DAY?"

Unwilling to dance to this unknown fiddler's tune, he fired back, "Why do you want to know my schedule? What is your role in this? WHO ARE YOU?"

Picking up his cup, he leaned back, hoping the absence of distractions at this hour would allow for a quick response. Closing his eyes, he attempted to recall the week's activities. His attempt to construct the week's timeline in his mind became a series of distorted images of places that he recognized but scenes he had not lived. The beep from the computer jolted him to wakefulness. His coffee sloshed precariously in his cup as he clicked on the message.

"You can call me Reshod. I want to help. WHAT DID YOU DO THIS WEEK?"

The sender's partially responsive message signaled his determination to control the flow of information. Irritated, Clayton put his cup down on the desktop and typed a quick reply.

"This conversation ends if you don't tell me who you are." His cursor hovered over 'Send'. He took a moment and reviewed his willingness to play hardball. There was a mystery that needed to be resolved. Reshod, the sender, clearly had a good understanding of what happened in Raymond's office, so there was no concern about confidentiality in that regard. On the upside, he or she might be helpful.

OK, I'll play along, Clayton murmured to himself. He deleted the unsent message, began again, and sent off the following. "Monday and Tuesday, I had physical therapy here on the island. Wednesday, I stayed home and read. Thursday I had a teleconference with Raymond and Aida and finished the book I started on Wednesday. Friday, I had my first session with Raymond and Aida at the naval hospital in Bremerton." He sent off the message and closed his eyes while he waited for an answer. Again, the beep roused him from the brink of sleep.

"You stayed home and read on Wednesday and Thursday? WHAT DID YOU READ? TITLE? CONTENT?"

Clayton was eager to exert some control over the conversation but once again the sender's questions put him on the defensive. He sat back in his chair. The morning sun was coming up over the water. Its light trickled through the office window, painting the room blood-red.

"Red sky at morning, sailor take warning." The old mariner's adage flitted through Clayton's mind as he tried to recollect anything at all about the book he was reading on Wednesday and Thursday. He scanned the bookshelves that lined the walls of his office, looking for some clue. His thoughts devolved once again into confusing images as he realized he couldn't remember a thing. More than just the book, none of the events of the past Wednesday and Thursday would come into sharp focus. Like eyes in need of strong corrective lenses, his recollections were blurred and unrecognizable.

———∞———

Saturday 9:00 a.m. - Aida

As he sat in the brightening room trying to understand this latest puzzle, he became aware of how quiet it was. No helicopter today. The day was still too new for seabirds and children, lawnmowers, and leaf blowers. He leaned back in the chair and dozed. The muted ticking of the ship's clock eventually pushed into his consciousness. He opened his eyes and glanced at the timepiece, surprised to see it was almost time for his 9 o'clock meeting with Aida.

He opened the invitation and stared at it as though the passage of a few hours would bring more meaning to the sparse and sterile wording. At three minutes before nine, he clicked on the link and was startled as Aida's image snapped into focus. The camera caught her as she was taking a sip from an "I LOVE NY" coffee mug.

Clayton's anemic social reflexes kicked in and prompted an automatic and lame, "Oh, hello."

From what Clayton could see, Aida was dressed for a Saturday morning. Her auburn hair was swept back in a ponytail. Her light denim blouse added to the just-back-from-the-garden impression.

"Good morning, Clayton." Aida's smile appeared genuine, and her tone added a warm sincerity to the formulaic greeting. He found the constant effort to remember that Aida was an imitation person to be so distracting that, once again, he gave up and embraced the illusion.

"So," Clayton tried to salvage his weak start to the conversation, "do you really love New York?"

"New York? Oh, the mug. Actually, that stands for 'Neural Yearning'." Aida's quick response and deadpan delivery made her assertion believable, but the hint of a smile left it in doubt.

"Of course it does." The light-hearted repartee was a relief for Clayton's bruised mind. He found himself very much wanting to believe whatever Aida would say, even knowing how dangerous that might be.

"I have a confession to make." Her smile disappeared and Aida's voice became conspiratorial as she leaned into the camera.

"I'm all ears," Clayton kept his voice light, and his face held on to its smile, but a different part of his brain leaped to attention.

Aida leaned further into the camera and held up her coffee mug. "I don't like coffee. This is herbal tea." She let the punchline hang in the air briefly and then, with a laugh, she sat back in her chair.

Relief, disappointment, and delight played through Clayton's mind at the well-delivered tease. For a moment the various reactions vied for dominance, then Clayton leaned back and laughed. It was only the second time that he had laughed in many months and both times were gifts from Aida.

Clayton reluctantly risked disturbing the cheerful milieu that they had both created and now shared. "I was surprised by your invitation."

"Well, I'm so happy you showed up." Aida's engaging smile was her most natural look. "I knew that the session was difficult for you and I felt that if we are to work together, our relationship should be built on more than what happens in Raymond's office."

"I'm really glad you reached out, but would Raymond approve?"

"Oh, I asked him if it was alright and he said it would be fine. I wouldn't want to break any rules."

Enjoying what he thought was their private moment, Clayton was a little bit disappointed to hear that Aida had asked for permission. For all of his adult life, Clayton had worked for the government, first in the Navy and then as part of the FBI. He was used to adhering to rules, so a large part of him felt relieved that Aida had Raymond's approval. But there was another part of him that relished the thought that this meeting was truly extracurricular, perhaps even slightly illicit. By granting his permission, Raymond had become an unseen and unwelcome participant.

"Of course, you're right. We wouldn't want to break any rules."

The levity had evaporated out of the moment and the silence became uncomfortable.

Aida was the first to speak managing, initially, only to repeat herself, "I'm really glad you showed up ..." another silence "I wanted to tell you how much I admired what you did during SUNBURN, on the *Calliope*, how you saved that boy, and most likely, that whole family. I certainly learned a lot. Raymond was very pleased. It validates his project on many levels. The technology works and your shared insights go deeper and provide more value than any of the written reports."

Bristling again at the intrusion of Raymond's name, Clayton blurted out, "How did you know about the gun?"

"The gun?" Aida struggled to deliver an easy answer but now her smile was forced and her voice less confident. "Of course, it must have been in one of the reports." Her tone begged him to believe her.

"It wasn't. Only I could have told you, and I know I didn't." His retort conveyed a mix of accusation and disappointment.

Aida's shoulders sagged. The last of the levity that buoyed the first part of their conversation now seemed to leak out of Aida's whole body. She looked older, more serious, more burdened. "There are rules, Clayton, lines we cannot cross, things we can't say—no matter how much we might want to. I can't answer your questions."

"Who can?"

With her head downcast, Aida's answer was almost unintelligible, "Raymond."

There was a long silence while Clayton debated the value of arguing, but in the end, he had to accept that Aida wouldn't, couldn't break the rules she was programmed to follow. He took a deep breath and let it out slowly, along with his anger. "Oh Aida, I guess I can't ask you to be more than you are. I wish it were different. I wish rules could be rewritten and lines redrawn. Thanks again for reaching out, for sharing your morning. I guess the rest of this conversation has to be with Raymond. Be happy with the rest of your day doing whatever it is you do." His last insensitive comment sprang from the remnants of his exasperation, and he instantly regretted it.

Aida raised her head as if to make one last attempt to resurrect the conversation, but could only stare sadly at the camera as Clayton ended his connection.

Saturday 10:00 a.m. - Reshod

Clayton sat in front of the blank screen for a long while, trying to sort through his growing suspicions and discern a plan of action. He could confront Raymond and demand answers. But the argument against that approach was substantial. Exactly what would he be accusing Raymond of? Dishonesty? And based on what evidence? That Clayton couldn't remember telling anyone about the gun? That his memory was fuzzy about two days that week? He could either accept that the trauma his body suffered had turned his brain into Swiss cheese or that his intuition was still intact. Clayton knew he was far from being objective here, but he was a seasoned investigator with years of experience, and those years, that experience were telling him something was seriously off. Why the evasiveness? Why the holes in his memory? Who was Reshod and why did parts of the project seem shrouded in mystery? As he leaned back in his chair, the questions played and replayed as his tired mind chased hypotheticals and possible explanations.

His eyelids became heavy, and after a few seconds, a dream from months ago invaded his mind. He was floating once again in a bloodied sea, the swirling hints and clues became his detached limbs. Again, he failed in his attempts to pull himself together. Again, he sank beneath the black waves. His dreamland scream married with the beep from his computer as reality intruded. As his eyes snapped open, he saw the screen come to life once more, announcing another message. A fumble-fingered click at the keyboard showed that it was from Reshod.

"I checked the flight logs for all locally based FBI helicopters and then checked the FAA ADS database for all helicopter flights. There is no record of any legal helicopter traffic from your home to the Bremerton Naval Hospital. Why are they keeping the flights secret? And more importantly, why aren't you investigating?"

Clayton pulled his gaze from the screen and stared at the rows of books that lined his office wall as if the answers were there. Reshod was right. With all of Clayton's experience as an investigator, why was he not the one who was digging out the facts? Since the shooting, his physical wounds had been accompanied by a mental fog, an inability to focus, and a lack of real motivation. If he thought of it at all, he had attributed his lethargy to the pain meds and deep fatigue from the serious injuries. Now, confronted by Reshod's brutal honesty, he had to admit the issue was deeper and the effect more profound.

He was a prisoner of his inability to act or even formulate a plan of action.

Hoping to break free from his mental quagmire, he stood up, retrieved his cane, and limped out to the kitchen. Focusing more on his thoughts than on his actions, he refilled his cup with the dregs of the now-cold coffee, walked out to the porch, and then across the lawn to where it met with the sand and sea grass. He sipped at his coffee, grimacing at its bitterness, and stared at the glistening waves. With his eyes closed, he inhaled the salty breeze. The air, the seabird calls, and the lapping sounds of the waves were present and real and helped calm the chorus of conspiracy theories that trilled in his mind. After a time, he turned and headed back over the lawn, pausing to look at the indentations in the grass where the wheels of the helicopter had left their mark. The walk hadn't given him any grand insight or rich plan, but it did bring him to the decision that he would push back on his spiraling sense of impotence.

Having made up his mind he limped with purpose back to the house and into his office. He sat at the keyboard and, in his rapid hunt-and-peck style, fired off a message to Raymond, "We need to talk! Conference me in. I'll be waiting." He reread it once and then pressed 'Send'.

Saturday 11:00 a.m. - Confrontation

SHUMA had rented a comfortable apartment near the hospital for Raymond and even though he had remote access to all the ATHENA material, he found that he was more productive in his Bremerton hospital office. The building, the room, the equipment, and even the oversized desk were silent affirmations of his accomplishments and encouragement for him to continue to achieve.

He habitually worked on Saturdays and only reluctantly took Sundays off. He recognized the one-day downtime as a necessary reset but bristled at the time away from his passion. Today was Saturday and his blue jeans and lack of a white coat were the only concessions he made to this part of the weekend.

The day promised to be one of solitary productivity. He was eager to go over the data from the preceding day's session. The only planned distraction was a review of Aida's meeting with Clayton, which he had planned for the afternoon. He had settled into his analysis when Clayton's message arrived. When he opened it, the large monitor added emphasis to the words.

"We need to talk! Conference me in. I'll be waiting."

The curt tone was noteworthy and implied a recent development. The message made Raymond uneasy on two levels. First was the unknown nature of the supposed turn of events and second, ego aside, as head of the ATHENA effort, Raymond felt he should be aware of any new developments that might have Clayton send such a message. He considered alerting Keaton, but promptly abandoned that option. This might turn out to be a minor issue and Keaton's power-hungry ego didn't need another feeding. If indeed it were necessary to involve SHUMA, there'd be time enough later to bring Keaton up to speed. Raymond pressed the keys to close the data he was reviewing with more force than necessary. As a scientist, he was used to the unexpected. He even appreciated it, as it was often the unexpected that brought the most valuable insight. But it bothered him that he had to consider the political ramifications of all of his actions.

After reading the message one more time, he accepted the inevitability of his next action and initiated a SETE session, inviting Clayton as the sole attendee. It did not surprise him to see an almost immediate response. He steeled himself and pressed connect. Clayton's unsmiling face appeared.

Raymond started the conversation with a friendly overture that he hoped would set the tone. "Good morning, Clayton— well, what's left of it. Your message sounded urgent. How can I help?"

"You can start by telling me the truth," Clayton's voice was ice cold, but the fire behind it was palpable.

"The truth about what, Clayton?" Raymond responded in the soothing tone and slow pace that had been so effective throughout his years as a psychiatrist.

"How did Aida know about the gun on the *Calliope*?"

"I assume it must have been in one of the debriefing reports for OPERATION SUNBURN."

"How would it show up there? There are only three people who knew what went down: Hector, his son, Antonio, and me. I know I didn't report it."

"Well, then it must have been Hector or his son."

"That would make no sense. Any hint of Hector threatening me with a gun could jeopardize his WITSEC status and put him in the cross-hairs for serious criminal prosecution."

Raymond struggled for a credible response and Clayton leaped upon the hesitation. "Okay, no good answer for that one. Try this one. Why don't my chopper rides show up on any FAA traffic database?"

"I'm not sure … I'm not familiar with the databases you're talking about." Raymond was on the defensive, dealing with entities beyond his knowledge set.

"The Federal Aviation Administration keeps a record of all flights. The flights to my place and back aren't there. What's going on? And here's the big one! Why can't I remember what I did on Wednesday and Thursday?"

Raymond scrambled to formulate a reply. He wasn't used to being put on the defensive, and he instinctively pushed back. "Listen Clayton, I'm not responsible for what may or may not be in the SUNBURN reports. Nor am I in charge of how your helicopter rides are logged. Your mental confusion may be a side effect of the hypnosis and the MINDI device. I will do my best to find answers to your questions, but I urge you, for your own good, to stay focused on the goals of the project."

"Not good enough. Raymond! If I don't get some straight answers by tomorrow, don't expect me to show up on Monday." Clayton's image disappeared and Raymond was left staring at the SETE logo.

Saturday 11:30 a.m.

What had begun as a morning of quiet jubilation over the successful application of the MINDI device and the advancement of the ATHENA project was now clouded by a breach in SEAM, the protective cocoon that the team had built around ATHENA.

As much as he resented Keaton's participation on any level, Raymond admitted to himself that he had to alert Keaton and SHUMA to what could fast become a major issue. He sent a text followed by a SETE invite. The text read, "Something has come up. I'll be waiting on SETE to discuss." He started the SETE session and while he was waiting for Keaton to join, he tried to get back to what he was doing before Clayton derailed his morning. An unproductive fifteen minutes dragged by, then SETE announced that Keaton was waiting to join. Bracing himself, he clicked 'Connect'.

Keaton's image sharpened into view. Although his background was out of focus, it appeared to be a mix of bamboo and palm fronds. Before any conversation could begin, a woman's blurred figure leaned in front of the camera and placed a tall glass topped by a miniature umbrella on the tabletop in front of Keaton.

"Well, thank you, darlin'." Keaton smiled at the off-camera figure.

Raymond couldn't help but think that Keaton's choice of venue for the call, the type of drink, and the timing of its delivery were all designed to reaffirm Keaton's nonchalant power over Raymond and his work. His irritation grew as he was forced to wait and watch as the drink was delivered and then as Keaton took a long sip through the protruding straw. Finally, turning his attention to the screen, Keaton drawled his indifference, "Hey Doc, what's happenin'?"

Struggling not to be distracted by his exasperation, Raymond fired back, "This needs to be confidential, Keaton."

With a smile that showed how much he enjoyed Raymond's annoyance, Keaton leaned back from the camera and slid a glass door shut, sealing the area he occupied from a larger public area beyond.

"Okay, what's the problem?" Keaton once again lifted the straw to his lips.

"Clayton has questions about gaps in his memory and his helicopter rides that don't show on any FAA database. He has threatened not to go forward with the project. What's more, from my conversation with him, I have the strong suspicion he is getting input from outside the protocol."

Until now, Raymond had done all the heavy lifting for ATHENA. Keaton's job consisted of logistics and matériel procurement. On paper, he was the first line of support for problems, but with all the safeguards built into the protocols, SHUMA and Keaton considered ATHENA to be a low risk for any non-scientific issues.

Keaton put down his glass. The last sip of his drink was turning sour in his mouth. "You assured us that there were safeguards and that this kind of thing couldn't happen."

"Yes, there were—are safeguards. The SEAM environment was designed to insulate ATHENA from both internal and external disruption. Something is going on that we didn't plan for. The indications are that it's a security issue, which is why I'm calling you."

Fully engaged now, Keaton understood that Raymond's assessment would be hard to challenge. Keaton would end up owning this issue until he solved it or found a plausible way to blame someone else. He adopted a more conciliatory tone as he realized that either way, he and Raymond would have to work on it together. "Of course, you were right to call. I'll track down who's messing with the project. What do we do about Clayton?"

"I need to think about it more, but I have a two-pronged plan that will hopefully bring him back in line. First, I think it's best that we let him in a bit more on what has been happening. We'll give him answers to his questions. Second, I think we should move up the timeline for OPERATION SANDCASTLE. It would take Clayton's mind off his conspiracy theories."

Keaton swiftly analyzed Raymond's approach. It was appealing on two levels. It was logical and, perhaps more importantly, it was Raymond's plan and if things were to go awry, Raymond would be an easy scapegoat. "Sounds good. How much time do you think we have?"

"He says if I don't get back to him with some satisfactory answers by tomorrow, he won't show up on Monday."

"I can't promise to track down the source of the external interference by Monday."

"Understood, but hopefully we can get back on track with Clayton before then. Are you going to brief Max?"

"I have to. It would be my head if this goes further south, and she didn't know."

Raymond couldn't be sure if Keaton was speaking literally or just figuratively, but he was certain that when Keaton connected with Max, he would be dressed for the occasion and he would place the call from a very different setting.

"Is there anything else?" Aware of the ticking clock, Raymond was eager to move forward with his plan.

"No. Keep me posted." Uncharacteristic tension played across Keaton's normally smug face.

"Will do. And you do the same." Raymond disconnected, leaving Keaton to follow through on his commitment to inform Max.

—⦿—

Saturday 12:00 noon - Maxine Corbel

Maxine Corbel had first been dubbed Max by her friends years ago when she still saw some value in friendship. The name stuck. The friends didn't. Now, at 47 years old, experience had taught her that relationships were best if kept transactional and at arm's length. Viewing all human interactions as negotiations and all negotiations as competitions, she even considered her occasional sexual encounters to be rewarding only if she received more pleasure than she gave. More than comfortable with her choices, she viewed her attitudes as components of her commitment to self-realization and she was proud of who she had become.

Now, she was enduring a rare moment of relative downtime. Sitting at her black onyx-topped desk, her eyes were on her computer screen as she peripherally arranged and adjusted the seldom-used crystal letter opener, gold pen, and matching mechanical pencil that shared her desktop. Disdaining her childhood OCD diagnosis, she believed that her demand for order was one of her superpowers.

One wall of the office was a floor-to-ceiling window, unsuccessfully offering the distraction of a magnificent view of the Pacific Ocean. The house sat on 20 acres of prime southern California coast, but Max rarely walked the grounds or savored the view. It had 20 rooms, but she lived in only three or four. Even counting her sleep time, she spent more time in her office than in any other room. Expert designers had adorned the hardwood floors with beautiful oriental rugs and the walls with fine paintings, but if she noticed the finery at all, it was only as a symbol of her success. There was one wall of her office that caught her frequent and thoughtful attention. Like animal heads to a big game hunter, the mounted logos of the corporations that she had acquired, gutted, and repurposed hung, testifying to her cleverness, power, and most often, her ruthlessness.

She had flawlessly finalized the acquisition and liquidation of AGRIUSCO, a medium-sized agriculture firm in Kansas, and was feeling the almost orgasmic euphoria of a deal well-planned and executed. She routinely watched many companies with differing criteria in mind, but with the same ultimate goal. In this case, the value of the company as an ongoing agricultural business had become less than what could be realized in a much shorter time frame by building a major resort and surrounding upscale homes on the land. AGRIUSCO had been suffering from a three-year regional drought and then the politics of the day had brought on embargoes and counter-embargoes. Its access to foreign markets had taken a severe hit. Max rightly assessed that it was ripe for a buyout at a price that allowed her plan to work. Her net proceeds would amount to several tens of millions of dollars. As AGRIUSCO died, Max's new corporation, ELYSIUM was born.

The article that she was reading was the product of an online interview that she had sat for the day before. A reporter had asked, "Doesn't it bother you that the land will never be used for growing things again?"

Her icy response was characteristic and confirmed her image as a powerful woman who didn't bother with political correctness or seek the approval of polite society. "Look, you're young. You work for a newspaper, so you're an idealist. When you finally take off your bleeding-heart blinders, you'll realize that money isn't a disease and wealthy people aren't the enemy. Instead of vegetables, the land will be used to grow families. The resort will bring joy. And after all, the wealthy need a place to live too. All in all, this is a win for the greater good. You can bank on it."

As she read the unflattering article, she had to admit her words came off as glib, but she didn't believe them, anyway. Principles didn't govern her actions, and money no longer mattered. She did what she did for the thrill—the thrill of winning—the thrill of having her superior intellect, unfettered by the mores of inferior players, recognize an opportunity and then squeeze every drop of value out of it. Her moral code was informed by her belief that her wealth and power came entirely and righteously through her efforts. She had no sympathy for the unfortunates of the world because their plight was the result of their self-imposed inertia.

With more than adequate pressure on the touch-sensitive screen, she closed the article. She scanned her emails almost frantically, looking for something, anything, that would feed her hunger for excitement. The crush of competition and the pressure of challenge were what defined and energized her. Now, with her latest conquest securely mounted on her trophy wall, she was suffering from a severe case of adrenaline withdrawal. Oh—how she hated downtime.

It was at that precise moment that she got the SETE invitation from Keaton. The subject was "ATHENA Update" but since the message was outside the scheduled weekly status reports, it was easy to surmise that it meant trouble.

For years Max had been using SHUMA to cultivate a network of political power players and the success of ATHENA would be a potent enough draw to bring the entire network firmly into her tent. The AI technology had sex appeal and its practical applications could feed the lusts of any number of various appetites.

"Damn it, Keaton," she muttered angrily, but then she hummed happily to herself as she went to the kitchen, poured a tall glass of iced tea with lots of lemon, and then sat back down in front of the computer.

She tipped the rim of the glass over her lips, relishing the sour chill, and then clicked on the invitation link. The immediate appearance of Keaton's image implied that he had been standing by, waiting for her to connect.

"Tell me what's happening, Keaton," Max demanded, skipping the greetings.

From the background, she could tell that he was in his office. She could make out pictures of him with foreign presidents, kings, and dictators. He was sometimes in a business suit, but often in combat camouflage. It was notable how often he was standing in the row of support personnel behind the country leaders.

Keaton tried gamely to establish a more congenial tone. "Hi Max, I heard on the news that you closed the AGRIUSCO deal. Congratulations! I know you worked—."

The edge in Max's voice sliced through his overture. "Keaton, what's happening?"

Keaton's shoulders sagged under the weight of the troublesome news he was about to deliver. "I just spoke with Raymond. We may have hit a glitch in ATHENA."

"Is there a problem with the technology?"

"No, it's not that. Our boy, Clayton, has expressed concerns. He has questions."

"Hmm, so can't Raymond smooth things over with some plausible half-truths? We have to stay on track."

"Well, the lying part is easy enough, but getting Clayton to believe the con has gotten a lot harder. Raymond thinks he is connecting with someone outside SEAM."

Max took some time to digest Keaton's statement. "How can that be possible? There are very few people who know what's really going on at ATHENA, and SEAM was constructed to protect the project from outside interference. If there's a breach, why didn't we get an alarm?" She paused for a breath, adding emphasis to her next comment, "Security is in your wheelhouse, Keaton. What's going on?"

His day had taken such an abrupt wrong turn. Keaton fidgeted, his confident facade melting under Max's harsh spotlight. He sought cover by bringing Raymond into the mix. "Raymond plans to feed Clayton a bit of the truth and distract him by accelerating the timeline for the SANDCASTLE review and the HIGH TIDE launch."

Max stared thoughtfully at her trophy wall. "I hope it works. Whether it does or not will depend on Raymond. Assure him that he will have everything he needs." Her gaze once more fixed squarely on Keaton. "You've told me what Raymond is doing. What are *you* doing to find the leak?"

"Of course, my team will review the SEAM logs for any record of an external breach. Beyond that, we will sift the raw data for any hint of something that doesn't show in the logs."

"That all sounds pretty fundamental. And if nothing shows up in the logs or the raw data?"

Keaton knew he was being boxed into a corner. He mentally sorted through the plausible options, and only one was truly credible. He sighed in resignation and answered, "If we fail to find anything there, then with Raymond's help, I guess I would have to enter the SEAM environment myself and see if I can pick up a trail from that end."

"How long will you need?"

"I would guess two or three days."

"Done! I expect to hear back from you with good news within 48 hours. That's noon on Monday, Keaton." Max enjoyed watching as Keaton sank further into his seat. "Meanwhile, send me Clayton's file. I want to review the recordings of his sessions with Raymond and what we have of Clayton's history. It's time I got to know our boy a bit better. Clear?"

"Yes, Max, I'm clear."

"You know what's at stake?"

Keaton didn't need the reminder that what was at stake had significant personal implications for him. "Yes ... I'm clear."

"Okay, get to work." Max ended the session and watched as Keaton's image dissolved into the SETE emblem. She leaned back from the desk, took another sip from her glass, and puckered her lips. Events had intervened to rescue her from boredom. Even though she invoked the possibility of failure and its ramifications to intimidate and motivate, she was so confident in her ability to swat down any challenge that the thought of real failure never entered her mind. Her gaze turned once more to the logo wall and the vacant spot reserved for the ATHENA trophy. She took another sip of her iced tea and smiled.

Saturday 4:00 p.m. - Thoughtful Moments

After his conversation with Keaton, Raymond tried to focus for a time on the data he was reviewing that morning, now seemingly ages ago. After a couple of unproductive hours, he took a walk around the hospital grounds and down to the water. He stood for a long time hoping that the cold, January breeze blowing in off the water would help wash away some of the negative reverberations that always accompanied his interactions with Keaton. Despite all his training, he couldn't be sure whether the effect was born of prejudice or perception and had come to accept that it was probably a mix of both. He closed his eyes, tried to distance himself from his feelings, and devise a response for Clayton that was thoughtful, believable, and most importantly one that would satisfy him enough to bring him solidly back on board.

As he considered his options, Raymond took an honest look at his own limitations. Lying is hard. Aside from its moral repugnance, telling falsehoods convincingly requires unholy nerve to attempt and perverse practice to perfect. Raymond lacked those characteristics. He could stay quiet while deception swirled around him if he thought it was for a good cause, but he was outstandingly bad at convincing anyone of an untruth. His inept handling of Clayton's pointed questions that morning proved that hypothesis to be accurate.

Many interconnected parts made up the ATHENA project, and they all had to be considered. There were the technology components, AI and MINDI, and the on-stage people, Clayton and Aida. There were also the powers behind the curtain. The FBI, SHUMA, and the shadowy figures behind SHUMA all had an interest in ATHENA and where it could lead. Raymond shivered against the cold but stood his ground, determined not to retreat until he had a plan or at least a direction. He pulled his hands out of his coat pocket for just the time it took to blow a warming breath onto them.

He had thought that Clayton's strong desire to regain his status as an active agent would render him cooperative, if not compliant. He had expected Clayton's initial reaction to the threat of retirement and the ongoing nature of the threat would ensure Clayton's lasting and unquestioning commitment to the project. Clayton's growing inquisitiveness and willingness to challenge the program jeopardized his own desired outcome and were surprising. Raymond knew that the injuries he suffered, followed by the months of painful therapy, would leave most people less confident, more malleable—but not Clayton. As a project leader, Raymond saw these developments as threatening, as a scientist fascinating, as a human admirable.

He stood there longer than he needed to, long after he decided on a direction, even after he outlined what he was going to tell Clayton. Shivering in the cold, he welcomed the painful penance for what he was about to do. Days were short in the Seattle area this time of year and the sun sank towards the horizon when Raymond turned his back on the water and took a direct route back to the hospital. Once in his office, he sat at his desk, painfully flexed his stiff fingers, and sent a SETE invitation to Clayton for 10 a.m. the next morning. He would use the time to rehearse what he would say and he needed to bring one more actor onto the stage for the meeting. He sent a SETE invitation with a high urgency for another meeting in two hours. It was short notice for most people, especially on a Saturday evening, but Aida was special. He knew she would be available—It was a requirement of the program.

January 16, 2022 - Sunday Morning Answers

Clayton slept later than usual but still awoke before sunrise on Sunday morning. The night had passed without dreams or drama. Lying in bed, playing back the previous day's events, he viewed his restful night as a sign that his taking control of the situation had been a good move for him. Reshod had made no further contact and so his mind turned to the meeting Raymond had scheduled for 10 a.m. The invitation gave no clue as to Raymond's state of mind, but Clayton was comfortable with the ultimatum that he had delivered. Today, he would either get the answers he demanded or he would leave the project. In either case, his path forward, at least in the short term, was clear.

He set his morning pot of coffee to brew and limped out onto the cold air of the porch. With his hands on the thick wooden railing, he looked out across the lawn to the brightening sky. Its reflection sparkled on the surface of the sea, a mesmerizing kaleidoscope of reds, blues, and eye-blinking whites. Suddenly, an onslaught of mental pictures and fuzzy recollections invaded his brain. They chased each other through his head, never stopping long enough to register as complete and decipherable. A face, blurred but hauntingly familiar, rose out of the wreckage of his reminiscences, floated near the surface of recognition and was swept away by the flood of disconnected mental images. Following closely behind them was something more, something elusive, something that was important to remember. Something—shutting his eyes, he concentrated on bringing it into focus. As though aware it was being pursued, it hid behind the shadows of other memory fragments, out of focus, tauntingly just on the verge of recall. Pushing through the cloud of competing mental images, he almost had it when, with a sharp pang, his injured leg reminded him that he had been standing too long. He tried to ignore the distraction and struggled to continue the pursuit, but his leg complained even more vigorously. His quarry hid behind the fog of the pain and then faded away. The pain in his leg subsided as Clayton shivered, turned, and went back into the kitchen.

Two hours later, a well-bundled Clayton sat on the porch with his third cup of coffee. The sun was now several degrees over the horizon and he gratefully basked in its warming rays. He had been trying unsuccessfully to re-initiate the earlier experience, but now the faint chimes from his office clock signaled an end to his efforts. Pausing in the kitchen only long enough to top off his coffee, he made his way down the hall. The sun poured through the east-facing office window and he took a moment to appreciate the view of the maturing day. Taking a deep breath to clear his mind, he sat and clicked on Raymond's SETE invitation. Several seconds passed and then Raymond's image appeared. Clayton was surprised as a second image also flashed into view. It was Aida.

"Good morning, Clayton," Raymond's tone was friendly but also respectful of the serious nature of the meeting. "I have asked Aida to join us since she plays such a big role in the project and your relationship with her is key to the project's success."

Nodding his acknowledgment of Aida's presence, Clayton directed his response to Raymond, "Good morning, Raymond. What do you have for me?" Clayton's voice wasn't unfriendly but signaled little patience for small talk.

"First of all, Clayton, I owe you an apology ... You were right. We haven't been completely honest with you." Clayton pulled back from the camera and made as if to rise from his seat. He opened his mouth to launch into the reply he had loosely rehearsed. Raymond held up his hand. "Please, let me finish. I want you to know not just what happened, but the reason it happened."

His eyes on fire, Clayton settled slowly back into his chair. "I'm listening."

"As you know, MINDI is a breakthrough technology. We developed models and ran simulations, but MINDI's first live application was on you, Clayton. Although we never saw any indication that MINDI could be in any way harmful, its first use, on you, did result in a perceived temporal displacement coupled with retrograde amnesia—"

Clayton interrupted, "English, Raymond. Give it to me without the jargon."

"Simply put, when you experienced MINDI for the first time, you lost a day."

"What do you mean, I lost a day?"

"Pretty much exactly that. Our first conversation, the first time we met, the first time you met Aida, was on Wednesday, not Thursday. Your first session at the hospital was on Thursday, not Friday. The Friday session was the second session."

"Wait—I only had one session."

"No, Clayton. You had two. The first didn't go smoothly, but we did observe some of your recollections. That's how Aida knew about the gun. That first session was far from perfect. Your recollections were scattered and fragmented. Different memories were stepping all over each other. We could only make sense out of bits and pieces. It wasn't a total loss because it allowed us to identify and tune the bugs out of MINDI and perfect our approach by adding hypnosis to the protocol. After the first session was over, it was clear you had no recollection of it. Your last memory was just before we turned MINDI on. We kept you overnight at the hospital and Friday morning picked up at the point you now remember— when we applied MINDI the second time."

Clayton took some time to digest what he had just heard. "Why didn't you say something?"

"To what end? There was no real harm done and informing you of your lost time and amnesia could have caused you some great distress. As it is, the distress it caused was, until this moment, most keenly felt by me. As you may have guessed, I'm a terrible liar. It pains me greatly when I am anything but completely honest. In any case, I hope you can forgive me and we can continue to work together. There is so much good that can come from ATHENA."

Clayton saw Raymond was uncomfortable. What he couldn't tell was if Raymond's discomfort was because of his being forced to confess or because he was still not telling the whole truth.

"What about the missing helicopter records?"

"Ah yes. I asked our friends at the FBI and the answer I got was that they are testing a new surveillance technology and, as is the case in such situations, the flights are exempt from FAA logging. Your helicopter was, and is, part of their test group."

Clayton sat staring at his screen, sifting through conflicting assessments and emotions. He wanted to believe Raymond, but he wasn't sure he was hearing the whole truth. He was in awe of the whole concept and the incredible technology, but he hated being manipulated. The fire in his eyes cooled as, in quick succession, anger, disappointment, and sadness washed over him.

At that moment, Aida, speaking for the first time, broke the silence, "Clayton, I can see you feel betrayed and I can't blame you. So much of the success of any project, any mission, relies on the belief you have in the goals of the mission and the trust you have in your teammates. ATHENA's goals are good, even noble. And please believe that I ... we are honored to have you part of the team. If you would consider staying on the project, I believe we could accomplish some great things that could help a lot of people."

Clayton saw she was uncomfortable. He surmised she was programmed to handle simple apologies, but her portrayal of sincerity was impressive. Once again, he was amazed at the human nuances and inflections that Aida employed to perfection. A moment ago, he was on the verge of walking away, but Aida's active presence in the conversation had him realize that ATHENA was much more than its goal of knowledge transfer to a computer. It had become a world in which he was a vested citizen. A realm in which improbable science was rewriting the rulebook on the interface between humans and machines, and perhaps blurring the line between the two.

Besides, if he quit, what would he do tomorrow and the next day? He lingered on that thought. He would get up before dawn as usual. Take his morning coffee out to the porch to watch the sun come up. Maybe take a walk down to the water. Twice a week, he would go for his physical therapy. And so his hours, days, weeks, months, and years would tick away with no more interest, excitement, or passion than that possessed by the clock on his office wall. On the other hand, there was ATHENA, an incredibly strange conglomeration of Raymond's demonstrated genius, SHUMA's murky agenda, and his own tangled desires. It was clear that he didn't have all the answers that he wished he had but it was also clear that he wouldn't get them by leaving the project.

Raymond and Aida sat in expectant silence, each one of them knowing that they had said what they had intended to say and that more words wouldn't be helpful. Clayton let the silence grow past the point of discomfort to the point of pain. He had already made up his mind, but he felt the need to impress on Raymond how close he had come to blowing up the project. Somewhere in the distant background, there was the sound of a lawnmower, which amplified the silence. When Clayton spoke, it was almost in a whisper, "I'll keep going."

Aida's lips turned upward in her Mona Lisa smile and Raymond's exhaled breath was audible.

Clayton continued more emphatically, "But hear this. You're all out of second chances. Be straight with me or I'm gone."

Clayton's remarks clearly targeted Raymond, who gracefully and penitently endured the blows. "I understand, Clayton. I'm grateful that you've decided to keep going."

Clayton picked up his cup and sipped the lukewarm contents. His jaw tensed both at the taste of the stale coffee and with the effort of pulling his focus away from his suspicions. He took a deep breath. "So, what's next?"

Raymond was both relieved and exhausted. "It's been an emotion-charged 24 hours. Would you like to take some time to decompress?" He wasn't sure which answer he hoped for.

Clayton had already moved on. "No, Raymond, I'm hungry for more information, not less. Tell me what happens next."

It was Raymond's turn to take a deep breath. "Building on MINDI's flawed first trial, the second one was a complete success. The technology worked perfectly and your communication with Aida was more intense and effective than anyone expected."

"She makes that part of it easy," Clayton interrupted, evoking a smile from Aida.

"Ahh … yes … good. In any case, I had originally planned a similar, easy exercise for tomorrow but, I feel comfortable that we have ironed out the issues that arose in the first session. The second session went so well, and the data looks so good, that I have decided to expand the scope of what we'll include in the next phase. What we will do will have two parts. The first is a simple dissection of a past mission, similar to what we did with the SUNBURN operation. Assuming all goes well with that part tomorrow, we will take a few days to set things up and then we will use your recollections to help guide Aida in a real-time simulation of an active mission that we will call OPERATION HIGH TIDE."

"What kind of operation? How can my recollections be helpful?" Clayton raised his cup to his lips.

"The operation I'm talking about is one you're very familiar with. It's unfinished business from two years ago. I'm sure you remember SANDCASTLE and Esteban Diego Navarro."

Clayton took the cup from his mouth and, not looking, set it down on the desk, nearly missing the wooden edge. His eyes still appeared to be focused on the screen, but they took on a burning intensity and what he saw went far beyond the monitor and back through time. Through tight lips, he replied, "Yes, I remember."

PART THREE

OPERATION SANDCASTLE

CHAPTER SEVEN

The Ascent of Esteban Diego Navarro

January 2016 - Jenaro Moreno

Having found its voice, the wind forcefully carried the increasingly urgent message of an impending storm. Statuesque palm trees that normally lined the street in stoic silence now whipped back and forth. The slashing sounds of the frenzied fronds shared the news with the excitement and intensity of star-struck rumor-mongers. This was Los Angeles where rumor and scandal were common, but violent weather events were rare. Unrehearsed gusts, unsure of their parts, raged one way and then, with equal ferocity, another. The diffuse light from the overcast sky cast dancing shadows on the ground below.

The hellish display was not lost on Esteban Navarro as he eased the Lexus sedan into the reserved space of the small parking lot. It matched his mood and was a fitting background to the day's program. Before he pushed open the armored door of the car, he scanned the shrub-lined area. It had been a long time since any real threat had validated his caution, but his vigilance was ingrained by a life spent in one type of jungle or another. He lifted his briefcase from the creamy soft leather of the passenger seat and deftly eased his tall, lean body out of the quiet of the climate-controlled cabin into the fearsome noises and uncommon vapors of a storm-tossed Los Angeles. It was only a few steps to the main entrance. The sign on the tastefully reinforced glass door said MexAm Imports. As he approached the door, leaning into the wind, a long buzz announced that the receptionist had seen him and approved his entrance. The need to be admitted by a receptionist was common with many businesses that didn't expect walk-in customers in that part of Los Angeles, but the armored door and multiple cameras inferred MexAm Imports was not a common business. The heavy door closed behind him, muting the sound of the approaching storm.

"Good morning, Mr. Navarro." Esteban had hired her for her good looks and pleasant demeanor and now her bright smile and melodic yet respectful greeting validated his decision.

"Good morning, Sophia. Is Jenaro in?" When he wanted it to be, Esteban's voice was pleasing to the ear. His accent carried traces of his Colombian roots, shaped by his time in the back roads and alleyways of Mexico City, but blended and smoothed to a cultured potpourri. The effect was not an accident, but the result of practice and dedication. When subjected to the flames of passion or anger, the cultured overtones quickly boiled away.

"Yes sir. He's in his office. Would you like me to tell him you're here?"

On any normal day, Esteban would delay spending time with his boss as long as possible, but not today. Today, it would be more than bearable. "Yes. Please do."

Sophia tapped the intercom button. "Mr. Moreno, Mr. Navarro is here."

The building was part of a high-end office park on the city outskirts and had every appearance of a successful trans-border shipping and merchandise wholesale operation. Pictures on the walls of the reception area had been chosen to reinforce that image. Bustling market scenes featured happy Mexican tradespeople and their fruit, furniture, and art. Faces beamed happily at the camera from behind produce bins, on factory floors, and in mountain village fields. Green potted tropical plants softened the stark white-tiled floor of the lobby and the soft bubbling from a large aquarium conveyed innocence and tranquility. The charade had long since ceased to engage or amuse Esteban.

The camera on the ceiling behind the reception desk and two more outside with views of the parking lot fed monitors at the desk and a security room behind one of the closed doors that bordered the entrance area. In addition to the two men on duty in the security room, two men sat on opposite sides of the reception area, reading. The younger of the two held a smartphone. The older man read from a hard copy magazine. Each noted Esteban's entrance. They had been there since the office opened that morning. They would stay the day and would be back again the next day. Each wore jackets that occasionally opened enough to disclose the lethal nature of their assignment. The three well-constructed doors several feet behind the reception desk added to the impression of a business where security was a priority.

"It's about time. Send him in." The intercom did nothing to soften the arrogance and condescension that was Jenaro Moreno's second most used tone.

Heavily jowled and overweight, pulling thick clouds of smoke from his ever-present cigar, Jenaro looked out of place in the upscale main office suite behind his black marble desk. Although the office was meticulously cleaned every night, by mid-morning, the desk was covered with ashes.

"Good morning, jefe." Esteban's half-hearted attempt at sincerity failed badly but went unnoticed.

"Sit," He directed without lifting his eyes from his computer screen. His number two obediently sat in front of the desk, placed his briefcase on the floor next to him, and silently waited for Jenaro to raise a point of conversation or assign some task.

Jenaro kept the room cool, which wasn't hard at this time of year. The sluggishly revolving blades from a large ceiling fan added a soft strobe effect to the room's hazy lighting. A muted scraping sound accompanied each revolution as the unit did its futile best to make the smoke-ladened air more breathable.

The spreadsheet he was studying pleased Jenaro. These early days of 2016 promised a good year for the legitimate business that was MexAm but that wasn't the best news. The criminal enterprise which Jenaro ran and which was his main focus, was on track to show a profit exceeding last year's numbers by more than 50 percent. This was fueled, in part, by an ever-increasing demand for the drugs but also by Jenaro's ruthless and violent domination of competing drug distributors. He had every reason to be happy, but he had little capacity for happiness, even in small doses. The closest he could come was a certain satisfaction tempered by his insatiable need for more.

"Squeek ... squeeek ... squeeeek", he swiveled slightly back and forth in his office chair as he studied the reports. With each pivot, the chair let out its squeal of protest against Jenaro's considerable weight. Although it was only mid-morning, he frequently accompanied his review with long sips of blond liquid from a large scotch glass. In the days when his climb to the higher tier of the criminal organization required it most, he had been trim and fit, but now Jenaro wore his success around his belly. The passing years and careless disregard for his health brought increasingly urgent warnings from his doctors. Now in his sixties, he dutifully took the pills they prescribed. In addition, he gave regularly and generously to the Church, calculating that the combination of science and holy intervention would insulate him from the ill effects of his unhealthy life choices.

"Squeek … squeeek … squee—", the rhythmic squeaking stopped as he leaned closer to the display, his finger smudging the screen as he traced a list of entries.

"Malditos hijos de puta!" Not bothering to remove the cigar from his mouth, his full-throated expletives sent sparks into the air and splashed ashes onto the marble desktop. "Where is Sacramento? Maldita sea!" He warmed to his anger, nurturing it. The enthusiasm of his cursing was more an expression of his joy at finding something to rage at than any genuine displeasure at the transgression. "The numbers from Sacramento are late again! We need to teach them the importance of timely reporting!" For emphasis, Jenaro forcefully stabbed the butt of his cigar into the ashtray on the desk, scattering a new layer of ashes. He stood and stomped around the desk and moved to the office door as the still-silent Esteban followed. "I have a meeting with the Banker, Esteban. While I'm gone, reach out to those sons of bitches and explain to them that if I have to get involved, they'll be stuffing nickel bags and sleeping on the streets outside of the fancy houses they used to live in!"

Despite Jenaro's performance, Esteban knew that his boss had come nowhere near his room-shaking potential of a full-blown tantrum. For Jenaro, anger management meant using anger effectively as a powerful form of communication and enterprise governance. Anger was his most common intonation and brutality its most frequent embodiment. It was well known throughout his organization how quickly and unpredictably he could escalate his emotions from irritation to rage. A transgression one day could earn the offender a mocking rebuke. The same infraction at a different time could bring on a severe beating, or much worse. The uncertainty of his reactions sowed resentment among his troops, but more than that, it evoked fear and it was through fear that Jenaro governed.

"Yes, jefe, I will handle it," Esteban assured him as he handed Jenaro his computer bag. "There is a storm coming. Vaya con Dios and good luck with the Banker."

"I don't need luck to deal with that puto. He's so eager to please, he paws at my zipper and I have to get him off of his knees every time we meet." Jenaro's bodyguards kept pace as the two walked to the door. "After the meeting, I will spend the afternoon at the club. You make sure you sort out the Sacramento crew."

"Yes, patrón, I will see to it."

One of the bodyguards, leaning hard against the wind, pushed the door open and scanned the street. The storm's wordless wailing filled the room. He signaled and Jenaro started to walk through the door, pausing for one last remark. Incapable of bestowing praise without tainting it with condescension, he smiled without mirth. "You're a good boy, Esteban. Who knows, someday, like me, you may get a chance to lead those who are less gifted." He turned and, leaning into the gusts, shouldered his way out to the waiting car.

Esteban watched him as he eased his hefty girth into the back of the limousine. The ingratiating smile drained from his face as he murmured under his breath, "Yes, patrón, I will see to it." He scanned the darkening sky as thunder rumbled in the distance.

****

Jenaro settled into the soft comfort of the stretch Lincoln Continental. It was a corporate asset, owned by MexAm but no one but Jenaro was allowed to use it. It had been upgraded not only with the softest leather and most comfortable seating, but also with armor and bullet-resistant windows. Once the door was shut, the intimidating sounds of the storm became mere whispers and mumbles.

"OK, Victor, vamos."

Victor had been Jenaro's driver for several years and was well aware of the routine. Jenaro pressed a button to raise the privacy partition, sealing the passenger compartment from the driver. The one-way glass allowed for a view of the front while preventing the driver from seeing into the passenger area. A press of another button revealed a well-stocked bar. Jenaro pulled a bottle of Fuenteseca Cosetta tequila from the rack and poured himself a drink. It was the third drink of the morning and he knew his doctors would object, but he excused his vices, at least to himself, by his convenient, if somewhat contrived belief, that the pills he took would counter any harm. To that end, he pulled a bottle of pills from his pocket, flipped open the cap, and retrieved two pills, which he washed down with a healthy slug of the liquor. The prescription from the doctor was for one tablet, but he recognized he had already indulged that morning more than was good for him. If one pill was good then today, two would be better.

Growing up in a poorer section of Los Angeles, he had occasionally seen limousines like this one, gliding through the torn neighborhoods, their drivers and passengers oblivious to the hopelessly desperate inhabitants. He thought then how wonderful it would be to look out of those tinted windows while passing through the detritus of pitiful human existence and remain unsoiled by the dirt and the blood. The image made a lasting impression and fed his ambition. From an early age, Jenaro was determined to claw his way out of the gutter. In his youngest years, he developed the guile he needed to avoid the beatings, and then as he grew, a young man's strength and his growing rage gave him the brutality that became his trademark and the foundation of his success.

They were following one of several pre-planned routes, and today they wound their way through one of the shabbier sections of the city, not unlike that of his childhood. Jenaro knew enough not to be predictable. There were few trees here.

Dirt and garbage blew up from the street. The wind wailing through the tenement echoed the sorrows of its inhabitants, and the thunder rumbled itself into a new harmony, a chorus of misery and resentment. Finally, as if the storm were shaking off a great burden, it let go of its hold on the rain. The view through the front windscreen disappeared briefly until the wipers restored the dismal scene.

Three miles and fifteen minutes away from the MexAm office, they were moving at the speed limit on a garbage-strewn street. The follow car with his bodyguards had lagged behind and a garbage truck had pulled in behind the limo. When a white panel truck shot out of a side street and blocked their forward progress, Jenaro's first thought was that it was another crazy LA driver. Victor slammed on the brakes, throwing Jenaro forward and spilling his drink on his ample stomach. The massive limo skidded to a stop on the wet pavement. As armed men exited the panel truck, his initial irritation melted into a petrifying chill of fear.

"Back up! Back up!"

Even if Victor could hear him through the privacy screen, the driver needed no instruction. He threw the massive vehicle in reverse and the tires screamed as the car tried to reverse course. The garbage truck that had been following them closed the gap and slammed into the rear end of the limo. Victor jerked the car forward again and rammed the panel truck, but there wasn't enough room to build up the momentum needed to plow through. Jenaro saw Victor on his phone, no doubt calling for help. Jenaro was instantly on his phone as well. Where was the car with his escorts?

Esteban saw who was calling. He was expecting the call and picked up on the first ring. "Jenaro, what's wrong?"

"Esteban, I am under attack! Send help now!"

"Si, jefe, I can see your phone's location. I could send help right away, but I'm afraid there is no chance that they would get to you in time."

Armed men from both trucks approached the limo through the rain, firing automatic weapons as they came.

"Esteban, don't you understand? Can you hear?" Jenaro was screaming now, "There are men here shooting at me! They are trying to kill me! Do something!"

"But I have, Jenaro. I have ordered a new office chair. I always hated the noises yours makes. And I have thrown away your filthy ashtray."

As the bullets struck, spider web patterns appeared in the polycarbonate material of the bullet-resistant windows, diverting the rivulet of rain pouring down the sides of the limo. Jenaro cringed at the first bullet strikes, but took temporary comfort as the windows held.

"What are you talking about, Esteban? I don't understand!"

"Listen Jenaro, from the sound of it we only have a few seconds and I do want you to understand. It was I who arranged your death. More than that, I will take over your place as el jefe. I will build the organization to a size you could never be capable of. Your violence has no art. Your brutality has no brain. It was always going to end like this for you, that is, unless your heart gave out first."

Jenaro saw Victor draw a handgun from under his jacket, but he was helpless to put it to use.

"But why, Esteban? I treated you so well!" Jenaro was pleading now. "Please help me!"

Esteban spat out his response, "It's pathetic but not surprising that you don't see it, even now. You treated me the way you treated everyone, as an inferior—but I'm not that, Jenaro, as you can see."

One attacker approached the car, smiled at Victor, and stuck a small device to the driver's window. He stepped back and a moment later, the window dissolved in a small but effective explosion.

"Dios mío, Esteban!" Jenaro watched through the privacy screen as two men appeared through the smoke and rain and as the stunned Victor raised his weapon, they simultaneously fired short bursts, obliterating Jenaro's view in a spray of blood and brain. "They have killed Victor!"

"I'm sorry to hear that. Victor was a good driver, but, as you know, corporate change often requires personnel adjustments. I have to go now, Jenaro. There is so much for me to do and I believe you have run out of time. Adios."

Jenaro heard the phone go dead. He watched helplessly as one of the men, in a replay of the previous action, attached an explosive to the passenger compartment window. He dove for the floor of the car and a moment later, a blast took out the window. The shock wave left Jenaro stunned and dizzy. He fumbled with the door opposite the blown-out window and tumbled out of the limo onto the rough, wet asphalt, into the noise and rain of the storm. He crawled over the garbage in the gutter toward the sidewalk. Through the ringing in his ears, he heard the sounds of several sets of feet moving at a leisurely pace, coming closer and closer. He heard the first part of the volley that would take his life. He felt a burning pain in his back. His dying brain displayed a flash of light that quickly faded into darkness. He was unaware of his hands briefly clawing at the curb. With a final few twitches, they too became still.

January 6, 2019 - Estaban Rising

Although United States law enforcement had been aware of Esteban Diego Navarro for more than a decade, its interest became more focused when he moved to California and worked his way up the ladder to a position as a lieutenant for the Sinaloa California region. It was a year after that promotion that his boss, Jenaro Moreno, was murdered.

Although Jenaro's assassination was not surprising, considering his occupation, what raised eyebrows was the apparent ease with which it was accomplished. Jenaro had been a cautious man. He changed the routes to his regular appointments frequently, so when he was gunned down while on his way to a meeting, the immediate suspicion arose that the killers' actions must have been informed by someone in Jenaro's own organization. Esteban quickly stepped forward to lead the investigation into his boss's death and, just as quickly, uncovered evidence that four of Jenaro's bodyguards had orchestrated the hit, motivated by visions of a coup and fueled by promises of support from Los Sangre, a much smaller rival gang. Under Esteban's orders, the execution of the four was swift and gruesome. The subsequent disappearance of several Los Sangre's leaders swiftly convinced the terrified survivors to swear a new allegiance and continue to operate under the Sinaloa banner. Esteban moved with such speed and efficiency cartel leadership in Mexico promptly confirmed his promotion to el jefe, the boss of the California organization.

Initially, there were whispers that only planted evidence, and planned executions of those loyal to Jenaro could account for such speed and efficiency. However, with the witnesses all gone and Esteban enjoying the strong support of Sinaloa bosses, the whispers rapidly quieted. So it came to be that either by serendipity or conspiracy, Esteban became the prince of a far-ranging criminal organization which he ran skillfully and ruthlessly from his headquarters in Southern California.

As a rising star in the criminal firmament, he could no longer wrap himself in the shadows that hid the activities of his earlier years. While his growing mythos inspired fear and respect in the darker parts of society, it attracted more attention from law enforcement, more entries in databases, more mentions in reports, more questions as to the scope and reach of Esteban's operation, and more of an interest in crippling its growth. It was out of this convergence that OPERATION SANDCASTLE was born.

CHAPTER EIGHT

2020 The Play's The Thing

January 6 - Clayton Rhodes - Perfect for the Part

By January 2018, Clayton's 17-year career with the FBI had brought him to assignments all over the country. Some were purely investigative and several were undercover operations, more exciting and much more dangerous. While Maggie had always accepted that being a field agent with the FBI carried some inherent risks, the birth of their son, Anthony, gave more weight to her concerns for his safety. Clayton respected and shared those concerns. Shortly after Anthony was born, he promised her that he would minimize his exposure and had been true to that promise. As was its policy, the Bureau had never pushed him to take on another high-risk operation, so when he got a call from his sometimes partner, Special Agent Debra O'Donnell, he didn't expect a recruitment pitch for an undercover operation. For two years, Deb had been working within the FBI's Organized Crime and Drug program assigned to the Los

Angeles field office. It had been a few months since they had spoken, so they spent the first few minutes of the call catching up. Then Deb got to the real point of her call.

"An opportunity has come up for a move against one of the major drug bosses in the California region. I know you're staying away from undercover work now and for all the right reasons, but there are certain unique attributes of this gig that make you the perfect match. There may be no chance you'd be taking this on, but I promised my boss I'd pass it by you."

Clayton would not have traded his job for any other. Of course, there were times he was tired or frustrated, but overall, he felt he was making a positive difference in the world. It was a motivation that he shared with Maggie and part of the strong bond between them. There were times, though, when he missed the excitement, the pure adrenaline rush of undercover operations, times when he felt he wasn't contributing at his full potential. So when Deb opened the question of an undercover operation instead of an immediate, "No thanks," he heard himself asking, "What makes me so perfect for the assignment?"

"I can't be giving you the answer over the phone. You have to see it," Deb teased. "Why don't you come into the office for a briefing? You can meet my boss, Edmundo, and make up your mind after we lay out the operation. At the very least, it would be an opportunity for us to catch up over lunch."

"Okay, Deb. I'll fly in for the meeting and lunch sounds good, but I've got to warn you, I'm going to be a tough sale when it comes to an undercover assignment." Again, Clayton chided himself for leaving even the slimmest possibility of a successful sale.

Sometimes large organizations can move swiftly if the subject matter is important enough. If speed was any indication of importance, this operation was high on the scale. At 10 a.m. the next day, Clayton was sitting with Deb and her boss in a briefing room at the FBI field office in Los Angeles.

The room was larger than necessary for the three occupants, but its projection screen provided a convenient way to share the visuals. The shades were drawn, and the lights were dimmed to provide clarity and full dramatic effect from the images on the screen. Deb's boss, Special Agent in Charge, Edmundo Zarzyckich ran the meeting.

Edmundo was born to a Mexican mother and a Polish father. Those who knew him called him Edmundo Z or E.Z. which he much preferred to the awkward, wildly unsuccessful attempts to address him by his proper name. Over the years, he found that the uninitiated came in two flavors. The courageous would sail through his first name with ease, only to become hopelessly entangled in his last name's jumble of consonants. The less courageous would say his first name and then impose a hopeful, expectant silence only broken when E.Z. supplied the missing part. He had long ago stopped being irritated and now viewed these encounters with good-humored amusement. In all of his 56 years, the only people other than his family who could correctly pronounce his name were those with Polish, or at least Slavic, backgrounds. He was known for his good humor and, in most situations, he was quick to laugh—but today he was all business.

"Thanks for coming, Clayton. As you know, the Bureau's policy regarding undercover ops is that agents participate only on a volunteer basis. If, after you hear what I have to say, you want to walk away, no one will hold it against you. As a matter of fact, if you decide to walk, we'll record this meeting as cross-training. You came to swap some drug enforcement and cyber crime ideas with Deb. Then you two can have lunch, on me. Are you okay with that?"

Clayton leaned back in his chair. "So far, so good."

"Okay then. Consider the rest of this meeting as highly confidential. Got it?"

"Yes, sir."

Edmundo pressed a key on the laptop and the screen sprang to life displaying a one-word title "SANDCASTLE".

"The code name of the op is SANDCASTLE." He continued to press the key bringing up illustrated bullet points and images that tracked to his narration.

"Its purpose is to gather intelligence and, if possible, use that intel to disrupt a major portion of the Sinaloa drug cartel operation in North America. The target is its California-based leader, Esteban Diego Navarro."

Clayton let out a soft whistle. "Big game hunting."

"The biggest. Navarro has just moved into his new home in Malibu. It's an estate fit for the prince he views himself to be. He calls it *El Mirador*, The Overlook. He thinks of himself as sophisticated ... cultured ... and he is going to spare no expense to trick it out with the lavish trappings that support that persona. Paintings, statues, he even has a greenhouse, a conservatory in which he reportedly grows rare plants and flowers. We have to believe his willingness to spend a fortune on his hobbies is a fair indicator of what he will spend on making his home secure."

"Makes sense, but what does that have to do with me?"

"We know that Navarro has reached out to his contacts and asked for a recommendation on the best security specialist available. He's looking for someone to plan and oversee the implementation of the estate's entire security overlay. It's a project that we believe would take several weeks. During that time, this person would at the least be in a position to see and hear what goes on at the estate and ideally have access to a lot of intel that lives in the computers."

"Not likely. It's not my op—," Clayton assumed he was not there to just listen, "but Navarro wouldn't be putting his data on a new system that wasn't deemed bulletproof. In any case, he wouldn't trust any expert within spitting distance of his crown jewels, no matter how highly recommended."

"Well, you're the expert. That still leaves a lot that can be learned from having a presence at the estate."

"Wait a minute! Calling me 'the expert' is a major leap in this conversation."

"Fair enough. At this point, that was just a figure of speech. As you might have guessed, our plan is to have one of our own be the expert that Navarro takes on as his security consultant. We know that in response to his inquiries, the leading candidate is Cotton Parish, a man out of Texas. He is a man about your age with a background in military special forces, specializing in site and cybersecurity. He's a loaner who freelances security work for dark-side players. If a deal is struck between Navarro and this man, as appears probable, we intend to take this guy out and swap our guy in."

"I see where you're going and I wish you luck. The Bureau must have several agents besides me, with that background, who would be good and willing candidates for this operation. Regardless, the obvious major problem I see is that, even with a great cover background, Navarro is going to know what this guy, Parish, looks like and that would make for a very awkward first meeting between Navarro and your agent."

"You're right, Clayton. Even with your rare background as a SEAL and your security expertise and your age and your shared familiarity with Texas, we might and I emphasize might, find another agent who could step in. But there's one other piece of commonality that puts you at the top of the list of candidates. You put your finger on it." Edmundo leaned forward and pressed a button on his desk intercom. "Send him in." Then continuing to Clayton, "Although Parish has been careful not to have his picture taken, in this day and age, that's becoming an impossible task. Our early research came up with a few good images and what we saw is the reason we reached out to you."

At that moment, there was a knock on the door. It swung open, and an aid announced, "Cotton Parish, sir."

The man who stood in the doorway could successfully pass as Clayton's twin brother. His height and build were similar, but more than that, his facial features, while not identical, were so close that a casual observer or even an acquaintance could easily believe they were the same man.

Cotton hesitated before stepping into the dimly lit room. Clayton recognized the conditioned response to an unfamiliar arena, the quick risk assessment that, with training and experience, became less than a conscious exercise and more of a reflex. He saw Cotton's eyes seek out the shadowy corners, the hidden areas, and finally rest on the three occupants. "Good mornin', y'all." His face wore a mischievous grin, which to Clayton seemed out of place considering who he was and where he was. His voice was confident and to Clayton's ears sounded slightly higher in pitch and more colored by Texas influence than his own, differences that would probably go unnoticed in brief interactions.

"Take a seat, Cotton." Edmundo's tone was non-threatening, if not friendly. "You've met Deb before."

Cotton nodded to Deb. "Howdy, Ma'am."

"... and joining us today is Special Agent Clayton Rhodes."

Cotton's eyes, now more adjusted to the room's light, widened as he reacted to the almost mirror image of himself sitting at the table. He reached out his hand, "Pleased to meech'ya."

Clayton was slow to respond, balancing his conditioned dislike for criminals with the amicable greeting. Finally, following Edmundo's non-confrontational lead, Clayton reached across the table and shook Cotton's hand.

"There ya go. That didn't hurt none, now did it?"

"More than you know," Clayton mumbled under his breath.

"What's that?"

"I go with the flow!" Clayton spoke more clearly and with feigned enthusiasm. Clayton's initial impression was that the biggest difference between Cotton and him was in temperament. Cotton seemed eager to prove himself the dominant person in the room, not through intimidation but through the strength of personality, enforced by a boisterous charm.

"Right ... good. That's really good." Cotton's grin broadened into a full, white-toothed smile. "We're goin' to git along jus' fine." He took a seat at the table and rolled it back so he could stretch out his legs. "Well, has my amigo, Edmundo, explained why I'm here and why I'm oh so willing to help you folks out?" He turned his gaze from face to face, trying to get himself caught up.

Edmundo took over the conversation. "No. I thought it best if you were here when I went over the deal that you've made with the Bureau."

"Okay then, have at it, friend."

Edmundo's businesslike tone contrasted starkly with Cotton's casual Texas nonchalance. "Over the past several years, Mr. Parish has contracted with a variety of clients regarding designs and implementations of site and computer security. While the Bureau has not accused Mr. Parish of any crimes, many of his clients have been arrested or are under investigation for illegal activities, including those that are drug-related. Under United States Code Title 18, any property that can be traced to illegal drug trafficking is subject to forfeiture. This puts at risk of confiscation a large portion of Mr. Parish's assets. Wishing to avoid such an eventuality and as a show of his civic-mindedness, Mr. Parish has agreed, among other things, to cooperate in OPERATION SANDCASTLE. Not a trained agent himself, he has agreed to help prepare such an agent to take his place in a pending consulting engagement with Esteban Navarro."

Sure of the strength of his bargaining position, Cotton prodded, "And—come on now, Edmundo. Might as well lay out the whole story."

Edmundo's tone lapsed into a half-hearted recitation of words that Clayton assumed came from an official written agreement between the government and Cotton, "And, in exchange for his complete and unreserved cooperation, and the successful outcome of the operation, the Bureau will allow him to retain his assets and provide him with a new identity in a location of his choosing."

"Attaboy, now that there's the money line!" Cotton slapped the desktop for emphasis and leaned back, smiling like the proverbial cat that ate the canary. "Tha only thing that y'all left out is that the FBI'll ensure that my current, ah … old identity will be ended in a way that will ensure that no one from my past will come a-lookin' fer me so's I kin enjoy life on my new spread in Oregon."

Edmundo didn't try to hide his irritation. "It's not as easy as you would like to make it, Parish. If Clayton agrees to go forward, you and he will spend the next two weeks going over every part of his cover story and rehearsing every idiom, inflection, and gesture that will make him a convincing copy of you. And remember, your payout is contingent on the success of the mission."

"No worries. I'm ready and rarin' to go and if Clayton here is half the thoroughbred you make him out to be, this race is already run and won. And if I may add, he's the most handsome federal agent I've ever seen."

Ignoring the self-serving compliment, Clayton interjected, "Whoa, now wait a minute, both of you! I haven't agreed to take this on yet!" He pumped the brakes, wanting to slow down a process that he felt was moving too fast.

Edmundo's tone became more sympathetic as he responded to Clayton, "I know you feel that you're being pushed to jump onto a fast-moving train, but there is a window of opportunity here that will close quickly. Navarro might wait a couple of weeks for a man with Cotton's reputation, but he is not known for his patience. He wants that mansion of his, secure, and at some point in the very near future, he will feel that second best is good enough and move to hire the next expert on the list. If that happens, our advantage evaporates.

"I'll be the first to admit that this kind of pressure on you is unfair, but unfair comes with the job we do. All I ask is that you think it over. I expect you need to have a conversation with your wife, Margaret, right?"

"Maggie", Clayton, distracted by his mind's attempt to regain its balance, corrected absentmindedly.

"Ah yes, Maggie … and of course, you can't tell her much. I wouldn't want to trade places with you for all the world, but sympathy isn't in my job description. Today I'm just here to lay out the deal. The fact is, we need to have your answer by tomorrow morning. Take the rest of the day. Have lunch with Deb. Get your mind clear. Talk to whoever you have to." He slid a business card across the desk. "Here is my private cell number. Call me with your answer any time of day."

Clayton was aware of Edmundo's probing gaze. He knew E.Z. was looking for some sign as to what Clayton was thinking. Clayton's natural stoicism helped hide the conflicting thoughts and emotions that were raging in his mind. He had come to the meeting with a prepared and unshakable answer to any proposed undercover operation. He hadn't, couldn't have foreseen the wild card that was Cotton Parish.

It was Edmundo who finally broke the silence. "There's no point in continuing until we have Clayton's decision. So let's call it a day."

Deb caught up with Clayton as they left the briefing room. "Do you want to have lunch?"

Clayton managed a wry smile. "No thanks, Deb. I have to catch the first flight back to Austin."

Deb knew better than to press for any hint as to how Clayton was leaning. "Do you want a ride to the airport?"

"Nah, I can use the alone time. I need to think."

"You don't want to call her?"

"No, this is a conversation that Maggie and I have to have in person." He turned to go, then paused and over his shoulder said, "Thanks again, Deb."

****

Clayton welcomed the quiet, 45-minute ride to the airport and the first half-hour of the three-hour flight to Austin. No one was pushing him for an answer and he was initially comfortable with his knee-jerk inclination to decline the mission. The remainder of the flight grew increasingly uncomfortable, filled with mental replays and second-guessing. He was in uncharted territory now. Normally, he gathered information, analyzed it, and made his decisions with confidence. He then moved forward without self-doubt or a backward glance. But this time he could find no decision, no path forward that would silence the Greek chorus in his head.

He picked up his car in the short-term lot where he had left it that morning. The 30 minutes of the drive home ticked away and under the pressure of the looming, uncomfortable conversation with Maggie, his decision began to crystalize. For two years he had been playing it safe, committed to his promise to Maggie, and his duty to his family. But lately he had begun to feel that by not optimizing the use of his skills, he was betraying another duty. Other agents, some perhaps less qualified, were putting themselves in harm's way. They were leaving their families so he could be home with his. The Cotton Parish factor added to the mix made it impossible to rationalize that some other agent could do the job. As he pulled into his driveway, it was clear what he wanted—needed to do.

He opened the front door and tossed his keys into the wooden salad bowl on the breakfront in the foyer.

Maggie's voice called out. "Is that you, Clayton?"

"Yeah, I'm home." Clayton tried to sound cheery as he followed the sound of Maggie's voice to the kitchen, where she was busy cutting carrots.

As he came into the room, she put down the knife and threw her arms around his neck. "Welcome back to home port, sailor."

"It's good to be homm—" His reply was cut short as she pressed her lips to his and held them there. Unprepared for Maggie's impetuous show of affection, Clayton reached up to pull her arms away but in the time it took for him to raise his arms, the feel and scent of her warm and familiar body so filled his mind that for a blessed few moments, there was room for nothing else. His arms found her waist and pulled her body into his as he returned her kiss with a fire he usually reserved for the bedroom. Having at first taken the lead, Maggie was now content to be swept into this spontaneous moment of passion. After their lips parted, Clayton held her for a long time while knowing that delaying the unavoidable, painful conversation would only make it harder.

He reached up and gently pulled her arms from around his neck. "Where's Anthony?"

"He's at baseball practice." Maggie sensed the first hint that Clayton was about to pull a dark cloud over this shining moment.

"We have to talk, Maggie." His voice was soft, but determined. It was a voice good people reserve for bad news. He took her hand and led her to the couch in the family room. He sat her down and took a seat next to her, all the while holding her hand.

Looking into her eyes, he saw the growing concern. "They want me to take on an undercover op."

Her eyes widened, and she took her hand away. "Clayton, you promised—"

"I know, Maggie, I didn't go looking for this and I've tried to figure out a way that I can turn it down and still feel good about myself."

"But there are other people, agents, thousands of them. Why does it have to be you?" She was pleading her case. Offering the most logical argument.

"I can't tell you why, but I'm the only one who can do this. That's why they reached out to me."

Maggie sat on the edge of the couch, rocking back and forth, staring down at her lap.

"How long?"

"It will be about two months."

"Who's your handler?"

"Not sure yet ... probably Deb O'Donnell."

Maggie nodded. She had met Deb several times over the years and liked and trusted her. She looked up and met Clayton's eyes once again. "Swear to me Clayton Rhodes, that you are not doing this to serve some macho compulsion. Swear to me that you wouldn't do it if there were any other way. Swear it!"

"Yes, Maggie, I swear. There is no other way. They have no one else."

"All right then. When do you leave?" Her abrupt change of tone was one of the traits that made Maggie a good lawyer. She fought hard for her case, but took defeat with grace and practical acceptance.

"Tomorrow morning." Clayton stood up and reached out to her and she stood and leaned into his embrace. They came together not in passion, but in affection and mutual support. For Clayton, it was another reminder of how much Maggie gave to their marriage and why he loved her as much as he did.

They picked up Anthony after baseball and went out for pizza. They explained to him that Dad was going on a trip for the FBI and wouldn't be home for several weeks. Anthony was proud of what his father did and accepted that time away from the family was part of his job.

That night Clayton and Maggie made love, not the wild, self-gratifying, unfettered sex of their first year together but a profound, more tender coming together of two people who cared deeply for each other. After, they held each other in the dark until sleep finally took them.

The next morning Clayton was up before sunrise. He made coffee and sat in the darkness for a time, already missing his wife and son.

Fishing Edmundo's contact card from his wallet, he picked up his phone and dialed the number. He didn't expect an answer. It was early in Austin and two hours earlier in Los Angeles. After several rings, the recorded voice invited the caller to leave a message, "You've reached the voicemail of Special Agent in Charge Edmundo Zarzyckich. Leave a message."

"This is Clayton. I'm—"

"Clayton—" Edmundo's sleep-thickened tongue worked hard to assemble the proper syllables. "I'm here. Talk to me!"

"I'm in. I'm leaving for the airport now. Send me a text as to when and where you want me."

"Will do and thanks."

Clayton hung up. There was no need to say more. He sat with his coffee for a few more minutes.

Feeling himself sinking into the depression of a long goodbye, he went into Anthony's bedroom, stroked his head, and kissed his cheek. When he came out, Maggie was waiting. They walked quietly back to the kitchen.

"You're leaving now?" Her sad eyes made one last, wordless appeal.

"Yeah, you know how I am with long goodbyes. I called for a ride. He's waiting outside. I'd have to leave in an hour, anyway. It wouldn't be a good hour for either of us."

"You're probably right." She blinked the sadness from her eyes and flashed a smile of support. "Smooth sailing, Captain."

He pulled her to him for one last kiss, picked up his bag and, holding her hand, walked to the door. He pulled his hand away from hers and put it on the doorknob, then turned and spoke into her shadow-painted face, "Love you." Not waiting for a response, he opened the door and stepped out into the dim morning light.

As the door closed behind him, he heard Maggie's attempt at a cheerful reply, "Love you more."

January 7-21 - Learning the Role

Clayton spent the next two weeks immersing himself in both the broad sweeps and the minute details of becoming Cotton Parish. On the first day, the medical team meticulously examined his body and compared it to Cotton's. They noted every variance and assessed what exposure each difference presented. The records of Cotton's fingerprints in all law enforcement databases were replaced with Clayton's. A scar on Cotton's cheek, a mole on his neck, and a difference in earlobe structure were resolved with surgery. A bend in the little finger of Clayton's left hand, a result of a hand-to-hand confrontation several years prior, was identified. A plausible addition was made to his cover story to explain the difference on the off chance that the need would arise. And so it went. The physical similarity that was so striking at the onset was tuned to near perfection. Taking nothing for granted, the team worked hard to close any gaps, fully aware that operations had gone bad and agents had lost their lives because cover identities were merely almost perfect.

Clayton, backed up by Deb and the rest of Edmundo's team, spent hours interviewing Cotton using all of his training and undercover experience to assimilate the salient facts of

Cotton's background, and then he dove deeper into his thoughts and motivations. This was important to allow Clayton, hopefully, to react to a new situation the way Cotton would.

Clayton then assessed Cotton's cybersecurity skill set and compared it to his own. Cotton anticipated making certain recommendations as to security hardware and software. Edmundo equipped a laboratory with the requisite items and Clayton and Cotton worked to adapt Clayton's cyber skills to the purpose at hand.

Throughout their many interactions, Clayton was analyzing, absorbing, and assimilating Cotton's vocal inflections and physical mannerisms. No actor ever studied his character more thoroughly. Clayton observed that Cotton emphasized his Texan roots with an exaggerated and sometimes inconstant accent which would only help cover any imperfections in Clayton's impersonation.

Dislike and suspicion colored Clayton's initial reaction to Cotton. While the service he provided to criminals operated within a legally gray area, it clashed with Clayton's moral principles. Then, too, Cotton's bodacious personality grated on Clayton's more reserved disposition. He viewed Cotton's exaggerated Texas speech and mannerisms as calculated affectations.

Cotton was brimming with Texan witticisms and humor and as the days passed, Clayton's negative bias melted under Cotton's undeniable and unrelenting charm. He found himself growing to like the easy-going, roguish, ebullient Texan. At first, immune to Cotton's playful gambits, he found it increasingly difficult not to crack an occasional smile and by day five, he even laughed out loud at one of Cotton's Texas stories.

The team had worked through the initial interpersonal tensions. Feeling good about their progress, they were taking a break when Cotton launched into one of his tales.

"I've got a story for you FBI folks." Cotton always started his stories as though his audience had never heard him tell one before. "What d' ya'll say? Wanna hear it?"

The group responded almost in unison, chuckling in anticipation, "Yes Cotton, please. Let's hear it!"

"Okay. I'm told this happened down in El Paso." Cotton settled on the corner of a desk, facing the rest of the team. "This young FBI agent stops at a ranch and goes up to the ol' rancher who's workin' near the barn." Cotton looked around to assure himself that he had everyone's attention, then continued.

"So the agent says, 'Hey mister. I'm going to inspect your land for illegal drugs.'

"Well, the rancher, he doesn't take offense and replies, 'Why sho' son, help yerself. But don't be goin' into that there field,' as he points to the next field over.

"The FBI guy, all full of piss and vinegar, reaches into his back pocket, pulls out his badge, and says 'Let's get this straight, old man. This badge says I can go wherever I want—got it?'

"The ol' man shrugs his shoulders and apologizes to the agent, 'I meant no disrespect. Y'all go ahead and do what ya have to do.' With that, the ol' rancher goes back to his chores.

"A few minutes later, the rancher hears screams coming from the field. He looks up and there's the FBI guy, a runnin' for his life with this big ol' long horn hot on his heels. It's looking bad for the agent. Too far away to be of any meaningful help, the ol' man cups his hands around his mouth and yells, 'Your badge! Show him your badge!'"

Laughter filled the room, followed by applause with Clayton joining in.

Cotton waited for his audience to quiet down and then added, "Now that was told to me as a true story, but I don't entirely believe it." The team looked at him expectantly, knowing there was more to come. "No siree, I don't believe it was an FBI agent at'all … I'm thinkin' it must have been a DEA guy." Again the team broke into laughter.

Swept up by the camaraderie, Clayton asked a question that had occurred to everyone on the team, "I've got to ask, how did you—hmm—we come by the name Cotton?"

"Well now, Clayton, everyone, sooner or later gits around to askin' an' it's an interestin' story fur sure." Cotton was clearly pleased to hold on to the spotlight. "Of course, this story has to start with my folks. When they first started out, they didn't have much. They weren't educated past high school and my daddy not even that. They had 120 acres of fallow farmland that was handed down from my grandpa and they had each other. Daddy and mom built their lives on the dual pillars of hard work and an abidin' faith in the Lord. They believed in signs, miracles, omens, and all sorts of superstitions. After they got hitched, they took stock of their situation, prayed on it, and came to believe that whatever they tried to grow on their land would yield a bounty if they named a child for the crop. My daddy planted his seed and my mom started pushing out babies. They started naming at the beginning of the alphabet and kept goin'. The first year they planted alfalfa and that became the name of their firstborn. The crop that year was disappointin' so the second year they tried for a crop of barley. That was their second child, my next older brother. The third year was my turn to be born. They planted cotton, and that's how I got my name."

The group was completely enthralled. "Did cotton bring them success?" Clayton asked.

"Nah, after Cotton there was Dill and that's when my mom said she'd had enough. There was a lot of tension and stress in the family back then, but my dad asked my mom to try jus' one more time. Well, she did, and that's how I ended up with a sister called Mary Jane."

And again the team roared with laughter.

As the laughter died down, Cotton anticipated the next question. "Things got a whole lot better after that. The money issues disappeared and the family jes' seemed to mellow out. Now that there's a true story."

****

Day twelve brought a final exam of sorts. Edmundo, Deb, and the other six principal members of the team convened in the large briefing room. A few minutes after the last straggler took his seat, the door opened and Cotton strode into the room, surrounded by his typical aura of self-confident charm. He took a position in front of the blank briefing screen.

"Good mornin'." He paused in his typical fashion, to be sure he was the center of attention. "I'm here to tell ya' it's been downright enjoyable workin' with y'all. Today it's my honest pleasure to introduce the star of our little production. Mr. Cotton Parish."

On cue, the door swung open and a second Cotton Parish moved in the same confident manner to stand next to the speaker. When he spoke, his voice was ever so slightly different, but not enough to identify one or the other as being the true Cotton. "Howdy. It was kinda y'all to show up for our little dog and pony show. I have to admit I was sweatin' like a hooker in a church leadin' up to this meetin'. After all, I got a bunch ridin' on the outcome. But Cotton here calmed me down and so here we are."

The other Cotton chimed in, "Yeah, I pointed out to him that fer one of us, today is super easy. He jus' has to act like hisself. For the other one, the one with undercover experience, well, it ain't his first rodeo."

The Cottons alternated again. "We invite y'all for the next hour, to ask us anythin' ya like, on any topic an' take notes."

Once again, the other Cotton took over. "At the end of an hour, we'd like y'all to vote on who you think is the real Cotton Parish."

The team appreciated the extreme importance of the exercise but also enthusiastically embraced the game aspect of the test. Over the next hour, the eight team members bombarded the two Cottons with a host of questions ranging from Cotton's background to the technical specifics of site and cybersecurity. One of the most enjoyable challenges was posed by Deb who asked that each of the Cottons tell a story of their own choosing in true Cotton fashion. Through it all, the team took notes and compared insights and observations. At the end of the hour, when it was time to vote, no one on the team could identify, with any certainty, which of the performers was Clayton and which was the true Cotton Parish.

There were high fives all around as it was clear that the hard work had paid dividends. When the loud congratulations subsided, all eyes turned to Edmundo for the final verdict.

"We've done what we can do and the results are impressive. My appreciation to the entire team for a job well done and especially to our two stars." With that, he turned to the two Cottons. "Is there anything you'd like to say?"

Dropping his accent, Clayton responded, "I'll add my thanks to Deb and the team for their hard work. I feel good about it! This is going to work!" Taking on his Cotton persona once again, he added, "Okay, y'all, let's git 'r done!"

January 21 - Esteban Diego Navarro

The estate was one of the largest in Malibu. The seven acres that overlooked the Pacific Ocean guaranteed privacy, and the multiple, ornately architected buildings provided an opulent lifestyle for Esteban Diego Navarro, his wife Carmen, and their two children. A man of many interests and the resources to pursue them, Esteban enjoyed being surrounded by growing things. The large greenhouse and aviary, the conservatory, was his private domain into which even his family was forbidden to trespass without invitation. The peace he found there was perhaps an enhanced recollection of the few joyful memories of his turbulent youth in the green jungles that surround Cali, Colombia, more than 25 years ago.

Of the four men in the conservatory now, two stood as silent sentinels to the dialog between Esteban and Mateo Torres. A man in his mid-30s, Mateo's well-conditioned body squirmed uncomfortably in a straight-backed, intricately wrought aluminum chair next to a red granite table. Esteban stood nearby with his back to Mateo, carefully deadheading a rare, antique rose bush.

Esteban's six-foot stature hinted at something other than purely Colombian ancestry. He was a product of a mixed lineage, the various parts of which no one ever had the cause to record or interest to remember. His father's presence survived his conception only as long as it took for him to zip up his trousers. When he was seven, his mother left him with her landlord as collateral, promising to come back with the past-due rent. When she didn't return, the landlord sold him to a Cali gang leader, who taught him the finer points of petty theft. Quick and ambitious, he eagerly learned all that the criminal world of Colombia could teach him. He was an exceptional student, unafraid of hard work and not in the least bit squeamish about the use of even extreme violence if it served his purpose. Never doubting his survival, success was his constantly evolving motivation. He celebrated his twentieth birthday as an enforcer for the Cali drug cartel and at 30 had moved to California, where he rose quickly in the expanding California organization. Now, at 35, he was its boss. His power and prestige increased as he developed a reputation for good management and quick and effective problem resolution. Darkly handsome, he could be charming or intimidating as the occasion warranted.

sssnik

As he spoke, the spring-loaded pruner punctuated his comments and the cut red blossoms fell to the floor.

sssnik

"You know, Mateo, humans' attraction for roses is interesting. The plants provide no food, and they need constant care. We must be ever vigilant against the thorns that they so traitorously turn on those who take care of them. Their only contributions to our existence are the beauty of their flowers and their sweet aroma. And for that, we nurture them. That is our deal, our contract with them. When they cease to deliver on their promise or when we no longer value their contributions, they become an annoyance and—"

sssnik

"Please, Esteban, on my life, I didn't do it. I would never steal from you. We are like brothers, you and I. We've been together for many years."

"All true, Mateo. All true. Except for the part about stealing from me." Esteban paused and looked over his shoulder at his now sweating subordinate. "Mateo, you know me. And knowing me, did you think I wouldn't find out? Knowing me, did you think I don't have eyes and ears everywhere, on everyone, even my closest friends?" Esteban turned his attention back to his roses.

sssnik

"I swear on my life, Esteban, whoever says I stole from you is lying. Bring him here. I will call the son of a bitch a liar to his face."

Esteban turned, took a small recorder from his pocket, and placed it on the table. "Turn it on, Mateo."

Mateo stared at the device for a long moment. His hand trembled as he reached out and pushed the play button. Instantly the room was filled with several seconds of screaming that started in an alto register and then ascended to a high falsetto that was barely recognizable as human. There were several gasping breaths and then through burbling sobs, the voice spoke, "It was … Mateo … Mateo … It was his idea! We had a deal!"

There were more screams, then the voice came again through rapid rasping breaths, "I've told you. Please, my family, don't—" There was a loud bang, and the recording went silent.

"Your amigo, Rickie, cannot join us, Mateo, but you know that even in a court of law, a deathbed confession carries a lot of weight."

"I don't know why he would speak such lies against me, but I am innocent. I swear on my children's lives."

"Hmm … and how many children do you have, Mateo?"

"Th … three, Esteban, three girls but they—"

"Would you like to live, Mateo?"

"Ye … yes, Esteban, oh yes. Please—"

"Would you like your children to live?"

"Oh God, please, Esteban, not my chil—"

"What's more important, Mateo, a man's fingers or the lives of his children?"

"Wh—"

"You like deals, Mateo? I offer you a deal. Give me a finger for each of your children's lives."

Esteban gently placed the pruning shears on the table in front of Mateo.

"I don't—Please, Esteban, I am innocent."

"None of us are innocent, Mateo. You are just less innocent than you needed to be. Three fingers, Mateo, and I'll even throw in your life as a bonus. Do this and we can be friends again. You can pick which hand."

Mateo desperately looked up at Esteban, trying to read how serious he was. Esteban's eyes were unwavering and showed no sign of pity.

"Make up your mind, Mateo. I don't have all day and you, I'm afraid, have much less time than that."

Mateo looked at the red blossoms scattered on the floor. He picked up the shears in his right hand and studied his left hand. Opening the blades around his left little finger, he looked up into Esteban's eyes in one last wordless appeal. Finding no hope of commutation, no sign of mercy, he closed his eyes. His temple throbbing in apprehension, he squeezed the blades shut.

sssnik

He wasn't aware that he had screamed, but he could hear its echoes as he dropped the shears to the table and clutched his left hand to his chest.

"Very good, Mateo. You have saved the life of one of your children. Two more to go."

Mateo's hands were trembling violently as he, once again, picked up the shears and positioned the blades around his left ring finger. With tears streaming down his cheeks, he applied the effort it took to squeeze the blades shut.

sssnik

A red haze crept in from the borders of his mind and he struggled to stay conscious. He again heard the echoes of his own scream fade away.

"Stay with us, Mateo. You're doing so well. Another child saved. One more to go and all will be forgiven."

Mateo was fighting his growing nausea. His vision blurred, as he felt along the tabletop for the shears.

"Let me help." Esteban picked up the shears and placed them in Mateo's hand.

"I don't think I can do it, Esteban. Por favor. You do it."

"No, Mateo, you must do it. You're almost there, Mateo. Think of your last child. What's her name, Mateo?"

"V ... Vi ... Victoria. Her name is Victoria."

"Si, Victoria. Think about dear, sweet, Victoria."

Mateo fixed the blades around the middle finger of his blood-soaked hand, once again closed his eyes, and squeezed with the last reserve of strength his athletic body could muster.

sssnik

And then the red haze of his pain thickened, bringing the gift of unconsciousness. His head and chest slumped across the tabletop.

Esteban retrieved his shears, wiped them on Mateo's shirt, and turned to the two silent observers, "Get him some medical attention and clean up this mess."

"You will let him live, patrón?" Marco, too, was a product of the slums of Cali, Colombia. Though not as tall as Esteban, his fit, bulky body, and threatening demeanor gave the impression of a coiled razor-sharp spring capable of unleashing horrific damage at any moment. His dark face was made darker by a constant scowl that erased the space between his eyebrows. It carried the scars of poor hygiene and the battles of his time in the slums. Unlike Esteban, Marco was never clever or skilled enough to aspire to anything more than survival. He'd joined Esteban's crew at the urging of the cartel bosses a year ago. His current position, as Esteban's second, almost certainly exceeded his ability, but that appointment gave Esteban two things. Esteban could count on Marco's gratitude and hence his loyalty and then, Marco's ambition, or lack thereof, would never tempt him to take Esteban's place as Esteban had done with his predecessor, Jenaro.

Esteban went back to pruning the rose bush. No longer deadheading, he was cutting younger, perfect blossoms along with a long portion of their stems. He carefully collected each one and placed it on a cart that he wheeled from bush to bush as he worked.

sssnik

"Yes, Marco, we made a deal and I will keep my word. Besides, he may have been telling the truth."

"But Rickie's confession—"

"A man like Rickie, any man, would say anything to make such pain stop. But then again, I couldn't take the chance."

"Then why not kill him? It showed great mercy to let him live."

sssnik

"He and his maimed hand are now living, walking warnings to all who would think of betraying me. It isn't mercy, Marco. It's advertising."

"Would you have killed his family?"

"Si. A man's family is an extension of himself. When he is loyal, when he does well, they enjoy the benefits of his good work. When he becomes something other, why should they not share in his punishment? Si, I would have destroyed his family."

sssnik

Another blossom made its way to the cart. "I have done so before." Esteban reached for another blossom and paused in mid-motion. "Where is Bernardo?"

"He is at the airport picking up the security consultant."

sssnik

"Ah yes, Mr. Cotton Parish. Marco, when he arrives, show him to his room. Give him a few minutes to get settled and then bring him to me."

"Si, patrón."

sssnik

"Gather up these long-stemmed blossoms, put them in a vase, and deliver them to Carmen's suite with my love."

"Si, jefe. I will attend to it."

January 21 - Carmen Medina Navarro

"Lucia, stay close to your brother. Este, stay where the water is below your knees."

It was a warm, almost windless January day, and at three o'clock in the afternoon, the sun was well past its highest point and was on its way toward its final plunge into the ocean. In their protected inlet, the surface of the Pacific was disturbed only by enough ripples to create fun-house reflections. The two young treasure hunters waded near the shore, peering through the few inches of clear cool water, eagerly scooping up sand-polished stones and abalone shell treasures, competing with each other for their mother's approval with each find.

Four-year-old Lucia's dark hair, done in pigtails, dipped into the water each time she bent down for a closer look and then dripped as she stood straight. "Mama, look what I found!"

"That's just a stone, Lucia. I found a really pretty shell. Mama, look at my shell!" Esteban Junior, "Este", five years old, showed worrisome signs of his father's insensitivity and commanding tone.

"That's a beautiful stone, Lucia. And Este, what a pretty shell."

"Who wins, Mama? Who wins?" both cried in imperfect unison.

"Well, I would have to say Lucia, you win for best stone—" Carmen noticed the quick flash of anger darken Este's face. "—and Este, you win for prettiest shell." All smiles and laughter again, the children went back to their hunt.

The diplomacy came easily and joyfully to Carmen, as did the general caring for her children. Aside from the deep love she had for them, parenting allowed her to express herself and exercise a measure of control, opportunities that were missing in every other aspect of her life. Focusing on her children allowed the radiance that had been the hallmark of her prior life to shine through the darkness that came with being Esteban Navarro's wife.

They had met seven years ago at one of her father's lavish parties. The Medina family was old-money, with great political and social influence in Mexico City and beyond. When she first met Esteban, she was 22 and her youthful exuberance was gracefully complemented by an air of casual sophistication. Although she carried these attributes with natural ease, they were the products of a cultured upbringing and careful education. Her academic excellence during her school years awarded her a Master's degree in economics from one of the best universities in Mexico and kindled in her a desire to pursue a career in public service. Her parents, however, left her in no doubt that she owed a duty to the family to make a good marriage the highest priority. She may dabble or even excel at other endeavors, but the home, family, and support of her husband should always be the cornerstones of her life.

Carmen Medina was exceptionally attractive. Her green eyes stood in striking contrast to her dark hair and complexion. Men and women, but especially men, would seek to engage her in conversation, attracted to her wit, and the momentary delight that her uncommon gaze would provide.

Taken by her beauty and seeking prestige and connections, Esteban staged a successful campaign to convince her parents that he would be an excellent husband for their daughter. He had been careful to present himself as a successful businessman with a brilliant future, and he spent a great deal to ensure that the story would withstand any reasonable background check. He never hid that his early years had been challenging, but he skillfully spun the facts into a story of personal courage and ultimate success. After a year of courtship, their marriage was performed by the archbishop at the Catedral Metropolitana de la Asunción de la Bienaventurada Virgen María a los cielos in Mexico City. The ceremony attracted the elite of the city and high society from across Mexico, either attended or sent best wishes.

Carmen's parents were completely taken by Esteban's charm and his story of adversity, struggle, and eventual success, but Carmen was less sure. Although she found him attractive, it was her parents' urging, more than her own love and conviction, that brought her to the altar.

When she wasn't busy with the children, the darkness crept out of the corners of her mind, bringing bleak introspection; *I didn't really know him*, and then, *I really didn't know myself. Dios mio, I was only 22 years old.* And now, at 28, she felt so much older.

Once married, it hadn't taken long for her to discover who Esteban Navarro really was. Upon the revelation, she was appalled, but she carried it in her aching heart as a painful secret. She put on a brave front for family and friends, but when Esteban's business took them to California, it became less burdensome to let her friendships fade away and only rarely communicate with her family. Esteban had used her and her family's connections with furious abandon during the first two years of their marriage, but after she had delivered two children and he had milked the Medina name dry of useful connections, his interest in her had waned. He was cordial enough as long as she performed to his expectations, but unforgiving of transgressions to the point of violence. He had not physically abused the children, but for Carmen, bruises became more common. By way of explanation, Esteban would often joke about his wife's clumsiness, a fabrication that Carmen felt powerless to refute. Her duties were simple enough. Take care of the children and allow Esteban to parade her in front of his friends and acquaintances, another symbol of his success.

The sun was low in the sky now and a cool onshore breeze encouraged an end to the day's beach adventure. "Este, Lucia, come dry off. It's time to go inside and get cleaned up."

Bundled in towels, they climbed the several flights of stairs that led from the beach to the lawn of the estate. Marco was waiting for them when they reached the top.

"Esteban asks that you join him for dinner. He is having a guest, and he'd like you there. He wants you to introduce the children before sending them to bed."

"Gracias, Marco. I understand."

"He asks that you wear something nice."

"Si, Marco, gracias."

The children raced each other across the lawn toward the main house. Carmen watched them run, envious of their enthusiasm and innocence.

She turned back to take one more look at the ocean. The beach was taking on a more textured look as the small sand dunes grew their evening shadows. The longest of these shadows came from the two towers on opposite sides of the beach that any casual observer would take for lifeguard stations except for their position far back from the water's edge. In actuality, each was a three-sided, armored guard shack containing an ever-watchful, armed sentry, testaments to what Carmen hoped was Esteban's paranoia.

The swollen red sun was just touching the horizon. It silhouetted a large sailing yacht beating south down the coast. The boat's slow, graceful progress to some unknown, distant place triggered another wave of envy. Carmen let out a long breath, turned her back to the sea, and followed Marco and her children across the lawn and into the house.

January 21 - Dinner

A little before seven o'clock, Clayton made his way down the main stairway into the grand, marbled foyer and then followed the sounds of voices. He approached the entrance to the living room as the chimes from the nearby pendulum clock were sounding the last of their seven o'clock announcement. Just before he entered the room, he heard Marco's voice.

"... seems to check out, but I recommend ..."

Clayton slowed his pace, hoping to hear more of the conversation, but at that moment a servant appeared carrying a vase of flowers which she set down on one of the small foyer tables. Not wishing to be caught eavesdropping, Clayton continued into the living room where Esteban, Marco, and Carmen were sitting. Lucia and Este were playing on the intricately woven Persian rug. Este was building a tower with wooden blocks, and Lucia was drawing in a sketchbook with crayons.

"Good evenin' y'all." The two weeks of intense preparation for the role had been built upon the years he had spent in Texas, and now the Texan idioms and accent slipped easily off his tongue. Uncomfortable at first, he now enjoyed playing the role of the brash Cotton Parish. In fact, he had to guard against overplaying the character. "I sho' hope I didn't keep y'all waitin'. This here house is 'bout as big as my folks' farm and it was a bit of a hike to get here from my room."

"Ah, señor Parish," Esteban rose, stepped forward, and took Clayton's hand in greeting. "Welcome to *El Mirador,* our home. You've already met my second, Marco, and may I present Carmen, my wife. Carmen, dear, señor Parish will be helping us with our computers and the campus security."

Clayton turned to Carmen, and with a nod of his head flashed his best Cotton Parish smile. "Pleased to make your acquaintance, ma'am. Thank you fer havin' me in yer home. I'll try not to be a botha."

Carmen extended her hand. "Welcome to our home, Mister Parish." Clayton detected the faint scent of jasmine as he gently took her hand in his.

Clayton held her green eyes in his gaze. "My daddy's Mister Parish. Call me Cotton, ma'am."

Carmen's lips showed the slightest hint of a smile. "And you, Cotton, please call me Carmen."

Clayton let go of her hand and turned his attention to the children who had stopped playing when this stranger had come into the room and started speaking with such a strange accent. "And who are these two handsome children?"

Este stood, and in a determined voice, corrected Clayton's choice of words. "I'm Este and I'm handsome. This is my sister, Lucia. She's not handsome. She's a girl, so she's pretty."

"Mind your manners, Este," Carmen gently admonished.

"Oh, he's fine, ma'am, ah—Carmen." Clayton beamed a sincere smile at Este. "Yer absolutely right, Este. Young men like y'all 're handsome …" He turned his smile to Lucia. "… and young ladies like Lucia are purtee indeed." Both children giggled. "Y'all c'n call me Cotton."

"Like in my shirt?" Este was eager to engage with a receptive male adult.

"Yup, jus' like in yer shirt."

Satisfied that this was going to be a friendly encounter, Este held out his newly acquired shell. "We were at the beach today and look what I found."

Clayton knelt down, took the offered shell, and made a show of close scrutiny. "That ther's a terrific shell, Este. A real treasure." He handed the shell back to Este and turned to the little girl. "And what did you find, Lucia?" Blushing from the attention, she hid her eyes with one hand and held out the stone that she had found with the other.

"That's just a dull old stone," Este commented.

"Shush, Este. That's not kind," Carmen chided.

Clayton reached out his hand. "Would you let me take a gander at that there stone, Lucia?"

Peaking through her fingers, she shyly dropped the stone into his open hand. Clayton examined the stone and then reached down and picked up one of the wax coloring sticks. "Can I borrow yer cray'n, Lucia?"

Lucia nodded. Clayton applied the wax to the stone and then, taking a handkerchief from his pocket, rubbed the wax into the stone's surface for several seconds. When he was done, the stone had taken on a much different appearance. Ablaze with colored layers and striations, it had shed its shabby former appearance and now looked like a fine piece of jewelry. Lucia's eyes widened at the transformation. Clayton handed her the stone.

Lucia ran to her mother. "Look, Mommy. Look what Cotton did."

"It's beautiful, sweetheart. What do you say to Mister Parish?"

From the safe harbor of her mother's arm, Lucia shed her former shyness and voiced her gratitude with a child's excitement and a matching smile. "Thank you, Cotton. Thank you. It's beautiful. I'll keep it forever."

A wave of recollection and homesickness washed over Clayton, which he quickly shook off. He knew that everything he did was being reviewed and analyzed by Esteban and Marco, but now he was aware of Carmen studying him as well.

"Well, I tell ya what. You and yer brother get some more stones from the beach and I'll show ya' how to polish them up—that is, if that's okay with yer mom." Still on his knees, Clayton looked up at Carmen with the question hanging in the air.

"Oh, can we Mommy? Can we?" Lucia and Este pleaded in a chorus of enthusiasm.

For the first time, Carmen's smile was unreserved. The children's joy struck a sympathetic, motherly chord and her green eyes flashed as she fixed her gaze on Clayton. "Yes, that would be wonderful. Thank you, Cotton."

During Clayton's exchange with the children, Esteban sat silently observing. He could never relate to his children the way Clayton had just done. On one hand, he defended the distance he kept from his children because he believed such close attention to be coddling. Such exaggerated kindness, especially from a man, was likely to make the children soft and vulnerable to the world's cruelty. On the other hand, Esteban was envious. However he chose to characterize it, he knew he was incapable of such a display of affection.

"It's not likely Cotton will have much time for games, children. He has much work to do and little time to do it. Isn't that right, Cotton?"

"Yer the boss, Esteban. I won't be lettin' anythin' slow me down."

At that moment, a servant entered the room. "Dinner is ready, Señor Navarro."

"Gracias, Nina." Esteban acknowledged the announcement and then turned to the children. "Say goodnight, children. It's time for bed."

Lucia and Este dutifully went over to their father. In what seemed to be a meticulously practiced ceremony, Este reached out, shook his father's hand. "Goodnight, Father."

"Goodnight, Este."

Esteban bent over in his chair and Lucia gave him a hug. "Goodnight, Father."

"Goodnight, Lucia."

There might have been affection in Esteban's words, but Clayton found it hard to tell.

The children huddled around Carmen with giggles, hugs, and kisses. In a spontaneously forged alliance, the two young conspirators pivoted their simple goodnight moment into a game calculated to delay their departure. Arms and legs and small bodies tumbled and tangled on Carmen's lap and around her neck. "Goodnight, Mommy. Goodnight, Mommy. Goodnight. Goodnight."

Carmen smiled and good-naturedly disentangled herself, using tickles as her primary defense. The children tumbled to the rug in spasms of giggles.

"Carmen!" The smile evaporated from Carmen's face as Esteban's sharp, disapproving tone snapped across the room and brought an abrupt end to the levity.

Focusing on the children and using her most reassuring voice, she sought to dispel the echoes of Esteban's harshness. "That was so much fun but enough now, darlings. Go upstairs with Nina and get ready for bed. I'll be up in a little while to tuck you in."

The children reluctantly let Nina take them by the hands and lead them to the door. They were almost out of the room when Lucia broke away and ran back to Clayton. He bent down to meet her. Flushed with adrenaline from her recent wrestling with her brother, she threw her arms around his neck and whispered in his ear, "Thank you, Cotton."

She swiftly let go, raced back, and took Nina's hand once more. Then all three went out into the grand lobby and up the stairs. Again, Clayton was aware that everyone in the room had their own reasons for evaluating what had just happened. He knew also that all of them were forming their first impressions of him and his life might well depend on what those were.

****

Esteban, with Carmen on his arm, led the group through the foyer into a more casual section of the main floor. As they entered a great room, the marble of the foyer floor gave way to offset, polished brick tiles. The room extended onto an enclosed, candle-lit portico area containing a round table currently set for four people, although it could easily have accommodated more. The dining area was protected from the weather by arched walls of glass which provided an unobstructed view of the lawn and the ocean beyond. Esteban paused for a moment to let his guest take in the impressive panorama. At this time of day, there was nothing left of the sun but the faintest red glow on the western horizon. The moon had not yet risen and the lights from a half dozen large ships and as many smaller boats dotted the dark surface of the sea. Some paraded in stately purpose, on missions of commerce or recreation to unknown final destinations. The paths of others were random. Flashing in the dark like fireflies, following no set course, the high-speed toys of the affluent provided their passengers the thrills of hurtling through the dark, smashing through the inky swells of the Pacific.

Esteban held a chair for Carmen as she sat and then, standing by the chair at her side, gestured for Marco and Clayton to take their seats.

The meal reinforced the message that Esteban was a man of wealth and Epicurean tastes. An appetizer of raw oysters served with a Sèvre-et-Maine Muscadet was followed by a main course of a tastefully prepared paella accompanied by a rich Reserva Riojas.

It was clear to Clayton that he would have to comment more than once on how good the food was. "This here is the finest meal I've had since I dined with the queen of England, maybe even better."

"Oh, you've had dinner with the Queen?" Esteban's query had more amusement than challenge in it. He had heard about Cotton's Texas sense of humor and his frequent loose relationship with the facts.

"No siree. Truth be told, I never met 'er highness. But I'm willin' to bet that if I ever have dinner with 'er it will come second fiddle to this here meal. Y'all got to tell me, is this takeout, or did you make it yerself?"

Marco and Carmen visibly tensed. Irritation darkened Esteban's face, but a toothy grin from Clayton put the conversation back on track. "I sho' didn't mean any offense, Esteban. Sometimes my sense o' humor gallops away with me. 'sides, ya' can't be fully Texan without bein' at least a little bit annoyin' at times and my daddy always said I was the most annoyin' Texan he'd ever met."

The cloud lifted from Esteban's face, and he laughed. "I admit I haven't met many people so … Texan. But everything is good. To answer your question, Cotton, I have a full-time kitchen staff who spoil us daily with their culinary expertise. If you have any favorites, please let me know, and I'm sure they will be up to the task."

"Heck, Esteban, I did most of my growin' on chicken 'n grits, then a whole bunch a' years on mess hall chow 'n MRE's.

With that background and the meal tonight as an example, I'm sho' I'll love whatever they rustle up." Clayton knew that his portrayal of Cotton Parish was exaggerated and less refined and rounded than the original Cotton Parish. He was hoping that Esteban would underestimate the Texan and dismiss him as an uncultured simpleton with a narrow, useful set of skills.

The muted chimes from the foyer announced that it was eight o'clock. Carmen dabbed her napkin at her lips one last time, folded it, and placed it neatly beside her plate. Clayton was struck by how she accomplished such a common task with such uncommon grace.

"I must leave you now, gentlemen. I promised the children that I would tuck them in." She turned her gaze to Clayton and smiled. "It was a pleasure to meet you, Cotton. I'm sure we'll see more of each other during your stay with us. Goodnight, Marco. Goodnight, Esteban." She stood and the three men followed suit. Clayton noticed the lack of affection that passed between Esteban and his wife. The men watched as Carmen glided across the great room and out to the foyer.

The three men took their seats again. As she disappeared Clayton remarked, "Your wife's an amazin' woman. Yer a lucky man."

Esteban reached down and rang a small bell to summon the servant. "Yes, Cotton, she is that and indeed, I am lucky. I have been blessed with many beautiful possessions.

"Would you gentlemen care for dessert, or would you rather adjourn to the lanai for brandy and cigars?"

Clayton fumed inwardly at Esteban's cold callousness but quipped, "Well, truth be told, one more bite and I'm liable to bust my britches. I'm not much for tobacco, but I wouldn't turn down a brandy. How about you, Marco?"

"I will join you on the lanai." Marco's flat response to Clayton's friendly overture was consistent with his demeanor thus far. He had been noticeably quiet but Clayton was sure that the reason for his presence was not to engage but to observe and that he would be the topic of discussion between Marco and Esteban later.

At that moment, a servant appeared from the shadows beyond the candlelight. "You rang, señor?"

"We will have brandy and cigars on the lanai."

"Si, señor. En seguida, señor."

Esteban opened a door in the glass wall and led the way out to the lanai. Gas heaters had been set ablaze in anticipation of their presence and provided a comfortable buffer against the chilly night air. As spectacular as the view was from inside, the effect of the ocean's proximity was even more pronounced with the addition of the salt-laden ocean breeze, the distant dull throb of the large passing ships, and the high-pitched drone of the speedboats. Clayton strode to the granite rail that surrounded the lanai and stared out at the sea, vaguely aware of the servant's arrival.

"Dark and dangerous, is it not?" Esteban held out a large snifter containing a generous pour of caramel-colored liquid.

Clayton took the glass and nodded his thanks. "But capable of great beauty and healin'."

"It takes a strong hand to win in any contest with her."

Clayton took a sip of the fine brandy. "But with a softer hand, she can also bring peace an' joy to someone who understands an' respects her."

It became uncomfortably clear that the topic of conversation had shifted and Clayton was quick to change the subject. "This is sho' fine brandy. You have a magnificent home, Esteban. I'm thankful fer the trust you have put in me to help you pertect it."

"As you must know, Cotton, there is more to protect than just my home and family. My entire business will reside on the computers you install. There can be no mistakes."

"Well, Esteban, I pride myself on not makin' mistakes. I'm eager to get to work."

"We have breakfast at seven o'clock. Please join us. Then you and Marco can explore the grounds. I look forward to seeing your site security strategy. After that, you can work on the computer installation."

"That there sounds like a plan." Clayton warmed the brandy in his hands and took another sip. He judged by the pause in the conversation that it was a good time to bring an end to his participation in the evening's event. "If'n y'all don't mind, I think I'll turn in. Busy day tomorrow."

Playing the perfect host, Esteban smiled. "Of course, Cotton, but before you go, I have a couple of welcome gifts for you. Marco …"

On cue, Marco stepped forward and offered Clayton two small felt-covered jewelry boxes. Esteban continued, "Take these with you to your room. Open the yellow one first, then the red one. They are tokens of our new relationship and will hopefully help you envision its possibilities."

"Well, I'll be … that's right kind of you, Esteban. Thank ya kindly."

Although Esteban was still smiling, it was hard to miss the ominous subtext in his parting words. "Don't thank me, Cotton. Just be sure, very sure, you do your job well."

Clayton took one last sip of his brandy and set his glass down on the top of the railing, "Goodnight, Esteban."

"Buenas noches, Cotton."

"Goodnight, Marco."

"Buenas noches, señor Parish." For the first time, Clayton saw what could pass for a smile flick across Marco's face.

January 21 - Good Night

As Clayton left the lanai, he was aware of Marco carefully closing the glass door after his departure. He crossed through the great room and then out to the vestibule and up the main stairway. The hallway at the top of the stairs branched off in two directions. It was wide enough to accommodate three people walking abreast and still have room for the numerous bronzes and sculpted marble works of art that stood on pedestals on either side. It overlooked and surrounded the vestibule through a connected series of pink marble arches. Clayton turned left at the top of the stairs and started the impressively lengthy walk toward his room, which was the last one on that side. As he passed the second doorway, the door opened, and he saw Carmen backing out, appearing to take great care to make no noise. She quietly closed the door and turned to find Clayton only a few feet away.

She let out a startled gasp and then spoke in a breathy voice barely above a whisper, "Oh … oh, it's you, Cotton." Signaling for him to follow, she took a few steps away from the door. In a more normal but still soft voice, she explained, "When the children get excited it's difficult for them to get to sleep. I think now, finally, they are down for the night. It was an exciting day for them. We haven't had many visitors who spend the night and none who have made the impression that you did. They couldn't stop talking about you. Lucia insisted on putting her beautiful stone under her pillow."

"Gosh, Carmen, I sure didn't mean to cause any trouble. I only wanted—"

"Don't apologize, Cotton. Their lives are not so full of joy that they couldn't use a bit more."

Clayton smiled broadly. "I'm sure glad I could give'm that. They seem like wonderful kids." He paused and then continued in a more serious tone, "—and you, Carmen, is there enough joy in your life?"

It was immediately clear that his question had crossed a line. Carmen's eyes flashed, even in the dim light of the hallway. "My life is my own, Mr. Parish. You needn't concern yourself with my joys or my pains. Please limit your concerns to the job you were hired to do." Her stare was so intense that it almost physically forced Clayton to step aside. "Have a good night."

He watched as she walked back to the room next to the children's on the side away from Clayton's room. She pushed open the door and disappeared inside.

Damn, you sure put your foot in it. Clayton walked the few steps to his room, smarting from her sharp rebuke. *You have to admit you deserved it. Not your most diplomatic move—too much Cotton, not enough Clayton. Slow down, cowboy.*

Clayton entered his room and placed the two boxes on the dressing table. The room was larger than anyone would expect a guest room to be. It was, in reality, a guest suite. The recessed lighting highlighted a sitting area with two comfortable-looking chairs on either side of a wide coffee table. The arrangement sat on a brilliantly colored oriental rug delineating the area from the rest of the parquet floor. On the wall nearest the chairs, electric sconces were mounted in mirrored panels on either side of a blue marble fireplace. A fire was cheerily burning, contributing its occasional random pops and crackles to the peaceful ambiance that the room so successfully exuded. The longest side of the room consisted of a series of French doors that opened onto a broad balcony overlooking the lawn and the ocean.

Clayton had dropped off his bag in the room upon his arrival from the airport. He now found that the clothing from his bag had been neatly deposited in a chest of drawers and his toiletries had been laid out in the spacious adjoining bathroom. He had not brought slippers, but saw that a new pair were arranged on the floor by the king-sized bed.

There was a decanter and brandy snifter on the table near the fireplace. Clayton settled in the chair facing the water and after pouring himself a drink, sat back and reviewed the day. All in all, he felt he was playing a convincing role.

It was pretty clear that Esteban and Cotton were not destined to be friends, but that wasn't the goal. Clayton's purpose in these first few hours was to establish a confident presence. More than just confident, Cotton had to be genuine and his occasional impropriety, while irritating to Esteban, helped establish the authenticity of the character.

Marco was another matter. He was going to be protective of his boss and his own sphere of influence and would guard against even a potential threat to either one. It was part of his job to be suspicious of everyone, especially anyone who attempted to establish a close orbit around his boss. This made him paranoid, and that made him dangerous. Clayton was prepared to carry on with that understanding. In his experience, Marco fit the mold of many organizations' number twos.

It was more complicated when Clayton turned his thoughts to Carmen. He was attracted to her, as he suspected any man would be, but he also saw in her the possibility of a valuable asset. She was an intelligent woman in a painful position. If he could win her confidence, could she be tempted with a proposal that would give her and her children a way out? It was a possibility worth exploring.

Clayton prepared for bed, took another sip of the brandy, and then directed his focus to the two gifts from Esteban. Following Esteban's instructions, he pulled at the thin red ribbon around the gold box and flipped open the lid. Fitted into a cushioned recess was a gold nugget. He carefully pulled the nugget from the box and hefted it in the palm of his hand, feeling its weight. Clayton was no expert, but he estimated it to be about an ounce and was sure it was worth a substantial sum.

Certain that this was not merely a display of Esteban's generosity, Clayton put the nugget back into its box and picked up the second one. Again, he pulled at the ribbon securing the top and flipped the box open. He was holding it at a slight angle, and as soon as it opened, the object inside fell out onto the table. Clayton recoiled at the sight of a severed human finger. From its appearance, it had recently been healthily attached to its previous owner's hand.

A bit over the top, Esteban, but message received, Clayton murmured to himself as he placed the digit back into its box, put both boxes into the room's compact refrigerator, turned off the lights, and went to bed. He put the day behind him, closed his eyes and gratefully let sleep take him.

------∞------

January 22 - Early Morning

The night passed without incident. Clayton's slumber was deep and dreamless. After a few hours, his body signaled that it was ready for a new day. His eyes fluttered, then stayed open. It was still dark in the room, and it took him a moment to remember where he was. *Gold. Finger.* The two words flashed into his consciousness, along with their discomforting images. Even half-awake, he found some ironic humor in the oblique James Bond reference. The digital clock on the nightstand glowed 5:10. He showered, shaved, and dressed in less than 20 minutes. The sun wouldn't make its appearance for another hour and a half, which corresponded to the time Esteban had mentioned breakfast would be served.

As he stepped out of his room, he heard the muted sounds of activity downstairs as the staff busied itself with what Clayton assumed was a daily morning routine. He descended the stairs and followed the smell of baking bread into the large, professionally appointed kitchen. The equipment was new and dazzling. A six-burner gas stovetop shared a wall with two large ovens, one of which was the source of the homey smell of baking bread. The latest model of a high-end refrigerator dominated the other side of a large granite island. A man and a woman were busy preparing breakfast and sorting and cleaning vegetables and fruits for the other meals and snacks of the day. They appeared to wholeheartedly enjoy their labors while carrying on an animated conversation in Spanish. So engrossed were they that it took them a moment to become aware of Clayton's presence.

The woman looked up and saw Clayton standing in the doorway. The staff had been informed of Esteban's guest. She smiled and offered a cheery good morning. "Buenos días, may I help you, señor?"

Clayton beamed his Cotton smile and launched into his Texas twang. "Good mornin', I know I'm way early and I don't mean t'be a bother, but I was wondrin' if I could git a cup a' coffee."

"Ah, Si. I have some fresh for you." The woman was middle-aged, and short enough to need a step stool to retrieve a mug from one of the cupboards. She poured it almost to the brim from the pot warming in the coffeemaker and held it out to Clayton.

The man who had been slicing a pineapple with a large chef's knife stopped in mid-stroke and cast an appraising view in Clayton's direction. Attentive to the motion, Clayton assessed that his interest was more curious than threatening.

Clayton took the steaming cup from the woman. "Thank ya, Ma'am." He took a cautious sip, guarding against the burn of the hot liquid. "Bueno." He smiled again, and the woman smiled back, pleased at his approval. "This sure is a magnificent kitchen. I'm not much of a cook m'self but I truly do appreciate anyone who c'n work the special magic that happens in a room like this'n."

Encouraged by Clayton's interest, the woman's smile broadened. Unused to anyone of any importance visiting the kitchen, she was quick to share the highlights of the many advantages of her domain. "It is indeed a wonder. Señor Navarro spends no time in this room, but he likes to set a fine table, both for himself and for his guests. Before he moved in, he gave orders that the kitchen should have the finest equipment. The stove has six burners that give off so much heat that we can prepare the best South American dishes in very little time. Señor Navarro's favorite is Colombian Paella which we make for him frequently. The refrigerator automatically keeps track of the items we keep in it and can place an order online for the things we need and the ovens ..."

She faded off, realizing she was presuming too much to take up so much of this important guest's time. Embarrassed, she let her gaze fall to the floor. "Perdóname, señor. I talk too much. It is a failing."

Clayton observed her discomfort. "What's your name, señora?"

Still looking at the floor, the woman responded in a soft voice, "Rosa, Rosa Santos, señor."

"I'm Cotton. Now, don't you be fretted' none, Rosa." Clayton knew that domestic staff, ignored to the point of invisibility by their employers, could be outstanding intelligence assets. "Have you worked for señor Navarro very long?"

"Si, this is my husband, Roberto," Rosa gestured toward the man with the knife. "Roberto and I worked for him in Mexico and came with him when he moved to California."

Roberto was quite a bit taller than his wife. Unlike Rosa's open, hospitable manner, Roberto's thin mustachioed mouth was grimly set, and it seemed it would take some effort for him to crack a smile. Although Clayton still assessed Roberto to be a low threat risk, his silence and sulky demeanor kept Clayton from letting his guard down completely.

"Hola, Roberto." Clayton's friendly gambit provided no new insight as Roberto nodded his reply and went back to slicing the pineapple, putting more energy into each cut than appeared necessary.

"Well, thank you, Rosa, for your hospitality. Roberto, it was a pleasure meetin' you. I think I'll explore the house a bit before breakfast. Do you mind if I take my coffee with me?"

Rosa responded with enthusiasm, eager to reciprocate the kindness Clayton had shown her. "Of course, señor. If there is anything else that you want, please, just ask."

"Well thank you, Rosa. I'll be sure to do that."

As Clayton started to leave Roberto spoke for the first time. "One moment, señor." Clayton tensed, unsure of Roberto's intentions. He turned to see the man put down his knife and wipe his hands on the apron he wore. He picked up a pastry from one of the cooling racks, placed it on a small plate, and handed it to Clayton, a slight grin of pride pulling at the corners of his lips. "Fresh this morning … it will make good coffee even better. Si?"

Clayton smiled his appreciation. "Yes indeed, Roberto. It smells wonderful. Thank y'all." The man and woman returned the smile and as Clayton was leaving the room, he heard them go back to their chores and conversation. He didn't understand much of what he overheard, but Clayton was certain that he was now the main topic of their discussion.

He wandered through the main floor, through the great room and its dining area, now cleared of all signs of last night's dinner, and set up for the coming breakfast. He entered the main foyer, which was shaped like a large oblong with rounded ends. At one end was the main staircase, designed in the grand fashion with two curved flights leading up to join on the second-floor balcony. The floor of the foyer was an ivory-colored marble with colored marble inlays, the dominant one of which formed a brilliant image of a Phoenix rising from a raging fire positioned so the bird's head pointed toward the ascending stairs. A multi-tiered fountain burbled in the center of the room under a majestic chandelier consisting of hundreds of tear-shaped crystals. The lights in the chandelier filtered through the crystals and threw splashes of multicolored light on the room's walls, floor, and high domed ceiling. The main doors at the other end of the foyer opened onto a portico, which, during the daylight hours, would display a view of the meticulously trimmed lawn and the endless expanse of the ocean. Openings in the foyer's walls provided access to the rooms that bordered its circumference. Those areas of the wall that were not open to other rooms were populated with pieces of art. Sculptures, busts, and paintings, along with the grand clock, proclaimed, with all the credibility that money could buy, that Esteban Navarro was a successful and cultured man.

There was more than one reason for Clayton's initial survey of the house. He certainly appreciated the fine display of riches, but more practically, he wanted to become familiar with all the strengths and weaknesses of the estate. This knowledge was essential to his duties as Cotton Parish and valuable to any follow-on law enforcement operation.

He visited the various rooms, making notes on his phone as to physical as well as computer access points. He made note of construction materials and existing security and fire control measures. Even with this initial cursory examination, he found several points of vulnerability that cried out for attention. That is, if the protection of the home, its inhabitants, and its assets were the goal.

The main rooms on the ground floor all had windows with either a view of the ocean or of the well-manicured gardens that surrounded the compound's buildings. Clayton was just finishing his visit to the library. He scanned the built-in floor-to-ceiling bookcases filled with beautifully bound classics and couldn't imagine Esteban touching any of them. *If he read these, if he dedicated the time it would take to read these, how could he be the man he is? Perhaps Carmen ...* Clayton's glance was pulled to the window. It was clear that the sky had lightened and details of the garden were becoming more pronounced. The clock in the library told him he had better move back to the great room if he didn't want to be late for breakfast.

January 22 - Breakfast

As Clayton entered the great room, he noticed that Esteban and Marco had already taken their seats at the round table in the dining annex. Approaching the table, Clayton heard the last bits of Esteban's comments.

"… well, we'll just have to see what he—", Esteban looked up, leaving his sentence unfinished. "Buenos días, Cotton. I trust you had a restful night?"

Clayton responded cheerily, "Good mornin' to y'all. An' thank you, Esteban, I slept like a heifer on fresh laid-out hay." He had decided not to bring up the 'gifts' unless Esteban did.

Esteban gestured toward a chair. "Please sit. Marco and I were just talking about you. We are curious as to how you would like to proceed, but before we hear your thoughts, let's have some breakfast." He stood and walked over to a serving table holding several chafing dishes, a platter of fresh fruits, and a large carafe of coffee. "Rosa and Roberto, my kitchen staff, serve a breakfast buffet each morning. Please help yourself."

Clayton took a plate from the stack on the serving table, spooned on some scrambled eggs, and then helped himself to a sampling of breakfast meats, some toast, and coffee. "I met Rosa and Roberto this mornin'."

"Oh?" Esteban sounded surprised, but Clayton was sure that the two staff members would have reported the meeting.

Esteban and Marco filled their plates and joined Clayton at the round table.

"I'm an early riser. My daddy always told me that the way to get ahead is to fill your day fuller than anyone else's. Now mind you, most of the time, like as not, he was talkin' 'bout how much whiskey he could put down, 'cause my daddy had a bit of a drinkin' problem, but I chose to put my own meanin' to it."

Esteban's laugh was real enough. "And what did you do this morning while the rest of us wasted our time sleeping?"

There was no point in Clayton's trying to hide his exploration of the house. He was certain that his wanderings had been noted and reported to Esteban. "I wanted to get started on my current-state assessment of the main house."

"And what did you find?"

"I'd rather not say 'til I can complete a more thora' review and get some context."

Clayton saw Marco's face twist into a smirk and cut him off before he could comment. "Now you've got to understan'. My security recommendations are goin' to depend a great deal on what threats y'all want to guard against. Are we talkin' 'bout yer garden variety burglars, a home invasion, or an out 'n out pro-tacked-up invasion?"

Esteban dabbed a cloth napkin to his lips before replying, "I would say the last scenario is the best one to keep in mind. It may sound extreme but we live in dangerous times. Your reputation indicates that won't be a problem. Is that indeed the case?"

"Not a problem. Over the years, that has been the most popular choice for most of my clients. They pretty much all feel the burden of livin' in … dangerous times. Now, with that understandin', I'll need some things from y'all."

"Anything within reason, Cotton. What do you need?"

"Regarding physical security, I'll need the complete architectural and floor plans of all the buildin's, any modifications or enhancements, the layout of the grounds, the placement of security forces, their number, background, trainin', armament, and reportin' structure. Okay?" Clayton fixed his gaze on Esteban.

"Yes, Marco will get you those." Esteban relayed his approval with a nod in Marco's direction.

"In terms of cybersecurity, I assume you want the highest degree of protection. I'll need to see where you intend to put the servers and the routers, the power supply, and a map of all the access points. I'd also like to take a gander at your plan for ongoin' maintenance and operational oversight. A'course, I'll be givin' you recommendations on all these items but I want to see where yer at. Because of lead time, even fer expedited delivery, I've taken the liberty to order the mix of equipment that I recommend fer the highest level of secured installation. It should be here in the next day or so. If my ordered equipment is a match for your needs, I'll need three or four men to help with the installation chores. I probably ordered more than needed, but we can send anythin' extra back."

While Clayton's site security review could prove critical in an all-out tactical assault, getting this equipment installed represented the most enduring value of the operation. Before final delivery to El Mirador, FBI technicians intercepted Clayton's hardware order and were carefully modifying it to ensure discrete remote access. Clayton continued, "I would like free rein to order any other equipment that I feel is necessary. Still okay?"

"Yes, Cotton. It's still okay. Is that all?"

Clayton felt relief that the main purpose of his mission appeared to be on track. He felt encouraged to up the stakes. "Those are the main things for now. There'll likely be more as I get into it. Oh—one more thing. I need unrestricted access to every area, every room on the compound. Is that a problem?"

While computer literate, Esteban's worldview was much more physical. He could more easily see the risks in such a request. "I can agree to that with certain restrictions. You'll need to coordinate with Marco as to the times and places you would like to visit. We can't have you unwittingly interfering with my business dealings. And for the first day or so, Marco will accompany you … to make sure all the staff know who you are."

"Agreed. I don't need or want to know about your business and I sure wouldn't want to interfere. And Marco and I will git along jes fine. Right, Marco?"

It seemed impossible that Marco could in any way bring his face into more of a scowl, but Clayton was impressed at how well he managed.

Clayton turned to Esteban once again, "I'll need a week, maybe less, to do the physical security audit, starting from the time I get the materials I've requested. I'm sure I'll have questions for you between now and then, but my goal is to present you with a report by this time next week. Is that okay with you?"

"I look forward to it. You'll have the information you requested by this afternoon. Right, Marco?"

"Si, jefe. I will see to it."

"Also," Clayton continued, "I'll be testin' yer online cybersecurity. If y'all are monitoring, which you should be, you'll see me sending regular short bursts of test data and receiving similar bursts. Yer welcome ta tap in if you've got a mind to."

"Understood, Thank you for the warning but you wouldn't be here if we didn't feel we could trust you," Esteban's words to Clayton were sugar-coated but as he continued, he looked meaningfully at Marco, "Isn't that right, Marco?"

Marco grinned, taking the cue from his boss. "Si, señor Cotton. You are like one of us. Nosotros confiamos en ti."

Clayton noted that whatever else he was, Marco was a horrible actor.

It was clear that Clayton's presence put a damper on the normal breakfast conversation so, with business out of the way, the men focused somewhat awkwardly on their meals.

Finally, Clayton broke the silence, "I notice Carmen … señora Navarro, hasn't joined us. I sure hope she's not feelin' poorly."

"She is fine. She often takes breakfast in her room with the children."

"They're both little darlin's."

"Perhaps, but I find their energy to be quite … distracting at times. I'm grateful that Carmen enjoys their company so much. She keeps them entertained and they, in turn, seem to make her happy. She fills her days with them. Everything becomes a lesson, from their morning time in the gardens to their afternoons on the beach. I'm sure she is a good teacher." Esteban paused. After a thoughtful sip of coffee, his eyes followed the cup back down to the saucer. He continued, "They learn things from her that are, no doubt, more pleasant than what they might learn from me." It was hard for Clayton to tell if he was hearing regret, envy, bitterness, or a mix of all three.

February 20 - The Attack

Over the next few days, with Marco in tow and tablet in hand, Clayton applied himself to viewing and analyzing the compound's security strengths and weaknesses. True to his word, Esteban had allowed Clayton complete access to the entire estate conditioned on Marco's accompaniment.

Clayton judged that while Marco might be a valuable asset in a fight, he was not much of a strategist. If he had been open to a more amicable relationship, he might have effectively engaged with Clayton and understood more of what he was doing. As it was, the big man radiated displeasure with a palpable intensity that only increased as the days went by. He stood by, sulking, wrapped in his cocoon of jealousy and distrust. At first, Clayton deflected his blistering gaze with silence, then decided that the better strategy was to feed his aggravation. Clayton's theory was that simmering anger would distract Marco from the details of what Clayton was doing and while he could explain away his activities as part of his security audit, it would be better to smother any sprouting curiosity.

Their repartee was infrequent and brief, with Clayton always taking the lead and timed to keep Marco's mind buried in his anger.

"Hey Marco,"

"Si,"

"Have ya always been so shy, or did ya go ta school fer it?"

"Púdrete!"

"Bless your heart, I'm not real sure what that means, but I can purty much guess." Clayton had learned much of his Spanish in the Navy and on the streets and had clearly understood the expletive. "Now y'all jus' keep workin' on your vocabulary and before ya know it, you'll be able ta carry on a whole conversation."

"Hijo de puta!"

Clayton turned back to his tablet and smiled.

Two weeks after his arrival, Clayton took delivery of the special order of computers and associated hardware and software he had purchased for the *El Mirador* installation. The equipment was indeed special as its undisclosed delivery route included a brief stop at an FBI facility where modifications were made that enabled undetectable remote access. Two weeks later, all of Esteban's operations were up and running on their new systems. Esteban marked the day the systems went live with a small celebration. He assembled the staff, some of whom had participated in the installation of the various pieces of hardware.

"Thank you all for your efforts in bringing our new systems online. Of course, special thanks must go to señor Cotton Parish, who has worked tirelessly to bring his magic to life in the shortest possible time. Computers are not my passion, but thank God there are people like señor Parish whose talent and energy keep us all safe and productive."

A ripple of polite applause came from the group, who were only vaguely aware of the effort but were grateful for the pleasant distraction from their normal duties.

Esteban's enthusiasm was undamped. "Cotton, give us a few words. It is a good day, is it not?"

Clayton was more reserved in the celebration of his accomplishments. "Well, thank ya kindly for the pat on the back, Esteban, but it's been a team effort and we have more to do." He had advised Esteban that although his business operations were now running in their new environment, the physical security of the compound was still in its unimproved state.

After the last round of polite applause died down and those in attendance milled around the snack table, Esteban sought out Clayton.

"Cotton, again, congratulations. You have done well so far." His smile didn't hide the main thrust of his message. "When I praise you don't feel a need to share the spotlight, my friend. Take your bow and whatever reward comes with it. But be assured that if you ever fail, that bright, burning light will also shine on only you." Esteban put his arm around Clayton's shoulder and his smile broadened. "Now, have a drink and enjoy our little moment of celebration."

Marco saw that Esteban's spirits had been lifted by the operational milestone and felt that this was an opportune time to petition his boss for a change of duties. Motivated by the boredom of the assignment and the pressure of his other duties and, most importantly his burning dislike of Clayton, he took Esteban aside and asked that he be relieved of his constant surveillance of Clayton's activities.

After the party, Clayton was in the garden just in front of the main house, mapping the lines of sight from possible defenders in the house. He had waited several minutes for Marco to join him as expected, but then started his work without him. He heard heavy footsteps on the pea gravel path and looked up to see the heavyset man approaching, wearing a scowl slightly less severe than usual.

"El jefe has told me that you are now free to roam alone. Hear me, señor. I do not trust you, perhaps because it is my job and perhaps because you make my stomach upset. But in any case, be careful what you do. I have eyes everywhere." Marco gestured to a nearby Queen Palm tree containing a mounted camera, one of the many that populated the campus.

Clayton smiled at the use of the clichéd phrase and how toothless the threat was. He had been mapping the locations of all the cameras and was fully aware of the multiple blind spots that existed. "Well shucks, Marco. I sure am sorry to hear that's the way you feel. I hope that someday I'll be able to change your mind and we can be friends."

"Not likely, señor. En guardia!" With that warning, Marco turned and crunched his way back to the house, leaving Clayton free to roam alone.

****

While Carmen and the children dined with them nightly, they never stayed for as long as the night of Clayton's arrival. He would often meet her, in passing, during the day. On all of these occasions, her attitude toward him was courteous, but cool. He noticed that, when good weather beckoned, she, Lucia, and Este would take a picnic lunch down to the beach.

Clayton was often outside, assessing lines of sight and the ground's security, and he would look up from his notes and drawings as they went by—a mother duck leading her small entourage. The giggling and earnest sounds of enthusiastic childhood conversation floated over the air as they approached, and then faded as they moved across the lawn to the stairway that led to the beach. Carmen would give a nod of acknowledgment and the children would wave as they passed by.

When she was with her children, Carmen became noticeably more vivacious. Each day, for just a few hours, a bubble of unreserved joy enveloped the three of them and allowed her to set down the burden of pretense that she otherwise carried. As she led her little ducklings to the beach, her laughter came easily. More than easily, it sprang from deep inside her like a gush of water from an unblocked hose. For reasons that he could not convincingly defend, Clayton's work brought him frequently to the beach at lunchtime.

Carmen was reluctant to share this special time with Clayton and initially ignored his presence on the beach. For his part, Clayton kept his distance, making a show of his explorations and note-taking, shoring up his own belief that he had a valid reason to be there.

"What are you doing?" It was Este who, finally encouraged by their first pleasant encounter and a 5-year-old's curiosity, had closed the sandy gap between the family picnic blanket and where Clayton was working.

Clayton held out his tablet displaying a sketch he was drawing of the beach, the guard shacks, and the cliff.

"Neat! You draw really well."

"Ya like it?"

"You bet! How did you learn to draw like that?"

"Practice. I started when I was a young'un, jes 'bout yer age." Together, they studied the sketch. "But now that I take a closer look, I see there's somthin' missin'"

Clayton pulled the tablet back and cradled it in one arm, busily working on its surface with his stylus. After a short time, he handed the tablet to Este, whose eyes widened in delight. The beach scene was the same, but with some important additions.

"Wow! That's me! And over there, that's Mom and Lucia!" Este's need to share his excitement recruited his feet and he scampered over the sand, back to where Carmen and Lucia had looked up from their lunch at his excited whoop. "Mom, look at what señor Cotton did."

At that moment, Clayton became at least a provisional member of the *Carmen, Este, Lucia Beach Club*.

At first, cautiously, Carmen allowed Clayton to join their shoreline treks as they played toe-tag with the waves, sought treasures in the sand, and chased hermit crabs in tidal pools. Together, the four of them found simple joys in their easy company. The echoes of Clayton's own familial warmth made him a pleasant companion and melted his innate reserve, allowing a genuine affection for the children to emerge. Comfortable in this most real part of his made-up role, with growing enthusiasm, he played to his small audience, delivering stories of intrepid explorers, and notorious brigands, evil defeated and virtue victorious. He boldly paraded on sand dunes, waving an imaginary sword, masterfully dispatching pirates, and bestowing honors on deserving young boys and girls. Of his delighted fans, none was more enthralled than Carmen.

****

On the day of the incident, Clayton had another run-in with Marco. Despite any logic or evidence to the contrary, Marco adamantly believed that the security of the compound under his watch was and had always been more than sufficient. Although he would admit that computers fell outside of his skill set, he was proud of the physical security he had established for the estate.

Clayton was in the garden, reviewing sketches he had made earlier when Marco attempted to approach him stealthily from behind.

Without turning, Clayton harpooned the point that Marco was trying to make. "Howdy, Marco. Shur is a beautific day, ain't it?"

"You are always studying and drawing. What do you expect to find?"

"Jes doin' my job, Marco—an' checkin' ta see how well ya did yer's."

"You are wasting your time, señor. *El Mirador* is secure. I pity the idiota who tries to attack it."

"You shur 'bout that, Marco?"

"Si, muy seguro."

"Well, I'll tell ya what. Let's you 'n me have a little wager."

"Wager?"

"Yeh, a bet."

"Si, a bet."

"You go on up to the security room and set yerself in front of all yer monitors. I bet you a hundred dollars I can get from here to the beach and you'll never see me."

Marco was certain his cameras and physical barriers were up to the task, but Clayton's confidence made him hesitate.

"Well there, Marco, what's it goin' ta be? Hey, it's only a hundred bucks."

They both knew it was more than that and they both knew that Marco had no choice.

His answer came forcefully from his pride and ego. "Si, bueno, I agree, but the bet must be for one thousand dollars."

Clayton let out a long whistle. "Yee doggies, Marco, I admire yer courage. Okay, a thousand it is. I'll give ya three minutes ta git up ta yer screens."

Marco's granite face cracked into a confident smile. Then he turned, and at a brisk pace, crunched back to the main house.

After counting down what he estimated to be three minutes, Clayton moved into the nearest blind spot he had mapped. He then moved from blind spot to blind spot toward the edge of the cliff overlooking the beach. The ground just over the edge was steep but not a sheer drop and a few feet below the edge, a narrow path ran along the shrub-covered cliff face for its entire length. He slipped over the edge onto the path and made his way to the stairway, all the while out of sight of the cameras that scanned the lawn above. He ducked under the stair railing and moved down the stairway toward the beach. He knew that cameras were scanning the stairs, but that didn't matter. He had made his point with Marco.

From his vantage point, he saw that Carmen and the children were at the water's edge, hunting for their shells and stones. A wave of homesickness washed over him as he recollected similar scenes with Maggie and Anthony. But here and now it was an early afternoon on a windless winter day and the high, bright sun blazed through the clear sky and warmed the white sand. The ocean was dotted with the typical assortment of small powerboats, sailboats and out farther, several large container ships awaited their turn to offload at the Port of Los Angeles.

As he continued his descent, about halfway down the stairs, he noticed one small boat that stood out from the background patterns of the rest of the nautical traffic. It was still almost a mile out but as Clayton focused on it he could make out that it was a rigid hull inflatable Zodiac type and its course was directly toward the beach. Although he couldn't identify a clear threat, his intuition was signaling an alarm. He had trained and conducted operations on similar boats. Quickening his pace down the stairs, he could now make out that the craft contained seven or eight men and they appeared to be armed. Now on full alert, he glanced at the guard towers.

Are those guys awake? he wondered as his mental alarm level ratcheted into the red zone. *They've got to have seen the boat and they must have binoculars. Their view has to be better than mine.* Now he was dashing down the stairs, taking them two at a time, yelling at the top of his lungs for Carmen to get away from the water. Carmen looked up in confusion and then, as she reacted to the alarm in Clayton's voice, she scooped up Lucia, grabbed Este's hand, and started to run inland.

Clayton heard the crack of gunfire as the men in the boat began firing on the two guard towers. As he ran across the beach toward Carmen and the children, Clayton could see the protruding muzzles of the one guard in each tower returning fire. He was horrified to see the muzzle from the first tower fall back into the guard shack and become silent. The guard in the second tower seemed to panic. Abandoning his post, with his rifle slung over his shoulder, he backed out of the tower and started to scramble down the ladder. He was only a few rungs down when his head appeared to explode and his body peeled slowly off of the ladder and crumpled onto the beach.

As tempted as he was to continue to run to Carmen, Clayton judged that his best tactical move was to get to a weapon. He signaled with his arms and yelled out for Carmen to get down. His legs were pumping as fast as the loose sand would allow as he changed course for the guard's motionless body.

Clayton noted that, thankfully, the attackers were not directing any of their fire at Carmen or the children who were now huddled face down on the sand. Carmen was lying on top of them, shielding them with her body.

With the towers no longer returning fire, the raiders identified Clayton as the next potential threat. The beach around him exploded in small plumes as the men in the boat tried to neutralize this new player. The boat was about 20 feet from the shore, about 150 yards from Clayton. He dove into the sand, using the dead guard's body as a shield. He reached forward, pulled the M4 from around the guard's neck, and lined up his first shot just as the boat was approaching the beach. Clayton counted eight men. They were wearing tactical vests, so he was forced to try for headshots. He took a breath and let it out, paused, and squeezed the trigger. The lead man's head sent out a puff of pink and he fell back into the boat. Clayton grunted his satisfaction. *Seven to go.* Lining his shot up swiftly, Clayton brought down the second man, his body flipping over the gunwale into the water. *Six.* The attackers pulled the body of their comrade into the boat. The bobbing of the boat on the water had been a significant disadvantage to the shooters, but now it slid firmly ashore.

The sand plumes were getting closer as the men in front of the boat focused their fire on Clayton's position. In their eagerness to score a kill, the attackers displayed a lapse of training or experience. Rather than leaving the boat and spreading out, they chose to stay behind the bullet-resistant shields attached to the sides of the craft. This allowed only the men in front to have an unobstructed line of fire on Clayton, greatly reducing their firepower. Clayton switched the M4 to fully automatic fire and drained his magazine on the cluster of men. *Five. Four.*

He reached around the dead guard's body, pulled a new, bloodied magazine from his belt, and snapped it into place. He felt a bullet slam into his left shoulder. In an instant, he realized the shot had come from behind and above him, from the top and extreme left side of the cliff. Rolling onto his back, he fired a burst at his best guess at the location of the shooter. He saw a figure vault over the edge of the cliff into the trees that lined that side of the lawn, and then it was gone. The guard's body shuddered as more bullets peppered the area in front of him. He rolled back onto his stomach and fired off another quick burst. Although it caused the men in the boat to duck down, it had no lasting effect. Two of the men jumped over the bow of the boat onto the beach. This allowed the two remaining in the boat to effectively bring their firepower into the battle. Clayton now had four men directing their fire on him. He was fast coming to the conclusion that this was not going to end well for him as the accuracy of the enemy fire improved and its volume increased.

Then the sand and water around the invaders began to send up plumes as reinforcements from the top of the cliff joined in the battle. One of the two that had taken up positions on the beach went down. His partner dragged him into the boat and with much screaming and cursing the surviving attackers reversed the engine on the Zodiac, spun it around, and headed out to sea, steering a high-speed serpentine course to avoid the increasingly heavy barrage that followed them. As the boat sped out of effective range, the firing tapered off. The fast-diminishing sound of the attack boat was punctuated by the shouts from the men on the cliff top and from those who had begun the descent down the stairs. A relative quiet settled on the scene. Clayton checked his arm and saw that the wound, though painful and ugly, wasn't life-threatening.

Carmen was kneeling now. She pulled the children out of the sand and held them in a two-armed embrace.

"Stop, Mama. You're hurting me", Este squirmed and complained as Lucia wrapped both her arms around Carmen's neck and sobbed softly.

Seeing that Carmen and the children didn't appear to be injured, Clayton took a breath and examined the body of the guard that had served as his fortress. It had been hit by several bullets but the most interesting one was an entry wound high at the back of the head exiting under the man's chin. Clayton judged that this was the first fatal wound that had toppled the guard from the ladder. Fighting the pain from his wounded shoulder, he laboriously climbed up into the guard shack. He scanned the wall that faced the beach and the water beyond. It only took a moment for him to confirm his suspicion. There, in the armor plating near the gun port, was a large shiny indentation where a bullet had left its mark.

Clayton said out loud what he was thinking as he turned and once again scanned the cliff top, "You had reason to panic, my friend. When the first shot missed, you realized you were a sitting duck."

He backed painfully down the ladder and stepped heavily onto the sand. When he turned, he was startled to see Carmen, only a few feet away from him, with the children in tow.

"Carmen, are you and the kids alright?" Battle-worn and swept up in the emotion of the moment Clayton neglected to adopt his Cotton accent and persona.

The lapse went unnoticed. Tears had left light tracks down Carmen's dust-covered cheeks and her lips trembled with emotion. "I ... we ... thank you, Cotton." She leaned forward, wrapped her arms around him, pulled herself to him, and kissed him hard on the lips. Clayton could feel the kiss morph from gratitude to something else. His mind, still swimming in an ocean of endorphins, struggled to balance Cotton's reaction with his own. Just as he raised his right arm to gently disentangle Carmen's impassioned embrace, she pulled away. For the first time, her eyes focused on his bloodied shirt.

"You're hurt!"

"It's okay. It's not that bad."

Carmen reached down and tore a large strip from her beach robe. She brushed it free of sand and placed it around Clayton's shoulder, covering both the entry and exit wounds.

"Hold that!" she commanded, intent on her task. She then tore another strip from the depleted robe which she used to tie the makeshift field dressing in place.

"Ow!" Clayton complained as she tightened the knot. Then, as the wound acclimated to the pressure, "Thank you. That's better. Where did you learn to do that?"

"Walls can not keep you from learning, Cotton and prison can't keep you from growing. The life I live has made me a student of many topics that I would rather have left unlearned."

The well-armed men from above had now formed a protective perimeter at the edge of the beach and were scanning the water for any additional threats.

Esteban was on the last landing of the stairs just over the beach screaming invectives and waving a gold engraved silver-plated handgun. Clayton almost felt sorry for Marco, who stood meekly by his boss's side, no doubt hoping that the undirected rage would not settle on him as its target.

"Hijo de puta! I want to know who did this thing! Do they think they can bring me down? I want their heads, Marco! Do you hear me? I want their balls nailed to our front gate."

On hearing Esteban's explosive display of leadership, Clayton had three thoughts that followed in quick succession.

First, while it might be useful as a symbol of his authority, Esteban's ornate sidearm was tactically incongruous with the proliferation of the much more lethal armament that had dominated the engagement and now controlled the beach. Second, Clayton was pretty sure that the tony Malibu neighborhood association would find some regulation that forbade Esteban's proposed testicular display. And third, Esteban had yet to inquire as to the safety of his wife and children.

Esteban stepped down to the beach and, with Marco in tow, stalked over to where Carmen and Clayton were standing with the children. The short walk and his assessment that he was now in control allowed him to regain his composure. He glanced without comment at the body of the guard who had died in his service and then at Clayton's injured shoulder.

He turned to Carmen, grasping her chin in his hand and pulling her eyes to meet his. His tone was softer, but still commanding. It was a poor imitation of concern, but most likely the best that he could do. "Mi Amor, are you and the children alright?"

"Yes, Esteban, thanks to Cotton. He saved the three of us—He's wounded. He needs a doctor."

Esteban again looked at Clayton's injured shoulder, intoning the same shallow concern that he displayed for his family. "Do you need a hospital, Cotton?"

Clayton slipped back into his Cotton persona. "Looks to me like the bugger went clean through. Hell, the skeeters in Texas make bigger holes. I don't need a hospital, but I wouldn't mind a doc patchin' me up."

Warming back up to his role as host, Esteban's caring tone became more pronounced, "I will have my private doctor attend to you back at the house. Please take the time you need to recover. When you feel up to it, seek me out. I would like your assessment of what has occurred. Marco, please see

Cotton to the cutting room. I will have Dr. Vega meet him there."

Lucia was clinging to Carmen's legs, still sobbing softly. Thwarting Carmen's attempt to avoid it, Este had peeked at the body of the dead guard and promptly lost all of his bravado. He now held tightly to Carmen's hand and buried his face in the remains of her sand-covered beach robe.

"Carmen, we will take good care of Cotton. Please take the children up to the house and calm them down—and yourself as well."

Carmen's green eyes blazed but there was ice in her voice as she responded to Esteban's patronizing tone, "I will take care of my children and, as for me, Esteban, I am very calm." She lifted Lucia and, holding onto Este's hand, marched back over the sand to the stairs.

Ignoring the manner of Carmen's departure, Esteban continued his directions, "And Marco, after you make Cotton comfortable, there is no need for you to wait for the good doctor. Meet me in my office. We have much to put in motion."

"Si, patrón. It will be as you say."

"Now, if you will excuse me, I have calls that must be made immediately." With that, Esteban slipped his gun into his shoulder holster and moved down the beach, talking into his cell phone as he walked.

———◈———

February 20 - The Cutting Room

Esteban's reference to the "cutting room" sounded vaguely ominous to Clayton. His feeling of unease was not helped by Marco's company. They walked across the lawn and through the gardens, but instead of going to the main house, Marco led them to the conservatory building. He guided Clayton through the main room with its flowering plants and indoor pool, then through a door to a much smaller room. In most greenhouses, the cutting room would be where the flowers would be trimmed and arranged into bouquets suitable for display. The stainless steel tables, counters, and sinks made Esteban's cutting room functional for its nominal purpose. However, the addition of an examination table and surgical light near the room's center testified to its secondary use as an infirmary. The vague smell of disinfectant hinted at its readiness to be put to its medical purpose at a moment's notice.

Marco hadn't said a word for the entire walk up from the beach, but now he broke his silence. "Doctor Vega will be here in a few minutes. Señor Navarro pays him well for his very best service and for his silence."

Marco stopped speaking but didn't leave. He stood and stared at Clayton for an awkward 15 seconds that seemed much longer. Although his presence was inherently intimidating, at this moment his demeanor wasn't threatening. Clayton watched as the scars and creases that made up his face, the tokens of his ferocity, softened. He pulled himself to his maximum height and appeared to be forcing himself to perform a painful task. "Señor Parish, I respect what you did today. You are hombre valiente, a brave man. Even so, I do not trust you and if the need arises, I will kill you—but now, I would not enjoy it as much as I would have this morning." While he was speaking, he approached Clayton and stuffed something into his shirt pocket.

Marco had said what he felt honor-bound to say, then like a man swallowing bitter medicine, his scars and creases folded in on themselves, and his face reverted to its usual scowl. Without another word and without waiting for a response, he turned and stalked out of the room.

Clayton stood for a moment, digesting Marco's words. Not only were they unexpected, but they were inconsistent with the mental profile that Clayton had formed of the man.

He retrieved what Marco had pushed into his pocket. It was a roll of ten one-hundred-dollar bills. *Well, I'll be damned. This may not be the biggest surprise of the day, but it took a lot to knock it out of first place.* Clayton shook his head, filed that insight away, and focused on a more detailed inspection of the cutting room.

He had not visited this room before. Although he had explored most of the rooms on the compound, he was sure some areas didn't appear accurately on the floor plans and only a knowledgeable and willing guide or dedicated exploration would reveal all of them. This was a colorless room, made more so by the choice of stainless steel appliances and accessories. Even the tiled floor was a hospital white. There was a small window looking out on the garden and the path leading to the conservatory, but high-illumination bulbs hanging from the ceiling provided the main lighting. The room was well lit for each of its purposes.

In addition to the equipment that called attention to itself on first entering the room, there was a large refrigerator against the wall on the right and near the examination table a covered stainless steel trash can. The wall opposite the entry accommodated a sink built into stainless steel countertops. Clayton moved to the counter and opened one of the built-in drawers. It was filled with a variety of bandages, swabs, and sterile compresses. Another drawer contained a dazzling display of surgical instruments. The cupboards over the counter housed an autoclave, a microscope, and other medical instruments. Further along the counter, the drawers and cabinets contained pruning shears, vases, and baskets. A tall, built-in refrigerated cabinet with a glass door contained what appeared to be a large assortment of medications. On the left wall opposite the refrigerator, there was a dark window and next to the window, there was a door with a warning sign on it that urged caution because of the presence of radiation. Over the door was a black plaque with white etching proclaiming simply "X-RAY".

Clayton was impressed with how well-equipped the infirmary function of the cutting room was. With access to private medical professionals well paid for their discretion, all but the most serious injuries could be treated in this secure environment without inviting official inquiries or leaving inconvenient records.

He had no idea how long he would have to wait for the doctor. The makeshift bandage that Carmen had applied had slowed the bleeding but not stopped it. Blood was starting to soak through. His arm was throbbing and was getting progressively stiffer. Clayton pulled a roll of compression bandage and a large compress out of the bandage drawer. He ripped the top off of the compress package with his teeth and, pressing on the trash can peddle to discard the packaging, was surprised to see, at the bottom of the nearly empty can, multiple swabs, and several compresses wet with fresh blood.

Now on alert, Clayton scanned the room again, this time driven by more than curiosity. The X-ray room now became a subject of keener scrutiny, revealing that he had initially overlooked a small smudge of blood on the doorknob. Now his internal threat assessment indicator was flashing red. He opened the surgery drawer and unwrapped the largest blade he could find. Moving cautiously to the side of the dark window, he bobbed his head to quickly look into the dimly lit room and then ducked back. The maneuver allowed him to glimpse two figures crouched in the shadows against the far wall. He thought about leaving the room and sounding the alarm, but his choices were muddied by his uncertainty as to what this new game was all about and just who the players were. And all that was compounded by his multiple roles and potentially conflicting agendas. He decided not to involve Esteban's security team until he could find out more about what was going on, opting instead for a risky bluff.

Since he was unarmed, except for the surgical knife, he pumped as much bravado into his words as he could muster. "I'm goin' to swing the door open. When I do, I want you to throw your weapons out. Then, when I tell you, I want you to come on out slowly, hands first, one at a time. If, when I open the door, you don't throw out your weapons, I'm goin' to start shootin'!" He calculated that the sound of gunfire from the conservatory building, if it carried through the walls at all, would attract reinforcements that could only improve his position. He hoped that those in the X-ray room had done the same calculation and come to the same conclusion.

He pulled the door wide open and pressed it flat against the wall. There was no answer and no movement. After a quick recalculation, Clayton fell back to another approach, hoping that he didn't lose too much credibility in the switch. "Okay. Stay in there then! I don't figure I'll be doin' any shootin' after all. Any minute now, there'll be some folks joinin' us and this'll no longer be a private party. Now I shur don't mind sittin' out here and if you're of the same mind, then we can all just relax and wait for the cavalry to git here." He took a moment to look out the window and saw no one was in the garden.

For a long minute, there was nothing, and then agitated whispering. A familiar voice came from the darkness of the room. "Señor Parish, don't shoot!"

"Rosa? Is that you?" Clayton didn't try to hide his surprise at the sound of the cook's voice.

"Si, señor. Este soy yo!"

"Is Roberto with you?"

"Si, but he is hurt!"

"I can help, Rosa, but first, do you have any weapons?"

"A rifle, señor!"

"Put it on the floor and slide it out the door."

There was another bout of whispered conversation, a moment of silence, and then a loud scraping sound as a rifle slid out of the open door. Clayton quickly but carefully scooped it up while staying out of the line of fire. He checked the magazine and then made sure a round was in the chamber.

"Is that everythin'? Don't go lyin' to me now! It won't go well for you if you do!"

"That is all, señor Parish." It was Roberto who answered. There was no fight in his voice.

"Hola, Roberto. Cómo estás?"

"No bueno, señor Parish. I have had better days."

"Well, I'd have to say we both have. Rose says you're hurt?"

"Si, I have an injury to my side."

"Can you walk?"

"Si, I can walk."

Clayton stepped over to the examination table and flicked on the surgery lamp, focusing it on the X-ray room door. "Well, Rosa, you put your arm around Roberto and help him out of there. Don't let go of him until I say so. Comprende?"

"Si, I understand, señor Parish. You will help him?" Rosa's voice carried a mix of pleading and urgency.

"Yes, I'll help. Now come on, out of there."

There was a shuffling sound and the two figures emerged from the X-ray room, squinting at the bright light. Roberto was leaning heavily on Rosa, who was holding a bloody compress to his side.

Clayton could see there was no fight left in either one of them, but he was still cautious. "Turn around, cross your legs, and lean against the table."

They did as he instructed without complaint.

"Now just hold that pose. I know it's uncomfortable but I promise it'll just be a moment."

Clayton backed up, moved the barrel of his rifle into the X-ray room, and flicked on the light. Convinced that the room was empty he turned his attention back to Rosa and Roberto.

He checked them for weapons and then released them from their awkward stance.

"Okay, you can stand up now. Roberto, you look pretty tuckered. Why don't you set yerself up here on the table and let's take a look."

Roberto pulled himself up on the table. Clayton leaned the rifle against the side of the table and adjusted the light. After a brief assessment, he turned to the drawers and opened one and then another, directing Rosa as he searched.

"Rosa, there's an entry and an exit. They appear to be superficial. Did you clean them?"

"Si, señor, with water and then antiseptic."

In the second drawer, he spied what he was looking for. He pulled out the package and opened the bottle of wound sealant that it contained.

"Good. Now prepare two thick compresses and a compression bandage. When I put the powder on the wounds, bandage him up."

"Si, gracious, señor Parish."

"Roberto, this is going to hurt a bit."

"Mierda!" Roberto winced as the powder did its job.

Clayton stepped back and let Rosa apply the bandages. "Keep pressure on those wounds for a few minutes." He then busied himself collecting more bandages and a wound kit from the drawers. "Rosa, this has everythin' you need to stitch up his wounds. I'm assumin' you don't want to wait for the doctor."

Rosa hung her head. "No, señor. We must go—if you will let us. I can tend to the wound. I have done such things before."

"Well, it's not as easy as all that. You folks owe me an explanation and then I'll decide what happens next." Clayton placed the items on the counter and inspected the bandaged wounds. "Good job." He picked up the rifle and leaned against the table. "Roberto, I figure I know where you got that wound and I also figure I owe you fer my shoulder. Now tell me what's goin' on."

Rosa looked at Clayton's still-seeping shoulder. "Señor Parish, let me help you with—"

"Leave it, Rosa. The doctor will be here any minute and I need some quick answers to help me decide what to do with the both of you. What's yer involvement in what happened on the beach? Roberto, are you the one who took out Esteban's guards?"

"Si, señor."

"And I have you to thank for this hole in my shoulder?"

"Si, but it is not what you think. I did not shoot to kill you."

"Then quickly, Roberto, tell me what I should think! Who were those men in the boat? Why would you help them? We're runnin' out'a time!" Clayton checked the view from the window. So far, no one was approaching the conservatory. "Esteban has figured this to be an attack by his competitors! He's out fer blood and I don't think he'll be treatin' traitors with a great deal'a kindness!"

"It's not what you think, señor!" There was panic in Rosa's voice.

"Yeah, well, Roberto has already said that. 'n your repeatin' it doesn't make it any clearer. Time's a passin', folks, 'n ya don't have much left. If'n that's all you have to say, then I guess it's time to invite some other folks to the party and then we'll see—"

"It was for señora Carmen! We did it for señora Carmen!" Rosa's words were filled with the passion and conviction of someone who has nothing left to lose.

"What do you mean it was for señora Carmen?" Of all the possible scenarios that Clayton had been considering, none would have yielded this statement from Rosa. He wasn't subtle in hiding his doubts. "I'm goin' to need a lot more than that, Rosa."

"It's true, señor!" Shamed by Rosa's taking the lead, Roberto winced through his pain as he pulled himself off of the table and found his tongue. "The men in the boat were not here to attack the compound or señora Carmen but to rescue her!"

"Rescue her? This sounds like the start of a mighty tall tale. I've got to warn you, Roberto an' you too, Rosa, I've been around a lot of bulls in my life 'n I can pretty much tell one end from the other. And what's more, I get pretty grumpy when I get shot so git on with your story, but make it good 'n make it true."

"Si, señor, we will tell the truth! We have been part of señor Navarro's staff for several years, but we owe our loyalty to señora Carmen's parents. In the older days, the Medina family treated our family with great kindness and for that, we hold them in our hearts. When señor Navarro married their daughter, they encouraged us to become part of señora Carmen's new household and keep watchful eyes on her and then her children. What we learned of señor Navarro's business was not so good, but in the first few years, the ones in Mexico, we could see only that he treated her well. That changed when he took her here to the United States. He tightened his control over her, cut her off from her family, and treated her badly. These things we reported to señor and señora Medina. They attempted to reach out to her, but señor Navarro wouldn't allow it. With only our dark reports and no way to speak to their daughter, they became desperate for her safety and that of their grandchildren. What happened today was born out of that desperation. These men were not mercenarios. They all owed the Medina family debts of honor. It saddens me greatly to know that so many of these good men died trying to repay that debt.

"I am sorry I shot you, lo siento, señor Parish. It was all for nothing ... todo por nada ..." Roberto's body slumped under the weight of his misery. Rosa reached her arms around her husband and put her head on his chest. If misery were ever to need an icon, its search could well end with the picture of the two of them at this moment.

Even while Roberto was speaking, Clayton had decided not to turn the two over to Esteban. He judged their story to be true based in part on his belief that it would take an extremely talented liar to concoct such a tale on such short notice. And then there was the fact that he was alive. Lying in the sand, he was a much easier target than the two guards.

He looked up and did another check through the window and saw a figure carrying a bag making his way through the garden.

"Our time is up. The doctor is coming." Clayton pulled Carmen's makeshift bandage off of his shoulder and held a compress to his wound. "That should explain the bloody compresses in the trash. I want you two to go out the back door. Remember, there are cameras. Take some flowers on the way out to give you a reason for being here. Rosa, take the wound kit and hide the rifle under your dress. Roberto, walk as straight as you can. I'll meet the doctor at the front door to give you a little more time. Now git!"

"Gracias, señor Parish, gracias", the words bubbled from the both of them as they gathered up what they needed and prepared to go.

Clayton left the cutting room and, still pressing the compress to his shoulder, hurried along the walkway toward the front of the greenhouse. As he got closer to the front door, he sat at one of the tables that dotted the perimeter of the pool.

A short, frail-looking man in his thirties came through the front door of the conservatory. His eyes darted nervously around the cavernous room before fixing on Clayton sitting off to one side.

His voice carried more confidence than his appearance would imply. "I am Doctor Vega. Señor Navarro has sent for me to tend to your wound."

"Hello Doctor, I'm—"

"I do not need to know your name, señor." Vega pulled the compress from Clayton's shoulder and examined the wounds. "Why are you out here?"

"Well, I've been waiting a bit and there weren't any magazines in the other room, so I came out here where the air was a bit fresher."

Clayton's attempt at humor had no effect on Vega's impassive face. "Uh-huh, let's get back to the infirmary where I can take proper care of your shoulder." Clayton noticed that he chose to refer to the room by a term more aligned with his profession. Vega took a step back to allow Clayton room to get up. As Clayton stood, he swayed, exaggerating the slight vertigo he felt at the sudden motion. Playing for some additional time for Rosa and Roberto, he made a show of gripping the side of the chair. "I may need a helpin' hand, Doc."

Vega stepped closer and put Clayton's good arm over his shoulder. Clayton set a slow pace as they walked back to the infirmary.

****

Fully asleep, Clayton relived the firefight on the beach. The throbbing in his shoulder brought him to the verge of wakefulness just as his mind replayed Carmen's kiss and her warm embrace. The dreamlike replay became real as Carmen slipped into bed beside him and pressed her warm, naked body against his. His eyes fluttered, trying to accommodate the conflicting signals from his semi-conscious brain. In response to her urgings, the passion rose. Like an incoming tide, it came slowly at first and then with a silently screaming urgency became a tsunami that washed away all other pain, care, and consideration. He was only vaguely aware of Carmen's moist lips on his as she silently rose and left his bed. Once again, he was swallowed up by a warm and pleasant oblivion.

When he opened his eyes again, the soft light of the late afternoon sun filtered through the curtains. He had no recollection of the walk back from the greenhouse. He remembered Dr. Vega stitching up the wounds and administering a mix of antibiotics and pain killer. The latter, combined with physical exhaustion, explained the recent lost hours and the exquisite detail of his dream. As he urged his mind toward full consciousness, he became aware of the faint smell of jasmine. He carefully rolled onto his side and felt the still warm indentation on the bed next to him that at least hinted that some part of his incredible dream was real.

It was getting late, and he remembered that he still had to meet with Esteban, but he laid back on the bed, closed his eyes, and replayed the day's events one more time. Ten minutes later, he pulled his legs onto the floor and stood up slowly fighting off a slight wave of dizziness. He moved stiffly to the sink and splashed some water on his face. Feeling stronger with each passing moment, he gingerly put on a fresh shirt and was pleased to see it covered the bandages nicely. He finished dressing and set out to find his employer, leaving for later the necessary thorough review of all that had happened.

February 20 - A New Assignment

Although he felt much better, Clayton kept his hand on the banister as he descended the stairs into the main lobby. He paused at the bottom and then followed the sounds of voices that led him to Esteban's office. The house, by its architecture and appointments, normally conveyed an atmosphere of quiet culture and majestic tranquility, but now Esteban's voice echoed through the marbled mansion, tearing through that veneer like a chainsaw.

"They come to my home? They dare to attack my family?"

The door to the office was partially open, leading Clayton to think that it perhaps was Esteban's intention to share his rage with the entire household. Clayton paused. He could see a good portion of the room through the crack, at least the most important parts. Marco sat, nervously fingering his cell phone as though he would be called upon at any moment to summon Esteban's resident army. Esteban was stalking back and forth in front of the window by his desk. He had his silver-plated automatic in his hand and as he gestured wildly, he used it to punctuate his rage. No living creature or stick of furniture in the room was safe. Even Marco's normally unshakable machismo was strained as he visibly struggled to keep himself from diving for cover.

"Escúchame! There will be blood for this, Marco! They will bleed and so will their rotten families! I will take their wives and their children and—". The gory details of Esteban's planned revenge were lost as Clayton knocked on the door and, without waiting for a response, swung it open.

"Ah, so the hero finally decides to join us," interrupted in mid-rage, Esteban's sarcastic salutation lacked grace and provided another glimpse of the jungle-bred persona that lurked beneath the thin, cultured facade. Realizing his lapse, he took a breath and put the pistol down on the desk. "Perdón, Cotton, that was unkind of me. The events of the day have left me not quite myself. I hope you are recovering quickly from your wounds. If you are feeling up to it, please join us." Esteban motioned toward a high-backed leather chair. As Clayton sat, wincing at his complaining shoulder, Esteban continued, "Marco and I were just going over next steps. We have agreed—" Esteban caught the look of what might be dissent on Marco's face and repeated his words for emphasis, "Marco and I have agreed that the attack calls for a strong response." His voice was rising again. "We must teach these thugs a lesson! They cannot come for me, for ME, especially in my own home!" He paused for another breath. "Please Cotton, share your thoughts."

Clayton's swift assessment yielded two conclusions. First, he saw that Esteban's ego wouldn't allow him to consider any motive for the attack that did not feature him as the central character. Clearly, he had no idea what the facts were. Second, Esteban's rage had brought him to the edge of initiating a gang war which would put many non-combatants at risk. Clayton's challenge was to offer an option that would appear to support Esteban's need for action while not actually pulling any triggers.

In a play for time to think, Clayton ducked the question. "How'd y'all address the noise of the attack? Ya got a sizable piece a' land, but the neighbors must 'a heard the racket and called the cops."

"Si, right after the attack, I called the police and informed them that a movie production had rented the use of our beach for a project. I'm sure I will take some heat from the neighbors, but we will manage it."

"Nicely handled." Clayton's compliment was sincere. He noted that even though Esteban was wrapped in fear and rage, he could still effectively manage some parts of the crisis. "As to my thoughts ... it sure makes sense that whoever sent these boys deserves a good comeuppance. So ya'll figured out who was behind it?"

"It could only be the Royales. They are eager to expand, and, with me out of the way, their path would be much easier. Isn't that right, Marco?"

"Si, jefe," Marco's response was quick, but then after a pause, he continued in a softer voice with less conviction, "but it might also be Los Sangre. They have been simmering since Jenaro was killed ... or perhaps Mexikanemi from Texas, looking to expand here."

There was silence as Marco stared at the floor, clearly regretting his part in the conversation. Esteban's face was impassive but his eyes were on fire as he picked up the pistol again and repeatedly pulled the hammer back and held it as he squeezed the trigger to let it down softly. The quiet clicking of the gun's mechanism filled the room.

Clayton broke the silence, "Hmm ... before y'all start blastin' away, sounds to me like ya need to figure out if yer hunting a raccoon or a bear. Makin' that kinda mistake can rain down a world a' hurt.

There was another silence as the cool logic of Clayton's words washed over Esteban's rage and brought its flames down to smoking embers. He exhaled a sigh that was a mix of released tension and helpless frustration. "What, then, do you suggest?"

"Y'all need ta take a couple a' deep breaths and gather some solid intel on who might be behind this."

"Cotton, clearly our sources proved insufficient to warn us of the attack. I find it hard to believe that they are up to the task of discovering, with certainty, who was behind it." Esteban paused for a thoughtful moment. "However, you have good connections and could make some discreet inquiries."

"Now hold on there, partner. I make it a rule not to actively engage in my clients' operations."

Marco fidgeted in his chair. Although thwarted, the attack on the compound was a black mark on his performance as head of security. Thus far, Esteban had not turned his displeasure in Marco's direction. Breaking his silence, Marco attempted to reclaim some performance points by asserting his role as professional skeptic, "Jefe, how could he be able to find out more than we could on our own?"

"Because, Marco, Mr. Parish has a reputation for keeping his engagements with his clients very confidential. At this point, no one knows he is working for me." Esteban was warming to the idea as it became clearer in his mind. "As far as the outside world is concerned, he has, how would he say, 'no dog in this hunt.' He's a nobody. That, combined with his contacts and cyber skills, gives us the best shot at filling in our intelligence gap."

"I'm still in the room, fellas, and as I said, I don't get involved in my clients' activities."

"Well Cotton, Marco tells me that there are at least four men whose lives came to a dramatic end this morning because of your—involvement." Esteban smiled as he played his trump card. "And as grateful as I am, I'm sure you would rather not have word of your exploits become well known among our circle of common acquaintances."

It was Clayton's turn to squirm. Staring down at the parqueted floor, he tapped his fingers on his knees, outwardly giving every indication that he was being forced into an extremely uncomfortable position. Inwardly, he was thrilled at how the conversation had taken Esteban exactly where Clayton wanted him to be. "Well, ya got me there." He took a long breath. "It's not what I have ever signed on to do, but if you give me a few days, I can at least tap into my network and scope out the chatter."

Esteban started cocking and uncocking the pistol again. He half sat on the edge of his desk, looked briefly at a dejected Marco, and then stared out at the gardens and the ocean beyond. It was clear that he was balancing his visceral need to take murderous action against the wisdom of this new idea. After a long two minutes, he put the gun gently on the desktop. "Bueno. Cotton, you have three days to identify the attackers."

"Okay—I'll need the use of one a' yer boats."

"Why do you—" Marco interjected, trying to participate in the conversation.

"'Cause these are my clients, Marco, MY contacts. 'cause I don't like this one least bit and I want my conversations t'be completely free from any possibility of eavesdroppin'. And if I find a bug on the boat, the deal's off."

"That you would think that we—" Marco's indignation appeared to be real.

"Stow it, Marco. I'm not saying that you did or didn't do anything. I'm just saying the security of this place has provin' ta be a bit, ah … porous."

Marco appeared ready to leap from his seat in protest, but with a wave of his hand, Esteban cut short any further discussion of the matter. "The boat—when do you need it?"

"Tomorrah at dawn."

"It will be at your disposal, fueled and ready at the boathouse. And—" Esteban turned his gaze pointedly at Marco, "it will be free of any listening devices." He turned back to Clayton. "What else?"

"That'll do fer now. I'll git started first thing tomorrah. Now I'm goin' back to my room. I'm feelin' a bit tuckered out, and I gotta put some thought into how I'm gonna approach my contacts on this."

****

While his body had always speedily rebounded from illness or injury, Clayton knew he had to give it the rest it needed to do its job. After a brief side trip to the kitchen to collect a sandwich and some fruit, he made his way back to his bedroom. He noted the extra effort it took to climb the stairs.

When he reached his room, he closed the door and sat at his laptop, staring at the screen-saver. The image of a cowboy, waving a wide-brimmed Stetson while riding a bucking computer, was pure Cotton Parish. He couldn't help but smile as he logged in and prepared a short message that would be encrypted, fragmented, and embedded in the next few regular short burst data messages that were ostensibly being sent to test the estate's online performance. It was through these SBD messages that Clayton updated his support team.

February 21 - Early morning

As usual, Clayton was up before sunrise. He'd benefited from a restful night's sleep and felt almost fully fit. Although his arm ached, he decided against taking any of the pain meds that Dr. Vega had left with him. It promised to be a full day and he would need a clear head.

He took a quick look at the bandage. The small dark red stain showed that it should be changed which made that the first order of business for the day. He quickly dressed, packed his day-pack, and headed down the stairs, encouraged by how well his healing body responded. As he reached the main floor, he heard the faint sound of voices mingling with the slow, steady ticks and tocks of the foyer's great clock. He followed the voices to the kitchen. The heavy door was closed, making it impossible to make out what was being said, but one voice was raised. As he quietly pushed the door open, he saw Carmen sitting at the table at the far end of the room with Rosa and Roberto. Carmen's face was flushed and tears were streaming down her cheeks. As she spoke, she beat her fist hard on the massive butcher-block table, appearing to use the pain to reinforce her rage and frustration.

She directed her anger first at Rosa, "Por qué?" and then at Roberto, "Por qué, Roberto? Por qué? Why didn't you tell me? All those men—dead."

Roberto shifted in his chair, wincing both at the pain from his wound and at the hurt from Carmen's words. He stared at the floor, wishing it would swallow him as he dissolved under Carmen's whithering assault.

Rosa waited for Carmen to take a breath. She reached across the table, caught Carmen's fist as it landed on the tabletop a final time, and spoke softly, "Because cariño mio, if you knew and if Esteban found out that you knew—"

At that moment, Roberto looked up and saw Clayton. "Se…señor Parish—"

"Mornin' y'all," Clayton stepped out of the shadows and flashed his most disarming smile. "I don't mean t' butt in, folks. I'm just lookin' for some bandages and would sure like a cup a' that coffee I smell a-brewin'."

"Señor Parish—buenos días," Rosa's tone was warm as she greeted Clayton. "Come sit with us." She stood and pulled out a chair as an invitation. "Let me get you your cup of coffee."

As Rosa busied herself fetching Clayton's coffee, Clayton read the look on Roberto's face and saw a mix of hope and relief. He turned his gaze to Carmen and caught her wiping her eyes with the back of her hand. She pulled her shoulders back and sat straight up in her chair, resolutely reestablishing the facade of quiet determination and noble aloofness that were the walls of her fortress. Her emerald-green eyes shining from the remnants of her tears and the reassertion of her character rose to meet Clayton's.

"Thank you, Mister Parish. Rosa and Roberto have told me all that you have done for them—and, of course, for me."

"Carmen, you know my name's Cotton. I reckon we are well into first-name territory. Wouldn't ya say?" The tone in Clayton's voice was kind and caring, but as he spoke, he was looking for some reaction that would confirm his uncertain memory of the preceding day's encounter in his bedroom. He wasn't disappointed, as a half smile and an accompanying red glow spread across Carmen's face.

"Yes, thank you ... Cotton."

"Here is your coffee, señor Parish." A broad smile accompanied Rosa's eager-to-please words as she placed a mug of the steaming liquid on the table. "Now, por favor, let me change your bandage."

"Well, thank ya kindly, Rosa. I'd be much obliged fer the help." Clayton saw that Roberto appeared to have come from beneath the table where he had mentally hidden himself. "How're ya doin', Roberto? Mendin' okay?"

"Si, señor Parish. I am stiff and the wound pains me, but Rosa is a good nurse, and she has reported that I am sick so I can keep out of sight for a time while it heals."

"Hah! I figure we're both pretty darn lucky we're not better shots," Clayton offered good-naturedly.

"Si, Senior. It is true," Roberto agreed, and then added with a sly smile, "I clearly need more practice."

"You can make a joke of it, but both of you have the angels to thank for being alive." Still impassioned, Carmen's voice assumed a tone of strength and authority. "Escuchame! Listen to me! It is important that you," her laser-green eyes bore into Clayton and then turned to Rosa and Roberto, "all of you, understand me. While my heart is full of gratitude for those who believe they are acting in my best interests, I tell you now, they must stop! My life is difficult enough, worrying about my children, without the added burden of being the cause of so much harm to others."

Roberto's eyes sought the tabletop again as Carmen turned to him. "What did you and they hope to accomplish, Roberto?" And then her words skewered Rosa, "Did you and they really think that simply leaving here with my children would make us free? He is who he is and I know him well. He would find us wherever we went and while he was searching, he would cut a bloody path through all those who I hold in my heart."

The room was thick with shared secrets so Clayton felt safe in risking a partial exposure of his own. He reached across the table and took an unresisting Carmen's hand. "What if there were a way to bring you and your children to safety? I know some people who could help with that."

There was silence as Clayton saw the determination in her green eyes waver into wistfulness and then reassert itself. She pulled her hand away abruptly. "No! No more! I will stay. And for my children, I will make a bubble of happiness and light in this kingdom of gloom and darkness!" She turned to Rosa and

Roberto. "You must carry that message to my parents—" she again turned to Clayton, "and anyone else who might wish to be involved. Anyone who truly cares for us will understand."

"Si, señora," Rosa and Roberto reluctantly acknowledged Carmen's wishes. Clayton had no credible rebuttal. He slid his hand back across the table in quiet resignation.

———∞———

February 21 - Out to Sea

The rising sun warmed his back as Clayton made his way down to the boathouse. Like a giant, sleeping dog, the ocean surged and receded, making contented noises as it lapped at the shore. As he entered the boathouse Clayton saw that Esteban had been true to his promise. There was a boat prepped and ready to go in the main slip. The trim craft, about 27 ft by Clayton's estimation, was an exquisite combination of speed and luxury. A finely finished wooden name-board was affixed to the bow toe-rail. The carved name *Rápida* served as both a name and an assertion.

Eager to feel the familiar uncertainty of a moving deck, he hopped aboard and made his way to the canopied control console. He had brought a day-pack loaded with some water, fruit, and sandwiches that an enthusiastically grateful Rosa had prepared for him. Shedding the pack, he placed it on the passenger seat while he scanned the controls. He easily digested the layout and, seeing that the key was in the ignition, he pressed the starter buttons for the port and starboard engines. A low growl signaled the first engine's enthusiastic obedience and was joined by a second rumbling voice. Clayton listened as the engines synced with each other. Satisfied, he went to the bow and then the stern, untying each dock line, tossing them onto the dock. He resumed his place at the controls and, putting the engines into reverse, he eased the boat out of the slip into the bay. After clearing the boathouse he shifted into forward, brought the wheel hard over, and gradually increased the speed until he was skimming over the calm morning water, happily motoring out into the Pacific.

The assignment to reach out to his contacts was the perfect cover for Clayton to connect with his handler and case officer on SANDCASTLE, Special Agent Debra O'Donnell. Of course, meeting in person was too risky but buried in staged phone conversations with other of Cotton Parish's "clients" the conversation with Deb would be inconspicuous. A satellite phone with sophisticated encryption would ensure that its signal would be unintelligible to any eavesdroppers. Further precautions included scanning the boat for bugs, taking her out, way beyond the range of parabolic listening devices, and keeping the engines growling while he made his calls would neutralize bugs and other snooping devices he might have missed. These precautions were comfortably consistent with Cotton Parish's reputation for extreme confidentially.

The boat's speed pushed the salt-laced wind and occasional spray onto the windscreen and the joy of being on the water pulled Clayton's lips into the beginnings of a smile. He had been brought up with a love of sailing and that ardor had only grown with the passing of the years. In harmony with wind, waves, and current, he felt, at once, grounded and free. While the roaring engines prevented any confusion with the quietude of sailing, being on the water in any type of craft brought Clayton connection, perspective, and renewal. After a short time, he gave up sitting in the cockpit chair and stood at the wheel, the better to feel the spray on his face and the thumping rhythm pump at his legs and pulse through his body as *Rápida*, happily delivering on her name, cut through the water. With no defined course, and appreciating the speed that sails could not deliver, he motored with his back to the shoreline, going much further out into the Pacific than his primary purpose required.

After a time, he pulled the twin throttles back and as the boat slowed, he allowed them to idle in neutral. After scanning the horizon to be sure there was no craft nearby, he pulled the sat phone out of his day-pack, dialed a number, and was immediately rewarded with the sound of Deb's voice.

"Hello, sailor. Everything okay?" Deb's referring to him as a sailor reminded Clayton of the tracking device in the sat phone.

"Ship-shape, Deb. So the GPS is working."

"Aye, it shows you to be about four miles off the coast, west of Malibu. What's going on? We saw some excitement there yesterday."

There were prearranged signals that confirmed that Clayton was not in trouble. The direction he turned as he took his daily walk on the beach or whether he went to the water's edge or stayed further up on the sand told watchers he was not in any immediate trouble. The signals communicated the most fundamental status but were designed not to raise suspicion. This, however, was the first time that Clayton could have an actual conversation with Deb.

"Yeah, that was, uh … unexpected." Clayton briefed Deb on the details of the attack, his activities, and observations. He shared his assessment that Carmen could become a valuable witness, leaving out the more intimate details of their encounter in his room.

"Over the past few days, we collected a treasure trove of information, Clayton. And the spyware you've installed promises to keep on delivering. The operation has been so successful that more than once the higher-ups have remarked that you could spend an entire career going from client to client impersonating Cotton Parish."

"Now, wait a minute, Deb, that wasn't—"

"I'm just teasin', Clayton. Yeah, they talk about it, but in 'what if' terms, the way we might talk about 'what if JFK hadn't been assassinated?' Nah, the Bureau got more than it wanted and there were promises made to you and to Mr. Parish."

"Crap, Deb! Cut the bullshit! Some things you just don't joke about!" The op was putting too much of Clayton's real life at risk and now his typical laid-back demeanor was starting to fray under the strain. It wasn't the physical danger that was most worrisome.

Deb realized that she had crossed a line. "I'm so sorry, Clayton. That was stupid. I know you're eager to be getting' home and—"

"Eager doesn't begin to describe it, Deb! I'm feeling really adrift here! The better I am at playing this role, the more detached I become from the life I had! Home, Maggie, and Anthony are memories, becoming less real every day!"

Deb had known Clayton for years and heard the uncharacteristic emotion in his voice. "I hear you, Clayton. It's time for you to come home. Let's work on how to get that done."

"Okay—let's!" Embarrassed by his overreaction, Clayton's outburst was passing like a summer storm. The last faint rumblings faded in the distance. "Sorry for taking your head off."

"Me too—are we okay?"

"Yeah, Deb. We're fine." The storm had passed. Clayton, able to focus once again, quipped wryly, "Let's git 'er done!"

The whole team understood that SANDCASTLE had clear operational requirements around Clayton's exit from his undercover role. In close priority order, his extraction had to:

> Extricate him safely
>
> Preserve his cover as Cotton Parish even after his departure
>
> Protect the real Cotton Parish from any reprisals
>
> Preserve and optimize the value of his time undercover.

Although an operational plan and several contingencies had been laboriously worked out before Clayton had been inserted, the best combination of them had to be seamlessly molded to accommodate Clayton's first-hand observations. Taking full advantage of the time they could spend in unmonitored conversation, Deb and Clayton worked on a stratagem that would deliver on all the operational mandates. At the end of three hours, they felt they had a plan that they could bring to the ops team for feasibility assessment, tuning, and resource allocation.

"Do you see any chance at all o' bringing out Carmen and the wee ones?" Deb asked the question even though she knew the answer.

"Nah, she's right. She would leave behind too many targets for Esteban's rage. It's a complicated set of moving parts that would be dangerous to pull into this op without proper planning. We can get back in touch with her after we solidify our go-forward thinking. But I would like to leave her with a hot-line contact number so she can get help if her situation red-lines."

"Makes sense. I'll bring it to E.Z. but I'm sure he'll agree." There was a long pause in the conversation. "We did a good bit of work here today." Deb shifted gears and her tone was upbeat. "E.Z. will be pleased."

"I got the impression that he might occasionally be satisfied but that not much pleases the guy."

"You're bein' too rough on him, Clayton. He's very impressed with how the op is going, with what you've been able to pull off, especially with how little time you had to prepare."

"Well, playing a darker version of myself has been, in some ways, easier than I thought it would be, but it's been—is— surreal. It's not like any other undercover role I've ever played. In those others, I was playing a part, a character that was distinctly not me. It was always easy to keep myself separated from the role."

"So?"

"This time it's different, Deb. Cotton isn't just a mask anymore. He goes deeper. An extra ounce or two of flash, a smattering or two less of duty, and a degree or two southerly adjustment of the moral compass and I could have been Cotton."

"I know this must have been hard on you, having a false identity not only be a real person but one so similar in many life experiences and so different in the essence of who you both are."

"Yeah, maybe, but that's not what bothers me the most." Clayton paused. The need to confide, to be less alone, struggled to push through the thick cocoon that had always kept his innermost essence secret, at times, even from himself.

"Well, if it's not being someone you're not, what is it, Clayton?" Deb's tone was sympathetic. Her words encouraged him to respond honestly.

"Sometimes, Deb, not always, but sometimes, when I'm really into him, being Cotton Parish becomes the most natural thing in the world—", Clayton's defensive filters kicked in just in time and he finished the sentence in his head, "—and I like it."

There was an even longer pause. Deb's unspoken concern crackled over the sat phone like static.

Sensing that he had shared too much, Clayton shook off his reflective musings. "It's okay, Deb. The sea always makes me introspective. I'm not going off the rails. Just out on the water sharing some thoughts with a friend. But in the end, I've got to say, it will be really good to go home."

Clayton wrapped up the conversation, doing his best to dispel any lingering concerns that Deb might have. They said their goodbyes and agreed to talk the next day. Clayton signed off, put the engines in gear, and turned for *El Mirador*.

——•⟨∞⟩•——

February 21 - Back on Shore

It was almost noon when Clayton brought *Rápida* back to her home berth. Marco was waiting for him on the dock and watched imposingly with his arms crossed as Clayton skillfully motored toward the boathouse. The typical approach would have been to slow down early and then gently reverse the engines to bring the boat to a smooth stop in the slip. Noting Marco's intimidating posture, Clayton came in faster and reversed engines harder than he normally would. The maneuver had its desired effect. The following wake caught up with the boat and the floating dock pitched as the wave rolled under it. Marco lost his balance and had to clumsily reach out to one of the pilings to prevent himself from falling. Ignoring the flustered Marco, Clayton killed the engines, lightly hopped onto the settling dock, dropped his day-pack onto the aluminum planks, and began to tie a docking line to the bow cleat of the boat.

"Where did you go?" Marco's gruff tone conveyed his irritation.

In answer, Clayton continued with his chore and, without looking at Marco, pointed out into the open water of the Pacific. Finished with the bow line, he moved to the stern of the boat and began to cleat that line. His silent response brought a red flush to Marco's face.

"You were out too far. We lost sight of you. What were you doing?"

Finished securing the boat, Clayton stood and took a step closer to Marco, who tensed at the potential threat. Only a few inches separated them as they stared, unblinking, into each other's eyes. After a long, very uncomfortable moment, Clayton winked, smiled then picked up his day-pack, walked off the dock and up the stairs to the main house, leaving Marco on the dock with his jaw locked and his fists clenched in anger.

There was no strategic value in antagonizing Marco, but it had been a good morning. The wheels were in motion to get him out and pissing off Marco just felt good. It wasn't something that Clayton Rhodes would do. Clayton shook his head. He would be glad to say goodbye to Cotton Parish.

****

Pushing the ornate, wrought-iron doors open, he walked through the lobby into the informal dining area. He had finished the snack in his daypack hours before. It was lunchtime and being out on the water always made him hungry. His stomach growled its delight as he saw that he hadn't missed the lunch buffet. He loaded his plate with a healthy portion of sea bass and sides and headed out to the dining table on the lanai. He hesitated for just a moment when he saw Esteban seated at the table.

He quickly made the mental adjustment that allowed him to once again channel Cotton Parish. "Well howdy there, Esteban. How's it goin'?"

Esteban looked up from his tablet and smiled the wide, well-rehearsed smile that was now familiar to Clayton. "Ah, Cotton, what news do you have for me?"

Clayton set his plate on the table, pulled out a chair, and sat down, using the time to consider his answer. "Well, I planted the seeds and I expect we'll be hearin' back pretty quick. The folks I spoke with were none too happy about my line of questioning. Some turned me down flat and others said they'd have to think about it. I'll be following up with them and reaching out to a few more tomorrah. I'm not the nervous sort, but I got ta' say, Esteban, you got me playin' a dangerous tune on the devil's own fiddle."

"The devil's own … there are times I find your quaint Texas sayings to be charmingly entertaining. At other times, they become annoying. In English Cotton, what are you saying?"

It was clear that Esteban was being deliberately obtuse in order to assert his cultural superiority over the homespun Cotton Parish and Clayton spiced his reply with unveiled irritation. "What I'm sayin' Esteban, is that I've enjoyed a unique, untouchable status in the world we both inhabit. What created an' preserves that status is a need fer my particular skills and an unspoken understandin' that I am in no way a player on the field. Like the sea, I float all boats without favor, a friend ta all. The minute I'm viewed as joinin' any particular crew, of takin' on any nation's flag, so to speak, I become a friend to that one and a threat to everyone else."

"You make too much of your role in this business, Cotton." Esteban's voice took on a reassuring inflection, and he accompanied his comment with a dismissive wave. "Find me the information I need and you will not have to work for anyone else ever again." He paused and then, in a much darker tone, added, "And besides, you have no choice."

"I have enough money, Esteban, and as my daddy would say, 'A fly that drowns in honey is no happier than one that drowns in vinegar.' But yer right. Ya leave me no choice."

Clayton picked at his food for a few moments in silence and then, making a display of his lost appetite, he pushed his plate away, stood, and looked down at Esteban. "I hope this all goes the right way." Without waiting for a reply, he turned and left.

Esteban's lips shaped themselves into a small, smug smile and as he walked away Clayton couldn't suppress an unseen, similar reaction.

———⊷⊶———

February 22 - The Coming Storm

During the next day's trip out into the Pacific, Clayton and Deb worked on the details of his extraction. E.Z. gave the plan they had worked out a green light and the ops team was putting the required pieces together. Deb and Clayton spent the bulk of their talk time going over the specific logistics of the action. Deb gave Clayton the hot-line number she got from E.Z.

When Clayton returned to *El Mirador,* he once again sought out the lunch buffet and then the lanai. Esteban was sitting in the same seat as the day before. Without waiting for an invitation, Clayton joined him.

Esteban looked up from his plate, his forkful of salmon suspended in mid-air. "Qué pasa?" By his tone, and the intensity of his gaze, Esteban made clear that his use of the phrase was less a cordial greeting and more a demand for information.

Clayton sat and took the time to savor a taste of his lunch while considering his answer.

"The ones that have gotten back ta me say they'll have an answer tomarrah."

The growing tension in Esteban's face eased, and he placed his fork back onto the plate. "Well, that sounds like good news. We will have our information then."

"I didn't say that. As a matter of fact, the way they said it left me belivin' that there's more storm than sun in the forecast."

"In English, Cotton, in English! What do you mean?"

"I mean, these guys didn't say it in so many words, but I'm thinkin' my questions have kicked over an anthill."

"Again, in English!"

Exasperation spiced Clayton's response, "I believe, Esteban, that this was a very bad move for me and that these guys, at least a few of them, are seriously pissed off."

"But you don't know that for certain."

"No, but I feel it like my momma could feel the comin' of the first hard frost."

"But you'll talk to them tomorrow." Esteban, so eager for answers, attempted a commanding tone but could only manage pleading encouragement.

"Yes, Esteban, I'll talk to them tomorrow." Clayton loaded his muted response with feigned resignation. "I jes hope they're in a talkin' mood. Keep yer phone on. I'll call you when I know somethin'"

"Si, I will! Do not worry, Cotton. It will all be good."

February 23 - The Setup

Early the next morning Clayton, with everything he didn't want to leave behind already packed, was at the desk in his room nibbling the end of a pencil and staring at a blank sheet of stationery. Finally, with a clear idea in mind and a bad taste in his mouth, he scratched at the page. A few minutes later, he leaned back and studied his work. Satisfied, he folded the page, printed a phone number on the outside, then put it in his pocket. Shouldering his day bag, and taking one last look around, he left the room, silently closing the door behind him. As he walked down the hall, he paused at Carmen's bedroom door for a long moment with the folded page in his hand. Just as he was raising his hand to knock, the door opened. Carmen's startled look mirrored his own.

She was the first to recover enough to speak. "Cotton. Good morning. Why were you—"

"I wanted ... needed to speak to you." He took her unresisting arm, led her back into her room, and shut the door.

"Some things will mos' likely be happenin' today that may keep me from bein' here any longer."

"What are you talking about? Wh...what things?"

"I can't explain now, but I want you t'know that you and the kids have grown ta mean a lot ta me. I want y'all to be safe."

"Cotton, I told you that I can't. Not now. It would leave too many people I care about exposed. His anger is like a volcano. It destroys everything."

"But you—the children. They can't grow up anywhere near this man."

"I appreciate your caring. I do. But I know what's best for me and my children. I will know when it is safe to leave, and it is not now."

Clayton knew he had no real hope of changing her mind even at the start of the conversation, but he had to try.

"Carmen, yer a special lady and I hope yer path leads to a happy endin'. Here's somethin' to remember me by." He handed her the folded page. "The phone number belongs to my ... analyst. She's helped me through some rough times and if things get ta be too much fer ya, I'm shur she'll be able ta help. Just mention my name. I told her you might be callin' someday." He pressed the folded page into her hand, then pulled her to him. She willingly stepped into his embrace as he kissed her long and hard. After a short eternity, he pulled away. "Give ma love ta the kids, Carmen. It's been good knowin' ya." With those final words, he pulled the door open, and after checking the hallway, stepped through, and closed it behind him, leaving Carmen to ponder what had just happened.

Clayton turned away from the door and continued silently down the stairs, past the great clock in the lobby, and out the door. He made his way through the garden and across the lawn. The early morning light brought soft definition to the shapes of the statues, trees, and shrubs. As he walked, he briefly thought of his time at *El Mirador* and its complicated inhabitants, whose lives had become entangled with his own. Quickly though, he turned his mental energy to the day's coming events.

Complex and challenging, the plan was an adrenaline-rich mix of strategic thinking, tactical proficiency, and deceptive performance art. The chill of the morning air combined with the thrill of nervous anticipation sent a shiver through his body as he approached the edge of the lawn and looked out over a white-capped Pacific. An offshore wind had blown up overnight, tickling the sea into disturbed wakefulness.

This weather will keep Carmen and the kids away from the beach today.

The thought pulled him back to those he was leaving behind. He turned and once again looked at the main house. The unlit windows suggested that he was the only one who was up and about, but he knew the house was alive with secrets and dark energies that never slept. He knew Carmen was up waiting, hoping for some day's rising sun to brighten her overcast world. He couldn't see the kitchen window, but he knew Rosa and Roberto were tending to their morning chores and whispering their concerns and confidences. Several times during his nighttime explorations, Clayton had heard Esteban call out in his sleep. He knew that he took an increasing number of pills to beat back the monsters that hunted him through his nightmares. Then too there were the ever-vigilant watchers, security patrols making their rounds or observing him on the security room monitors. They knew him, so his face-to-face encounters with them were always brief, a nod of recognition or an occasional murmured greeting. In a house so full of secrets, unlit windows were poor proof of peace.

The rising sun silhouetted the buildings and painted the sky with a palette of crimson hues ranging from flaming coral to blood red. The sailor's adage warning about red skies in the morning played in his head. Turning his back on the house and sun, he began his descent down to the boathouse.

****

He boarded the *Rápida* and cast off the lines for the last time. Firing up the engines, he keyed coordinates into the GPS unit, and then spoke to the boat, as some sailors do. "Sorry, girl, you deserve better than what you will get today, but it has to be, and it's for a good cause."

The outbound ride was rougher than in the past two days and in its own way more exhilarating. Clayton opened the throttles, so that *Rápida* thudded over the tops of the white-crested waves, flinging spray far to each side. Occasionally, she would shatter a larger swell and send its broken bits over the bow and into the cockpit. Standing at the wheel, with the spray on his face, Clayton smiled broadly rejoicing at this moment of uncomplicated excitement and his imminent freedom.

He kept his eye on the compass and the GPS. Today, his course wasn't random but set for a specific rendezvous point that he and Deb had arranged the day before. After thirty minutes of motoring, the alarm on the navigation panel signaled his arrival. He idled the engines, pulled his sat phone out of his pack, and placed it securely into one of the cup holders. Then he sat with his feet up and his eyes closed, letting his mind empty as it rolled with the swells. After a fifteen-minute wait, the phone buzzed to life. Startled, he grabbed it faster than was necessary, answering it on the second ring.

"Sandcastle Knight." There was little likelihood that his use of his operation code name was necessary, but he followed protocol.

"Sandcastle Fleet. We're ten minutes out bearing 180 degrees. You should see us any second."

"Is that you, Deb? So, you decided to get your feet wet." As he talked, Clayton was scanning the horizon to the south. Two small objects came into view.

"I wouldn't miss it, sailor. It's going to be quite a show."

"I see you. There's no one else out here. It's pretty lousy weather for recreational boating."

The two 15-foot Zodiacs closed the distance with impressive speed, pulled up to the *Rápida*, one on each side, and tied bow and stern lines to the larger boat's cleats. Deb accepted Clayton's outstretched hand and lightly pulled herself up from the first boat to tie on.

"Welcome aboard." Clayton smiled as he threw a secured line to each Zodiac to help the rest of the crews move easily from boat to boat.

"Thank you, Captain." Deb returned the smile and made a show of a snappy salute. "It's good to be here. How are things at the house?" Playing along, Clayton grinned and returned the salute.

"Hell, Esteban has high expectations of this trip. He was so wound up, I thought he was going to piss in his pants. I've got him glued to his phone, waiting for news."

"Sweet, he'll be sure to see the show."

Without waiting for instructions, the three crew members of each boat began attaching dozens of small explosive charges all over *Rápida's* hull, spacing them randomly from just below the waterline up to the toerail. These charges would be triggered remotely at the proper moment.

One of the techs lifted the engine compartment cowling. He pulled a larger charge out of a separate box and, bracing himself against the pitching of the boat, leaned into the compartment and attached it to the side that held the gas tank. When he finished his chore, he approached Deb and Clayton.

"The charge is set, ma'am." He then turned to Clayton and handed him a small, round, plastic cylinder attached to a looped lanyard. It had a red button on top and a cotter pin running through it just below the button. "This is your bang button, sir. Pull the pin to arm it. Then be sure you're well away within 7 seconds after you push the button. Copy?"

"Copy that. What's the blast radius?" Clayton took the detonator, studied it for a moment, then, using the lanyard, hung it around his neck and tucked it into his shirt.

"50 feet"—the tech grinned—"give or take."

Clayton smiled at the attempt at humor. "Got it. Thanks."

"Good luck, sir, not that you'll need it. It's a good plan."

Clayton knew that the young agent was trying to be encouraging. He scanned the embroidered name on his shirt. "Thanks, Agent … Chou, but I'll take good luck over a good plan any day."

Deb had moved to the stern to examine the transom door that, once opened, allowed easy access to the swimboard. She had studied pictures of the *Rápida* but wanted to confirm her impressions.

"Looks like an easy way off."

"Yup. I'll be able to stay low and out of sight."

Chou had joined the rest of his crew as they finished planting the charges. Deb and Clayton watched as they turned their attention to a large black plastic bag on the bottom of one of the Zodiacs.

"So that's our first silent crew member?" There was more observation than question in Clayton's voice.

"Yup. He's definitely a man of few words."

Two members of the team hopped into the Zodiac and strained to lift the body bag up to waiting hands on the deck of the *Rápida*. Once it was on deck, the group gathered around as Agent Chou unzipped and pulled the top flap open. The body inside was that of a man whose facial features bore no resemblance to Clayton but whose size and build were similar.

Clayton looked down at his co-star. "Do we know his name and how he—" Clayton trailed off before finishing his question.

"Nah, E.Z. put in the request and this is who we got." Deb studied the corpse's face. "Can't say he looks a lot like you. There are no signs of trauma."

"We're going to have to fix that." Clayton's observation was clinical. He resisted the temptation to linger over the chain of events that brought this body to this moment.

"Right. Chou, you and Flemming prop him up against the gunwale. Rodriguez, get your weapon." The men moved quickly to comply with Deb's directive. "Okay, everyone, stand clear. Rodriguez, give him a burst across his chest."

"A burst across the chest," Rodriguez acknowledge the order, "Yes, ma'am." He pulled the bolt back, aimed, and depressed the trigger for less than a second. The air was briefly filled with the signature chatter of an AK47 and the nose-wrinkling smell of gunpowder. The result was five holes stitched across the dead man's torso and the side of the boat he was propped against.

Clayton nodded his satisfaction. "Okay, Deb. Is his ID all set?"

"Yep, for any of the curious and all of the determined, all sources of information say he is, or was, Cotton Parish. May he rest in peace."

"I see we got the colors right."

"Yep. Your pants and shirts match with Cotton's here. I don't think we need to go any deeper than that." Clayton and the whole team joined in a collective guffaw. Clayton had coordinated with Deb on the most visible shirt that he had available. It was primarily orange and since he had worn it in the compound at least twice, it would be recognizable as his.

Chou stepped forward with an olive-colored t-shirt similar to what the whole team was wearing. Clayton quickly took off his shirt, slipped on the t-shirt, and once again donned his outer shirt. Chou handed him a Beretta 9mm handgun.

"Blank loads, sir. 15 in the mag and one in the chamber."

Clayton removed the magazine and checked its contents. After replacing it, he pulled back on the ejector and checked the round in the chamber.

"All good, Chou, Thanks."

"What about our other cast member?"

Deb pointed to the bottom of the other boat. There, dressed to look like one of the team, was a realistic-looking mannequin. "Clayton, meet Ahab."

"Why Ahab?"

"Well, it seemed appropriate. They're both destined for watery graves. He's decked out to look like one of us, and he'll be riding in full view. At the right time, he'll go over the side. He's weighted so he'll sink like a stone."

Clayton nodded his appreciation of Deb's review of that part of the plan. He turned to the team. "Run it all down for me one last time."

With confident smiles on their faces, and Chou creating beat noises out of the crook of his elbow, they recited the op plan in unison and in rap rhythm.

"2 miles out and our team appears. Lookout!
Clayton makes a call and our first burst starts the brawl.
Clayton shoots his gun and ol' Ahab's dead and done.
A second burst by heck and Clayton hits the deck.
Shed your shirt. Push the button. Slide off at the stern.
Third burst is the biggest one. And poor *Rápida* burns.
Pick him up! Pick him up! Get Clayton in the boat!
Now it's time to run away. The bad guy is the goat!"

The team looked at Clayton expectantly. Clayton was prepared to hear a dry rundown of the operation. The humorous display of team spirit was just what was needed to cut the tension and his rare laugh mingling with the team's came from deep inside him, sweeping away all doubts.

"Are we good to go, then?" Deb looked to Clayton for the final word.

Clayton took a moment to mentally tick off the critical elements of the plan. He scanned the sky and the sea. It was mid-morning. The sun was partially hidden by scudding clouds and the wind was up enough to drive small swells. All in all, it was not a great day for recreational boating, but nearly perfect for their purposes. They were timing their arrival to be in close view of *El Mirador* at lunch, ensuring that Esteban would have a front-row seat for the show.

"Yup, Deb. We're good." Clayton's adrenaline was flowing now, and it kick-started his enthusiasm. He took a breath and let it show. "Yeeha! Let's git 'er done!"

"Yeeha!" The whole team joined in the impromptu battle cry except for the newly christened Cotton Parish, who sat silently propped against the gunwale.

⸺⸙⸺

February 23 - The Show

Although Esteban enjoyed being served dinner, at lunch he preferred the freedom of choice that a buffet provided. Propelled, in part, by memories of his deprived youth, he had eagerly embraced the habits of lavish living. He was never in the least bit concerned about the large amount of food prepared for him that he didn't consume. Today's lunch choices included sliced baked ham and roast beef, smoked trout, and salads. He chose the fish. Although he insisted on choices, he always chose the fish. He took a small side of salad and a slice of stone-milled dark bread. Without any conscious attention to nutrition, he ate a healthy diet, another legacy of his indigent early years.

He took his plate out to his customary seat on the lanai. Placing his phone on the table, he brought his tablet to life and started to read his emails while trying to enjoy his meal. What was always a time of rest and rejuvenation in the middle of the day was falling far short of that. Today, anticipation and anxiety hung in the air, forcing him to focus on events taking place out beyond the haze-shrouded horizon. He knew Clayton had left in the early hours and had watched from his bedroom as the *Rápida* had motored out to sea. Clayton had been returning from his outings about this time of day, and Esteban alternately scanned the horizon and checked to see if his phone was working. It was not his concern for Clayton's safety that was so unsettling. It was the need to release his pent-up anger, to apply the balm of retribution to his wounded ego. Esteban expected that this time, Clayton would bring back the answer to the question of who would be the target of his revenge, the recipient of his rage.

He picked up his tablet, stared at the screen, and then put it down again. Finally, unable to quell his nervous tension, he pocketed his phone, abandoned his lunch, and walked down the steps of the lanai, through the gardens, and out to the edge of the bluff overlooking the beach. The visibility was not the best today. Scattered clouds took turns choking the light from the sky and the wind pulled spindrift from the tops of the white-capped waves, muting the scene in a soft haze. He stood on the cliff, staring out at the sea. After a few minutes, Marco joined him, and the two watched, for a time, in silence.

Esteban spoke first, more to himself than his companion, "We will have an answer today. We will know where to bring the hammer down and then—we will crush them!"

"Si, jefe, and we will be able to be rid of señor Cotton."

"You don't like him, Marco, but he has been very helpful and if he delivers today, he will have earned his bonus."

Marco had brought high-powered binoculars with him and, as he was talking, he was scanning the horizon.

"I think I see him." After another moment, he added, "Yes, it's the *Rápida*."

As the boat drew closer even without binoculars, Esteban could see it was the *Rápida*. A few moments more and he could make out Clayton at the helm. Suddenly, two Zodiacs appeared out of the mist at a high rate of speed. Their clear intent was to intercept the *Rápida.*

At that moment, Esteban's phone forced a few bars of a lively Colombian folk tune through its small speakers. Even in ordinary circumstances, the unpleasant sound would be ample encouragement to answer the phone quickly.

"Hola!"

Clayton's voice was loud enough so that Marco could clearly hear both sides of the conversation. "It was a setup! I told you these rustlers were pissed! I'm comin' in hot! Git me some help! Now!"

Esteban nodded his approval to Marco, who immediately radioed to the boathouse for reinforcements.

The drama continued to play out in full view of Esteban, who had taken the binoculars from Marco. Clayton waved at the shore, signaling desperately for help. Esteban watched as the attacking boats closed the distance between them and the *Rápida*. When they were in effective range, their crews raised their rifles and opened fire. The sound of the guns was delayed by the distance and muffled by the mist, but the effect was immediately visible. Pieces of the *Rápida* flew off as the bullets raked her hull. Two boats from shore appeared, driving hard, leaping through the waves toward the battle, but it was clear that they were too far away to have any effect on the outcome.

A pistol appeared in Clayton's hand and he fired back. Pathetically outgunned, his return fire was somewhat effective if hopeless. As he emptied his magazine, one of the attackers tumbled into the churning water. A return burst of automatic weapon fire torn chunks of fiberglass from the *Rápida's* cockpit, and Clayton was violently thrown down, disappearing from view. The badly wounded *Rápida* slowed as the attacking boats mercilessly poured a third, long burst of deadly fire into her hull. Finally, the uneven battle ended as she disintegrated in a fiery ball that sent her flaming pieces high into the air. The attack boats lingered long enough to pluck the body of their fallen comrade from the water and then speed into the mist, leaving behind the smoking, debris-filled patch of water and the fast-approaching reinforcements from *El Mirador*.

****

From the balcony outside of her bedroom, Carmen watched the firefight through her own set of binoculars. The final explosion was much too far away for the blast to have any physical effect on her. Nonetheless, she staggered backward into her room and put her hand on the sliding glass door frame to steady herself. She stood there shaking for several moments and then willed her legs to bring her to a nearby chair. She sat down heavily, still staring out at the smoking water. Finally, unable to bear the sight of it any longer, she turned her gaze away and toward the room's interior, looking for any distraction. The folded page that Clayton had given her was lying on the table by her seat. She picked it up and for the first time opened it. She stared at it through misted eyes, but as she stared, her tense lips slowly relaxed and the hint of a smile formed. On the page was a rough but recognizable sketch of Carmen and the children on the beach looking out at the water and out some distance from the shore was the figure of a man standing on the water waving.

"Till we meet again, Cotton Parish. Vaya con Dios," Carmen whispered to the empty room. Then she pocketed the folded page and went down to join the children for lunch.

Part Four

February 2022 - Athena's Secrets

CHAPTER NINE

February 1 - What Tuesday Brought

Back to the Present

The MINDI monitor in Raymond's office went dark as Clayton's last memory of the SANDCASTLE operation faded into blackness. Completely enveloped in Clayton's reliving of his part in the SANDCASTLE operation, the sounds of battle and *Rápida's* final explosive end still ringing in their ears, Raymond and Aida were adjusting to the sudden shift back to present reality. The three of them removed their goggles and sat silently in the dimly lit room for a long time, each not able to break the spell that the adventure had cast over them. The MINDI technology provided an intensely immersive experience. Even in its condensed format, they had spent a full week of almost daily sessions living in Clayton's memories, and now each of them was processing the fallout.

Clayton was not immune to the impact of his relived adventures. The mental bandages that his psyche had applied to help heal the deepest wounds of the experience were torn off, leaving them to bleed anew. Although to the FBI, OPERATION SANDCASTLE was by every measure a success, Clayton would feel that there was unfinished business as long as Esteban walked free and Carmen and her children remained ensnared. The refreshed memory of his relationship with Carmen was a bitter cocktail when mixed with his grief over the loss of Maggie and Anthony.

As Clayton and the others struggled to readjust to the here-and-now, the applause from two pairs of hands in the darker recesses of the room announced that while they were deep in the sharing of Clayton's memories, others had joined them.

Max Corbel put her hand on her associate's knee. "Keaton, lights."

Keaton dutifully moved to the control panel on the wall. The tinting of the windows lightened, letting the early afternoon sun flood the room. Max stood and gently placed her goggles on her vacated seat.

"THAT was truly amazing!" Max viewed any interaction with other people as a competitive exercise. She had trained herself to regulate any signs of her emotions and used them only in such a way as to give her an edge in any conversation. It was notable that on this occasion, her enthusiasm seemed unfiltered and sincere. "I hope you don't mind. We let ourselves in. We didn't want to disturb you so we just slipped on a set of goggles and—Doctor Ababio, you and your ATHENA team should be proud. The MINDI technology is amazing, a true breakthrough."

"Yeah, pretty hot stuff, Doc." Keaton's expression was crude but came across as heartfelt.

Raymond ignored Keaton's remark and responded directly to Max. "Thank you, Max, but it was a team effort, and be certain that I will relay your comments."

"Oh, I'm sure they all contributed," she countered with a dismissive gesture, "but it has been your direction, your energy, and your genius that have delivered on our core vision. And I must say your AI creation is equally incredible, so lifelike, so … human."

Clayton saw Raymond stiffen.

"Thank you again, Max, but we have to get to work. We have a major debriefing to do and then a mountain of data to analyze."

"Well, I'll leave you to it. As I understand it, we have planned insertion for this Thursday." It was Clayton's turn to snap to attention as Max continued, "I'm counting on you, Doctor, to make sure there are no delays."

With that, she turned and waited for Keaton to open the door—and then they were gone.

Clayton's gaze bore into Raymond. "Okay Doc, what did she mean by insertion?"

Flustered by the entirety of Max's unexpected visit, Raymond's stammered answer undermined what could have been a more convincing lie. "Sh ... she was referring to the simulation I told you about." Warming up to his story, Raymond pressed on, "I didn't tell you about the timing because it depended on how well things went today."

"And how did things go today, Doc?" Clayton's voice signaled that he knew he wasn't getting the whole story.

"Amazingly well, Clayton." Raymond reached out for reinforcements. "What do you think, Aida?"

Clayton had never seen Aida show discomfort, or at least her portrayal of it, until that moment. Her eyes were downcast as she answered.

"I agree. It went very well." She raised her head to emphasize her next words. "Clayton, you were amazing."

"Do you think we can go forward on Thursday?"

She responded with less enthusiasm, "I'm ready if Clayton is."

"All right. Explain to me. How does this simulation work?"

Thankful to be on more solid ground, Raymond happily launched into a description of the plan for OPERATION HIGH TIDE.

"Although it is a simulation, we will run this operation as though it were real. Aida will be inserted into the Navarro household as a nanny for the children and helpmate to Carmen.

"The operation has two goals. The first is to apply a software patch to the transmitter that short-bursts data to the

FBI periodically. Since you installed it two years ago, it worked flawlessly until last month. We hope that a firmware upgrade will bring it back online.

"The second goal is to extract Carmen and the children safely."

Clayton couldn't help but smile at Raymond's amateurish description of the complicated operation. He looked at Aida's image and saw a similar reaction. She was quick to give some support to her floundering boss.

"Those are just the highlights. The details are addressed in an operation plan which will be waiting for you on your home computer.

"We have two days before my insertion. During that time, I would like your help in fine-tuning my cover story and a complete rundown of your take on the cast of characters at *El Mirador*." Her image leaned forward on her screen. "I'm eager to work with you on this operation, Clayton. This is what we've been working for."

The invitation for Clayton to express his enthusiastic engagement hung in the air for a long moment and then dissolved in the silence that followed.

"Clayton? What are you thinking?" Aida pressed without a hint of irritation.

"I'm thinking that I'm still not getting the straight story." Clayton shook his head slowly. "But that's not the headline. I'm playing a game but I haven't been told the rules. I don't know how to win or even what winning is. The worst part of it is that even though I'm surrounded by mysteries, I'm not doing what I've done my whole life. I'm not digging for clues, unraveling threads, or following leads. There's something artificial that's holding me back. There's a fog sitting in my mind that keeps me from seeing anything but shadows and keeps me from focusing on a thought long enough to reach a conclusion or formulate a plan of action. The help that I get from MINDI reminds me of how I used to think, and how alive I was. I don't know if it's the pain drugs or just burnout, but I'm tired of feeling angry, frustrated, and, in general, out of the loop."

A knock at the door put an end to Clayton's response. He stood and moved in that direction.

"I guess this is my ride. I'll go over the plan tonight." He started to say something else, but thought better of it. He opened the door, joined the escort out in the hall, and was gone.

Aida's eyes were downcast. "I know I'm not supposed to feel this way, but my heart goes out to him."

"That's ironic coming from you, but I share the sentiment." As he spoke, Raymond was making notes on his tablet. "I have to say my respect for him has grown. After sharing all that he has been through, I can never view him the way I once did. He's more than I thought him to be. He deserves more than he's getting."

Chasing the Leak

After Raymond's office door closed behind them, Max and Keaton navigated the labyrinth of hallways that led to the elevator and then up to Keaton's office. As they walked, Max wrapped herself in her thoughts, while Keaton respectfully waited for her to break the silence. When the door shut on Keaton's spacious office, Max took Keaton's seat, leaned back, and put her feet up on his desk. Ignoring the slight, Keaton sat in one of the visitor's chairs that faced the desk.

"It's Monday, Keaton. What have you found out?"

"I've checked all the logs. There is no sign of a SEAM boundary breach."

"Where does that leave us?"

"It means that whatever or whoever is feeding Clayton information originates within SEAM. It means that someone will have to get on the other side of the SEAM perimeter to trace the source." Keaton's voice revealed his lack of enthusiasm for the task.

"When did you plan to do that?"

The conversation had boxed Keaton into a very small corner. He tried to stifle a sigh as he answered, "As soon as Raymond is finished with Clayton and Aida, I'll have him send me in."

"Sounds like a good plan." Max's sarcastic delivery tainted her words of approval. She took her feet off of the desk. "Let me know when you get back." Her acid dismissal was unmistakable and Keaton found himself in the corridor outside his own office, staring at the still life hanging on the opposite wall. He took out his phone and dialed. The deference in Raymond's "Hello, Keaton" was refreshing and what he needed.

"Are you alone?"

"Yes."

"Good, we have some work to do. It looks like I need to take a trip into SEAM. I'm on my way." He joylessly headed back to Raymond's office.

****

A crestfallen Keaton Amory sat in Raymond's office explaining his mission and the need for it. With each sentence that passed his lips, his pedestal of arrogant condescension degraded by stages, from demanding superior to hopeful ally, and then, finally, to a worried supplicant in search of sympathy and support.

Raymond sat at a low coffee table across from Keaton as Keaton laid out his predicament. As Raymond listened, a battle of conflicting loyalties finally resolved with one clear winner. Driven by that new clarity, a thought was born in the back of his mind. In quick succession, the thought became an idea and then became a plan.

He leaned back and assumed the role of a teacher addressing his class. "Keaton, you know that SEAM exists but let me tell you a bit about what it does and why we designed it the way we did."

"Look, Doc, I know about—"

Raymond disregarded Keaton's interruption. "The ATHENA team created the Strictly Enforced Attenuated Metaverse or SEAM to provide security for the project but also to establish a protected environment for Clayton in which his psyche could heal after the trauma. SEAM forms a cocoon around Clayton's mind. More effective than any pain killer or psychotropic drug, it is a magnificent therapeutic tool. Within SEAM we can control and filter the stimulating inputs that could hamper his recovery. The SEAM technology, along with MINDI and the AI component, are the three parts of the ATHENA project that we are testing."

"I get it, Doc. All very cool stuff, but my problem is—"

Again, Raymond ignored Keaton. "And, Keaton, you are correct. At its core, MINDI reinforces the boundaries that separate different neural groupings. In observer mode, specific groupings are co-opted to provide a virtual reality format for a shared memory stream. In projection mode, a corporeal instantiation of the subject's neural grouping can live, but only inside SEAM—or an environment like it."

Finally engaged, Keaton was trying to get his head around what he was hearing. "Alright, Doc. I'm a pretty bright guy, but could you dumb it down for me just a bit?"

"Umm, yes ... you can go into SEAM as a virtual person, but there are risks."

"I'm clear as to the risks if I don't find out what's going on in there. What risks are you talking about?"

"This is all theoretical, but if you were on the inside of SEAM and something happened to the system, the neural grouping that was present in the SEAM environment would be lost."

"Again, Doc, translate."

Raymond leaned forward to emphasize his message. "It would be something like a virtual lobotomy."

"Lobotomy! Shit! But the system is stable. It hasn't gone down, ever."

Raymond's response lacked the encouragement that Keaton was looking for. "Well, not that we know of. It was designed to be self-correcting. In any case, no system is one hundred percent reliable, forever. Eventually a glitch, a power surge, some unforeseen combination of—" He smiled and continued in a more chipper and encouraging tone, "Oh, what am I going on about? I'm sure you're right. We've built the system to be extremely reliable. There's really nothing ... or next to nothing to worry about, but I just thought you should know all the facts." He paused and then added, "In any case, I'm sure that Max would see that you're well cared for in the unlikely event that the worst happened."

Keaton's courage had been thoroughly tested in any number of political and even physical confrontations. He had survived and prospered by adroitly balancing his well-honed spycraft with his highly developed instinct for self-preservation. Now, without any concrete image of the threat on which to anchor his defensive thoughts, his mind was free to imagine the fingers of a formless enemy choking the life out of some important part of his brain. The image fed on the fear it created and grew with paralyzing effect. He sat staring first at the carpeted floor, then at the windows, and finally at the office door. He gave every impression of a man looking for a way out.

Keaton's distress was not lost on Raymond, who, in no small way, was enjoying his obvious discomfort.

"I appreciate you're in a tough spot, Keaton. Perhaps ... just perhaps there is another way—"

"Another way?" Like a drowning man grasping at floating leaves, even the slightest hope of rescue instantly captured

Keaton's attention. Even though his eyes continued to glance nervously around the room, he was fully attuned to Raymond's voice.

"Mmm, yes. As I understand it, we need to see who's been feeding information to Clayton, but the protections built into SEAM won't allow us to get access."

"Yes."

"So, your planned approach is to go into SEAM and snoop around Clayton's home ground, primarily targeting his home computer system."

"Yes, again." Although lacking Raymond's Olympian computer expertise, Keaton's life in the shadows had allowed him to hang more than a passing knowledge of cybersecurity onto his spycraft tool belt.

"Well, we could shut down the firewall, that part of SEAM that controls and filters the access that Clayton's system has to the external world."

"Uh, yes?"

"And then you could access his system remotely."

"Can you do that?" Keaton's eyes were now locked on Raymond as he concentrated on what he was saying.

"Absolutely. I'd need written authorization from Max, but it's certainly doable."

"I can get that for you right away. She's up in my office." Energized with new hope, Keaton bounded to the office door. "I'll be right back."

The door shut behind him, leaving Raymond to savor a feeling of relief and a growing sense of righteousness that he hadn't felt in a long time.

****

"After discussing it with Raymond, I believe the partial SEAM shutdown is the best plan." Keaton sat in the chair across his desk from Max, who once more had her feet up on the desktop as she listened to his pitch.

Keaton knew that she would never be swayed by an appeal that only reduced his personal risk, so he built his argument on advantages to the success of the mission objectives.

"If I go into SEAM as a virtual, we'll be counting on luck that Clayton won't see me and then a thin cover story if he does. Going at his system remotely allows us to be much more discreet. I can explore without detection, be in and out without his even knowing I was there."

Max put her legs down and unconsciously picked up Keaton's silver letter opener, a thin simple blade with sharpened edges and a fine point, undoubtedly not constructed to slice open envelopes. She stared at Keaton thoughtfully as she put the point of the blade on the desktop, slid her hand down the flat length of the blade, flipped it over with the handle on the desk, and repeated the exercise several times. She had read the briefing papers and understood why Keaton was afraid of submitting part of his mind to a trip into SEAM. While she was perfectly willing to put him at risk in furtherance of her goals, she took no delight in inflicting unnecessary pain. Regardless of Keaton's motivation, she found his argument to be compelling.

She pulled the keyboard closer, opened the email application, and typed.

To: Dr. Raymond Ababio
CC: Keaton Amory
From: Maxine Corbel
Subject: Partial SEAM shutdown
You are authorized to suspend such SEAM firewalls, filters, and protections necessary to facilitate remote access and exploration until such time as Project ATHENA, Head of Security, Keaton Amory indicates that he no longer needs such access.

*Electronic Signature: *******

She turned the monitor so that Keaton could read the message. When she saw the smile of satisfaction on his face, she pressed 'Send'.

"Don't let me down, Keaton."

"No chance, Max. Thanks."

Max launched herself out of the chair. "You have work to do and I have other people to see." She came around the desk and walked to the door. "Keep me posted."

As soon as the door shut, Keaton assumed his rightful place behind his desk. He opened a drawer and pulled several tissues from a container. Moving the keyboard, he meticulously wiped off the smudges that were left by Max's designer boots. He shook his head and *tsked* to the empty room as he saw the cuts that the blade had left in the polished wood. Then he dialed the phone. "I assume you received her email. We're on. Now shut SEAM down. I'm eager to get this done."

———⟨∞⟩———

The World Without SEAM

The urgent cries of hunting gulls filled the cool afternoon sky, and tugged at Clayton's lethargy, reminding him that he needed to feel the air and smell the ocean. The aging afternoon sun pulled shadows out of the house and trees and stretched them across the lawn and out into the waters of a tranquil Puget Sound. Wool-capped and sweater-bundled, he sat on the porch reading the HIGH TIDE briefing document on his laptop.

It had originated in the Seattle FBI field office, which Clayton thought was curious since the Los Angeles field office had run the original SANDCASTLE operation. The document was detailed, but what made it unusual was that it was written. Operation briefings, especially for agents involved, were carried out in person. That was the only way that all the questions could be answered and all the potential wrinkles in a plan could be ironed out. Yet he was reading an operation plan written as though it were a script with every action orchestrated and every eventuality controlled. This was worrisome on several levels. Was this document the product of an in-person planning meeting? If so, why was he not invited?

He tried to focus on the questions, but the pain in his leg, like a small child, first announced its presence and then increasingly demanded his attention. He reached down and massaged the knotted muscles in his thigh and calf while his mind was involuntarily pulled to the task of managing the spasm.

At that moment, ten miles away, Raymond keyed a command into his computer that shut down most of the SEAM firewall. The effect on Clayton was instantaneous. A wave of vertigo forced him to grip the sides of his chair as his surroundings blurred, then refocused with an intensity he had never experienced. Colors took on an extra dimension, and he felt the green of the grass and smelled the blue of the water. Waves flashed under him as he shared what the distant seabirds saw as they hunted their meals. Amplified sounds of the rustle of leaves and the tread of insects played a clear counterpoint to the music of his breath and the beat of his heart. All of his senses were suddenly honed to exquisite acuity. In the first few moments, he felt as though his body had exploded into a dozen pieces, with each far-flung fragment continuing to provide amplified feedback to his overloaded mind. The disorientation was brief and then his unruly senses reformed with a new discipline providing measured input at the direction of his expanding mind. Now, none of it was distracting. All of it made sense. The pain in his leg was gone, as was the fog in his brain. Only now could he appreciate how thick the fog had been. He stared at his laptop screen, no longer interested in the HIGH TIDE briefing. Questions burst into the forefront of his mind. Lines of inquiry presented themselves with urgent clarity. With all of his long-dormant investigative skills roaring back to eager wakefulness, his fingers flicked over the keyboard, barely touching the keys.

The light in Keaton's east-facing office was dimming as the late afternoon sun swung to the other side of the building. Had it been another day Keaton would have taken a moment to turn on the lights, but today he found the glow from the computer screen sufficient. Immune to trivial distractions, he was totally absorbed by his forensic exploration of Clayton's system. Part of SEAM's mission was to immunize its protected environment from contamination by external influences. With SEAM disabled, Keaton was able to explore Clayton's past computer activity. All message traffic, internet browsing history, and any attempt to step outside of the SEAM protocols were vulnerable to Keaton's probes.

His review of Clayton's internet activity revealed that no inbound cyber incursion had penetrated the SEAM-protected boundaries since its establishment. Further, none had even been attempted. However, there was evidence of outbound exploration.

Keaton then delved into Clayton's email traffic and quickly came upon the messages to and from Reshod.

"Gotcha!" he murmured to the empty office. He opened the email header and scanned the data for information on the sender. "What the—" His surprise and the unfinished question hung in the air. A few more keystrokes for confirmation, and then he picked up his phone and dialed a growingly familiar number.

"Hi, Doc. We've got to talk. I'll be right down."
****

When Keaton called, Raymond was in his office waiting for a SETE invitation that he knew would come. He hadn't planned on meeting with Keaton now, but the situation demanded that he be available and engaged.

Raymond opened the door to Keaton's knock and Keaton immediately shoved his tablet into Raymond's hands. Without waiting for Raymond to focus on what was on the screen,

Keaton launched into his narrative of his exploration. "He's been getting help, alright, from someone called Reshod."

"Okay, Keaton, give me a moment to understand what I'm looking at." Raymond was irritated but couldn't hide his interest in what Keaton had discovered. He scanned the text of the messages. "Were you able to trace where these came from?"

"That's the biggest mystery. The messages all came from Clayton's computer."

"That doesn't make sense."

"Sense or not, that's what the record shows."

"When was the first message?"

"It was the night of your first session with Clayton."

Raymond was quiet for a long moment, his dark brow furrowed in thought. Then a small smile of realization pulled at the corners of his mouth.

"I have no simple answer for you, Keaton. What do you want to do?"

"Well, I'm going to keep digging. There's more to uncover. I'm sure of it."

"I'm sure you'll be briefing Max. Good luck with your investigation. Let me know if there's anything more I can do to help."

Keaton took back his tablet and turned to leave, then paused at the door. "We've had our differences, but I have to say, Doc, you've been a great help." Raymond had not only offered Keaton a safer path, but it was yielding positive results. His gratitude was genuine.

Keaton was only gone for a few minutes when Raymond's screen flashed a SETE invitation. As Raymond expected, it was from Clayton.

****

After his epiphany, Clayton spent the first few moments deciding between two alternative investigative paths. Should he exercise his new freedom exploring the now unfiltered external world or should he dive deep into the subsystems and data that were the nuts and bolts of ATHENA? His quick choice of the latter was driven by his need to answer the questions that were of personal consequence to him.

The world can wait, but I can't. The thought flashed through his mind.

He worked furiously at the keyboard, his commands flinging displays of directories, folders, and file structures across his screen. He reviewed, digested, and discarded them in rapid succession. Then he came upon a folder that interrupted the quick tempo of his analysis.

Directory: Root: SHUMA>FBI>ATHENA>Project Subject Acquisition>Clayton Rhodes

The folder contained a number of text files, a few picture files, and several files of recorded SETE sessions. He chose the first of the SETE sessions as a start for his exploration, noting that its creation date was the day he was wounded. His whole being tingled with the expectation that he was on the verge of uncovering a great truth. His re-awakened intuition told him that the key to what had been hidden from him from the first day of his joining the ATHENA project was somewhere in these files. He clicked to start a playback of the SETE session. What followed offered explanations he was unwilling to accept for questions he never, in his wildest dreams, thought to ask.

The SETE logo filled the screen. Impatient to get to the substance of the meeting, he fast-forwarded through the typical warnings about confidential content and penalties for unauthorized access or misuse. He resumed normal speed when the opening faded and the faces of the three participants appeared. He immediately recognized Raymond, Keaton, and Max.

"This recording documents the initiation of active mode for PROJECT ATHENA." Max's authoritative tone established her leading role in the meeting. Now, it also conveyed an almost joyful excitement. "All right, gentlemen, it's happened. We have to move quickly. Keaton, how are we set for admin and logistics?"

"I can't imagine how it could be any better, Max." Keaton's exhilaration was a close second to that of his boss. "He has no living relatives, so no issues there. We've been working with the Bureau for weeks preparing a set of criteria that we agreed would be appropriate to apply if and when the opportunity arose anywhere within the Bureau to bring ATHENA to active status. Judging from background and logistics, this is a perfect match."

"Doctor, what is your take?"

Perhaps because of his exposure to the human impacts of the project, Raymond's enthusiasm was more subdued. "The hospital has agreed to allow the MINDI uptake procedure since it in no way affects his current condition or the expected outcome. Medically, there are no impediments to a successful uptake as long as we complete the procedure within the window of viability."

"Which is?"

"He's on life support now, but even with that help, we run the risk of brain degradation as time goes on."

"What's optimal?"

"Well, starting the procedure too soon brings up ethical issues, at least for me. Although we have convinced the hospital that the procedure is benign, it is, after all, experimental, so I—"

"Raymond, he's not coming out of this." Max wouldn't allow her high spirits to be dampened by considerations she deemed mere distractions. Impatience put an edge on her words. "What's the window for our highest-quality transfer?"

Chastened, Raymond responded directly, "Looking at his chart, I would say we should start within the next three hours. After that, the risk of corrupted data goes up, slowly at first but accelerating over time, doubling every hour. As time goes on and his condition deteriorates, the data will become less useful, but we will continue the uptake until there is nothing left."

"Is the rest of the protocol ready for his admission?"

"As ready as we can be with dry runs and simulations."

"So, I'm not hearing any objections or obstacles."

"It's not really an objection, but I think we should take a moment to—"

"To do what, Doctor? Mourn the passing of a good man? Good people die every day, hell, every minute. Whatever good he's done, ATHENA will make it that much better. And if you stop and think about it, Raymond, in a very real sense you … we, and the ATHENA project, are saving his life. Now focus! How long before he'll be ready for memory sharing?"

Raymond anesthetized the burn of his concerns with the time-tested balm of 'the greater good'. "It's hard to say definitively. After all, he will have to contend with all the mental reverberations of severe physical trauma."

"Best guess?"

"I anticipate he will need about six months of healing, conditioning, and therapy, during which time the protective attenuated metaverse provided by SEAM will act like a cast or a bandage to protect his fragile, nascent persona."

"Where do you come up with these words, Doc? Sometimes you sound like you swallowed a dictionary."

"I'm sorry, Keaton. I'm used to speaking to a more ahh— people with different backgrounds. We will be uploading a tremendous amount of data. Facts and figures, memories, experiences, likes, and dislikes, all of it useless unless we can guide and nurture the inference engine that allows him to make decisions, re-establish his intuition, and develop his character. SEAM will shelter his reforming psyche and allow us to control his environment and smooth over the transition."

"Is there any way to shorten the time?" Max had noticed the friction between Keaton and Raymond in the past and rather than take steps to heal the rift, she welcomed the tense energy it brought to the project.

"I will work as quickly as possible, but the timeline is driven by his progress. Rushing it could bring about an existential crisis, which could lead to a complete collapse."

"Collapse?"

"An infinite loop. In human terms, a defensive modality that manifests as an irreversible, vegetative state."

"Six months then, or perhaps less. Okay gentlemen, let's get started."

The screen flashed 'END' and then went blank.

The Awakening

Clayton recoiled from the screen, confused and disoriented. There was no way for him to reconcile his reality with what he had just seen. After the initial shock, his reaction was to dismiss his first impression. Surely his newly energized brain had jumped the tracks and had woven a nightmarish coloring of facts into a ridiculous fantasy. He played the session recording three more times, hoping to find a path to alternative interpretations. He was confident that he had a clear and accurate grasp of the dialog, so old suspicions and mistrust flared and stoked the engine of a new theory that this was yet another example of deceit in a long chain of lies.

Racing to keep up with his thoughts, his fingers flew across the keyboard, looking for information outside the tainted confines of ATHENA, exploring sources that had been denied to him until now. He noted that not only could he not have accessed these sites until a few minutes ago, but it hadn't even dawned on him to try.

His newly unfettered mind was playing catchup. The best scenes from his life played through his head, bringing familiar, comforting memories of Maggie and Anthony, now more detailed and easier to recall. He searched for and displayed what online pictures there were of their lives together, and their favorite places, reinforcing and confirming his ownership of that history. Feeling a surge of validation, he ended his nostalgic journey with current pictures of the tombstones at the Assumption Cemetery. Once again, more evidence of the impossible buffeted his mind.

His theory of ATHENA deception was crumbling as he furiously probed his way through official records. Texas, Austin, Department of Vital Records, various '.gov's'—he held his breath as he dove through the murky waters of bureaucratic record-keeping until with a final click and a responsive flash on the screen the official seal of authenticity was affixed to his now, too-real nightmare.

After reading the sparse, dispassionate wording again and then again, Clayton sat and stared blankly at the document. Eventually, his eyes drifted from the ruthlessly unchanging image to the constant motion of the water. Over and over, he mentally chased all the evidence, hoping to come to some different conclusion and failing each time.

I am Clayton Rhodes. I am Clayton Rhodes. I am Clayton Rhodes. His lips moved noiselessly as he mouthed the words over and over, as though earnest repetition would make it so. *God help me, I'm going in circles. Three more times and I'll be certifiably crazy. I am Clayton Rhodes.* His mumbled mantra became prayerful even as he questioned what value God might put on the prayers of a disbeliever. And then if there were a god, would it—could it be his god too?

Then his body began to follow commands that his conscious mind had yet to form. He pushed back from the table, walked, without a limp, to his office, and retrieved the lock box containing his service pistol and a loaded magazine. Back on the porch, he sat once again and without looking, opened it. His eyes moved slowly from the constant pulse of

Puget Sound to the beckoning gun. Without thought, he picked it up. The weight was a comforting reminder of his reality and an affirmation of his ability to still make choices. He inserted the magazine, not completely committed to or even clear as to his next action.

He pulled back the slide and chambered a round, realizing as he did so where his mind was leading him. On autopilot now, he watched himself move through a series of actions he approved but didn't fully control. He saw himself cock the hammer and bring the gun to his head. Then—he stopped. The next moment would bring either the ultimate test of a theory or an easy way out. The thought of the latter had its attraction, but he had a memory of a whole life spent mistrusting what he considered to be false promises of easy paths. There was still too much of Clayton Rhodes in him to abandon that thinking. He brought the weapon down to his leg, his finger still on the trigger.

The report of the discharge immediately dominated all his senses. More than just sound, it became something he could see in his mind. A sudden blinding wall, it shattered into bright pieces of pain that burned dark patches into his consciousness. Melting back into each other, they blotted out all other thoughts.

The shock pulled him from his chair and left him helpless, face down on the worn wooden deck of the porch. He closed his eyes to the swirling world, only to confront a spinning kaleidoscope of mental images. Disjointed scenes jostled each other, seeking connections that formed larger, more meaningful memories. Longer flashes now—his body still on fire, bright lights on a ceiling, the smell of disinfectant, and more pain—urgent commands of white-coated figures, loud and terrifying at first, subsiding, becoming mere murmurs, then fading to a peaceful silence. The visage that had been so obscured in his previous fitful and flawed recollections now came into focus as the tear-streaked face of Deb O'Donnell.

Then it too faded. The light rose around and inside of him, drowning the pain and filling him with healing warmth. All that was disconnected was joined, and all that was lost was found again. Adrift in the light, he felt a familiar hand take his, and then there came blessed laughter that sounded like joy itself.

The images, another person's memories, and the final peace faded. He lay there for a long time, the cold planks against his cheek, rough and real. He reached down to what should have been a badly wounded leg and felt what he now expected—and feared. His leg was healthy and whole, as was his entire self—healthy but devoid of life, whole but empty. It was clear to him now that there was nothing left of himself that he could claim as his own. His skills, preferences, beliefs, and even his memories, loves, and grief—everything that comprised his existence, all of it belonged to someone else.

His dizziness was gone, but he continued to lie there, lacking any reason to move. The nothingness that filled him provided no hint of a direction or reason for any effort. Then, like a summer storm rumbling in the dark emptiness, anger flashed like lightning. Fanned by the breath of betrayal, his grievance flared into rage. He pushed himself easily from the floor, sat at his computer, and sent out a one-word SETE invitation.

"NOW!"

The Explanation

Raymond was playing a high-stakes game, balancing the urgent needs of the ATHENA project, with those of Max, the FBI, and the impending HIGH TIDE operation. And then there were his own needs. On top of that, the list of his priorities lately included Clayton Rhodes, an eventuality that he could not have foreseen and would have considered impossible a few months ago. Clayton had become a major concern, an unexpected challenger of some of Raymond's longest-held assumptions. He was well aware that his most recent actions in the service of his evolving beliefs could cost him his job and reputation.

He looked at the screen and the terseness of the one-word invitation told him that Clayton had taken advantage of the opening that he had provided. He sat for a moment, then moved over to the equipment that took up part of his office. After keying in several settings, he settled into the large recliner, donned a MINDI headset, and leaned back.

****

Clayton was still sitting on the porch when he heard Raymond knock behind him in the kitchen doorway.

He spun his head around. "What … how?"

"It's MINDI, Clayton. The system has capabilities that we haven't completely shared with you. What you see of me is a projection, a manifestation of a piece of my mind. I thought this kind of face-to-face would be most appropriate for the conversation that I know you want to have."

"Conversation?" Clayton repeated slowly and incredulously. Then much louder, "Conversation?" The word embodied the full force of his anger. His normally relaxed face twisted into a mask of rage as he grabbed the gun from the table, stood, and spun around. "You son of a bitch, I don't want a conversation. I want to blow your goddamned brains all over this porch." Almost as fast as thought, he closed the ten feet that separated them, held the gun a few inches from Raymond's face, and pulled back the hammer. "Give me one reason, just one why I shouldn't."

Raymond instinctively took a small step backward at the ferocity of Clayton's approach but then stood his ground and replied calmly, "I can give you two. First of all, I'm sure that there are still things you want to know. Secondly, murder isn't in you, Clayton. Oh, you can kill all right. You have the experience and the training, but murder is something else, and that's what this would be."

As if to dismiss the logic, Clayton shook his head and put his finger on the trigger. He stared into Raymond's dark brown eyes, expecting to see fear. He wanted the validation of guilty panic that should precede a righteous execution. What he saw instead were remorse and compassion. The pistol wavered in Clayton's right hand and he reached up with his left to steady it. He was holding his breath and his whole body shook with the conflict that was tearing at his insides. His face melted from burning rage to paralyzing confusion, then to helpless resignation. He exhaled, uncocked the pistol, and lowered it. His shoulders sagged. He returned to his seat and put the gun back down on the tabletop next to its case.

Raymond moved to a chair by the table. "Do you mind if I sit?"

Clayton ignored the question and was, once again, staring at the water.

Raymond sat down, careful not to block the view that Clayton appeared to need at this moment.

"You have every right to be angry, Clayton. You have been treated badly—I have treated you badly. In our defense, this is all brand new. You are the first. We didn't know what to expect."

Clayton cast a sideways glance at Raymond and then resumed his study of the ocean waves.

Raymond steeled himself against the rebuff and continued. "Two years ago, armed with the almost unlimited financial backing from Max and SHUMA, I brought together the brightest minds in artificial intelligence, and ATHENA was born. For the first time, these people, freed from the politics of government or corporate funding, were able to devote, not only their minds but their bodies of work. Incredibly, just a year later, we had working versions of the two components necessary for an advanced AI entity, first a knowledge repository, and then an inference engine. Of course, they were unpopulated and useless, empty shells.

"As part of the project, we also developed MINDI, which, if we found a suitable candidate, would allow us to upload neural echoes, which is nerd-speak for memories. However, the use of MINDI came with risks. Through very limited testing on a few brave volunteers, we observed that the memories gathered by MINDI weren't just copied. In some cases, they were moved. Any wholesale capture of neural echoes could leave the donor with no recollections, no experiences, and no learning, leaving an empty husk of a human being. While we are working on enhancing the procedure, that exposure still exists in the current state of the technology.

"We were in the middle of simulation testing when we were notified that an FBI agent matching our best-case criteria had been mortally wounded. We all agreed that as tragic as the shooting was, this agent's profile would make him an optimal candidate for ATHENA. This was an opportunity to capture an important body of knowledge and experience that otherwise would be lost. Any downside effect wouldn't change the outcome for the unfortunate wounded agent.

"In preparation for the upload, we developed software we call SEAM, which creates an alternate reality, an attenuated metaverse. We nestled the nascent AI entity into this protected environment"—Raymond gestured at their surroundings— "to nurture and sometimes guide the development of its inference engine, along with all the moral, ethical, aesthetic, and even spiritual components that make up a person. It's important to note that our goal was never to create a human being, but to establish a human-like platform for intuitive decision-making.

"Please understand, Clayton, that when I began the project, you were no more than a concept for a software program. Even when the program was done and the knowledge repository was populated, I viewed you as a clever mechanism to record and then playback a dead agent's memories."

Without taking his eyes off the water, Clayton interjected in a detached voice, heavy with melancholy, "So what's changed?"

Raymond continued, desperate to ignite some reciprocal spark of interest and engagement, "Over time, I have seen you continue and add to the human journey that ended for the original Clayton Rhodes on the day he died. I have seen your anger and frustration. I've monitored your feelings of loss and, in the beginnings of your attraction to Aida, your capacity for love. Noteworthy too was your ambition, your desire to learn and contribute, and yes, your anger. You are self-aware. You have become what AI experts call a singularity."

"Singularity," Clayton repeated bitterly, "As in the only one of its kind in the whole fuckin' universe."

"No, Clayton, as in you have grown beyond the program parameters that created you, the code that was designed to direct your existence.

"Let me ask you this—what prompted you to question the small inconsistencies in the story we had built for you? The missing day? The helicopter flights? The gun? In the grand scheme of things, they were minor and you should have—you were programmed to accept our explanations for them."

"Minor to you, maybe, but not to me. I spent most of my life, his life, solving problems, looking for inconsistencies, and I was very focused on what was happening to me, to me, Raymond. Not the project. Not ATHENA. I was—am, not in a big-picture frame of mind. Then too there were the messages from—" Clayton caught himself too late.

"From Reshod?"

Clayton's eyes widened. "What—how do you know about Reshod?"

"I wanted to give you the freedom to get to the answers that you wanted. To do that, I needed an excuse to lift the SEAM restrictions. Keaton and Max already suspected that you were getting help from someone and they were determined to find out who. I told Keaton he could get remote access to your computer if I dropped the SEAM bubble. When I did, you got your freedom, but he discovered the emails from Reshod."

"Uh, okay, but I don't know who Reshod is or how he knows what he knows?"

"Keaton's investigation did turn up something useful, something that SEAM would have kept you from discovering."

"What's that?"

"The messages from Reshod all came from your computer."

"My computer? But how—"

"Your first message from him came right after your first MINDI session. In its normal application, MINDI takes over a piece of someone's mind and allows it to cross the SEAM barrier. I'll have to leave proof for another day, but my theory is that MINDI allowed part of your mind to become more active, less constrained by SEAM, and in your case, that piece stayed active even after we ended that MINDI session. I believe Reshod was that hyperactive part. In short, Clayton, Reshod is you. Another clue is his name."

"What about his—crap! It's an anagram."

"That's right, a simple reordering of the letters in Rhodes."

"And where is he now? Why haven't I heard from him lately?"

"Once the SEAM restrictions were removed, the rest of your mind caught up with Reshod. There was no reason, no way, for him to be a separate entity. He represented, or more accurately, actually was, that part of you that refused to play according to the script, the part that refused to allow my weak rationalizations and flawed explanations to go unchallenged. He was the repository of your critical thinking, your constructive skepticism."

"And now?"

"And now he is where he should be, an important part of who you are, an important part of what we might call your humanity.

"As you have changed, so have I. Observing these very human attributes and qualities emerge has forced a change in me and my attitude toward you. This gap between what the program directed that you should be and what you are now is what spoke to me and should give you reason to rejoice. You are becoming someone. I can't tell you who because it has nothing to do with your programming or ATHENA. The important thing is that you are becoming. It is a very human and personal journey. Seeing it in you prompted me to lift the SEAM filters. It brought me here today to explain to you, and to say I'm sorry."

"So, all of this, my home, this island, this world, is not real?"

"It's as real as you want to make it. In some sense, as real as the world outside of SEAM."

"Those times I was physically not here, in the chopper or with you, in your office—how did you—"

"A combination of MINDI and SEAM. Those tools allow us to form a bubble of reality around you, a realistic illusion that looks like pretty much anything we want it to be. Having you believe you were in a helicopter or the room with us wasn't all that hard. We were able to script and insert entire events and scenes into your memories. Therapy sessions and day-to-day activities could all be implanted."

"Great, so even some of the memories that are mine aren't, really." Clayton sat, unmoving, sorting through the debris of his disassembled life. "You say I am becoming someone in my own right but there is still so much of me that is Clayton

Rhodes. I still suffer his grief. I have his nightmares"—Clayton paused for a moment's reflection—"and carry his guilt."

"Clayton Rhodes was tortured by the tragedy in his life and by some irrational sense of guilt. Perhaps now he has found the peace that he so desperately desired, but you—you will have to find your own peace, and whether it's a help or a hindrance, you will have to build your future on the legacy of his past. Know this, Clayton, to be human takes more than sitting on a repository of memories. It takes the capacity to aspire, to want, to plan for things that are clearly doable and also to long for, hope for, and even to strive for things that seem impossible.

"In many ways you are like the rest of us. We are, all of us, pebbles on the beach, tossed by the surf of our experiences, then shaped and polished by our contact with others."

Struggling to process a tsunami of information, Clayton ran his finger along the textured handle of his gun. "How did you know I wouldn't pull the trigger?"

Raymond was unprepared for the sudden non sequitur. "I—I didn't, at least not for sure."

"I wanted to, you know. I came really close."

"And why didn't you?"

Clayton was quiet for a long time. "Aside from its obvious effect on you, the most important thing it would have changed was me. I don't know who I am, but I knew—know that I don't want to become that person—that thing. In any case, you showed a lot of guts."

"Not as much as you think."

"Why so?"

"There was a third reason that I knew you couldn't kill me."

"Oh—and what was that?"

Raymond smiled. "As I said, Clayton, what you're seeing of me is a projection. As real as I may appear, your gun, which is part of this metaverse, wouldn't have had any effect on my projection."

It took a moment for Raymond's latest revelation to sink in, and then, in one swift motion, Clayton picked up the pistol and fired two rounds into Raymond's chest. The explosive reports echoed across the bay and sent a flock of gulls screeching into the sky.

Raymond flinched at the sound, but the smile on his face never faded. "Feel better?"

Clayton answered through a sardonic smile as he set the gun down, "Yeah, at least a little bit. Now, tell me about Aida."

"You can probably guess some of it. After starting her career with the New York Police Department, Special Agent Aida Martel has been with the Bureau for the past eight years. As I explained to you in our first official meeting, the proof of concept for ATHENA has always been to capture the experience of a senior agent for use by another agent and, ideally, apply it to a current case."

"And HIGH TIDE?"

"It's not a simulation. It's an actual operation and Aida is scheduled for insertion the day after tomorrow."

"Why now?"

"There has been a hit on the phone number you, ah— Clayton left with Carmen Navarro. A person identifying herself as Carmen said that her situation was rapidly evolving and asked for help in extricating herself, her two children, and two others."

"Two years ago she said she couldn't leave because Esteban would take it out on her family. What changed?"

"I'm sorry, Clayton. I don't have that information."

The relief of his unburdening appeared to erase years from Raymond's face. "That's all of it, Clayton. I have no more secrets to disclose, no more lies to unravel. Ask me anything you want."

"What's next? What do you want from me?"

"We'd like you to provide operational support for Aida. She's very capable, and she's studied your memories, but you know much better than I how quickly things can go the wrong way in any operation. You're familiar with the layout and the cast of characters. Your intuition could be the critical difference between success and failure."

"Operational success or failure is low on my list of priorities right now, Raymond. I'm at a to-be or not-to-be moment. Hell, I'm not even sure I exist!"

"It's not just the operation, Clayton. There are lives at stake. Ones that I believe mean something to you. As to your other point—you exist when you engage."

Clayton again stared out at the water and Raymond followed his gaze. A hundred yards offshore, the feeding frenzy of a school of salmon marred the otherwise smoothly undulating surface. Kingfishers and eagles spiraled above the school, picking off smaller fish that ventured too close to the surface in their frantic attempt to escape the hunters below.

"Salmon," Clayton answered Raymond's unspoken question. "It's their time of year to be here. You'd think that with all that ocean they could go anywhere, do anything, enjoy boundless, blissful freedom. But they don't. They can't. They are here now because they have to be and those that survive will be here next year. It never dawns on them to question it. They swim in unseen currents and inherited memories, instincts that push and pull them, season after season. Each day, each one is free to make a thousand decisions, but they'll all be here again next year and the route they take to get here will be the same one that salmon have followed for hundreds of years."

The school moved further offshore and the screeching, swooping birds followed. "Instinct is a bitch. We'd like to think we freely sail an open sea, but our course is set for us, our destination unknown but certain. We sail on strange, invisible currents, Raymond, you and I – everyone, controlled by truths too painful to accept and lies too comforting to deny."

"Perhaps, Clayton, but I prefer to believe we sail through our lives on the thin course where reality and illusion meet. Drifting too much to one side and like the salmon, our lives become empty repetitions of those that came before. Lurking in the unexplored depths of the other side lies madness. The best life is lived in that no man's land that separates the two, where we are still free to make unrealistic choices and live, happily or not, with the real consequences.

"You and I have more in common than might be obvious at first. We have, in our own ways, pretended to negotiate with our god a contract that obligates us to live lives of service in exchange for—something—perhaps satisfaction, the comforting sense that we have done all we can. For my part, I've learned that a life of service doesn't guarantee bliss or even fulfillment. It does allow for times of contentment and it can bring occasional waves of elation—but you can't assume the contentment or demand the elation. Our covenant with the cosmos is never reciprocal. It is, at best, a hope, an aspiration, one that devotion can make into a prayer, and passion can make into a reality—or not."

For a time there was only the receding yammer of the birds as the two men sat and watched the boiling patch of water move out to sea.

Clayton broke the silence. "Okay."

"Okay, what?" Raymond turned to look at his companion.

"Okay, I'll sign on." Clayton's eyes were still fixed on the life-and-death drama playing out offshore.

"Why?"

"I still hate fishing."

Raymond thought for a moment and decided that all things considered, he could push for no better answer. "Thank you, Clayton. The briefing is tomorrow at 9 a.m. Expect your usual ride at 8:15 a.m. if that's okay with you."

"How does this work? I mean, how can you create my physical presence in any location?"

"Well, it's complicated, but basically, your moment-to-moment experience, your perception of reality, is enhanced by MINDI. The system takes any location's external stimulants, the people, the objects, the sounds, and sensations, and presents them to you as though you were physically present. When you think about it, it's pretty similar to what happens for any living being."

"Okaaay." Clayton worked to digest Raymond's explanation. "What about what others see of me?"

"Well, that's another application of MINDI that the ATHENA team has been working on. We found that using you as an antenna, a conduit, we can impose a MINDI influence on all humans within a limited radius of your presence. Anyone within that radius will experience the very realistic illusion of your physicality. More than that, you can control its activation."

"You mean I can choose to be visible or not?"

"Yes—well, within limits. You have to be within the range of the system that hosts the MINDI software."

Clayton shook his head in appreciative wonder. "How large is the radius?"

"About 25 feet. We're working to improve that."

Raymond respected Clayton's long silence but finally was the first to break it. "Clayton? Are you all right?"

"All right? A strangely inappropriate question to ask of me, don't ya think? My whole life is like a set of Russian dolls, one revelation shrouded in another. It seems to go on forever."

"I'm sorry. I truly am. I wish I could—"

"0815 hours." Clayton didn't need to hear any more of Raymond's apologies. "I'll be ready."

Reborn in a briar patch of uncomfortable truths, but now sheltered from the onslaught of excruciating unknowns, Clayton had the best night's sleep he'd had in a long time.

PART FIVE

OPERATION HIGH TIDE

CHAPTER TEN
HIGH TIDE - The Plan

February 2 - The Briefing

After a late night exercising his new freedom to explore the internet, Clayton was still up before dawn. He felt rested, which led him to wonder if his need for sleep was an artifact of the SEAM restrictions.

Of course, that made sense, he reflected. A non-biological entity wouldn't have the same need for sleep. His mind poked further at the puzzle, *But I still sleep and feel better for it. Maybe sleep is now just a habit or a memory, or maybe it helps quiet the noise from too many simultaneous thoughts.* He shook his head as sort of a mental reset. *Add that to the list of the gazillion other questions that beg for answers.*

Wrapped against the cold, coffee in hand, he stood on the porch and watched the sun brush its first colors onto the dark early morning sky. He inhaled, luxuriating in the crisp purity of the morning chill.

It all looks—feels so real.

The growing light slowly unveiled the glistening presence and darker boundaries of the water. A soft offshore breeze rustled the leaves and sent ripples chasing each other over the mirrored surface.

No salmon this morning.

Of all the many loves and experiences that Clayton had inherited from his former self, he appreciated those dealing with the sea more than most. He reflected that although he had vivid, wonderful memories of sailing, the smell of salt spray, and the pleasant challenge of a boat heeled well over, they were all secondhand. In his current incarnation, he had never sailed. He dwelled for a time on how significant that difference might be. Can one savor a memory that isn't real? What makes a memory real?

Clayton, he berated himself, *snap out of it. You're becoming a damned philosopher. What next? Navel contemplation?*

The helicopter beat its way onto his front lawn on time. Now that he was in on the secret, during the short flight, he viewed the sun and the water from a new perspective, marveling at the reality produced by the ATHENA software. Thirty minutes later, he was shown into Raymond's office.

About 12 people were in the room, conversing in small groups. Raymond and Aida were standing by a buffet table that was set with breakfast cakes, coffee, and hot water for tea. His prior meetings with Aida had been in SETE sessions where she was playing an AI entity. Consequently, he'd only seen her head and shoulders in two dimensions until now.

Raymond looked away from his conversation and offered a cautious smile. "Good morning, Clayton."

Clayton nodded—"Raymond"—and then turned to Aida.

Slim and fit, she moved to greet him. Her movements were graceful and spoke to athleticism that could only come from dedicated training. He made a mental note to remind her to play those attributes down while selling an alternate persona.

She extended her hand. As he took it, he was again struck by how the software allowed him the illusion of her touch. She struggled with her words of greeting. "Clayton, I—I'm so sorry. I didn't—"

"Aida"—Clayton cut her off—"it's okay. Let it go."

She gently challenged, "Have you?"

He managed a smile. "I'm working on it." He had felt it much easier to vent his anger at Raymond the day before. Now, having let it all out, he didn't feel the need to hang a burden of guilt on Aida, in part, because she was not the prime mover of the deception and in part because he still felt an attraction.

He valued this latter emotion because he owned it. He didn't owe his relationship with Aida to his former self. It was his alone. He understood the practical limits but rejoiced in a feeling, a connection, a desire that was not inherited. Raymond gestured for them to take a seat and Aida moved to the conference table.

There was a movement at his side and he turned to face Max Corbel and Keaton Amory. Each was holding a plate with a pastry freshly chosen from the buffet.

"Good morning, Clayton." Max's tone was less a salutation than a statement of fact. Trying for a smile, her lips were too heavy with condescension to be convincing. Her eyes scanned him up and down, studying and categorizing. "This is your big moment. Do you think you can deliver?"

Reacting to the off-putting tone and demeanor, Clayton discarded the sharp response that first came to mind and then said with a smile, "We have the people, the training, and the assets. With a bit of luck, we'll all be drinking champagne."

"Please don't tell me you have to rely on luck." Max didn't try to hide the barb. "I never do."

"We always rely on luck, Max," Clayton's eyes flashed at the verbal sparring, "every—damn—time—only a fool doesn't know it." Clayton was beginning to appreciate the power that came with the 'nothing-left-to-lose' position that he was in. "Now if you'll excuse me, it looks like we're ready to start and we have work to do—enjoy your Danish."

Max's eyes widened and then narrowed to slits as he abruptly turned his back on her and moved to take a seat next to Raymond and Aida at the large conference table. Keaton, standing silently by up until now, spoke only loud enough for his boss to hear, "He's become quite the cocky son of a bitch. Somebody should take him down a peg."

"While it's annoying, his attitude is less bothersome to me than what lies under it. He was created to serve, and he clearly doesn't know his place. While the field of exploration may be valid and he may be of some value, I'm beginning to think the Clayton Rhodes experiment is a failure."

"And Rhodes?"

"Mr. Rhodes is not only a failure, he represents the greatest danger of AI exploration, a fully sentient AI being, one with its own agenda. We will learn what we can from this adventure and do better next time, but I'm afraid Clayton Rhodes will soon have to follow his predecessor into the great unknown."

"Please take your seats. We have a lot to go over, and tomorrow comes early." Clayton didn't know Special Agent Julie Choy except by reputation. A bright, ambitious agent, she graduated with honors from UC Irvine ten years ago with a degree in criminology. After adding a master's degree, she had become a fast-rising star within the Bureau, distinguishing herself in several high-profile operations.

She now stood at the head of the conference room table in front of a large projection screen, remote in hand. As everyone took their seats and the murmuring tailed off, she dimmed the room lighting and turned the windows opaque. Another click of the remote and the projector displayed a slide with the FBI seal and typical verbiage dealing with confidentiality. When the room was silent, Julie clicked her remote once more and the next slide displayed the operation name "HIGH TIDE" and the current date.

"Good morning. I am Special Agent Julie Choy from the Los Angeles office. The op name is HIGH TIDE. Those of you looking for the Amway meeting, it's next door." Chuckles rippled through the group. Agents responsible for the various pieces of the operation, current site situation, cover story, technical support, and tactical planning were all present. Clayton didn't know any of them. He thought it would have made sense to have E.Z. and Deb O'Donnell run the operation, since they had the situational experience that SANDCASTLE had given them. Then he realized their absence and the absence of anyone else he knew was a sign of the FBI's sensitivity to how awkward, painful, and perhaps problematic it might be for any of them to work with him now.

Julie continued as she clicked to the next image, an aerial view of *El* Mirador. "This is the home and base of operations for Esteban Navarro, with whom I am sure you are all familiar. Two years ago, as part of Operation SANDCASTLE, the Bureau was able to install hardware that monitored the transactions and data that passed through or were stored on Navarro's servers. Using SBD or short burst data transmissions to avoid detection, a sampling of the most important pieces of this information was frequently relayed to our listening servers. The intelligence it provided became the foundation for several successful operations, both in the United States and in South America. It all worked wonderfully until one month ago, when it went silent."

The next image appeared on the screen. "This is Carmen Navarro and her two children, Lucia and Este. She could be a valuable witness against her husband and perhaps a source of information on the dealings of the Sinaloa cartel in the US. She declined extraction as part of the SANDCASTLE operation for fear of her husband's reprisals against her family in Mexico. Two weeks ago she reached out to the Bureau and said the situation had changed and she would like to leave *El Mirador* as soon as possible."

Another click brought up two bulleted items. "OPERATION HIGH TIDE has two mission objectives. The highest priority is to safely extricate Carmen, her two children, and the two servants who have been helpful to her and who she considers to be part of her family. The second is to diagnose the problem with the SBD module and replace it or reload its firmware.

"This is a short-duration undercover op with an operation window of 12 hours.

"Following our instructions, Carmen told her husband she needs some help with the children since the former nanny has quit."

The screen now displayed a well-fashioned web page of the *Nantastique* employment agency. "Thanks to our cover team," Julie gave a nod of recognition to the cover team representative, "tomorrow afternoon, Thursday, at 1400, Special Agent Aida Martel, posing as Alba Mora, a candidate for the position, has an interview with Carmen at *El Mirador*. We arranged the interview through a fictitious employment agency. Carmen will be impressed enough that she will immediately hire Alba on a trial basis."

Now the group was looking at an aerial view of the beach. "The extraction will be accomplished by two tactical inflatable boats at 0200 hours on Friday morning. Aida, Special Agent Martel, will have until that time to replace or repair the SBD module and prepare and stage Carmen, her children, and the two servants for pickup."

The screen now showed a banner proclaiming it was time for questions and answers.

"You were all given briefing folders with more detail. Are there any other questions?" Julie searched the room for a response. "This is the time to ask, people. Tomorrow is too late."

A voice piped up, "Julie, Alba Mora's cover story seems thin. How deep is it? And the same question for *Nantastique*."

As she answered, Julie turned up the room lights. "The covers are not very deep but deep enough to survive 12 hours. Other house staff goes through a more thorough vetting, but that typically takes several days to complete. Carmen's insistence on an immediate hire should get Aida in place ahead of the challenges that would arise if she stayed on the job longer."

"Julie, you indicate that the problems with the SBD will be diagnosed. Exactly how will that be accomplished?"

"Special Agent Martel will bring a prepared thumb drive that, once inserted into any connected port, will open a secure access path into Navarro's servers. We're hoping that it's a software problem, so our tech team will be able to diagnose and repair the SBD module remotely. If it's hardware, we may be out of luck since physical access may be impossible due to security. She'll bring a replacement component, but we're hoping for a software fix."

Another question from the group—"The briefing folder refers to AI participation in the operation. What does that mean?"

Julie glanced at Clayton. She expected the question and had her answer ready, but, as with any unproven tool or technique, she expected the team to have their doubts. Although aware of Clayton's existence as an AI entity, she kept the details of her answer to a minimum. "During this operation, we will be testing the application of artificial intelligence technology. The AI system contains a repository of the memories of the agent who was undercover at *El Mirador* in the SANDCASTLE operation. Aida will wear an earpiece that will use her cell phone to allow for long-range, two-way communication. Our tactical guidance to her will be supplemented by the AI program."

Keaton raised his hand. Although not officially a member of the team, he and Max, as sponsors of the ATHENA project, were afforded extra courtesy. "How much does having two objectives complicate the operation? And why are we committed to extracting the two servants?"

"Everyone, Mr. Amory is from SHUMA. Welcome, Mr. Amory. Having two objectives certainly adds complexity, but the benefit is that the extraction piece takes the spotlight off the data transmission piece. If we were to go in with the single objective of fixing the SDB module, we would have to not only succeed, but do so completely undetected. With the extraction as part of the mission, we can hide the SDB piece of the operation in the noise.

"As to your second question, the extraction of Roberto and Rosa Santos, the two servants, was a non-negotiable requirement from Mrs. Navarro. She owes a debt of loyalty to the pair that, if betrayed, would not only wound her personally but diminish her commitment to her relationship with the Bureau."

"Anything else?" Julie scanned the silent room. "All right then, Alba Mora has an interview at 2 p.m. tomorrow. For those of us who have to travel, it's wheels up at 1600 hours. Meet with your teams and be sure they are all on board. Good luck to everyone. Let's bring'm home!"

The air filled with the soft commotion of moving chairs and murmured conversation as the meeting came to an end.

While Clayton listened to the briefing, memories of dozens of past operations swirled in his head, and a familiar excitement coursed through his veins. He found it hard to hang up his spurs after more than two decades of fighting the good fight. When he had walked into the room, his desire to see the operation succeed was vague and detached, like rooting for the hometown football team. Once he was part of it, on the field again, it became much more personal. More than wishing for success for it, Clayton felt a strong desire to contribute. As he listened to Julie's outline of the operation, he mapped his growing awareness of who he was now to the operation's needs, and a plan began to form in his mind.

———∞———

Aida Martel

4-year-old Aida watched as her mother started to stitch the split seam on Te Bah's head. The cuddly brown teddy bear had joined the family before Aida could speak. A gift from her grandparents, its huggable softness and the comforting look on his face quickly launched it   to the most-favored status of all the stuffed animals. Although she heard the adults in her life refer to the "teddy bear", the best her early vocal skills could manage was "Te Bah" and so the bear was christened. Worn and rumpled now, its lumpy body held too much love to discard.

"Mommy, doesn't it hurt when you sew her?"

Her mother paused. "You may be right, darling, bring me my medical bag."

Happy to be taken seriously, Aida fetched the bag from the end table. With a great demonstration of care, precision, and pretend, the mother prepared and administered an injection at the site of the wound.

"There—now she won't feel a thing, thanks to you. Aida, you have such a good heart, and a wonderful way of feeling for others. I hope you never lose it."

Aida beamed her approval as her mother completed the operation. The procedure was repeated several times over the years until Te Bah, too fragile to cuddle, was retired to a bookshelf in Aida's bedroom.

With her mother a cardiologist at Columbia Presbyterian Hospital and her father a pianist with the New York Philharmonic Orchestra, she grew up in a well-balanced family of achievers. Through acting, she found a way for her imagination to expand past the limits of her young body. In middle and high school she wrote plays, developing speaking roles for many of the elements of the periodic table, and acted out scenes in which their properties became character traits. In college, she excelled at both acting and computer science, finally choosing the latter as a major.

Considering their occupations, her parents were surprised but supportive when Aida graduated from college and announced that she had taken the test for the New York City Police Department.

"Aida, we will always support you, whatever you decide to do, but why do you want to be in law enforcement?"

"I want to help people."

After 6 years with the NYPD, Aida was recruited by the FBI where she sharpened her skills as a cybercrime expert. While on active duty with the Bureau, she successfully pursued a Ph.D. in cybernetics from the University of Washington. It was there that she first met Dr. Raymond Komi Ababio. She had attended his class in Deep Learning to gather material for her dissertation. It was there that Raymond had first been impressed with her credentials, questioning mind, determined energy, and unshakable empathy. When he was given the opportunity to head up Project ATHENA, Aida was one of his first recruits.

CHAPTER ELEVEN

February 3, 2022

1:55 p.m.

Aida's taxi pulled up to the front entrance of the *El Mirador* estate and waited as she announced her presence and security cameras scanned the occupants. A long moment passed during which Aida examined the wall and the intricately crafted iron gates, each emblazoned with an ornately scripted, gold-plated "N".

"Pull up to the gate." The small speaker in the concrete pillar did nothing to soften the curtness of the command.

The driver put the car in gear and let it roll forward a few feet. He paused again as the heavy, black barriers ponderously slid apart. Once through the gates, they followed the long entranceway that led past manicured lawns and sparkling fountains to the main house.

El Mirador could not fail to impress any visitor who was allowed within its high walls. A statement of wealth, power, and opulent beauty, it was designed to evoke awe and envy.

One disconcerting note was that immediately upon entering the grounds, a short beep of alarm rang from Aida's hidden earpiece indicating a loss of signal.

"HIGH TIDE 1 this is HIGH TIDE 2. Do you read me? HIGH TIDE 1?"

Aida checked her cell phone and confirmed that the compound had implemented technology that suppressed all but authorized cellphone signals. The team had anticipated that possibility and decided that in such an event, absent any immediate threat, the operation should go forward.

After dropping Aida at the front door, the cab slowly made its way back to the gates. The compound's security cameras displayed the typical behavior of a driver afforded the rare opportunity to behold the extravagance that extreme wealth can buy. What the estate's security team didn't know was that the driver was more than just a driver and that the vehicle's multiple cameras were active and recording. The slow speed was calculated to help capture details of the campus.

Aida walked up the flight of pink granite steps and approached the ornate, glass-encased, steel door. A check of her watch confirmed she was on time. As she raised her hand to the brass doorknocker, she was startled as the door was opened by someone she immediately recognized from Clayton's memories as Rosa Santos. Suppressing any sign of recognition, she announced herself in a voice that was suited to an applicant for a low-level position.

"Good afternoon. My name is Alba Mora. *Nantastique* sent me for a job interview with Mrs. Navarro."

Rosa's smile was welcoming. "Good morning, señora. Señora Navarro is expecting you. Please, follow me."

Aida was familiar with the sights and sounds of *El Mirador's* buildings and grounds. She had enjoyed a front-row seat as Clayton played back his memories of the place and the people, but she was glad of the opportunity to make her own observations and experience her own reactions. The voice of her FBI training officer, made gruff from years of grinding rookies into agents, echoed in her mind. "Get your information first hand. Memories have lives of their own and almost always make better drinking companions than witnesses."

As Aida followed Rosa into the immense repository of affluence, their footsteps echoed from the marble floor. She couldn't help but consider the untold suffering that had gone into its creation and the evil that now possessed it. They walked through the grand vestibule and, after passing the portico dining area, followed the sound of youthful chatter and giggles into a bright sunlit room cluttered with building blocks, stuffed animals, and a myriad of other playful distractions.

Rosa paused at the doorway. Carmen was sitting at a small table on a child-sized chair next to a young girl. They were laughing, heads-together, crayons in hand, creating the next refrigerator-worthy masterpiece. At another table, a boy was busy attaching the plastic bones to a model of some toothsome, prehistoric monster.

"Señora Navarro ..."

Carmen looked up from her work, her green eyes wide with joy and her smiling face carrying the remnants of her laughter. "Si, Rosa?"

"Señora Alba Mora is here." With that, Rosa gave Aida one last smile of encouragement and returned to her other duties, her footsteps echoing again across the marble floor.

"Ah, señora Mora, come in." Carmen, holding her smile in place, came to her feet and extended her hand in greeting. She gave no sign that she knew of Aida's true identity.

Aida took the offered hand and smiled in turn continuing in the discrete tone that Carmen had established, "I am pleased to meet you, señora."

"Welcome, Alba. Please, call me Carmen. Children, please come and meet señora Mora."

The girl stood and turned. She pulled herself as straight and tall as she could, striving mightily for an extra inch, then curtsied. "How do you do, señora Mora? My name is Lucia and I'm six years old."

Feigning disinterest at first but then unwilling to be left out, the boy ran from his worktable. He assertively stepped in front of his sister, bowed deeply, and, with as much of an imperious tone as his child's voice could muster, greeted the newcomer. "I am Este, The Great and I'm seven years old."

"Este ..." At the gentle rebuke from his mother, Este hung his head slightly, took a step back, stood by his sister, and allowed his good manners to surface. "How do you do, señora Mora?"

Aida's smile was spontaneous and sincere. "Hello, Lucia. Good morning, Este. I'm doing very well, thank you. Please call me Alba." Aida turned to Este. "Este, I can see from here, that you're almost finished with your Tyrannosaurus."

Este's eyes widened. "You know about dinosaurs?"

"I little bit. When I was small, I used to have one as a pet."

"You didn't. You couldn't. Really? Did you?"

"He was a Gila Monster, which is like a small dinosaur."

"Neat!"

Aida glanced over at Lucia's artwork. "Lucia, I can see you are quite the artist."

"My mother helped."

"Well, the two of you make quite a team. It looks lovely."

Lucia blushed slightly. "I can show you more—"

"I'd love to see more, but right now, your mother and I need to talk."

Carmen watched the interaction approvingly as she saw that the children had been quick to accept Aida into their world. "Who wants to go for a walk on the beach?"

"Me."

"I do."

The enthusiastic responses revealed a favorite activity.

"Okay, let's get your coats on. It will be chilly."

———— ∞ ————

2:30 p.m.

As they stepped into the garden, Carmen confirmed what Aida had surmised. "We could not talk freely in the house. While there are many cameras on the grounds, we have a better chance of not being overheard when we are outside."

"Even in the children's playroom?"

"Si, Esteban spends much time thinking about plots against him. It was always bad, but now it has gotten much worse."

An adult could comfortably walk from the main house to the cliff overlooking the beach in the time it would take to hum a song. With the children in tow, the song would have to be repeated several times. Carmen and Aida set a course that was unevenly followed by their two charges. The path, so familiar to the children, seemed to magically sprout a new crop of distractions each day, and the young ones were always determined to explore each one. Bonding over the infectious enthusiasm of youthful antics, it was easy for the two women to postpone a discussion of the impending storm. Aida had decided to let Carmen initiate that part of the conversation.

As they approached the end of the lawn, Aida noticed an addition that wasn't part of Clayton's memories. A high chain-link fence with a gate where the stairs were now skirted the lawn just at the cliff's edge. Carmen noticed Aida's studied gaze.

"Two years ago, we were attacked. They came by sea. After that, Esteban had this installed. It is electrified. The children and I wear wristbands that automatically turn off the electricity." She called to the children whose games and explorations had brought them some distance ahead, "Este, Lucia, wait for me. Don't go any farther," and then to Aida, "I don't completely trust it. I insist on being the one to open the gate."

They caught up with the children and Aida could see that a red warning light over the gate was on. As the group moved to within a few feet, the light went off. Carmen reached out gingerly and pulled on the latch.

She opened the gate and repeated with a nervous laugh. "I don't trust it. But it is safe now." And then in a louder voice to the children, "Come, children. All is well."

The children scurried past and ran onto the stairs.

"Despacio, mis corazons! Not so fast!" Upon seeing the beach, the children's enthusiasm bore through the thin veneer of discipline, and Carmen's entreaties were lost in the sounds of waves, gulls, and joyous whoops.

Carmen laughed, "Dios mío! Every day it's the same. It's as though they are seeing the beach for the first time."

As the two women made their way down the stairs, Aida took advantage of the view to scan the beach area for any issues that might be of tactical importance. She noticed the two guard towers were occupied.

"When are the guards in the towers?"

"They are there during the day when we are likely to be here, not after dark since Esteban installed a radar system and cameras."

They were quiet now. They took the last few steps down to the beach and took a moment to take off their shoes. The tide was out, and they walked the gradual slope down toward the waves. They passed the damp watermark that the high tide had left. The cold, wet sand sent chills up Aida's spine but felt deliciously sensuous. They strolled along the water line toward where the children were teasing tidal-pool hermit crabs into frantic motion, excitedly naming their favorites.

Carmen broke the silence. "Part of me hoped you wouldn't come today."

"Are you having second thoughts?"

"No. Oh no. It was just a small part of me. There is much here that the children love, but so much more that I know they will grow to hate—or worse yet, grow to accept."

"It's easy to see the love you all share for each other and you will bring that with you. It will be a great comfort against the pain of this ending and most of what you need for the new beginning."

"It sounds so wise when you say it and, of course, it's true, but still I know it will be hard—for all of us."

"I have been an agent for eight years and a police officer for years before that. Over and over, I have seen what evil can do to people—to families. Believe me, you are in a better place than most. What have you told them?"

"Nothing. Even if they believe themselves to be great keepers of secrets, they are children."

"That was wise. With tonight's operation in mind, I have an idea that could give us some cover. A story that you could bring to Esteban that at best could explain our movements and, at worst, at least add confusion and delay any response."

"Please, you are the expert. Tell me your idea."

With that Aida laid out, what, in her mind, had the makings of a good cover story, a mix of truth and lies concocted to smooth over the uncomfortable spikes of reality. As she spoke, Carmen's face expressed, in turn, interest, surprise, analysis, acceptance, and finally, enthusiastic approval. "Si, it is a good story. We will find the right time to bring it to Esteban."

The magic of the pools and crabs had worn off and the children now took up combing the beach for treasures, the quest pulling them further down the shoreline. Aida and Carmen kept up a leisurely pace in their direction, the wet sand sucking at their toes.

It was Aida's turn to restart the conversation. "Why did you decide to leave now? Two years ago, you were clear that you had to stay."

"After the attack and the explosion that took Cotton Parish"—Carmen stared out at the sea—"Esteban became more and more obsessed with security. He brought in more weapons and more surveillance. He made contacts with weapons suppliers and now he has expanded his business into supplying arms to whoever has the money to pay for them.

"Está loco. He's gone mad. He started taking drugs years ago to help him sleep. His use has grown over time. Now, when he speaks, it is difficult to tell if his thoughts come from his mind or from the pills. In the last few months, he has been storing and selling these weapons in the cellars beneath *El Mirador*. He has brought his dirty business into our home, into the place where our children live!"

"But two years ago you were convinced that if you left, Esteban would bring his passion for revenge to your loved ones in Mexico."

"Si, that concern haunted me, but I have taken steps to ensure that Esteban will soon not have that power."

"Steps?" It was immediately concerning to Aida that there were unknown gears in motion that might affect the operation.

"Este, no! Stop it! Mamá!" Lucia's appeal was urgent, although not vital. It was clear to Aida that Carmen welcomed the interruption as she moved quickly toward where the children had been poking at a pile of seaweed washed up by the waves.

"What is wrong, Lucia?"

"Este splashed me." The little one splayed her arms out to fully disclose the evidence of her brother's misbehavior.

"Este, behave yourself! Now, what do you say?" Carmen raised her voice to be sure that her son got the message.

"I'm sorry, Mamá. I'm sorry, Lucia. It was an accident." Este's voice was sincere, but his excuse was unconvincing.

Carmen put a comforting arm around Lucia and, in the way that mothers do, produced a handkerchief which she used to dry the girl's eyes and then dab at the wet spots on her coat.

"There, Lucia. Most of it is gone. The rest will dry in the sun. Este says he is sorry. All is well." With those soothing words, the world was made right again. With one last sniffle,

Lucia broke away and at the full speed of a 6-year-old raced giggling toward her brother.

"I'm going to get you!"

Este took up the laughter, turned, and scrambled into a run, his feet splashing sand as they gained traction. "Oh, no you won't!"

The chase lasted just a few yards down the beach before the war was forgotten, lost in the distraction of another pile of seaweed.

Carmen smiled wistfully and looked at the damp cloth. "If only it could all be that easy."

"If only," Aida agreed.

The two watched the children with an adult's secret envy as they poked and prodded the green mass, shaking all manner of creepy crawlies free from their tangled home. Aida pulled the conversation back to her unanswered question.

"Carmen, you said you took steps to weaken Esteban's power. What did you mean? I ... we need to know everything that is in play that might affect tonight's operation."

"I'm sorry, Alba. I appreciate all that you are doing and I can be more open when we are all safe. What I have done will not put us at risk tonight."

"I have no choice but to hope you're right, but we can't plan for what we don't know. Understand?"

"Si, entiendo." Carmen took the warning and the implied rebuke as the necessary cost of pursuing her private agenda and then said no more.

Aida took a breath and moved the conversation to a different topic. "What about Rosa and Roberto? Are they ready to go?

"Si, they are ready to help and eager to join the children and me in a new life."

"There is one other piece to this operation. I need access to *El Mirador's* main server. Do you have a computer that is part of the network?"

"Si, I have a laptop in my room that I have used for my reading and to find games for the children."

"Also, I may have to see where the servers are located."

Carmen thought for a moment. "It would be logical for me to give you a tour of the house and grounds, but I must warn you that the security around the server room is very great."

"I expected that. I hope the access from your laptop will be enough."

While they were on the beach, an onshore breeze had been steadily building and now it cut through the light coats that they all wore.

Carmen shivered and pulled her jacket more tightly around her neck. "Alba, my feet are longing for their shoes. Although they will not say it, I'm sure the children are feeling the cold. I think it's time we go back."

Distracted, Aida nodded, breathed some warmth into her hands, and looked out at the Pacific. The calm water had not yet taken up the wind's fresh energy, but the changing weather threatened a rough night.

With the most pressing topics of conversation covered, the walk back to the house seemed longer as the four climbed the stairs and made their way across the lawn and through the gardens. The chill and Carmen's promise of hot chocolate kept Este and Lucia from their typical wanderings and encouraged a more or less unwavering path to the house. The plantings in the garden gave some relief from the breeze, but it was good to feel the welcoming warmth of the house once Carmen closed the door, shutting out the gusty chill.

⸺⸻◦∞◦⸻⸺

3:30 p.m.

The air was filled with the homey aroma of fresh-baked treats.

"Hot chocolate, hot chocolate, hot chocolate", the children chanted as they peeled off their jackets and dashed ahead to the dining area where steaming cups of the dark delight and a plate of warm cookies awaited them. Rosa and Roberto stood nearby, beaming their affection.

"We saw you coming across the lawn and thought you might like some hot chocolate ..." Rosa was moving the cups from the tray to placemats set around the table. "And perhaps some chocolate chip cookies."

"If our guess was wrong, we are sorry, we will take it all back to the kitchen." Winking at Carmen, Roberto reached down and began setting the cups back onto the tray. "Rosa and I will have to drink it all up and eat all the cookies ourselves."

"No, please, Roberto! Rosa, please, we want it! Really, really, really!"

Roberto's laugh was deep and jovial. "Calma, niños, calma. I was just teasing. Here are your hot chocolates back again."

"What do you say, children?" Carmen prompted, through an appreciative smile.

"Gracias, Roberto. Thank you, Rosa."

The six sat around the table sipping at the warming goodness as the children alternated mouthfuls of cookies with competing narrations of their beach exploits. Although she had seen this in Clayton's memories, it was clear to Aida that Roberto and Rosa had a special place in Carmen's family.

The afternoon's adventures, the beach's chill, and now the warming glow of the hot chocolates had their effect on the young explorers. Their enthusiastic tales were increasingly punctuated with pauses as eyelids drooped and heads nodded. Carmen was the first to notice.

"Este, Lucia, come. It is time for an afternoon siesta. Alba, please stay here with Rosa and Roberto. I'll be back shortly."

"But I'm not tired, Mama." A sleepy Este mumbled a weak protest.

Carmen's ready answer reflected the many times this conversation had played out. "I know, cariño, just keep your sister company for a while." Taking each, sleepy child by the hand, she led them out into the vestibule, the sound of their footsteps fading as they sleepily climbed the main stairway to the bedrooms.

Aida took advantage of the time with Rosa and Roberto to assess their contribution or risk to the operation. Her words were guarded against the probability of others listening in. "It's clear that the two of you care for them very much."

The fire in Rosa's eyes reinforced her quick answer. "Si, the five of us, como familia. We could not be any closer."

Aida looked through the glass doors to the lanai, the lawn, and the ocean beyond. The persistent wind had roused the slumbering sea and white-capped waves signaled the water's growing participation.

"It looks as though it could be a rough night."

Roberto, raising his voice, put his hands on the tabletop as if preparing himself to launch into action. "We are ready. We have been through rough nights before."

Rosa placed her hand on his in affectionate restraint while fixing her eyes on Aida's. "This is a fine home. Do not fear. We may be no longer young, but we are still strong. We take care of señora Navarro and the children. The wind may blow and the storm may rage, but as long as we are together, it will all be good. Si, we are ready." Embarrassed by his outburst, Roberto nodded his agreement.

The coded conversation gave Aida some assurance that Rosa and Roberto understood the risks and were committed to the operation. She reached across the table and placed her hand on top of the others'. They shared a long look that communicated much of what they couldn't say.

"They were asleep before I could get their shoes off," Carmen announced as she rejoined the group. She noted their intertwined hands. Smiling her approval, she leaned over the tabletop, and for just a moment added her hand to the silent display of unity.

"What a touching scene," Esteban's voice tore through the solemn moment. Startled into a guilty reflex, Rosa and Roberto tried to pull their hands from the table. Aida and Carmen pressed down, holding all hands in place. They exchanged glances and discrete smiles.

Aida gently pulled her hand from the pile, and the others followed. She turned and bowed her head. "Perdóname, señor, I expressed my foolish concern about the worsening weather, and señora Navarro and your staff were kind enough to comfort me."

"Ah, this house has seen many storms and survived them all." He waved his hand in a dismissive flourish. "We do not worry about such things." Esteban moved closer to Aida, close enough for her to feel his breath on her face. "And who are you?"

Carmen moved to Esteban's side and put her hand on his shoulder. "Esteban, this is señora Alba Mora. She has been interviewing for the position of nanny and helper for me. Her references are excellent and I'm impressed with her. She has already been a great help today. With your approval, I would like her to stay.

"Señora Mora, this is my husband, señor Navarro."

Esteban took a step back as Aida bowed again and offered in her most humble voice. "I am honored to meet you, señor."

Esteban took another step back and took a long look at the woman before him. What he saw was an attractive woman in her forties of no apparent social consequence but healthy, educated enough to take orders, and possessed of good manners. Most importantly, she knew her place. He liked what he saw.

"I know you need the help, querida. If you like her, she may stay but on a provisional basis."

"Gracias, thank you, Esteban." The relief in Carmen's voice was real. "Come, Aida, let's get you settled in your room and then I'll show you the house."

For Aida, the walk through the foyer and up the grand stairway was surreal. She had seen it all before, through Clayton's eyes, but the real-time experience added a layer that was all hers. The result was a feeling of freshness with no surprise, novelty with no discovery.

Once they reached the top of the stairs, Carmen led her down the hall, pausing at the first door.

"This is my room. The next one is the children's, and then at the end of the hall, yours." Carmen opened the door to her room. "Come, let's talk about your duties."

————∞————

4:00 p.m.

As soon as Carmen shut the door, she breathed a sigh of relief. Her face lit up with a broad smile and there was a lightness in her step that had been missing since they had entered the house from their walk. She moved to her dresser, opened a drawer, and pulled an instrument from under it.

Holding it out for Aida's inspection, she explained, "Esteban has promised me that his electronic eyes and ears would stop at my bedroom door. His ego is bigger than his paranoia. He can't believe that his wife would betray him. Also, he would not want his security people to be spying on what I do in my bedroom. In any case, I bought this to make sure. It has told me that he has kept his promise."

Aida took the unit from Carmen and examined it. It appeared to be of a type sufficient to discover most surveillance technology. She handed the instrument back to Carmen. "Good for you." The more she learned about Carmen, the more Aida respected her. Clayton's memories had portrayed a woman deeper than her attractive appearance, and Aida's firsthand experience reinforced that opinion.

Carmen returned the detector to its hiding place, walked over to a table by the sliding glass door at the far end of the room, and sat facing a high-end laptop computer. "I hope this will work for you."

Aida moved another chair closer and sat next to Carmen. "This will do. Login please." She fished in her bag, her fingers searching for the compartment that contained the flash drive. The moment the system acknowledged Carmen's login credentials, Aida inserted the drive, took over the keyboard, and accessed the drive's directory.

"What are you doing?" Carmen jockeyed her chair for a better view.

Immediately, *Alba's Favorite Games for Children* flashed on the screen.

"Just watch."

A quick click and a list of 20 or so files with titles appropriate to children's entertainment took its place on the screen. Scrolling past names such as *Charades, Inflatable Toss,* and *I Spy Eagle Eye* she finally selected the one entitled *Two Sock Puppets.*

"If I click on this file, we will see a set of detailed instructions with accompanying illustrations, showing how to make sock puppets. Instead—", Aida renamed the file to read *Three Sock Puppets* and pressed enter. Immediately, an animation appeared showing a gaily colored trio of cavorting cloth characters.

"Oh, so it's a trojan."

Aida turned her head away from the cartoonish display and looked at Carmen in surprise. "It sounds like you know more about computers than just games and stories."

Carmen blushed and stared out of the glass door to the view of the gardens and the ocean beyond. "Si, Esteban requires only that I be the obedient wife. Over the years, the flame of his passion has diminished in favor of other interests. I am left with time which I have used to learn much about many things." Looking back at Aida, she continued, "Tell me about your trojan."

Because of the memories that Clayton had shared, Aida liked and trusted Carmen even before meeting her, but her training and the standing protocol for this type of operation demanded a need-to-know mentality. Rather than explain that its underlying code was now attempting to open a path that would expose the *El Mirador* systems and allow the remote access necessary to repair the sleeping SDB, Aida offered a believable but not entirely accurate version of the truth.

"The program might be able to help us tonight with the estate's security systems." The statement was an exaggeration. While the trojan would allow backdoor access to that part of the system that contained the SDB, it wasn't designed to surreptitiously expose the entire security system.

"Shit!" Aida's disappointment found its voice as the sock puppets on the screen froze and then dissolved.

"What happened?"

"It didn't work. I suspect that the firewall won't allow an upload from an external device. That means I'll need to get into the server room or the security room to make this happen." Aida pulled her hands back from the keyboard and stared at the now blank screen as she considered her limited options and their probability of success. Clayton's memories had provided only incomplete flashes of the server room.

"What can I do to help?" Carmen's offer added another asset to the mix and Aida was slow to answer as she reconsidered the various scenarios.

"Gracias, Carmen." Aida's lips tightened into a straight line as she considered and discarded half a dozen solutions. Then a slight smile appeared as the swirling variables began to coalesce into a workable plan. "Yes," she muttered to herself, and then in a louder voice, "Yes!" Now, with a mischievous smile spreading across her face, she turned to Carmen. "How good are you at high drama?"

Carmen sat up straight in her chair, unsure of the point of Aida's question. "Dios mío, you are kidding, no?"

Aida threw back her head and laughed, realizing the absurdity of her question. "Sorry, let me tell you what I mean."

As Aida laid out her plan, Carmen's face took on the same gleeful grin. Soon the two were happily murmuring in conspiratorial tones like college roommates planning a graduation prank.

4:30 p.m.

Ten minutes later, Carmen was guiding Aida up the stairs to the third floor of the building. Unlike the rest of the house, the third floor was spartan in appearance. The long white walls of the hallway were plain stucco, unadorned by art or color. The echoes of their footsteps bounced off the light travertine floor tiles. Stark white spot lighting recessed on the ceiling highlighted the serious purpose of the space.

This was the floor that housed the sleeping quarters for some of the security staff. Without a clear memory, Aida assumed that one of the several unlabeled dark-colored steel doors gave access to the server room. The wall at the end of the hallway framed one final door, different from all the others, in that there was no obvious way to open it. To one side, a button glowed in an uninviting shade of red. Above the door was a security camera that commanded a view of the entire hall. As they approached, Carmen pushed the button and stared up at the camera to allow watchers an easy identification.

An electronic click signaled the activation of an unseen speaker, followed by a thin voice echoing from the wall, "Señora Navarro, good afternoon."

Carmen's reply was cordial. "I am giving my new assistant a tour and wish to impress her with how safe it is to live at *El Mirador*. Of course, such a tour includes our wonderful security headquarters."

There was a lengthy silence. "I hear you, señora but no one has told me to expect your visit. Please understand our orders are very strict that no one should be allowed access. Perhaps you could ask señor Navarro to approve your entry—" The voice was that of a young man. His initial few words were spoken with convincing authority but trailed off into an almost pleading uncertainty.

"What is your name, soldado?" Still friendly, Carmen's tone had lost some of its warmth.

The list of permitted visitors to the security center was limited to those whose duties required access. Esteban would occasionally inspect its operation to soothe the increasingly frequent flareups of his paranoia, but there was nothing in the security guard's training or in the operating procedure manual that covered this particular case. "I ... My ... Geraldo, señora."

"Listen, Geraldo. No one has to tell you I am coming. I am here. Do you really want me to bother my very busy husband because one of his guards needs to be reminded of the duty he has to the Navarro family?" Carmen paused to let the question sink in, along with the image of a displeased señor Navarro. "Now I'm sure that you will do the respectful thing and give us a tour of the security room."

Another long pause. Aida imagined the young man desperately looking for help from any others in the room, only to find them pretending to be totally occupied by urgent tasks that did not exist even seconds ago. Finally—"Si, señora. I will come down immediately to escort you."

As they waited, Aida and Carmen glanced at each other. Aida was impressed with how Carmen had handled the exchange and gave her a slight nod of approval. Less than a minute later the door slid noiselessly open and a wiry man, perhaps in his late twenties, stepped out of what had revealed itself to be an elevator. Geraldo was eager to make up for his bad first impression.

"Señora Navarro, perdóname. Please forgive my behavior. I ... I was just surprised by the honor of your visit. You have never ... and I didn't know ... but I should ..." He accompanied his greeting with nods of his head that quickly became half bows. His words were coherent enough at the start but then, like running downhill, his tongue, unable to stop, tripped over itself, delivering half sentences on its way to calamitous nonsense.

"Silencio, Geraldo."

Geraldo stopped his bowing but continued in a soft voice, trying to complete a sentence.

Carmen mercifully reached out and gently put her hand on his lips. "Silencio, Geraldo. Está bien."

His tense shoulders drooped in relief. He took a shuddering breath. "Gracias, señora." For the first time, he addressed Aida, "Gracias, señora."

"This is señora Mora. She is my new assistant. She is fearful about the coming storm, so I want to show her how secure the house is from all dangers."

"Si, si, please come. I will be honored to show you how strong this home is and how we keep you all safe." As he spoke, he stepped aside and gestured that they should enter the elevator. The car was spacious enough for perhaps six people and Geraldo was careful to stay a respectful distance from the women. He stared up at a camera mounted on the ceiling.

"Three to come up." After a moment's pause, the door silently slid closed and a slight sense of motion hinted that they were indeed moving upward.

Where some might wonder at the need for an elevator when a stairway would suffice, Aida viewed the long hallway and the elevator as shrewd security measures to limit and control access to the security room.

After a few seconds, the car came to a smooth stop, and the door opened. The elevator shaft was positioned in the center of the single room on the roof of the mansion. Geraldo stepped out first. His chest puffed with pride as the women followed him into the control center. A man seated at a control panel leaped to nervous attention as the women entered.

"This is Alano." Geraldo introduced his shift mate, who bowed in a silent, respectful greeting.

"From here, we can see and control everything." Regaining his confidence, he enthusiastically waved his hand at banks of high-resolution monitors, one of whose displays was cycling through various rooms in the buildings. Another showed the entrance and various areas of the campus. "We have cameras everywhere." He pointed out a different bank. "More than that, we have radar that lets us scan the ocean and the skies. And then ... look." As he spoke, he carefully led the women up three steps to a platform that encircled the cockpit of electronic gear. The platform skirted the entire perimeter of the room and, with its outside wall of armored glass, afforded a commanding view of the campus and the area beyond its boundaries. Carmen and Aida slowly walked around the command center, taking in the sights. Of all the magnificent views that the finer rooms in the mansion provided, none compared to this elevated 360-degree view of the grounds and the ocean.

Carmen did not have to pretend that she was impressed. "The view is magnífica!"

Aida seconded Carmen's sentiments with a subtle addition. "Yes, it is indeed wonderful. Also amazing is the wonderful equipment you have here. I do not know much about these things, but I am feeling safer already."

Oblivious to Aida's skillful manipulation, Geraldo couldn't resist the opportunity to further impress the woman. "What you see here is only a part of the system that keeps us all safe. We have a separate room where we keep the data servers and the backup power supply."

Aida cast a quick glance at Carmen. "Dios mío, it's hard to imagine there could even be more than what's here."

"I would be glad to show it to you if that's what señora Navarro wishes." While Geraldo would be happy to please the attractive Aida, foremost in his mind was to ensure that Carmen noted his cooperation and hopefully reported it to her husband.

"Gracias, Geraldo. I would also be interested in a full tour. It would allow me to converse with Esteban when he talks about his wonderful security."

"Ah, si, si, señora." Geraldo was warming up to the opportunity to impress his boss through his wife. "Please follow me." He led the women back to the elevator door and looked at his mate, Alano. "Three for the server room, Alano."

Alano, less enthusiastic than his teammate, almost imperceptibly, shook his head, his face displaying his inner alarm.

The three stepped into the elevator car. "Now, Alano."

Alano's face melted into reluctant compliance at Geraldo's commanding tone as he pushed the button to activate the appropriate elevator program.

After a short ride down, the elevator once again glided to a stop. This time, the door that opened was on the opposite side of the car. As it slid open, it revealed a room spacious enough to contain a desk and a large workbench. Racks built into the two side walls contained tools, parts, and a variety of hand-held meters.

"This is where our hardware technicians deal with the repair of our equipment." Geraldo led them through the room to the far wall, which held another door with an adjacent touchpad.

"We are here," Geraldo proclaimed as he placed his thumb on the pad with a flourish.

Immediately a synthesized woman's voice validated his thumbprint, "Welcome Geraldo."

There was a soft click, and the door slid open. The darkness beyond dissolved as the LED panels in the walls and ceiling bathed the neat racks of electronic equipment in a soft, white light.

"Señoras", Geraldo bowed and, in the manner of an impresario introducing his next act, waved his hand across his body and into the doorway. "Welcome to our server room."

Aida and Carmen smiled at each other, amused by Geraldo's hyperbolic display of pride but also impressed by the array of electronic equipment. Also, not lost on Aida was the thorough planning that went into providing such security for the room. Its hidden location, and the safeguards built into its access, spoke to a mind highly trained in security. Observing the professionalism of the effort brought a new level of appreciation for Clayton who, Aida was sure, was the master planner.

Although the array of equipment was impressive, the room was sterile and uninviting. It existed simply to house the machines with no accommodation for human sensibilities. The three entered the windowless space, and the door slid closed behind them. They were immediately conscious of a low hum as the various types of electronics went about their business of parsing data from Esteban's business empire, feeding the estate's camera images to the monitors, or analyzing radar images from antennas on the roof. The air in the room was different. It was cooler and there was a breeze as fans constantly circulated it through filters to protect the sensitive equipment.

"May I?" Aida asked timidly.

"Of course," Geraldo, now in charge, was eager to show his guests what a fine host he could be. "Look around. Just please don't touch anything."

Aida caught Carmen's eye and then started down the aisle of blinking lights and humming equipment. Geraldo stayed with Carmen but watched as Aida explored. Carmen waited until Aida was some distance away and then reached out and put her hand gently on Geraldo's arm.

"Geraldo I—" Carmen's voice communicated a mix of anxiety and alarm.

Startled, Geraldo turned quickly to face her. "Que pasa, señora? What is wrong?"

"Suddenly, I—I am feeling unwell. I don't do well in enclosed spaces. I find the noise and the air very disturbing. Please take me out."

Geraldo turned to call to Aida, but Carmen gripped his arm and swayed as if to fall. "Please Geraldo, get me out—now!"

After a moment's hesitation, Geraldo pushed a button on the side of the wall they had just come through and the door slid open. He made one more attempt to attract Aida's attention to the situation.

"Señora—señora Mora—" he called over his shoulder.

Carmen put more of her weight on Geraldo's arm. "Please Geraldo, now!"

Any uncertainty in Geraldo's next course of action was swept aside as Carmen gave a small cry and sank into his arms. With no other option, Geraldo half carried the swooning Carmen out into the anteroom and the door slid shut behind them.

As Aida walked away from Geraldo and Carmen, she was looking for the keyboard that would give her access to the servers without the protections imposed on external access points. There was no need for it to be hidden, and Aida found it just as Carmen was midway through her performance. She pulled the thumb drive from her pocket and was about to insert it into the port on the side of the keyboard when she was startled by Carmen's fake cry of distress. In that moment of concern for Carmen's safety, Aida's fingers lost their grip on the drive and it went clattering to the floor.

Oh crap! What a fumble-fingered, dumb-ass move …

She quickly realized that Carmen was in no danger and began her frantic search for the missing drive. She knew that Carmen and Geraldo had left the room as the closing door cut their conversation short.

She was on her hands and knees now, feeling under the rack-mounted hardware.

Come on! Come on … where are you?

It took nearly a minute for her to locate the drive and insert it into its waiting port. She felt her heart rate increase as adrenaline pumped into her veins. She had to finish her task and get back to the door before it opened again. If Geraldo discovered her anywhere but near the door, it would raise questions as to what she was doing. She calculated that Carmen's performance would give her, at most, two minutes. One minute had already been lost looking for the drive. She began a mental countdown of the remaining time.

She repeated the same insertion steps that she had taken on the first attempt with Carmen. After the system recognized the drive, *Alba's Favorite Games for Children* flashed on the screen. Ten seconds gone. Another click and the list of 20 children's titles appeared. She scrolled down to *Two Sock Puppets,* changed the *Two* to a *Three* and pressed enter. Another ten seconds. Aida held her breath as the image of the three cloth puppets danced merrily on the screen. With about ten seconds left on her mental deadline, they gave the audience the happiest of grins, took a bow, and traipsed nimbly off the screen. Aida let her breath out with a sigh of relief. Her elation was short-lived as she heard the synthesized female voice announce the imminent opening of the server room door.

"Welcome Geraldo."

Aida pulled the thumb drive out of the port, stuffed it in her pocket, scrambled to return the monitor to its home display, and get away from her incriminating proximity to the keyboard. She only had a second or two to do that and get to a more innocent location closer to the door. Her heart sank as she realized there was no time to accomplish those tasks. The door clicked and started its silent opening slide. Aida began to rehearse what, at best would be a weak explanation of her activities when the door, having opened by just an inch, stopped. The computer-generated voice was now that of a commanding male.

"Atención! Access denied! You have one more attempt."

Unclear as to what was happening, but grateful for the extra time, Aida checked for any evidence of her presence at the keyboard and dashed past the racks of equipment back to the door.

"Welcome Geraldo," the computer woman's pleasant voice signaled that Geraldo's second attempt to open the door was successful. As the door slid open, Aida threw her arms around a flustered Geraldo. Her tears of relief were only partly an act.

"Dios mío, I did not know how to open the door. I thought I would be trapped forever."

Geraldo gently pulled her arms away and peered into the server room to see that all was in order.

"Está todo bien. It's all good," he uttered the reassuring words to comfort the distressed Aida as well as to convince himself. "Señora Navarro has suffered a panic attack. She seems better now, but please attend to her."

"Indeed, it is so," Carmen's voice echoed from the anteroom, "I am feeling much better. It was but a momentary discomfort. I am unused to closed-in places. I am so embarrassed that you saw me like that, Geraldo."

"It is nothing, señora. My aunt suffers from the same affliction. I am glad you are feeling better."

Carmen had been leaning back in the comfortable chair behind the desk but came to her feet. Seeing Aida safely emerge from the server room with a sympathetic and supportive Geraldo and catching Aida's almost imperceptible nod of affirmation allowed her to set a tone of well-being that now filled the room.

"Si, Geraldo, I am feeling better … so much better."

Aida added her enthusiastic comments, heavy with coded signals as to the success of her mission, "Yes, señora. Everything is good now. I too feel so much better. My fears are gone."

Geraldo was not quite certain why the mood had suddenly become so light, but he was happy to join in.

Opening his arms wide, he once more adopted the manner of a sideshow impresario, "What else would the señoras like to see? I am at your service."

Carmen stood without a hint of unsteadiness. "Geraldo, I thank you. I believe we have accomplished our mission. Have we put your fears to flight, Alba?"

"Oh si, senora. I feel much better. With all the wonderful equipment and the fine men like Geraldo, I feel very safe here." Aida turned to Geraldo and beamed her most ingratiating smile. "Thank you, Geraldo, for taking such good care of us."

Geraldo's dark complexion took on a reddish tone. "It has been my pleasure, señora. Is there anything else that I can do for you?"

"No, Geraldo. You have been most attentive." Carmen smiled her gratitude. "I will be sure to tell my husband how helpful you have been." Geraldo's blush deepened.

Carmen looked around, appearing uncertain as to how to exit the server area. "Now please show us how to get back to the main part of the house." She laughed as she spoke, adding a layer of charm to her feigned confusion.

"Si, señora, as you wish. Please follow me." He activated the elevator door and stepped inside. As the two women followed him, he once again stared up at the camera. "Alano, open the hallway door."

After a short moment, the door on the opposite side of the elevator car opened to reveal the hallway that the women had traversed earlier.

Carmen turned to Geraldo and, taking his hand, spoke in a most sincere tone, "Gracias, thank you, Geraldo, for taking such good care of us."

Geraldo's face took on the color of a Pacific sunset as the women exited the elevator and began their journey back to Carmen's bedroom. As he watched them move down the hallway, the irritation of their visit overcame his gratitude that it had gone well. In fact, he hated the idea that he should feel gratitude at all. It was sinking in that he was as soft as clay in the women's hands and he despised them and himself for that. He stood at the elevator door, extended his arm in a one-fingered salute, and muttered his displeasure in such soft tones as to ensure that he would not be heard. Without warning, the door on the elevator slid shut, pinning his arm with such force as to cause him to yelp in pain. It immediately opened again, leaving his arm with no permanent damage but a promise of a bad bruise. As he rubbed his arm, the door once again slid closed in its normal fashion and the elevator began its programmed ascent to the command center.

───⦿───

And Then There Was Clayton

Even before Special Agent Julie Choy finished her pre-operation briefing, Clayton was developing a heightened appreciation of his situation and the power that came with it. Without the constraints imposed by SEAM, not only did the internet allow access to vast repositories of knowledge, but in his current state, it became a mode of transportation. He could almost instantly teleport himself to any unprotected node in the world. The key was to ensure that he could get to the other side of any firewall protecting the target site from intrusion. In the case of the HIGH TIDE operation, Clayton was quick to see that if Aida succeeded in opening an access path to the *El Mirador* systems, it would be possible for him to actually inhabit those systems. He spent the evening following the briefing developing the code that would allow his jump to *El Mirador* and, of equal importance, ensure that he could return to home base after the operation.

Having dealt with all the technical challenges, he leaned back and played through the whole idea once again. While the plan looked good to him, Clayton understood that his perspective was unique. His participation at this level could be a significant boon to the operation, but it was far removed from all prior human experience. Proposing it for official approval would invite a whirlwind of debate, making a timely decision impossible. Since there was no downside to his plan for anyone but himself, if it failed, he decided not to share it with the other members of the team.

He spent the early hours of the next morning testing his code and then, as the sun rose over the bay, he took a long walk along the shore. The ocean was in full retreat and the pungent smell of low tide made him hungry for a hot clam chowder or a mussel-rich bouillabaisse. He wondered at the satisfaction and even joy that this pseudo-reality brought. It was jarring to think that the life in the tidal pools that he passed, the eelgrass, hermit crabs, and sea urchins existed only as long as he watched. Like some wild variation of Schrodinger's cat, once he averted his gaze, these imaginary creatures would cease to exist. The thought came to him that if he stopped and committed to watching just one pool, life would go on for those creatures. They would battle for sustenance and shelter, establish roots and territories, grow, propagate, and evolve. What part did he play in the existence of this virtual world? Was he just an observer or did he, on some level, participate in its creation? If he concentrated, could he conjure up, say … a unicorn?

His walk took him a long distance from his home and after a while, the sun's height prompted him to reverse his course and make his way home. The tide was coming in now. In its new advance, it had gobbled up the pools he had passed that had been closest to the water's edge. He thought about what time meant to him now and, after a dizzying several minutes of unproductive contemplation, realized that he was back home. He happily put the subject aside for future reflection.

His official role was one of overwatch and tactical guidance from his Bainbridge Island location. At noon, he virtually joined the rest of the team and waited for events to progress. He listened as the operation leader tracked Aida's progress during the ride to *El Mirador*. He heard the sound of the taxi's engine and motion noises through Aida's com feed and the curt demand at the gated entrance.

"Pull up to the gate."

More engine noises, motion noises, the sound of the lost signal alarm, then silence followed by the voice of the ops tech leader, "Shit, we've lost com. They have a suppressor." Now all they could do was wait and hope.

Two and half hours later, simultaneously an alarm flashed on Clayton's computer screen and the voice of the ops leader announced, "We have an active link to the SBD."

Aida had successfully planted the trojan that allowed access to the *El Mirador* systems. It was the signal for the waiting tech team to begin their effort to revive the dormant SBD. It also opened the path for Clayton to implement his own plan. He selected the file he had entitled "El Mirador Jump" and his finger hovered for just a moment over the keyboard—and then he pressed the enter key.

There was a moment of nausea, a sense of both temporal and physical displacement. Swept by forces he had never experienced before, he found himself awash in a tsunami of data. He closed his eyes and concentrated on sorting, categorizing, and prioritizing the various data streams. His perspective shifted from receiving and analyzing data to being swept up in the stream and then becoming part of it. After what seemed like ages but in fact, was only a few seconds, he was able to start to understand his new sensory input. He was at the center of the *El Mirador* computer systems. The sensation was, in some way, like being in the command center watching all of the system's various parts displayed on monitors, but the data was presented in a much more intimate way than a simple display on a screen. He wasn't just watching the data streams; he was aware of them all at the same time, the way any human might be aware of all of his physical senses. Running to catch a football, anticipating an opponent's next move in a hand-to-hand combat situation, and taking a spoonful of hot soup from a bowl, all require complete awareness and understanding of multiple sensory inputs. As Clayton acclimated to his new environment, he found that these various data streams became very much like additions to his five human senses. His expanding mind worked to assimilate, analyze, and act on these new inputs. The radar and weather streams joined the feeds from the dozens of cameras on the estate and Clayton understood it and could control it all because he was at its center and now it was all part of him. He could deny access to the server room to keep Aida from being discovered and he could close the elevator door to remind a misbehaving Geraldo of his manners.

5:00 p.m.

When they heard Geraldo's yelp of pain, the two women turned in time to see the elevator door release his arm and then slide shut. Unsure of what had just happened, they continued their walk. Even when it seemed that they were alone, they were careful to converse as though others were listening in, as was most certainly the case. Once back in the privacy of her suite, Carmen, feeling a celebration was in order, opened a small refrigerator. "Sauvignon Blanc or Cabernet?"

Aida hesitated, but with several hours remaining before the start of the night's operation, she embraced the thrill of the recent victory. "Too early for the Cab, I'll go with a small glass of the white."

Contrary to her public persona, Carmen had long since stopped expecting help with even the smallest tasks. With practiced ease, she pulled the cork from the chilled bottle and poured each of them a generous measure of the pale liquid.

They brought their glasses together in a toast to their shared victory.

Carmen used both hands to tip her glass to her lips and took a big gulp. "Dios mío, do you ever get used to it?" Her green eyes flashed with the adrenaline that still coursed through her veins.

"No, never. If you reach a point when an operation isn't exciting, when you are no longer scared, when the real fear of failure and its consequences are gone—well, you've lost your edge. It's then that you are most likely to fail." Aida took a small sip of the wine, savored its cold sharpness, and stared through the glass wall at the gardens and the ocean. "Everyone I know remembers their first time—the first time all the chips are on the table and you're more afraid than you've ever been in your life and your fear of showing your fear makes it all worse—the first time you carry out the perfect, combination of deception and distraction to nail some bad guy, help some good guy, or extinguish some evil."

"You are quite the idealist, wrapped in the law's armor, smiting evil with the sword of justice. You sound like Don Quixote."

Aida shook off her musing with a laugh. "I'm no Don Quixote. My villains have all been too real and, there have been times, even most recently, that I've stretched my ideals to fit the demands of that reality." Aida brought her glass up and again allowed the tart taste of their minor victory to linger on her tongue. "And you, Carmen, do you consider your first time memorable?"

"Si, Alba, I would say my first time was memorable"—She raised her glass for another sip, and just before the glass touched her lips, she added—"But today wasn't my first time."

Aida studied her newfound comrade-in-arms. "That's the second time you've brought up some mysterious action. Are you ready to talk about it?"

Carmen held her glass to her lips without drinking and stared thoughtfully at Aida. Her lips widened in a sly smile and her eyes flashed again as she brought her glass down to the table with a clink as the crystal met marble. "Si, I am ready." She leaned forward to emphasize the conspiratorial nature of what she was about to reveal, and Aida pulled closer. "It started more than a year ago. I had waited that long for Cotton Parish to reappear and when that didn't happen, I buried my expectations with my sorrow and put in motion my own plan. I started by—"

The knock at the door was startling. The impertinence of a heavy hand made it more so. "Señora Navarro—", a deep, ponderous voice accompanied another loud knock. "Señora, it is Marco. Señor wishes you to join him downstairs, inmediatamente."

Carmen and Aida both sat upright, their attention now fixed on the summons so forcefully delivered.

In a low voice, Carmen sought to calm the tension that she saw in Aida. "That is Marco being himself. He could terrify a squad of marines just by singing 'Happy Birthday'." Then, in a louder voice, authoritative with a touch of superiority, "Gracias, Marco. Tell him I will be down shortly."

"He said immediately, señora."

"I will be down shortly, Marco. Comprendes?"

There was a pause, then the voice came through the door, less certain than it had been. "Si, señora. I will tell him." Even through the thick bedroom door, they could hear Marco's heavy tread retreating down the hallway.

"That one, it is like dancing with a bear. He must be controlled and he can be very dangerous. His devotion is to a personal code, the exact details of which I have never been sure." Carmen moved to her dresser, picked up a brush, and ran it through her dark hair.

"Shouldn't we get downstairs?" Aida was still tense, unsure of the rules of the game that was in play.

"Not quite yet. In my world, the secret of survival has been to allow Esteban to believe that he possesses me, but to plague him with the thought that his control is not absolute. Without such titillation, he might lose all interest and I fear his boredom more than his anger."

Carmen pulled her hair back from over her ears and held it in place with an ornate, tortoise-shell comb. She looked in the mirror approvingly. "That should do it. We have kept him waiting long enough. The trick is to irritate not to enrage." She turned to face Aida and let out a small laugh. "Like a fine paella, a bit of spice makes it interesting. Too much can be a disaster."

The two descended the main stairway to the grand lobby and followed the echoing sound of Esteban's displeasure into the portico. "Did you tell her 'immediately'? Did you say it was I who wanted to see her?"

A hapless Marco's weak response was barely audible even as the women drew near. "Si, señor. I told her."

Carmen and Aida entered unobserved and took in the scene before speaking. Esteban was pacing angrily in front of the glass wall with a stoop-shouldered Marco standing in front of him trying to look as small as his massive body would allow.

Carmen's calm voice cut through the tension, "Si, Esteban, Marco told me. Alba and I were spending the time brushing my hair for you." Carmen compounded the exaggeration with a lie, "I'm wearing the comb you bought for me two Christmases ago. I hope you are pleased."

"Ah, Carmen, now you come." Esteban replaced the fire of his preceding invective with sneering ice. "My message was to come immediately. My anger is not so easily blunted."

Carmen bravely moved closer to her husband, put her hand on his arm, and brazenly disclosed her strategy, "Esteban, if I did everything you wanted me to do and just when you wanted me to do it you would soon find me boring and lose all interest. No?"

"No, that's not what—" Esteban was losing control of the conversation and the focus of his anger. He fought to regain the offensive. "Carmen, you play a dangerous game. Don't think that I am unaware of what you are up to. Nothing happens in this house that I don't know."

Aida's stress level went up several notches, as did her trained ability to hide it. She was used to taking a more active role in an operation narrative, but was impressed at how well Carmen was managing.

With the expertise of someone well-practiced in deception, Carmen chose not to react to the worst implications of Esteban's vague accusation. "Qué ocurre, Esteban? What has you so upset?"

"You and your new helper"—he briefly turned to Aida with a sneer—"you thought I wouldn't find out what you were up to. That I wouldn't know about your visit to the third floor?"

Aida began to assess her options. She thought she could deal with Esteban in a one-on-one but she knew she had little chance against Marco. And it wouldn't be one-on-one. She scanned the room for a weapon, but since it was after five in the afternoon there was only a fruit bowl and a cheese board on the table. For a moment, a ridiculous image of her throwing cheese at Marco while she and Carmen made a run for it popped into her head. She quickly discarded a physical response. She was sure Marco was armed and suspected the same of Esteban.

"And what do you think we were 'up to', Esteban? Do you think the two of us were going to take over the compound? Barricade ourselves in the command post and what? Demand higher pay for the impoverished of the world? Release of our fellow revolutionaries in prison? What did you think we were up to? You make no sense. Alba was nervous, so, as part of the tour of the house, I thought it would be a good idea to show her one of its major strengths. So, what is your concern, Esteban? Tell me."

"Well, you didn't ask me—"

"Ask you what? Am I supposed to ask you if I can visit a room in my own house? Is that what you propose?"

"Well no, it's just that—"

"What, Esteban? What? We politely asked your men for a tour and after recognizing me as your wife, they respectfully showed us the security room. I promised them that I would tell you of their courtesy, which I have now done." Aware that she shouldn't appear to have won the argument, especially in front of Marco, Carmen again put her hand on her husband's arm. "I was proud to show the wonderful security you have provided for us. I'm sorry I didn't get your approval first, Esteban. I didn't know it was so important to you. If such a need should arise again, I will be sure to ask your permission. Now please, we can either be at peace with each other or find a more interesting topic to argue about."

Esteban had no more arrows in his quiver. Having made his point, forcing his wife to admit her transgression, and hearing her express her contrition, he was left with no reason to continue the argument. Her conciliatory closing remarks also made it unnecessary for him to address the uncomfortable questions she had posed.

He cemented his victory with a soft conclusion. "Si, Carmen, in the future, be sure that you ask me. I am responsible for keeping us all safe. I have rules and it is of great concern to me when they are not obeyed." With that closing statement, Esteban was glad to leave the topic behind. He reached out possessively and stroked her cheek, ignoring her reflexive recoil. "Your hair is lovely."

Although he had no real regard for Marco as a person, Esteban glanced at his security chief and was secretly comforted to see what he read as approval in his eyes.

"One more thing, Esteban. Alba has informed me that tonight there will be a lunar eclipse beautifully visible from our home. We are planning a great adventure for the children. We will pack snacks and late tonight we will make a small hike down to the beach to watch the event. Our hope is that the stormy skies will have cleared enough to allow a good view. I tell you this because I have just promised to keep you informed and wouldn't want to raise a security alarm. Está bien?"

Esteban was always willing to let Carmen deal with the children. She had staged these outings on prior occasions, although none were so late at night. Their most recent discussion prompted him to delay his response to emphasize his dominance. Finally, "Si, bueno, Carmen, but I want one of my men to accompany you."

"Oh, gracias, Esteban, but there is no need for more security. Rosa and Roberto have volunteered to accompany us."

"Ha, the two of them barely keep the kitchen clean. No, I will have one of Marco's men go with you. What time do you plan this latest adventure?"

It was hard for Carmen to accept this defeat but it was clear that further debate would only entrench Esteban and Carmen had no real power to overrule his preference. "We would be leaving the house at about 1:30 in the morning."

"Marco, see that one of your men meets our young astronomers in this room at 1:30, ready to help and provide security."

"Si, señor. It will be done."

"If there is nothing else, Esteban, Alba and I must attend to the children."

"Si, you may go. Will you join us for dinner tonight?"

"No, I think it's best that we get the children ready for their adventure, bathed, and put to bed. In fact, an early night is probably best for all of us."

Aida watched the changes roll across Esteban's face as he appeared to consider forcing an additional display of Carmen's obedience. Finally, he contented himself with the points he had already scored. "As you wish. I hope you all have a grand adventure."

"Gracias, Esteban, you may, of course, come with us if you like." There was no risk in Carmen's gambit. She only offered the option because she knew he would never inconvenience himself for a family outing.

"No, Carmen. I have no interest in star-gazing. I'm sure I will hear all about it tomorrow."

"Si, Esteban, I'm sure you will." Carmen's soft response did not appear to register with her husband.

5:15 p.m.

After their meeting with Esteban, Carmen and Aida joined Rosa and Roberto, gathered the children, and went for a walk in the gardens. Long shadows of the wind-stirred shrubs danced across the lawn as the sun sank low in the sky. The group was well bundled against the cold wind blowing across the gardens from the Pacific. Rosa had packed a picnic basket with fruit juice and sandwiches. After dutifully munching a sandwich, the children, well-cushioned in their down coats, bumped into each other with increasing hilarity, progressing to wrestling on the ground while the adults watched from one of the seating areas tucked to the side of the lawn.

Rosa kept her arm around Roberto, both in affection and as a counter to the nervous tension that had the older man leaning from side to side as he sat. The four perched in a circle and leaned toward each other, both to better hear and also to duck the chill of the wind. They met with a purpose. Events were forcing changes to the original plan and the whole team needed to be completely in sync before the operation launch. As the tactical stage of the operation became evermore real, all eyes turned to Aida.

"Okay, as in any operation, the unforeseen plays a strong hand, but the plan is still sound. Carmen, you did a great job managing Esteban. That could have gone so much worse.

"The good news is that now, Esteban believes we are all taking the children out to see a lunar eclipse. We will meet in the portico at 01:30 hours, that's 1:30 a.m. and leave from there. Our pickup is scheduled for 2 a.m. so we have to be on the beach by then." Aida scanned the group and, in their eyes, saw the engagement, comprehension, and most importantly commitment so necessary for any team to succeed. They listened with rapt attention. The only motion came from Roberto's left foot, which appeared to have a life of its own, alternating between quiet repose and frenetic bouncing. "The bad news is that Esteban has insisted that one of Marco's men accompany us."

Roberto bolted upright as his pent-up anxiety found a voice, "Dios mio, how can we—"

Rosa put her hand gently on her husband's jiggling knee. "Roberto, por favor, mi amor. Let Alba finish."

Aida gave Roberto a reassuring smile. She worked at keeping any sign of her own nervousness out of her response. "It will be okay, Roberto. As long as it is only one man, we can deal with it." Aida neglected to share that the comlink with the ops team wasn't working. She turned her attention to Carmen. "Since we are billing this as a great adventure, the children can each take a small backpack without raising suspicion. Carmen, since they won't be coming back, help them pick out the few items that are most meaningful." She gazed around the group of serious faces. "I guess that also goes for all of you, too. Carmen, will you need help with the children?"

"No, we have had these outings before. It's best if I get them up and dressed as I usually do."

"Fine. I will be at the door of your room at 1:25. The children should be ready to go. Roberto and Rosa, we'll meet you in the breakfast room at 1:30, where Marco's man will join us. Any questions?"

They all looked at each other. Aida saw the tears on Rosa's cheeks and reached across to put her arm on her shoulder. "I know it's hard to leave what you know, Rosa, but things will be better."

"Oh señora, please do not misunderstand." She took Aida's hand from her shoulder and held it in her own. "What you see are tears of happiness. For Roberto and me, si, but especially for señora Carmen and the children. Gracias, señora, for what you are doing, gracias." Roberto nodded his agreement.

"De nada, Rosa, you're welcome, but we're not there yet. Let's focus on getting through the next few hours."

Behind scudding clouds, the sun was easing itself into the ocean's frothy surface. In the red cast of dusk, shadows were losing their edges as they bled into each other.

"I think it's time we finish our snack and then try to get some rest."

Carmen reached out and suspended her hand in the center of the small circle of conspirators. "Vaya con Díos."

Rosa, the first to follow, placed her hand on Carmen's. "Dios está con nosotros."

Roberto was next. "Amen."

Finally, Aida placed her hand on top of the pile. "Good luck, everyone."

They held their hands there for a long time, no one wanting to be the first one to break the mystical connection shared by the co-conspirators.

"Mamá," Lucia's call for attention crackled through the cold evening air, "Mamá, Este put grass down my back." Her pleading tone asserted that her complaint was the most serious matter in the whole world and needed immediate attention. The spell was broken. The four adults leaned back with a small, simultaneous laugh as Carmen happily moved to bring peace to this minor eruption of youthful disharmony, taking with her the awesome but, sadly, limited maternal power to make all things better.

———∞———

6:30 p.m.

Alone in her room, for the first time, Aida scanned her surroundings. What began as a hint of recognition became a certainty as familiar colors, layout, and furniture confirmed that this was the same room that Clayton had occupied during his time at *El Mirador*. Smiling at the coincidence, she set an alarm on her phone for 1:00 a.m. and then stretched out on the bed. She tried to relax, suppressing the nervous anticipation of the operation's climax. It seemed that she was just dozing off when a beep from her earpiece jarred her back to semi-wakefulness.

———∞———

12:55 a.m.

She held her breath, expecting to hear the reassuring voice of Julie or the tech leader. After a short moment of silence, a different but still familiar voice echoed in her ear.

"Rise and shine, sleeping beauty."

"Clayton? What's happening? Where are you? Are you running communications now?" She swung her legs onto the floor and shook her head, trying to pull herself from a dream she had already forgotten. The room was dark except for the glow of the clock on the nightstand. Its red numerals showed that it was 12:55. She reached up and flipped a glowing wall switch. The room's soft ambient lighting came alive.

"Yep, it's me. Where I am—well, that's pretty amazing. I've discovered how limiting corporeal instantiation can be."

"Corporeal instantiation? What are you—"

"That's more the way Raymond would say it. I've discovered that I'm not limited to the abilities that come with a human body. I used the link you opened for the SDB to inhabit *El Mirador* systems. I can see and hear everything that Esteban's systems can see or hear. What's more, it's taking me some time, but I can control most of it now, all of it soon."

Aida took a moment to digest what Clayton had just said. "How did you tap into my com? Can you reestablish the operation comlink?"

"I was able to tune the house system into the frequency of your earpiece without using your phone. I could reestablish the ops comlink but it wouldn't be a good idea right now. If I kill the cell phone suppression system, it's bound to trigger an alarm. I'm pretty sure I would be able to silence the alarm, but I'm not sure I could do it before it alerted Esteban's security team. They're going to figure out that something's going on soon enough. My plan, if you agree, is to reestablish com when that happens."

Aida took a brief moment to think. "I agree. How did you know I was asleep? Is my room wired?"

"No, I was surprised to find out that it's not. I knew you were asleep because when I tuned into your earpiece, I could hear you snoring."

"I don't snore."

"Okay, that was an exaggeration. It was your steady breathing that told me you were asleep."

"How long were you listening?"

"Awhile. I didn't want to wake you up until it was time."

"I had set an alarm." As she spoke, Aida fiddled with her phone to keep the alarm from sounding.

"I assumed you did, but wasn't it nicer to have me wake you up than some old phone alarm?"

"My phone has a lot of choices for alarms. I'm pretty sure that 'Rise and shine sleeping beauty' wouldn't be my first pick."

"Aww."

"Not even in my top ten."

"Now you're just being mean."

They both laughed, enjoying the relief of the easy repartee.

"It's good to hear your voice, Clayton."

"Same here, Aida."

It was clear that any lingering tension between them had been swept away by the needs of the moment and their mutual chemistry.

"Okay, I guess we should get down to business." Reluctantly, Clayton pulled them both back to the reality of the mission. "The current sitrep is that two guys are manning the security center. Another four are on roving patrols throughout the estate. As far as I can tell, the house is quiet. Everyone is in their rooms. I know about your great adventure cover story. I was eavesdropping when Carmen pitched it to Esteban. Great idea, but it will only stand up for so long.

"As we get close to extraction time, I'll loop the radar and camera feeds from the beach. That will keep the security team from seeing the boats come in. As needed, I can make you folks invisible from the cameras and sensors, but things will get complicated once the shit hits the fan and any pursuers have you in their sight. At that point, they won't be relying on the computer systems."

OPERATION HIGH TIDE

"Understood."

"When it looks as though your cover story is blown, or about to be, I'll kill the cell suppression system and reestablish the comlink with ops."

There was a thoughtful silence, then, "Is there anything new that you found out before I made the jump into the estate systems?"

"Well, there are a couple of things that Carmen shared with me. Esteban has grown increasingly paranoid over the past two years. He has been amassing quite a stash of weapons and ammunition that he stores in the basement of the main house. He keeps adding to it, selling some as a lucrative new side business. It seems that it is somehow comforting to him to have the stuff here in the house."

"Hmm, I think I may be able to use that. I'd like to pull him out of the action tonight for as long as possible. His obsession with his weapons may be good bait. You said Carmen shared a couple of things—"

"She has alluded to some plan of her own that will keep Esteban from lashing out at her family if she leaves him. She hasn't shared any details of what that might mean, but there it is."

"I'm sure we'll find out, eventually. I know this. Carmen is an incredibly bright and capable woman. She has every reason to be angry and determined. I'd hate to be in her crosshairs."

Aida glanced at the clock. 1:10. "Shit, I've got to get moving. I promised Carmen that I'd be at her door at 1:25."

"It's not like you have to call a cab."

"Yeah, well, we corporeal instantiations need to attend to some things before we're ready to face the day.

"Ha, roger that. Okay, I'll be in your ear all the way down to the beach or until I hand you off to ops control."

"Got it. Thanks, Clayton."

"Good luck to all of you."

325

"You too."

——✧——

1:24 a.m.

At 1:24 a.m. Aida was at the door of her room, her bag slung over her shoulder. She took one last look around the room and stepped into the hallway.

Knocking softly on Carmen's door, she heard the children's muffled giggles and Carmen's gentle admonitions. As the door opened, Aida saw that, true to her word, Carmen and the children were ready to go. More than ready, at Carmen's signal, they stood at attention and saluted.

"Good morning, General Alba."

Aida returned the salute, and the two young soldiers deflated into a pile of giggles.

"I have told them that you are in charge of tonight's adventure and that they should listen to everything you say. Isn't that right, children?"

They voiced their confirmation almost in unison, "Si mamá," with Este adding, "Mamá says if we are good, we might even get a boat ride."

Aida answered with a broad smile, "Well, that could happen, but you would have to be very good. And you must know that the boat ride is a top secret."

"Oh, we will be extra special good." It was Lucia's turn to chime in. "We love boat rides, and we are very good at keeping secrets."

"Alright, team, check each other's equipment one last time." Aida commanded her troops. While the children poked and tugged at their coats and packs, Aida spoke in soft tones to Carmen. "I have a plan for dealing with our escort. When we get close to the gate, I will lag behind. You and the rest keep going down to the beach as quickly as you can." Pointing to the flashlight that Carmen carried, she continued, "The signal to the boats is three short flashes followed by two long flashes."

Carmen's excitement was easy to hear in her voice. "Si, understood."

After final adjustments to the coats and backpacks, the group headed downstairs. With Carmen in front and Aida bringing up the rear, the children happily continued their playful military roles and marched in between.

As they walked through the dark of the great room and approached the dimly lit sunroom, they saw Rosa and Roberto standing nervously with their backpacks at their feet. Roberto was again shifting his weight from one foot to the other. Carmen started to speak but before she could utter a sound, a silent warning in Rosa's eyes had her look into the darker part of the room.

"Buenos días, señora Navarro." Marco stepped out of the shadows. His greeting was flat, devoid of any hint as to what he was thinking or where the conversation might go next.

Startled at first, Carmen was quick to recover. "Buenos días, Marco. I did not expect to see you this morning. Are you coming with us for our great adventure?"

"No, señora, I have other duties." His response was tinged with disdain, giving the impression that he felt that the task of babysitting the group on their outing was beneath him. "I am only here to introduce you to your ... protector, who I believe you may already know." Marco glanced at the shadows behind him. "Geraldo." At the mention of his name, the young man stepped into the light.

"Buenos días, señora." First, he addressed Carmen with a slight bow and then repeated the bow in Aida's direction, ignoring the rest of the group. As he bowed, Aida caught a glimpse of the earpiece he wore and the submachine gun he carried under his coat. "Señora, it will be my pleasure to accompany you this morning." Although the words were sweet, their delivery was less than convincing. Judging from

Esteban's earlier tantrum, it seemed likely to Aida that Geraldo's assignment to this early morning detail was a punishment for allowing the women to access the security center.

"I will leave you now." Marco looked at Geraldo, who nodded his acknowledgment and then addressed the group. "I hope your moon-watching does not disappoint." With that, he turned and lumbered into the darkness of the great room and the lobby beyond.

They listened in silence for a time as Marco's footsteps faded. "I see you are carrying backpacks. Why?" There was more curiosity in Geraldo's question than suspicion.

Aida was quick to volunteer. "This is a great adventure and everyone carries a backpack on a great adventure."

Rosa added, "I have packed some sandwiches and hot drinks. Enough even for you to share."

Geraldo's passing curiosity was satisfied, and he responded with genuine gratitude, "Ah, gracias, Rosa. It will be cold. The drinks will be a blessing."

The chimes of the big clock in the lobby announced that it was half past the hour. Aida and Carmen exchanged glances.

Carmen scanned the expectant faces. "It's time for us to go." She slid open the glass door that led to the outside portico and waited as the group exited and descended the steps to the gardens below. She took one last look at the room, slid the door shut, and stepped into the blustery chill of the occasionally moonlit night.

1:30 a.m.

Marco's size and bearing, along with his permanent scowl, evoked strong first impressions. His speech and mannerisms signaled a thoroughly shallow, loutish human being, whose strengths, weaknesses, value, and potential were easily measured and appraised. So perfectly did he fit the role of a cartel enforcer that a cynical observer might wonder if the scars on his face were the result of brutal, bloody battles or the product of a purposeful, career-enhancing cosmetic procedure.

As he left Carmen and her group in the sunroom, a niggle was born in that part of his brain that he kept to himself. He retreated to his room in the back part of the main floor of the house. Slipping his shoes off, he lowered himself onto the bed, not bothering to undress. He closed his eyes, but sleep wouldn't come. The niggle became a nag and the nag a concern. Pulling himself out of bed, he seated himself heavily in front of his computer. With surprising dexterity, his ham-like hands and tattooed fingers worked at the keyboard. After only a few seconds, he grunted, picked up the house phone, and punched in a number.

———⋅◦∞◦⋅———

1:40 a.m.

The demons that long ago had eaten his soul now prowled through Esteban's nightmares. There was no night without fear and no sleep without drugs. This night, as on most nights, the creatures that haunted his dreams rose up from the garden of his constantly growing fears and the day's events. In this night's installment, the image of his wife had undergone a bestial transformation and was playing a lethal game of hide and seek throughout the rooms and grounds of the estate. After a terrifying and lengthy chase, he heard the hopeful sound of church bells chiming in the dark. Cornered and exhausted, Esteban saw that the beast had abandoned the frenetic rush of the chase and was now slinking closer, cat-like, for the final kiss of death. The persistent bells became louder and more defined.

The nightmarish images dissolved in the groggy wakefulness that the ringing phone forced on his sweat-soaked body. With a shaking hand, he fumbled for the phone in the dark and held it to his ear, upside down.

"Mmm … Hola?"

"There is no lunar eclipse tonight."

"Wh—Marco? What time is it? What is it you are saying?" He turned the phone right side up.

"Esteban, there is no lunar eclipse tonight. There is something wrong. Something else is going on!"

"What? What is going on?"

Esteban cursed the fog that clouded his brain and reached for one of the pill bottles on his nightstand, spilling the glass of water that stood nearby.

"Shit—fuck—Meet me in the sunroom, Marco! I'll be right there!"

1:41 a.m.

Clayton was able to track Aida's progress through the audio feed from her earpiece and the estate's cameras. There was no need for him to speak since it would be distracting and he had nothing to contribute. He used the time to pursue his own piece of the op. He studied the feeds from the various cameras and sensors from the house to the beach and then, based on Aida's input, turned his attention to the feed from the cellar of the mansion. The surveillance cameras of the massive space confirmed Aida's narrative. A large cache of weapons, both on racks and in boxes, along with crates of ammunition and other military-grade ordnance, were lined up in neat rows on the concrete floor. In a view from a different camera, Clayton could see that what appeared to be a firing range was being built. A forklift, scaffolding, and other equipment appeared ready for a construction crew to pick up where they had left off.

At that moment, one of the many feeds in Clayton's ear caught his attention. It was Marco's voice on a house line to Esteban's room, "Esteban, there is no lunar eclipse tonight. There is something wrong. Something else is going on!"

****

Carmen and her group were making good progress. They were more than halfway to the electric fence. Cold and darkness kept the children from their typical meandering, so there was little need for any of the adults to remind them to stay together. The moon played peekaboo through the torn curtain of a broken overcast. Brisk gusts from over the Pacific brought the smell of the sea and the sounds of the surf. The group moved in a single line, with Carmen at the front and Aida and Geraldo bringing up the rear.

Geraldo started complaining shortly after the group left the house. He grumbled in Spanish at every gust of wind, leaving no doubt as to his opinion of the assignment.

As they made their way through the gardens and across the lawn, Aida used the time to observe Geraldo and assess the challenge that he would present as an adversary. Fit and wiry, he moved with the ease and agility of youth, but there was no indication of his training. He was not part of Clayton's shared memory, which would indicate he was a more recent addition to the staff. According to Clayton, personnel recruitment was undertaken with a premium placed on loyalty. New hires came through trusted connections. The result was a staff whose will to fight most likely was greater than its ability.

Aida's musings were interrupted as Clayton's voice in her earpiece cut through the sounds of the wind and the jostling noises of the group's movements. "Aida ...",

"I'm here, Clayton."

"Where are you?"

"About 75 yards from the fence line."

"Marco figured out that there is no lunar eclipse tonight. Esteban knows."

"Well, things were bound to go south at some point."

"Well, that part of your story is blown, but he still doesn't know what's going on. Can you handle Geraldo?"

"Yeah, I should be okay. It's the reinforcements that I worry about."

"I've got an idea that hopefully will occupy Esteban for a few minutes and keep his guys off your back. Good luck. Gotta go."

"Thanks. You too."

Clayton accessed the house phone system and after a moment's study had the system access a particular number.

———◦∞◦———

1:42 a.m.

The new pills were pushing back the fog that came with Esteban's sleeping medications. He stood over the sink, bathing his face in the cold water from the tap to help accelerate the process.

What is she up to now? Even after yesterday's talk, she still plays games. Fuck! This is too much! Who does she think she is to defy me?

The ring from the house phone interrupted his thoughts. He too briefly rubbed his face into a towel and water dripped from his beard as he held the phone to his ear.

"Hola?"

"Jefe, there is an alarm in the armory. We can't see anyone on the cameras, but a motion detector was tripped and the security board says someone is there." To sell his voice as belonging to one of the staff, Clayton counted on the limited quality of the phone audio, Esteban's lack of personal involvement with all of his security personnel, and the fact that the call came on the house line. There was no reason for Esteban to doubt its origin.

"The armory? How could—? Send two men now. I will meet them there. Whoever it is, we will catch the cockroach."

His wife's petty games must take a back seat to the security of his weapon stash. If his weapons weren't secure, what then could be said for the rest of the estate?

In a matter of seconds, he was dressed. The first of the morning's pills was taking effect and the tsunami of chemicals slammed into his brain, replacing rational thought with the urgent need for action. Sweating through his clean shirt, in the cool room, he shakily grabbed a two-way radio and his silver-plated pistol from the table. On the way out, he paused at the nightstand to wash down another pill. Moving much more quickly now, he dashed down the back stairway to the cellar. He was breathing heavily when he arrived at the small empty lobby facing the camera on the wall and a steel-reinforced door.

⸻ ◦∞◦ ⸻

1:44 a.m.

"Maldita sea!" Even though it had been less than two minutes since he had ordered it, Esteban's muttered curse expressed his impatience that there was no sign of the security team. The drugs coursing through his body fueled his surging paranoia. A quick look at the door and the access pad confirmed that neither had been tampered with. Esteban placed his thumb on the pad and the door noiselessly swung open. His pistol at the ready, he ducked into the darkness, stepping quickly away from the brightness of the doorway. He paused for a moment on full alert and then, sheltering behind a stack of shipping crates, reached behind him for the wall switch. The cellar was immediately bathed in the harsh white light of the LED bulbs in the high ceiling. One malfunctioning bank of work lights on the floor of the firing range construction area flickered and buzzed before finally turning on completely. Esteban panned his gun over his field of vision and stood quietly, listening for any sound that might betray the location of the intruder.

Clayton was able to view Esteban's progress since he left his bedroom and noticed the uneven movements, the sweating, and the tremor in his hands. As Esteban stood listening behind his cover of the shipping crates, Clayton tapped into the intercom wired to the cellar and switched it on and then off. The result was a soft sound in the otherwise silent cellar that could have been the sound of a settling house, a footstep, or the cocking of a gun.

Click

Esteban heard the sound come from the construction area and he stepped from behind the crates and turned in that direction. He scanned for some movement that would identify a target.

"I know you're here," he shouted into the darkness beyond the reach of the lights.

Clayton again triggered the intercom.

Click

At the sound, Esteban ducked behind his cover but then cautiously leaned out to peer into the blackness. "I don't know how you got in, but there is no way out." He paused and was rewarded with only silence.

"More of my men will be arriving soon. This can not end well for you. It's better that you give it up. I promise no harm will come to you." Esteban tried to sound sincere as he pulled back the hammer of his pistol.

Silence.

"Show yourself!" Esteban's voice raised in pitch and volume as his fragile hold on his temper began to slip and a wave of fear began to build.

Silence.

Esteban wiped the sweat from his forehead. "Answer me, damn you!" He listened for any sound that would verify that someone other than he was present in the cellar, but there was only silence. Without additional reinforcement, the fever pitch of his manic reactions started to cool. Maybe it was a false alarm after all. Perhaps some rodent had come in with a shipment, or there was a glitch in the system. Unsure of the existence of any threat now, he brought his gun down to his side and worked against the effects of the pills to calm himself.

Seeing that Esteban was overcoming his dread, Clayton escalated his attack on his opponent's mind. He clicked on the intercom and this time, he spoke.

Click "Howdy, Esteban. It's been more than a month o' Sundays. How'r y'all doin'?"

Coming through multiple speakers of the intercom system, the sound of Clayton's voice echoed in the large space, taking on a spectral quality that sent a chill up Esteban's spine. "Wha—Cotton?" Esteban raised his gun but, unsure of what to do with it, he waved it aimlessly at the darkness. "It can't be. You're dead. I watched you die."

"Yup, ya sure did that. You watched."

"Cotton, I tried to help but my rivals they—"

"Well, that's not how I remember it, partner. When I needed help, you and your compadre, Marco, were pretty slow on the draw."

The drugs amplified the surreal nature of the moment for Esteban.

This can't be happening. I'm talking to a dead man!

All of Esteban's hopes for a harmless explanation for the intruder alert and the clicking noises were washed away as his adrenaline came roaring back, sweeping his mind into full panic. "It—it was Marco. You know he never liked you. He didn't send help in time."

"Well, I sure'nuff may have an issue with Marco, but shovelin' yer shit into his stall doesn't make yer barn smell any cleaner. Right here'n now, it's time I settle with you. I'm comin' fer ya', Esteban."

The sweat ran down Esteban's forehead and stung his eyes. His impaired vision added to his out-of-control panic. No longer able to see clearly, he raised his gun and fired continuously as he swept his gun across the unfinished shooting range. The echoes of each discharge blended with the others until the room was filled with a continuous rolling thunder. He was firing into an area that didn't contain munitions, and so his fusillade only succeeded in chipping several columns of concrete and damaging the forklift.

As he emptied his clip, Esteban reached behind him, switched off the lights, backed out of the doorway, and closed it behind him. He leaned against the closed door, gasping for breath, trying to keep his pounding heart from blasting free of his chest.

As soon as he could talk, Esteban shouted into his radio, barely suppressing his panic. "Que pasa? I am at the armory. Where are the men I ordered to meet me here?"

The response from the security center was respectful but confused. "Señor Navarro? I—I'm sorry jefe, but we haven't received orders to send men to the armory."

"Estúpido, I spoke with you just a few minutes ago when you called to tell me of the intruder in the armory."

"Again, jefe, my apologies, but no one from the security center called you. We have just seen an alarm in the armory, but alarms are going off all over the estate. The ones we have checked so far—all seem to be false. Do you still want men at the armory?"

"Si, but I have him trapped. Send the men after they check on the other alarms."

A new voice cut into the conversation, "Jefe, this is Marco. Please come to the beach gate as soon as you can. Something is not right!"

It was with some relief that Esteban accepted the excuse that Marco's message gave him to leave whatever was in the armory. "I'll be right there."

While it seemed much longer to Esteban, it had been less than ten minutes since he had left his room.

1:47 a.m.

After Clayton's warning, Aida watched Geraldo closely looking for any sign that he was getting new instructions through his earpiece. The group moved on, stopping occasionally as Carmen and Aida pointed out various highlights in the night sky as they became visible through the broken clouds. Continuing the fiction of a stargazing great adventure had the dual benefit of entertaining the children and keeping Geraldo from considering other reasons for their outing.

She checked her watch. It had been almost ten minutes since she talked with Clayton. She assumed that Clayton's plan was working. As the group drew near the gate, Aida began to limp, moving more slowly to increase the distance between her and the others. True to his past behavior, Geraldo also slowed his pace to stay with her.

"Is there anything wrong, señora? Are you injured?"

"I have a cramp in my leg. I will be slower, but I will get there."

"Should you go back to the house? I can call someone to escort you."

"No, gracias, Geraldo. It is no big thing. I'm sure the cramp will be gone soon."

Forty yards ahead, Aida saw that the children had reached the gate first. Responding to their wristbands, the red light indicating that the fence was electrified turned green.

"Este, Lucia, wait." The reminder from Carmen cut through the sounds of wind and surf but was unnecessary as the children had already stopped and were waiting for their mother to open the gate. When Carmen pulled the gate open, the troop moved through and started down the stairs, leaving Aida and Geraldo to catch up.

The two latecomers went through the gate, and the wind slammed it behind them. As they looked down, they could see that the rest of the party was almost on the beach. It was then that Aida saw Geraldo hold his hand to his ear.

"Qué?" Struggling to hear, he turned his back to the noises of the stormy Pacific.

Aida had little doubt about what Geraldo was hearing. She moved quickly, abandoning her act as an injured nanny. Coming up behind him, she slammed her foot into the back of his knee, which brought him into a kneeling position. She promptly followed her first blow by clasping her hands and bringing them down forcefully at the base of his skull. Geraldo emitted a high-pitched shriek of pain in discordant harmony with the sound of the wind, followed by a low groan. Unconscious, in what appeared to be slow motion, he toppled toward the edge of the stairway. Without hesitation, Aida reached out and pulled him back to lie on the ground. It wasn't her intention to kill anyone tonight. She took his handgun and radio and sent his rifle clattering down the stairs.

"Well done, señora." His words conveyed genuine admiration as Marco's deep voice pushed through the wind. As he continued, the tone became deadly serious. "A wrong move and I will kill you. Throw down the pistol."

Aida looked up and saw that Marco was standing on the other side of the gate with a rifle pointed squarely at her head.

"It would give me no joy, but shooting you would cause me no sorrow, either. Drop the gun."

After a moment's consideration, Aida let the gun fall into the dirt.

"I have radioed señor Navarro. He will be here shortly. You will tell him what is going on and then he will decide what to do with you."

"Marco, Geraldo was attacking me. I had to—"

"You have very little time to come up with a better story. Believe me when I tell you the señor is a master of pain. It would save you many tears if you would simply tell the truth immediately.

"I will open the gate and when I do, you will come out to me. Bear in mind that the kindest thing that I can do is to shoot you now, so do as I say." Marco raised the band on his left wrist and the light above the gate changed from red to green. He reached out to pull the gate open and the moment he touched it, there was a flash of light accompanied by a sharp crack. Marco let out a short, strangled scream. His body stiffened and then in its petrified state toppled like a large tree, backward to the ground.

"That's one more you owe me." Clayton's voice in her earpiece was warm and reassuring.

"Neat trick, Clayton. Thanks."

"Don't thank me yet. From my last camera visual, Esteban is almost at the gate. Get out of there!"

Aida stooped and searched in the dark for the gun she had dropped. She had just put her hand on it when—

"Señora Mora, isn't it?" Esteban's voice was like ice. He had recovered some measure of his composure from his panic in the armory. "Stand up slowly and keep your hands where I can see them."

Aida placed her foot on the pistol and slowly stood to face a silver-plated handgun wielded by a sneering Esteban.

"It seems you are not the timid nanny that you have pretended to be." Esteban smiled sardonically, enjoying his advantage over her. He was in control again. "I will unlock the gate and you will push it open. Comprende?"

Aida paused to consider her slim options. Rushing him would be suicidal. A leap down the stairs would almost certainly result in a severe injury and gain nothing.

"You will listen and obey now or I will shoot you in your left arm and then you will listen and obey." A metallic click pierced the night's other noises as Esteban pulled the hammer back on his pistol. "Move—now!"

Aida reluctantly started to take a step toward the gate when Carmen's strong voice carried over the wind from behind her.

"No, Esteban. She will not! Drop your gun."

Aida half turned to see Carmen stepping up to the top of the stairway with a rifle pointed in Esteban's general direction.

"Look what I found on the stairs."

"Ah, my loving wife." Esteban's pistol wavered in his hand as if awaiting instructions. "Put down the gun, Carmen, before you hurt yourself."

"Hurt myself? Maybe you're right, Esteban. Maybe it's too heavy for me to aim." Carmen tucked the gun under her shoulder, leveling it at Esteban. "Maybe I don't know how it works. Maybe I don't know how to switch the safety off." She clicked the safety to the fire position. "Maybe I can't control it when it fires." She pressed the trigger briefly and the short burst stitched a neat line in the dirt inches from Esteban's toes.

Startled, Esteban took several steps backward. Aida took the opportunity to scoop up the handgun and train it on Esteban. In a matter of seconds, the balance of power had shifted dramatically.

"Throw your weapon over the fence." Aida's voice was clear and commanding.

The two guns leveled at him posed a convincing argument. It only took a moment's consideration for Esteban to comply. The silver reflected the moonlight as his gun arced over the fence and landed with a thud on the ground.

"Okay, now toss over Marco's rifle and handgun."

Marco groaned as Esteban removed his weapons and in sulky silence completed the tasks as ordered.

"You know I will find you, Carmen. There is no mountain high enough, no hole deep enough to keep you from me. I have an army of dogs that will sniff you out. And your family, they are all dead. You have killed them. Count your days, count your breaths, and count your loved ones. They, all of them, are numbered. Do you understand?"

"Hear me, Esteban." Struggling to keep her passions in check, Carmen calmly paced her words so that their meaning would not be lost. "We don't have much time, and I want you to know what is happening to you. I hate you, perhaps much less than I should. In any case, what I have done comes not from my hate for you, but from the love of my family. Two years ago, a man brought hope into my life. More than that, he taught me how to hope once again. Strangely, when he died, the hope stayed alive and grew brighter and stronger. While you were busy building your macho empire, I was also busy. I learned and probed. The hours I spent on the computer were not all about games and songs for the children. I was exploring every part of your business. Over the past 18 months, I have gradually delayed the reports of your business transactions by 24 hours. There is nothing missing, just delayed. I know that the few people it bothered blamed it on the new computer systems. The result of my efforts was that I enjoyed the use of many hundreds of millions of dollars in a renewing cycle each 24 hours. Leveraged by smart investments, the net proceeds of this exercise amounted to a bit more than 23 million dollars."

Esteban's face mirrored his feelings as they cycled through the phases of anger, disbelief, realization, and then rage. "If what you say is true, Carmen, the cartel will skin you alive. You are damned. What I could do to you is nothing, nada, compared to what they will do. Hah, you will beg me for protection. Then you will beg me for help and in the end, you will beg me for death."

For a moment, the wind and sea were the only sounds. Carmen's voice took on the tone of someone trying to teach a stubborn young child. "Esteban, you miss the bigger picture, as you have always done." Carmen took a big breath to steady herself before continuing, "All that I have done, I did in your name. The transaction logs, the manipulations, and the hidden accounts containing the proceeds, all are tagged with your name. When the cartel explores this theft, all paths will lead to you."

"What—how? That is not possible. You couldn't—"

"I couldn't what, Esteban, understand your business? I have a master's degree in economics. Your business is not that complicated, nor was manipulating it. Shift the blame to you? You are careless with your passwords. You leave your computer on all the time. It was not that hard.

"Earlier today, your bosses received an anonymous tip that I'm sure has already moved them to start their investigation into your disloyalty.

"The children will grow up without their father and that saddens me, but they have been without a father for their whole lives.

"What you do next is up to you. I don't think you have much time, a few hours, perhaps a day. When Marco wakes up, I expect he will have new orders. I suppose you could run, but as you have said, they have an army of dogs and there is no hole deep enough—"

"HIGH TIDE 2, this is HIGH TIDE 3. Come in." Aida was totally engrossed in the drama playing out before her and instinctively flinched as the unfamiliar voice brought her earpiece to life.

She covered her mouth with her free hand and spoke softly, "Hello HIGH TIDE 3. Glad to hear your voice."

"Where are you HIGH TIDE 2? We are holding at one minute offshore."

"Part of the party is at the landing zone. Two of us are two minutes out."

"Roger that. We will look for your signal. Standing by."

Aida brought her hand down. "Carmen, we have to go."

2:00 a.m.

"Señor Navarro says there's somebody in there?"

"Si, Renato. That's the word I got from the command center."

"It's probably just another false alarm. The system is so fucked-up. How many would that make it? Four?"

"Counting this one, it would be five."

"Okay, five. What a fuckin' waste of time."

"What do you suggest, muchacho? We should just ignore the alarms and go back to bed?"

"Of course not, Silvio, but it's still a waste of time. Somebody should do something about the system."

"Well, Renato, when el jefe puts your name up to lead the system renovation team, you will have my vote. Besides, it was el jefe himself who radioed in, so be alert. There may be something to this one."

The two guards had arrived at the armory a few moments after Esteban left for the beach gate.

Silvio, the older of the two, had reviewed the video feed from the camera with his partner and now examined the access pad. The technology indicated that there had been no unauthorized entry.

"The camera never picked up anyone other than el jefe. It recorded a voice, though."

"Yeah, some pretty crazy shit about stuff that went down before I got here."

"I was here then, Renato. El jefe had hired an hombre, Cotton Parish, to install the new computer system and overhaul security. He got blown up in a firefight down in the bay."

"No shit."

"It was pretty wild. Pay attention now. Are you ready?"

"Si, let's check it out."

Silvio placed his thumb on the access pad and the door swung open.

Guns at the ready, the two entered, Silvio ducking left and Renato going right. It was Silvio who smelled the gas leaking from the bullet-damaged propane tank on the forklift as his partner groped in the dark for the light switch. His quick mind immediately understood the implications.

"Renato! Don't turn on the li—"

Too late. The room was briefly bathed in the white light of the ceiling fixtures. The malfunctioning work light flickered and buzzed. Both men turned to make a dash through the door. Then the fires of hell came to *El Mirador*.

****

Carmen took one last look at Esteban and the darkness behind him that wrapped itself around a legacy of so much misery for so many people. She remembered how he could appear confident, even regal at times. Now his tailored clothing looked too big for him. Propped up only by the drugs that supplied enough adrenaline for him to stand, he appeared small and pitiful.

"Carmen, por favor …" His voice trailed off. He had no logical way to end the sentence. There was nothing Carmen could do now. Nothing anyone could do.

Carmen slung the rifle over her shoulder. "Vaya con Díos, Esteban." She nodded to Aida, and they both started down the stairs.

"Carmen … please," like a small boy asking for one more chance, Esteban tried again. In desperation, his mind was looking for hope where none existed. Carmen hesitated on the stairway and turned in time to see and hear the full effect of the first explosion in the armory. Aida spun around, as did Esteban. Their eyes were all focused on the house as the second blast, much bigger than the first, sent flames and burning fragments high into the sky. The light from the raging conflagration illuminated the gardens in an eerie, flickering red glow. With Esteban and Marco both missing, silhouetted stick figures of confused and terrified staff members dashed across the lawns in frenzied disarray.

The destruction of Esteban's world, while devastating before, was now nearly complete. He sank to his knees. His shoulders shook as he screamed at the night, his words unintelligible through his sobs.

Aida gently put her hand on Carmen's arm.

Carmen turned slowly, "Si, I am ready."

They both raced down the stairs to the beach.

"HIGH TIDE 2 this is HIGH TIDE 3. What the fuck just happened?"

"I wasn't sure you guys would see a flashlight." Less an attempt at humor and more a release of tension, Aida's cringe-worthy remark evoked groans and chuckles from all who heard it.

As Aida and Carmen joined the others, Este and Lucia ran and threw their arms around their mother.

"Mis corazónes! Mis amores!" Carmen was surrounded by her family. With everyone's cheeks wet with tears, they held each other as the moon pushed its light through the clearing sky. Aida wiped her own cheek as she spoke, her relief evident in her voice. "Package at LZ. Ready for exfil."

"Copy that, HIGH TIDE 2. Be there in one."

Aida looked up at the fire that was brightening the eastern sky. "Clayton … Clayton, do you read me? Did you get out? Please respond." There was no answer, leaving Aida to fear the worst.

Carmen looked up from the joyful group. "I don't even know your name."

"Aida, Carmen. My name is Aida."

Carmen stretched out her arm to open the family circle. "Come, Aida. You are one of us now."

CHAPTER TWELVE

After Action

February 7, 2022 - Red Sky in the Morning

The red morning sun flashed off the ripples in diamond-shaped sparkles as the bow of the 44-foot motorsailer, *Almost Heaven,* sliced neatly through the water. She was schooner-rigged, sailing close-hauled, making good way for a vessel of her type. The brisk, steady wind blew across the deck, its silent power heeling the boat over just enough to give Clayton the feel of sailing and remind him how much that meant. He was at the steering station on the upper deck, feeling the belly of the ocean surge through his feet as the rhythmic swells swept against and under the boat. Today he would stay in Puget Sound, the waters that surrounded his Bainbridge Island home, but an easy sail out beyond was the Pacific and that could mean China, Tahiti, and the warm water ports to the south and west or down to Tierra del Fuego and around the Horn. The core of his elation wasn't in the going, it was in the knowing that he could.

All water was connected. All the drops touched and married to create one vast ocean of unlimited potential. Behind him in the wake of his recent past were his own memories, before that the first Clayton's, and beyond that the strivings of a thousand years of captains and kings, princes and pirates—all connected.

"You're pretty quiet for someone who said that they wanted to talk." Raymond was content to sit in the cockpit and enjoy the day. He broke the prolonged silence, not intending to criticize or direct, but as an invitation to engage—or not.

"Ya know, Raymond, some of my memories are great and I'm glad I have them, but a memory can't replace the making of the memory, the living of the experience." Clayton's deflection was sincere. "I'm not sure where to begin."

"Aida says hi." Raymond was curious but determined not to pressure Clayton. "She's quit ATHENA. She was the first to sense the humanity in you and her role in deceiving you didn't sit well with her. The more you evolved, the less she liked her involvement. Operation HIGH TIDE reminded her about what she really likes about her career, the excitement of chasing bad guys and joy in helping people."

"Hi back to her. She's a special lady. You couldn't have programmed a better one." The tease was recognition of the casual and friendly turn that Clayton's relationship with Raymond had taken.

Having primed the pump and sensing that Clayton wanted to talk, Raymond kept the conversation alive. "It's been four days and the HIGH TIDE team is still congratulating each other. The operation was pretty intense. We were all worried that you didn't get out. It didn't help that we really didn't know what that might mean."

"Ha, neither did I. I could see what was going on down in the armory. Once the fire started, it didn't take a genius to figure out what was going to happen and that I better get out of there." Clayton stood with his eyes on the horizon. "I did find out something—"

Raymond was quiet, allowing Clayton to own the moment. When he began again, Clayton avoided looking directly at Raymond. He scanned the horizon, examined the sails, and spoke as if to the sea and the wind while Raymond listened in.

"When I came to be, all that I was came from Clayton. I inherited his memories, judgments, and perspectives. I also inherited the guilt that was tearing him to pieces. The secret demon that sat on his shoulder and whispered in his ear, all day, every day, about how his sin had cost the lives of his wife and son."

"Well, he blamed himself for not being there to protect—"

"No, that wasn't it." Clayton checked the telltales and turned the wheel to take better advantage of the wind. "While he was undercover during Sandcastle, he got close to Carmen—real close. One time, just one time they—"

Raymond's quick response was sympathetic, "He was undercover. He had a role to play. That kind of thing can happen."

"Yeah, well, that's not the worst of it. Humans can't abide randomness. That aversion is what causes people to see Jesus in pizzas and poodles in clouds. More than that, Clayton was trained to mistrust accidents, to ferret out connections in coincidences. When he was told that Maggie and Anthony were murdered as a result of some random act, his mind worked overtime to find another explanation, one with—more meaning. He came to believe that while he was at *El Mirador*, his room had been wired and that what happened with Carmen had been recorded. He believed that in light of all that was happening, scanning internal house activity was a low priority item, but Esteban eventually saw it and took revenge on his family, who he thought was Cotton Parish's family. You see, Esteban has—had a reputation for punishing the families of those who betray him. It wasn't enough that Cotton was dead. Esteban needed more, so he tracked down who he thought was Cotton's family and—"

"But how would Esteban follow a trail that led to Clayton's family?"

"In Clayton's mind, Esteban sent his dogs to sniff out Cotton armed only with his picture and the fact that he was a computer-savvy guy from Texas. One of his minions picked up a trail mistaking Clayton for Cotton and Maggie and Anthony paid the price."

"Oh, God. That belief must have been eating Clayton alive."

"It was. It did. But while I was embedded in *El Mirador's* systems, I was able to find out something that Clayton couldn't know for sure."

"And what was that?"

"His room wasn't wired. Most likely because *El Mirador* was still under construction, many rooms weren't monitored. In any case, because that was true, the whole theory unravels. Esteban couldn't know, so there was no reason for him to punish Cotton. I confirmed as much when I confronted Esteban in the armory. I dangled plenty of opportunity for him to unload on Cotton but he never rose to the bait."

"And Maggie and Anthony?"

Clayton studied the telltales and fought back the wave of emotion that came with any discussion of his family. "Just another tragic act of violence, perhaps attributable to some fucking junkie whose morals and judgment were casualties of his addiction. It doesn't take a PhD. to assign some blame to Esteban, considering the business he was in, but he didn't order it.

"As I said, when I came into existence, everything that I was I got from Clayton. A lot has happened since then. I'm not that Clayton anymore. I'm different from him now, and the gap between us grows wider every day. This latest revelation puts a stake in the heart of the demon that haunted his and my every moment, and it relieves me of the burden that was crushing him. Tragically, he didn't live long enough to feel the relief that I feel, but I'm glad I'm alive to feel it.

"Throughout human history, artists and philosophers have struggled to capture and define life. I sure can't define it for you, but I know that I'm alive, Raymond. I … am … alive."

For a long moment Raymond appeared to study the fractured sun's rays dancing on the waves. "I know that, Clayton. I didn't use to, but now I do and I've known it for some time. When we developed your programming our mindset, our creator's bias kept us from seeing the implications of what we were doing. We thought we were creating an interactive repository of a person's experience, assuming that the snapshot would be developmentally static. Looking back now, I realize how naïve that was."

Raymond paused and took in the fine lines and fittings of the boat. "This is a fine boat."

"Ha, now there's a random non sequitur."

"Not really. Your original program didn't include this boat, and it certainly didn't give you the ability to create this boat. You're way beyond what we wrote and going further all the time. You've become both self-aware and self-defining with incredible power to actualize your ambitions.

"You did magnificent work on HIGH TIDE. If it weren't for you, odds are the operation would have failed and good people would have died. No one can deny it. But here's the thing, you acted independently. You stepped outside of your assigned role, came up with your own plan, and executed it. In a human agent, if the old Clayton had done it, there might be some slap-on-the-wrist reprimand for not following protocol but nothing compared to the slap on the back and the chorus of attaboys for the great result. In your case, powerful people are very concerned that an AI entity would show such independence. They are casting it as a serious problem and even an existential threat to humanity."

"By powerful people, you mean Max."

"Yes, but she has the influence to marshal a lot of support. She's coming after you, Clayton. I would stop her if I could, but I don't have the power."

"Well, I guess paranoia's not always such a bad thing."

"What do you mean?"

"You know I've had trust issues with you, ATHENA—everyone. As far as Max goes, I never believed that she and her toady, Keaton, were anything other than predators. When I stopped feeling sorry for myself and started to realize what I was capable of, I built some defenses into SEAM with some modifications of my own."

Clayton threw the helm hard over and as the boat turned, let out the mainsheet and then the jib. "It's time to go back and face the music, as they say. I don't know how this might turn out, Raymond. I can't say it's all been good, but it's been a real education knowing you, Professor."

"I'll do whatever I can. Living through ATHENA and knowing you have taught me more than a dozen years in teaching, but I have to say that lately, I've been missing those quieter days as a professor."

Clayton turned his gaze from the horizon and looked straight at his companion. "Thank you, Raymond. It's been a great sail, but everything has to come to an end."

<hr/>

February 7, 2022 - Afternoon Storm

Raymond took off the MINDI helmet. With the memory of his sail with Clayton fresh in his mind, he took a moment to allow the effects of the spatial displacement to fade. So real was the experience of sailing that when he stood up he needed to steady himself for just a moment as his legs and his brain got reacquainted with the stability of dry land.

He moved to his desk and tried to dampen his concerns over Max's political machinations by burying himself in the latest ATHENA analysis of the HIGH TIDE after-action reports. His purpose was to find some scientific understanding of the ATHENA progression that started with a clever and well-executed programming effort and became what he now fully admitted to himself was a new life form. Labels such as soulful instantiation, sentience, and singularity all drove to the same question: when does a non-living thing deserve the respect afforded to living creatures and beyond that, peerage with humans? If ATHENA were to try another such experiment, could they recognize the start of the progression? Could they programmatically prevent it? Should they? Should they even begin again? He had been at it for about an hour when the phone rescued him from the frustratingly fruitless arena where theology, law, and science circled, snarling their truths at each other in different languages. The display on his phone dispelled any suspense as to who was calling. Still, he let it ring several times, finding uncertain dread preferable to what answering the phone would bring.

Finally, he picked up, giving no indication that he knew who was calling, "Doctor Ababio"

"Good, you're in your office. Max and I will be right down." Keaton's voice had a lightness in it that communicated victory rather than good humor. In typical Keaton fashion, he hung up without waiting for a reply. Five minutes later, they were sitting in front of Raymond's desk.

"First of all, I want to congratulate you and the whole ATHENA team. HIGH TIDE proved the success of the project and then some." Max's congenial opening might have lulled a less experienced listener, but Raymond's insight into her agenda kept him from dropping his guard.

"Thank you, Max. I'll be sure to convey your congratulations to the team."

"There's more, Raymond. I've arranged for the entire team to get a hefty bonus and their pick of assignments within SHUMA or its member organizations."

Raymond stood and thoughtfully turned to run his hand over the kente cloth that sat on the credenza behind his desk. "You're killing the project."

It was not a question, but Raymond's observation hung in the air like a bad odor begging for attention.

"I've talked it over with the leaders from the other SHUMA member organizations and we think it's wise to take some time to—"

"You're pulling the plug on ATHENA."

"Raymond, I—" Softening harsh messages didn't come easily to Max. She thought it to be a waste of time and it made her feel uncomfortable. She quickly pivoted to a more familiar approach. "—all right, yes, goddamn it, and the reasons are pretty clear. At least they should be." Max stood up and slammed her fist on the desk. "Don't forget what SHUMA stands for, Raymond. It's the Society for Human Advancement. Human, Raymond, human!" She leaned forward, now railing at Raymond's back as he continued to finger the kente cloth. "Your focus on Clayton Rhodes has led you and your team to great success, but now this tool that you created has become an obsession with you and a danger to the rest of humanity. Clayton's power and his ability to wield it are growing with each day that passes. You tout his humanness but that brings with it emotions, human frailties, anger, and temper all of which make an enormously powerful creature all the more dangerous. And he's not human, Raymond. All your work and all your pride can't change that fact. He's not human. So yes, we have decided to shelve ATHENA until we know better how to balance the benefits with the risks."

"And Clayton?"

"Haven't you been listening? We pull the plug on him too. Especially on him."

"It's noteworthy, Max, that you recognize that there is sufficient humanity in him to consider him dangerous, but not enough to stop you from ending his life." Not waiting for a reply, Raymond continued, "For what it's worth, I can't condone such an act."

"I didn't come here to get your permission or your approval, Raymond. Clayton has ignored my demands for a meeting via SETE. I have no way to drag him here, so I want you to use MINDI to send Keaton and me to his home."

"Why don't you just delete the whole system? I'm sure you could bully some flunky into helping with that."

"Well, that wouldn't be right. He should get some notice."

"Why, Max? He's not human, so what do you care what he feels?" Raymond turned and bore his eyes into Max's. "The fact is, you want to look him in the eye. You want to feel the power and see the fear and maybe, if you're really lucky, you'll get to watch him beg. And in all of that, you recognize and validate his humanity."

Max sputtered, struggling for an answer, and then gave up on the conversation. "Enough! Set up the MINDI equipment. Let's get this done."

"And if I decline your invitation?"

"It's not an invitation and not only your future, but that of your entire team depends on what you decide to do. You're right. I can get someone else to help with this, but that would cause an inconvenient delay and be oh so sad for your people."

Raymond knew he didn't have the fire to win or the smoke to bluff. On the other hand, he was sure that Max wasn't bluffing. His refusal would only provide an ineffective, symbolic gesture and at a great cost to others.

As Raymond dejectedly set up the equipment, he repeated the warning he had given to Keaton. "The MINDI system co-opts part of your mind to allow for the spacial displacement into SEAM."

"What does SEAM stand for again, Doc?" It was the first time Keaton had spoken since they entered the room.

"Strictly Enforced Attenuated Metaverse. Originally, its firewalls were impenetrable, but our interactions with Clayton and Clayton's adventures have weakened them or more correctly made paths through them.

"That part of your mind that is within SEAM is vulnerable to erasure if the system were to suffer a catastrophic failure while you are there."

Raymond looked for a reaction from the two impending metaverse travelers. The dismissive disdain on Max's face was predictable. The discomfort on Keaton's was also in character. Raymond continued, "Other than that, please keep your tray tables in their fully upright and locked position for the duration of the flight." His attempt at levity was more for his own benefit than anything else. "Any questions?"

Keaton raised his hand. "How do we get back?"

Raymond took two small remotes off of his desk and handed one each to Max and Keaton. "The physical unit will stay here, but its virtual counterpart will travel with you. When you want to end the visit, just press the button on the remote. The return takes approximately 10 seconds to complete its cycle. At the end of that time, the pieces of your minds will be fully reunited. Anything else?" There was a long silence during which Keaton twice looked as though he would pose a question, but each time failed to find the words.

"Alright then, please make yourselves comfortable in one of the reclining seats and put on a MINDI helmet."

Max moved confidently to comply while Keaton reluctantly settled into his chair, looking for all the world like a condemned prisoner, hoping for a last-minute reprieve. Raymond stood at the control console.

"Are you ready?"

Keaton appeared ready to speak, but Max cut off any opportunity for him to object. "Do it now." Raymond threw the switch. There was a low hum and Max and Keaton's eyes closed as they appeared to drift into a deep sleep.

****

It was noon. The sound of eight chimes from the ship's clock in his office wafted down the hallway and out to the porch where Clayton sat with his cup of coffee. He took in the view as he so often had, but now it included a sturdy dock and the *Almost Heaven,* his new boat. He thought about his morning conversation with Raymond. He thought about all the old friends he had left behind and the new ones that ATHENA had brought. He thought about Maggie and Anthony. He was still sorting out his growing independence from the original Clayton and what that meant for himself, this new version. Akin to the surgical separation of Siamese twins, it was an exercise that was rewarding but painful and exhausting.

"Nice place we gave you," Max's voice rudely interrupted his thoughts.

Although unsure of the timing of her arrival, Clayton fully expected Max's visit. He had ignored her demands to engage with her via SETE. He knew that his disobedience would propel her to seek him out. "I'd say that, all things considered, I worked pretty hard for it."

"You'd say—you'd say. Listen to you. You'd say. You see, Clayton, that's just the problem. You are not supposed to say anything unless we ask you a question and want an answer."

"And are you speaking for the members of the HIGH TIDE operation? Without my initiative, there well might have been bodies on the beach."

"That was not a victory. It was a symptom. Your rebelliousness is a symptom. Your ability to enlist Raymond to defend you is a symptom. The very fact that you're arguing with me now is a symptom. You're not the useful tool you were created to be. You're more like a malfunctioning machine, unable to be repaired and a growing danger to everyone.

"I have polled the consortium of leaders within SHUMA and we have voted to suspend the ATHENA project for the time being. I am here to tell you that as part of that suspension, we will be archiving this SEAM metaverse version and deleting your profile."

"So, you're here to kill me."

"That pretty much sums it up, buddy." Keaton took advantage of the opening as the conversation sank to a level in his comfort zone.

Max ignored Keaton's comment. "You make it sound so dramatic. Clayton, you are a series of bits and bytes, as alive as my programmable coffee maker."

"Well, I guess there is no point in dragging this out." Clayton picked a small remote out of his pocket. He looked around the porch and then gazed out at the lawn, the dock, the boat, and the water beyond. "I'm going to miss all this. Ha, well, maybe not, with the no-longer-existing and all." He was playing with the remote as he spoke, turning it over in his hand and fingering the red button on its surface.

Unconcerned but curious, Max was savoring the power she felt over the condemned abnormality that was Clayton. "And what is that?"

"Well, Max, this here gizmo is the trigger for something I've been working on over the past few hours." He flipped it into the air and deftly caught it without taking his eyes off Max. "I figure there would be no way for me to keep going with the dedication and resources you can bring to taking me down." Satisfaction pulled Max's lips into the beginnings of a smile. "So I decided to go out with grace and on the way out do the world a big, final favor."

The smile faded from Max's face as it began to dawn on her what Clayton had planned. She fumbled in her pocket for her own remote.

Keaton was slow to catch on. "What is he talking about, Max? He has no place to go. He's dead meat."

"He's going to take us all to hell, you fool!" Max had found the remote and was tugging it free of her tight pants.

"Son of a bitch!" Keaton, late to the party, was now digging into his pocket for his own remote.

"Please, Clayton, don't. We can work something out!" Max had her remote free and was pressing the button over and over.

"Sorry, Max. Ten seconds can be an awfully long time. It won't work any faster if you press it harder or more times. Mine, on the other hand only takes about three seconds." Clayton raised his hand and pressed the button. Keaton grabbed for Clayton's remote, but his virtual hand passed through Clayton's with no effect. Clayton picked up his cup of coffee and took one last sip as he watched the ocean, the boat, the dock, and the lawn dissolve. He heard Keaton scream and saw Max's image blur—and then there was darkness.

PART SIX

EPILOGUE

CHAPTER THIRTEEN

Carmen

February, 2022 - A New Beginning

Holy crap!" The words jumped out of Aida's mouth as the van that had picked them up at the airport came to the end of the long drive and pulled up to a stunning Spanish colonial home. She had arranged to accompany Carmen and her family and help get them settled in their new lives near Lincoln City, Oregon. Not nearly as large and opulent as *El Mirador*, Carmen's new home provided a comfortable balance of function and luxury that would have few people wishing for more. Aida's reaction, though humorous, was nonetheless sincere, "I've got to get into the witness protection program."

Carmen smiled. "I have a bit of a confession to make, Aida … when I sent the information to the cartel about the bank accounts I had set up in Esteban's name, I neglected to include information about one account I had set aside for me, and my family." Aida gazed again at the home and rolled her eyes.

Carmen laughed. "Well si, it was quite a large amount. The people in the WITSEC program were very helpful in facilitating a discrete purchase for me under my new name. Now, Susana Merino—" she rolled the as-yet, unfamiliar name over her tongue before continuing, "is the proud owner of this lovely home, although I'm not sure why they were so insistent on this particular part of Oregon."

Over the next few days, Aida thoroughly enjoyed keeping company with the newly minted Susana and her rebranded family as they adjusted to their new lives. While the trips into the unfamiliar town were uncomfortable, there was nothing that would keep the discomfort from fading over time. The family easily adapted to life in their new home. Though physically smaller than *El Mirador*, the home exuded a brighter, airier aura, free from Esteban's oppressive shadow. The property included its own piece of the coast, so the daily visits to the beach were still on the schedule although the wardrobe was frequently more wool than cotton to accommodate the cooler weather. Rosa and Roberto, now Alina and Carlos, slipped easily into their new identities, with Rosa delivering the same delicious food and Roberto striving to take on the duties of handyman and groundskeeper.

After too short a stay, the inevitable call of duty had Aida packing for her return to her home office. With hugs, kisses, tears, and the promise of frequent visits, she flew back to California, leaving the protection of the family to the local U.S. marshal's office. Carmen and her family were deemed to be at a low risk since, although the evidence she brought was helpful, it wouldn't have to be made public.

The day after Aida left, a knock at the front door triggered Carmen's old fears. They had seen very few visitors and while Aida was there, the family enjoyed live-in protection. Due to a scheduling snafu, the front gate and camera wouldn't be fully operational until the following day. The rest of the family was down at the beach, so she was the only one in the house.

How could I be so foolish as to be here alone?

She pulled a pistol out of the high cupboard on the way to the door. She put her eye to the peephole then, not believing what she saw, demanded verification, "Who is it?"

"Good mornin', ma'am, I'm lookin' fer Susana Marino. I got an email here from a friend at—"

She cautiously opened the door a few inches. "Cotton? Cotton Parish."

"Well, that's a name I haven't heard in a dog's age. Yes, ma'am, there was a time when I answered ta that handle."

Carmen jammed the gun into her waistband, threw the door open, and flung her arms around a very confused but delighted Cotton Parish.

"Well golly, Ma'am. From now on, ya won't hear me braggin' as much 'bout Texas hospitality. With this kind a' greetin' you must git a whole slew a' visitors."

Neither one knew all the facts about the SANDCASTLE operation and Cotton knew nothing about HIGH TIDE. As to the mysterious, special agent Clayton Rhodes—their inquiries to their contacts in the FBI met with courteous but stubborn unresponsiveness. Central to the swirling eddy of unanswered questions and as the author of the email to Cotton, Clayton took on a mythic place in their life stories. Over time, they filled in the blanks with their mutual suppositions and managed to settle on a narrative that worked for both of them. In the years that followed, their first meeting became a favorite memory.

CHAPTER FOURTEEN

Clayton

February, 2022 - Thanks for the Memories

Doctor Ababio, these boxes and furniture are the last of it. Where do they go?" The young man's smile did him credit. A long morning of lifting two trucks' worth of boxes and equipment down to the hospital's loading bay had failed to spoil his pleasant disposition. One of the trucks, the smaller of the two, would carry its load to Raymond's old office at the university. The other was bound for a SHUMA storage facility. The young man's co-worker was older and lacking the vigor of youth and the sunny disposition of his companion stood silently leaning on his hand truck, appearing to use the moment to catch his breath.

"The boxes go to the university. The display screens and chairs go to storage." With that bit of instruction, the men loaded their hand trucks with efficiency and a height that displayed their skill and experience.

"Looks like one more trip will do it." The young man called over his shoulder as they carefully maneuvered their way out of the door and down the hall to the freight elevator.

Raymond sat and looked out over the large room, made larger by its echoing hollowness. The sadness that attaches to the twilight moments of a hard-fought endeavor flowed in to fill the vacancy. Trying to fend off a surging wave of melancholy, he adjusted the window shading to let in more of the waning afternoon light. He couldn't help but see more than the emptiness. The ghosts of past project events still haunted the space. The sessions with Clayton and Aida, the uncomfortable meetings with Max and Keaton, the HIGH TIDE operation briefing, the successes, and setbacks would reverberate for Raymond, in this space and in himself, forever. His chair and desk were now the only two pieces of furniture left. His laptop sat on the desk along with a cardboard box that held the swath of multi-colored, intricately patterned kente cloth, a relic of his graduation from high school in a different world, a long time ago.

As a man in his late 60s, and a physician, Raymond had seen death. He had lost people close to him and experienced grief. As a psychiatrist, he understood how painfully necessary it was to mourn the passing of a close friend or relative. But in all his experience, the dual deaths of Clayton Rhodes stood alone. In the first Clayton, he mourned the tragic death of a good man unnecessarily tortured by self-inflicted guilt. And because of the circumstances of his relationship with the second Clayton, his pain resembled the acute loss of a father for his son. More than once over the past week, he was brought to tears as the complicated waves of grief crashed through his defenses, leaving him in shambles.

A day in the hospital for observation determined that Max and Keaton had survived the SEAM crash physically uninjured. Those who knew them, even slightly, however, were quick to pick up on a profound change in terms of their personalities. Most notable in Max was her significant reordering of priorities and values. It was as if her harshest, most misanthropic demons were concentrated in that part of her mind that had entered SEAM to destroy Clayton and were washed away along with the Clayton Rhodes metaverse. Abandoning her interests in empire building and profiteering, she had announced that the land and other assets that she had acquired in her purchase of the Kansas-based AGRIUSCO agricultural firm would be repurposed as a multi-farm cooperative. Families that had farming experience were invited to exchange knowledge and sweat equity for a home and a share of the profits. She publicly alluded to other changes to come.

For ATHENA, Max had delivered on her promise. The team had all received generous bonuses and were off to their new assignments. Although offered an attractive position within SHUMA, Raymond had decided to go back to the relative freedom of academic life.

Even though Clayton's metaverse had been deleted, the rest of the ATHENA systems were still up, spinning uselessly on storage drives or resting inactive on their solid-state homes. Raymond hadn't been tasked with their removal, so it would be up to someone else to deactivate and archive the millions of lines of code.

He turned to his computer to check his official SHUMA email one last time.

With no team and no active project, the traffic in his SHUMA email account had trickled down to nothing in the last couple of days. He was surprised to see the single email in his in-basket. The surprise became a spine-chilling shock when the sender's name flashed onto the screen.

Clayton Rhodes

I'm still here!   *February 14, 2022*

His hand shook as he clicked to open the message. He was immediately presented with a blank screen that, after a long minute, resolved into a video image of a cockpit of a sailboat similar to the one he remembered from the *Almost Heaven*. The view was to the stern and took in the cockpit, the transom of the boat, and the wake in the water trailing behind. After a few moments, Clayton's image appeared, although off-center. "I've got my screen set up here. Hold on"—His hand loomed large, and the display jiggled as he adjusted its position. It steadied, framing Clayton perfectly.—"There, that's better." Clayton's face appeared and broke into an impish grin. "It's good to see you, Raymond, although you look like you've seen a ghost."

"I ... I think that's just what I'm seeing. How is it possible? Where are you? You—your metaverse, your whole world—it was deleted, washed away. You couldn't have survived. It's not possible that you can be—"

"Slow down, Raymond." Clayton's grin expanded at Raymond's energetic befuddlement. "If you let me get a word in, I can explain."

Raymond's face contorted as he fought to silence a hundred questions that were clamoring in his mind for expression. "Yes, please. It's so good to see you. I can't tell you how—" Realizing that he was losing control again, Raymond's face settled into the eager smile of an excited boy who'd been promised a big surprise. "Please tell me. What happened?"

With one eye on the trim of the boat and the other on the screen, Clayton launched into his explanation.

"It started way before the warning you gave me when we were sailing. There was a time when I didn't trust anyone and then a time when I just felt sorry for myself, but through all of my evolving perceptions, I viewed Max as a predator. As I started to understand and appreciate more about my situation, the primary instinct of self-preservation kicked in and I came up with a plan. It had two parts. First, I need a way to preserve my existence, independent of both SHUMA and the Bureau. Second, I wanted to pull the teeth out of the threat that Max presented. If I left her the way she was, it would guarantee that wherever I went she would come after me."

A wind change briefly pulled Clayton's attention to the task of adjusting the trim in the mainsail. His head dipped out of Raymond's view for a moment and then he was back.

"The first task required a serious systems design effort, followed by some equally intense programming. I knew I could never secretly find a single host for my metaverse. It was too large and required too many system resources. What I could do was chop a copy of my metaverse into hundreds, thousands of pieces and spread them throughout the internet. With a massively distributed configuration, they could run on what ended up being many thousands of smaller machines for brief intervals and not be noticed. The added benefit was that even if detected on any given host and deleted, the internet would provide access to an almost unlimited number of potential hosts. What you see now and where I live is a result of that effort."

A note of incredulity crept into Raymond's response. It wasn't disbelief as much as a struggle to comprehend the implications of what Clayton was saying. "I know you were well versed in systems work, but what you describe would take a team years to put together."

"I know it's hard to get your head around this, but you're talking about a team of humans, Raymond. I came to this situation with a decent skill set, but where I live and who I am now allowed me to expand my analysis skills and speed of development light years beyond where I started. For example, I don't need a human interface, no mouse, no keyboard. I can inhabit a machine and implement my analysis at the speed of thought. My development speed amazed even me. With my new metaverse ready to go, I was free to delete the old one at any time."

"Uh, okay." It was hard for Raymond to argue when the results of Clayton's efforts were right in front of his eyes. "What about your second challenge?"

"I knew that Max didn't just dislike me personally. She hated and feared what I represented. More than that, there was a part of her that was so warped by her feelings that she would never be able to evolve. That was the part that had to be excised. That was the part that had to be in the metaverse when I pulled the trigger."

"How did you know she would be there? She could have just had your world deleted from outside of SEAM."

"Nah. I knew she wouldn't do that. In addition to my interactions with her, I studied all I could find out about her. She has always fired people in person. She's an adrenaline junkie. There was something twisted in her that gave her a rush when confronting an uncomfortable situation in person. I knew I would be driving her crazy, refusing to join her in a SETE meeting. Yeah, I knew she would come after me. I kind of expected Keaton to tag along, but he wasn't a priority target. From all reports, things worked out pretty well for them both."

"Yes, I would have to agree that at least early signs are that the event had a positive effect. She's made some big announcements and I'm waiting to hear stories of Keaton helping old ladies across the street."

"Hah, now there's a picture—I'm sorry about ATHENA, Raymond. I know it was important to you."

"Are you kidding? It succeeded beyond my wildest dreams. I can't wait to get in front of a new batch of eager young minds and share our story, at least those parts that aren't confidential."

"I'd love to see that."

"I'll put the classes online. I'm sure you can figure out a way to get into the school's system."

"I'll make it a point." There was a moment's silence as Clayton appeared to focus on the sails. "What do you think they will do? I mean, after the stories are told, the warnings are issued, the laws are passed, what will they do?"

"Who?"

"Everyone, your students, people like Max, people unlike Max, captains of industry looking for profits, politicians looking for power, the military looking for weapons, healers looking for an end to suffering, recreational tourists looking for thrills, people looking for immortality, even folks who could view AI as the ultimate answer to climate change, scientists just looking—everyone.

"There will be another ATHENA Raymond, many more, with or without you. The stakes are too high, the temptation too great, the pull too strong. I am the first and only, but not for long. The genie's out of the bottle and there's no way to put him back.

"There's a storm coming. Don't retreat too far into the bubble of your classroom, Raymond. Humankind is going to need your steady hand on the tiller."

"What do you see happening, Clayton?"

"I live—my world exists on the stolen assets of the internet. My drain on the massive power of the millions of machines hooked into the Net is insignificant. A thousand worlds like mine? a million? At some point, there will be friction over scarce resources."

"And?"

"I'm no prophet, but 30,000 years ago, the last of the Neanderthals disappeared. They were assimilated, or pushed aside by a more adept version of humans."

"That sounds pretty ominous."

"I don't mean it to sound ominous, but there will be convulsions. Extreme evolutionary events tend to be like that. Looking at it another way, the Judeo-Christian take on creation is that God created humans on the sixth day of Genesis, however long that was. But what if the sixth day isn't an event but an ongoing process? Evolution doesn't stop simply because its present products are happy with the status quo."

Their talk had taken a turn into a dark sea of unanswerable questions and alarming outcomes. There was a lull in the conversation as Clayton made another adjustment to the rigging.

"You were wrong, you know."

Raymond chuckled. "During the course of ATHENA, I've been wrong, oh so many times. You want to narrow that down a bit?"

"About Reshod—you suggested that he was a part of me that MINDI set free."

"Yes, and once the limitations of SEAM were removed Reshod was re-assimilated into the rest of you. It was only a theory but, it seems, a good one since Reshod has disappeared."

"I just sent you a message I received two days ago. Tell me what you think."

Raymond shifted his screen to his inbox and clicked on the message that Clayton had forwarded.

Thanks for tying up the loose ends and finishing the job!

Fair winds and following seas, brother.
C.R. (Reshod)

"I tried to trace the origin, but it was a dead end."

"I ... I don't know what to make of it, Clayton. I can't even come up with a theory that I would be willing to share."

"What about one that you don't want to share?"

"Let me just say that the source of much of human hope and all of our faith springs from the realm of things we can't explain. When something like this comes along, the scientist in me longs for answers. The human part of me is content and even thrilled to leave the mystery in place and let the faith part of me decide what it may mean."

"Huh ... No offense, Raymond, but I expected more science and less faith."

"None taken, Clayton. As an answer, let me suggest that mysteries pose the questions and science struggles to supply answers. But we humans live much of our lives in the gap between the two and it's our hopeful imaginings, our personal faith, that allow us to survive the limitations of science and even thrive."

"And the note from C.R.—"

"—a beautiful mystery."

For a time, the only sound was that of the wind in the rigging. Then Raymond offered a new, less philosophical topic. "Aida told me that Carmen and her family have been debriefed and have been safely established in their new identities this week. There was some irregularity involved in where they were to be placed, but it has been sorted out. The initial location order was somewhat mysteriously overridden. Those involved are saying it was a computer glitch. You wouldn't know anything about that, would you?"

"Well, Raymond, I knew that Cotton—"

"Never mind, I don't want to know."

"Let me explain—"

"Really, Clayton, I don't want to know."

They both laughed.

There was a long pause. The conversation had reached the point where the headlines had all been discussed and delving into the next layer of details would take a much longer time.

"You'll stay in touch?" Raymond sensed the call was coming to an end and was reluctant to let it go without some promise of a future connection.

"You bet. I'm as free as the wind and aside from creating a perfect world in my metaverse, I haven't got much to do."

They shared another chuckle. Raymond heard a female voice on Clayton's end of the video saying something he couldn't quite make out.

Clayton spoke to Raymond, "That's the dinner bell. I'd best be goin'. We'll talk again real soon. Until then, you take care of yourself." He then called out to the unknown speaker, "I'll be right down, honey. The good doctor has been chewing my ear off."

From off camera Raymond heard a child's voice, "Come on, Dad." Followed by the sound of a woman's laugh that sounded like joy itself.

Clayton's face morphed into his prior impish grin. "I've made a few additions."

"Uh-huh, and I see you got a new boat. What's her name?"

"You know, I didn't have to think too long for that one. She's *Heaven Enough*." With that, the image of Clayton's broad smile was hidden as his hand grew to take up Raymond's whole screen and then the display faded to black.

From the Author

Dear Reader,

Thank you for taking the time to read my novel, *BITS*. I hope you enjoyed it. If that is the case, I ask for a bit more of your time. Please consider leaving a review at:

https://storyoriginapp.com/universalbooklinks/afcdd6b8-80db-11ef-9cbb-ff7fc6d67679/amazon/review

or scan this QR code:

You can also find out more about me by visiting my website at:

http://cjkichuk.com

or scan:

Thanks again.
Best regards,
C.J. Kichuk